What people are saying about …

BRIDGE TO A DISTANT STAR

"I can forgive Carolyn Williford for making me care so much about her characters only because she restores my faith in the possibility of miracles. Hold on as you read, because she'll take you right off that bridge with her."

Nancy Rue, author of The Reluctant Prophet trilogy

"Compelling characters wrestle with heart-rending conflicts and disappointments, unaware of the incredible disaster ahead. With a tragedy ripped from the headlines, Carolyn Williford weaves a story of love, loss, and hope."

Ginger Garrett, author of *Wolves Among Us*
and *Chosen: The Lost Diaries of Queen Esther*

"Carolyn Williford's *Bridge to a Distant Star* is a tragic tale of
_e toward one fatal moment. Filled with
_sed with faith and hope."
_i **DePree,** author of *Into the Wilderness*

_ties at character development and
_ling of evangelical Christianity come
_g novel. Rooted in an actual event,
_he lives of three diverse families, each
wrestling with issues of life and faith. You will care about her characters and gain insight into a

true to life struggles we all may face. Carolyn's down-to-earth style and insightful observations will have you thinking about this story long after you have finished this book."

Perry G. Downs, professor of Educational
Ministries, Trinity Evangelical Divinity School

BRIDGE TO A DISTANT STAR

BRIDGE TO A DISTANT STAR

A NOVEL

CAROLYN WILLIFORD

David C Cook®
transforming lives together

BRIDGE TO A DISTANT STAR
Published by David C Cook
4050 Lee Vance View
Colorado Springs, CO 80918 U.S.A.

David C Cook Distribution Canada
55 Woodslee Avenue, Paris, Ontario, Canada N3L 3E5

David C Cook U.K., Kingsway Communications
Eastbourne, East Sussex BN23 6NT, England

David C Cook and the graphic circle C logo
are registered trademarks of Cook Communications Ministries.

LCCN 2010942525
ISBN 978-1-4347-6703-5
eISBN 978-0-7814-0625-3

The Team: Don Pape, Nicci Jordan Hubert, Amy Kiechlin
Konyndyk, Sarah Schultz, Renada Arens, and Karen Athen
Cover Design and Digital Illustration: Gearbox Studios
Cover Photos: Veer PHP3075584
123RF 4495136
Photos.com 87834995; 87765569; 87803509

Printed in the United States of America
First Edition 2011

1 2 3 4 5 6 7 8 9 10

032911

For you, Sweetheart
Come what may.

ACKNOWLEDGMENTS

This novel would still be a veritable mess of a file in my computer if not for the help and encouragement of several people. So I am delighted to put my sincere thanks in print to:

Steve Laube—my agent, who believed in my ability to write fiction, and started encouraging me to finish this book—how many years ago? Would you believe six?

Polly Lott and *Joann Gay*—both patient and loving friends who suffered through way too many rough manuscripts.

Don Pape—who also believed in me, and had the great sense to marry Ruth.

Numerous friends and family (one of those is you, Sharon!)—who pray for me on a regular basis, and would frequently prod, "How's the book coming?" Your gifts of friendship are invaluable.

My parents—whom I can count on to love and pray for me, no matter what. I cherish you both.

Bob—since he's my absolute favorite Big Brother.

Tucker, Abby, Tyler, and Nate—simply because you're the four most wonderful grandchildren in the world, produced by the four most amazing parents, *Robb* and *Tricia,* and *Jay* and *Rachael.*

Nicci Jordan Hubert—my editor, who put up with my whining, complaining, grouching, and arguing and yet still hung in there with me, vastly improving this story.

Craig—my love, my best friend and confidant, my partner in ministry. I love living life with you, Sweetheart.

Though my story is based on the actual, tragic collapse of the Sunshine Skyway Bridge on May 9, 1980, all details concerning time, characters, and incidents are purely fictional. My prayer is that all affected by this horrendous accident have found healing in their hearts, minds, and souls.

Then Jesus said to his disciples,
"If anyone would come after me, he must deny himself
and take up his cross and follow me."
Matthew 16:24

BEGINNINGS

A Friday morning in May 2009

The heavy fog moved toward him like fists pushing against the window. Using a frayed handkerchief, the solitary man reached up to wipe a mist-covered spot. Large, heavily muscled, he was an imposing figure accustomed to giving orders, commanding men and ships at will. But as he leaned forward, squinting jet-black eyes to peer out into the gloom of that dawn, he was aware that there would be no submission from the fickle weather, no acquiescence to his hope for an easier route ahead. The toothpick he absentmindedly chewed switched from one side of his bushy-mustached mouth to the other. And then he slumped backward in frustration, sighing heavily. Captain Ray Luis was a great believer in signs and omens. In his estimation, this beastly morning was a harbinger of nothing good.

Though inside the pilothouse and out of the wretched weather, Captain Luis felt the dampness envelop him like a soggy blanket. Usually the view out the window toward the waves filled him with a sense of pride; holding the well-worn, smooth wheel of the ship in his calloused hands could still produce a thrill. But on that particular morning, none of the familiar pleasures would lift his spirits. In good weather, he would trust no other crew member to be at the helm for the formidable journey up the Tampa Bay channel; in this weather, the responsibility of the job weighed on him—and him alone—even more.

Intently peering through the fogged windows, Luis tried to estimate the visibility ahead, shaking his head at his infernal bad luck. Reaching up to rub tired eyes and then scratch his chin, he felt the stubble of a three-day growth of beard. He'd taken all the necessary precautions before heading up the bay. Even so he reminded himself that his freighter, the *Wilder Wanderer,* was now without cargo and therefore significantly lighter; as a result, she would ride higher in the water, more at the mercy of wind and waves.

The bridge that worried him just ahead was the over five-mile-long Sunshine Skyway, a marvel of engineering—and beauty—that spanned the bay from St. Petersburg to Bradenton. The golden cables, designed to gently arch upward, proclaimed the elegance of her design, beckoning all who passed over or beneath to savor the symmetry. But wise captains weren't naive to her siren's song; they knew her spell was merely a facade, and a dangerous one at that. Beneath the beauty lay treachery for the unwary.

The stark reality was this: Every ship's captain faced a critical test of his skills by maneuvering through the passage, which measured 864 feet wide and 150 feet tall. On each side of the channel stood bridge piers made of steel and concrete; these structures supported the roadway above, providing a safe journey for people in the cars, trucks, and buses that crossed the bridge, going about their daily lives. All of them traveled blind to any potential emergency or danger from below. Unknowingly, they placed their trust not only in the worthiness of the superstructure itself, but also in the hands of every pilot who steered his ship under the bridge. Today their lives rested in the hands of Captain Luis.

Clutching the wheel of the *Wild One*—as he affectionately called the ship—Luis continued his search for the all-important buoys that marked the safe channel under the bridge. Any divergence from that channel was extremely dangerous; no captain wanted to entertain the possibility of that disaster. He felt his ship's over two-hundred-foot-long hull begin to pull slightly against his steering. He tensed his jaw in concentration and nudged the wheel more to the left.

When the thunder roared into the darkness, it caught Captain Luis off guard; his head jerked backward in unexpected alarm. The flash of lightning that immediately followed announced the storm was directly overhead. He cursed and then braced himself for the next assault that he feared was inevitable: a gust of fierce wind. It came just as he'd expected, forcing the ship directly into the path of the bridge's supports.

Grabbing the intercom mike, he shouted for his man in charge at the bow of the ship. "Jaurez! How bad is it up there?"

The garbled voice of Jaurez answered almost immediately. "Captain, they ain't no seeing in this!" Another crack of thunder with its accompanying lightning struck, and Jaurez mumbled under his breath. "Cursed channel! I swear it's haunted! Couldn't see a blessed thing before, and now it's even *worse*. Want us t' drop anchor and sit her out?" Jaurez and four other men were huddled beneath heavy slickers.

"No! Can't take the chance of being pushed into those piers." All the captain's past experience came into play, and he made a quick decision. "I'm cutting her speed to five miles per hour. Gives us a chance to see where we're heading in this muck. And let me know soon's you spot those buoys!"

Suddenly the winds increased again, approaching tropical-storm speeds of seventy miles per hour. The *Wild One* groaned and creaked in response. Feeling the first rise of panic, Luis glanced over at his radar just in time to see it blink out. For a few moments, he simply stared at the blank screen, uncomprehending. Just as he reached over to give it a useless rap, he heard Jaurez's shout over the intercom: "Captain! There's a buoy; we're passing it port side! We're headin' right down the middle of the channel!"

Luis kept his voice calm and radioed back, "Set tight, Jaurez. I'm thinkin' you're right. We'll take it easy … steer on through. But keep a close watch, you hear?"

"Yes, sir! I'll be mighty glad when …"

But Juarez's voice was lost in another reverberating thunderclap. Lightning followed, illuminating the seductive lines of the Skyway. That quick revelation also showed Captain Luis that the perspectives were off. *This isn't right!* Luis gasped, opening his eyes and mouth wide in sudden shock. *We're not in the channel, not at all!* In that hor- rific instant, Luis realized that the buoy they just passed must've been the one marking the *right side* of the channel. He froze as the realiza- tion shot like a knife through his gut: The *Wild One* was headed right toward one of the bridge's supports.

Grabbing the intercom with shaking hands, Luis shouted, *"Jaurez!* Hard to port! Let go the anchor! Ram the engines, full astern!" In a frantic effort to prevent the catastrophe, he attempted to stop the giant ship before she hit the bridge. But another show of lightning proved the futility of his efforts. The concrete pier loomed over the *Wild One*.

There was no stopping the inevitable. They were going to ram it.

"*Cap'n!*" was all he heard from Jaurez before the ship's bow and the concrete of the bridge met in a rage of violence. The first loud *boom!* was immediately followed by the howling of grinding steel, and the great ship groaned, as though she were personally injured. Splintering, wrenched roadway released overhead, and great blocks of concrete and warped, twisted steel plunged into the water and onto the deck of the ship.

The collision had thrown Captain Luis nearly off his feet, though he grabbed the wheel at the last moment to brace himself. He took one brief moment to pray, *God, oh please!—may the road overhead be clear!* Gathering courage to face whatever awaited, he ran out to the bow of his doomed ship.

On the road above, no one suspected that a dire rending had just occurred. If any felt the slight movement of the roadway, they assumed that strong winds were the culprit. The drivers merely adjusted for the pull, intending to continue on safely.

On the deck of his fated ship, Captain Luis froze at the desolation unfolding before him. He watched in terror as huge pieces of roadway dropped into the violently churning waves of black, murky water. But he and every member of the crew recoiled in horror when, all eyes compelled to follow the surreal scene before them, they watched a bus, a Mercedes, and a van launch out into a void of nothingness.

And plunge into the depths of the Tampa Bay.

Book One

DENY YOURSELF

April 2009
Suburb of St. Petersburg, Florida

"Emilie, face it. You've run out of *E*'s," Maureen needled her friend. "We've been through all of this before."

By habit, Maureen's gaze drifted toward the window to study the bluebird house in the backyard. The Roberts' home was typical of the coastal section of Florida: stucco topped by a terra-cotta roof, a sprawling ranch with St. Augustine grass precisely trimmed, flowering bushes and fruit trees dotting the yard. The early arrival of spring this year had been conducive to lush growth, and the bushes and plants were already threatening to overwhelm their prescribed boundaries.

Her attention distracted again, Maureen moved to the sliding glass doors overlooking the pool. It had been cleaned yesterday, and the feel of its soothing water, now marked and variegated with alternating lines of shadow and light glistening in the sun, beckoned to her. Glancing upward through the slats of the screened pergola, however, she caught a glimpse of ominous clouds in the distance.

"I know, I know," Emilie was saying, "But Ellie's off to first grade in the fall—"

"And she's your baby and you can't stand the idea of being alone," Maureen interrupted. "Listen to me. It has to stop sometime, Emilie. You can't continue having another baby every time a child goes off to school."

"But Emma's a *junior*. She'll leave for college in a little over a year."

"Emma's ready, you know that. A great student. Responsible. But wouldn't it be wonderful to have more time for yourself?—squeezed in between caring for Eddie, Ethan, and Ellie. Not to mention your husband, or even Eunice the wonder dog."

"Listen, I'm being serious now. Ed agrees with me."

"Really?"

Emilie cleared her throat. "He even said the number *seven* is a biblical number."

"You already have seven if you count the dog."

"Maureen, I said I'm being serious. I think God really wants us to do this."

Maureen sighed. Again sensing the weariness that had recently settled over her like a fog, she leaned against the sliding glass door, enjoying the coolness against her fair skin. Tall and willowy in build and movement, she had the usual coloring of an auburn redhead: freckles sprinkled liberally across light skin, with a concentration on her face, mostly across nose and cheeks. Which gave her a delightful eternally youthful and slightly mischievous look. What wasn't typical, however, were the hazel eyes flecked with darker accents. Rarely did anyone glance at Maureen without noticing those lovely eyes, and ultimately feeling drawn to look more deeply into them. Maureen's eyes promised a beauty and depth that few could resist. "I'm sorry, Em. I guess there's no question then. I mean, if Ed's on board and you're both sure that's what God wants …"

"Right. Although lately, Mo, there's been … well, somewhat of a dis—"

A slammed door and raised voices interrupted the conversation. "*Mom.* Aubrey's been in my room again and messed with my stuff." Maureen winced as she heard each of Colleen's words escalate in intensity.

"Emilie, I'm so sorry. But I have to go."

"Sounds rather umm … testy over there." Emilie chuckled, probably relishing the fact that the squabbles were currently at some-one else's home.

"Collie has *Rabbit.*" Aubrey's wail reached a fevered pitch that matched her older sister's, and Maureen's shoulders tensed in response. "Rabbit is missing and I had to finded him and …"

"Your dumb rabbit better not be in my room!" Colleen shouted.

"Rabbit is *not* dumb."

"Is so." Colleen pulled her features into a dramatic scowl. Aimed it like a weapon at her sister. "It's dirty and falling apart and smelly and …"

Willing calm, Maureen gracefully asked, "Girls, can you take this conversation into the family room, please? I need to say a quick good-bye to Mrs. Esteban and then I'll be right with you." Neither daughter budged, alternating glares at each other and Maureen. She pointedly turned her back on both of them.

Bobo, the family's pint-sized Yorkshire terrier, took that moment to come to Maureen, scratching at her calf and yapping, demanding to be let out. "All *right*, Bobo. Emilie, you still there? I'm so sorry. Honestly, why does everything have to … happen in …" She opened the door to the backyard, then nudged Bobo out with her foot. Never thrilled about walking on grass, he required a little encouragement. Glancing at Colleen and Aubrey, Maureen made a hasty decision to follow Bobo out, firmly closing the door behind her. The humidity was immediately oppressive, but less so than the tension she'd escaped in the kitchen. "Where was I? Why does everything happen when you're *attempting* to talk on the phone?"

Emilie chuckled again and Maureen pictured her friend's slightly crooked, impish grin. Emilie always pulled the left side of her smile slightly higher, which also created a distinct dimple. It was one of those infectious smiles that seemed to constantly hint that she was enjoying a private joke, and was merely waiting for you to catch on. "I know this doesn't sound like the most opportune time to present this argument, but Mo, I swear I wouldn't know what to do with myself if I weren't a full-time mom."

"At this point, friend, having grown children who've moved on in life sounds like heaven to me. Oh, almost forgot to tell you. I had a dream the other night that I was in labor and delivered a baby girl. When she popped out—yes, she *popped;* it was a dream, for heaven's sake—instead of crying, the baby yelled, 'NO.'"

Emilie exploded with laughter, the honking, no-holds-barred laugh that was distinctly hers. Maureen loved making Emilie laugh, fondly remembering the first time she'd heard the sound—at a dorm meeting when they were in college. Even a noisy room-length away, Maureen had caught that distinctive sound and found herself gravitating toward the source of the delightful outburst. And then promptly fell in love with the woman who owned it.

"Maybe I'd better start praying you have a boy? I suppose you could always name him Earnest. Or Eldridge," Maureen offered. She fleetingly thought about peeking in the window to check on the girls. Decided against it.

"See? You admit there are *E* names left."

"And there's Evan."

"Way too close to Ethan. I'd yell the wrong name constantly."

"Good point. I really should go, Em. Oh, almost forgot—see you tomorrow at the Vacation Bible School meeting? Nine o'clock, in the sixth-grade room. With the hours I'm putting in at the shop right now I feel a bit overwhelmed. But Bill and I agree I need to stay committed to VBS, no matter what."

"Yeah, Ed feels the same way, but I don't see him volunteering to cut out two hundred and forty baskets for baby Moses."

"Ha. But there *is* a payoff: The gang's going to lunch afterward, right?"

"Absolutely. Wouldn't miss it."

"Okay, see you tomorrow." Maureen clicked off the phone, squared her shoulders, and gingerly opened the door of the family room to face her daughters. Colleen's wrath had reached the crisis stage. Aubrey's lower lip began quivering. Full-blown tears wouldn't be far behind, and Maureen dreaded the shift from laughing with her friend to conflict resolution. Some days it felt like all she did was referee arguments between the two. Sending up a quick prayer—*God, give me wisdom*—she set to the task.

"Mom, you gotta tell Aubrey to stay out of my stuff. *Out ... of ... my ... room.*" Every word drawn out, driven home by a steely teenage stare at the three-year-old who glared right back—even though her lips were still trembling and her eyes were already glistening with the hint of tears. "I *need* my privacy," Colleen said.

Maureen looked from one daughter to the other in exasperation and disappointment. After Colleen was born, she and Bill had tried for ten years to have another child—years of bargaining and pleading with God to put another baby in their arms. Their prayers were finally answered when Aubrey joined their little family. Bill and Maureen were convinced that compliant, easy-going, sweet-tempered Colleen—about to enter the "turbulent teens," as friends had called it—would welcome her new sibling with nothing but loving acceptance and unbounded joy.

Had they merely been delusional? Or totally out of their minds?

"Aubrey, did you go into Colleen's room? You know you're not supposed to be in your sister's room without her permission."

Aubrey reached for a handful of her mother's sweatshirt as she gazed up at her. Her security seemed tied to a need to clutch things—satin on the edge of a blanket, the hem of her dresses (to her mother's exasperation, as Aubrey repeatedly revealed her own underwear), her daddy's pocket (she could reach just that high), and of course, the ever-present Rabbit. She whispered, "I hada finded Rabbit, Mommy."

"But why did you think Rabbit was in Collie's room?" Maureen whispered back.

Aubrey held out her hands, palms up, with eyes wide open in feigned innocence. "'Cause ... 'cause I fink he's hiding in there."

"See. I *told* you she'd been in my room. She's always doing stuff like this and getting away with—"

Trying her best to remain calm, Maureen interrupted. "Colleen, I'm handling it." She paused, took a breath, and looked at her eldest daughter. "How about you go read the first part of John 8? It's the passage about throwing the first stone."

The look Colleen gave Maureen hit like a direct punch to the stomach. "I'm sick of you throwing Bible verses at me, *Mother*." The name was saturated with sarcasm and disrespect. "Like you're one to lay that on *me*. I heard you talking about Daddy with Miss Mann the other day. I heard what you said about him. And then you act ... all loving-like with Daddy. And I heard what you said to Mrs. Esteban, too. You really don't think they should have another kid, but because they've decided *God* says they should, you're like, all for it suddenly. That's *sick*."

The accusation made Maureen feel ill, causing her to regret that she hadn't hung up the phone the instant the girls started arguing. *What on earth did I say to Sherry Mann? I can't remember.* Impulsively, Maureen reached out to pull Aubrey into her embrace. "Colleen, I—"

"I know exactly what you're thinking right now, too," Colleen spit out with a sneer. "You're worried about your friends, aren't you? What they would think of *you* if they could hear me right now."

Sickening silence. Maureen opened her mouth to defend herself, but no words came.

"Knew I was right." Colleen smirked and gave her mother one last disdainful, triumphant look before turning away. She walked down the hallway toward her room. "Here's the disgusting rabbit." A *thump* followed the pronouncement as it was thrown against the wall of the hallway, followed by the slam of her door.

"Mommy?"

A mommy again, not a *mo-ther.* "Yes, sweetie?"

"Can I get Rabbit now?"

"Sure."

Lured by the glimpse of a bluebird that had just landed atop the birdhouse, Maureen moved to look out the window. She identified him immediately as a male, for he was a radiant indigo. For a moment, she simply drank in his glorious color, grateful for the respite. But then, distracted by the erratically waving leaves of the palm next to the house, she lifted her gaze to the sky. It was a sickly yellow, the hue that often precedes a major storm.

Though the air conditioner was running—generally a must for Florida's climate—Maureen still noticed an uncomfortable mugginess. Absentmindedly she ran her fingers through her hair. Pulled a sticky shirt away from her neck and chest and used it to fan sweaty skin. The changing barometric pressure felt as though it were throbbing inside her head. And then, as storms along the volatile Florida coast tend to do, the rain rushed toward them with a force of its own, and raindrops struck against the window with a vengeance.

Maureen's attention shifted back to the bird. She hadn't realized that she'd been holding her breath, but now she exhaled, relieved to find the bird still there, protectively flattening itself against the birdhouse roof, feathers ruffled by the wind. *Please stay,* she whispered, pleading. *Go into the bird house, where you'll be safe.* But he flew off, battling the aggressive wind as he fluttered away from her.

Blinking her eyes, stretching out her tense neck from side to side, forcing herself to *do* something, Maureen moved to the mundane, the comfortably familiar—she started dinner, pulling out lettuce and vegetables. It wasn't until she nearly tripped over a small foot that she noticed her daughter hovering again. Aubrey grabbed a handful of sweatshirt, the need to clutch something heightened when she felt insecure. Rabbit was back where he belonged, none the worse for his ill treatment. *He couldn't get much worse looking anyway,* Maureen mused, blaming herself for not being firmer with Aubrey about dragging it everywhere. It was rare that Rabbit got tossed into the washer.

Maureen leaned down, meeting Aubrey's look at eye level. She gazed into eyes that were likewise unusual—considering Aubrey also had red hair—but unlike her mother's, Aubrey's eyes were a rich dark brown with matching dark lashes. Still, despite the difference in eye color, family and friends teased that Bill and Maureen had been given "one each" by God. Colleen took mostly after her father, sharing his darker olive skin and straighter hair, while Aubrey had inherited her mother's auburn curls and fairer coloring—though Aubrey's skin had less of a propensity to freckle. She did have a sprinkling across her nose and cheeks, however, which only served to highlight her eyes, like an ornamental frame around a picture.

"What's up, Lolly Pops?" Maureen asked, using Bill's nickname for Aubrey.

Dimpled fingers firmly gripped the stuffed animal against her chest. "Rabbit's wowied."

"About?"

"The storm."

Maureen took Aubrey's hand in hers and directed her toward the window. They stared out at the pellets of rain that were now striking fragile, budding blooms. "All the rain and thunder are out *there,* sweetie." Maureen lightly squeezed her daughter's hand. "We're absolutely safe here in the house. God's protecting us. Rabbit, too." She pulled Aubrey into her embrace, healing the worry, wishing, *If only I could do this as easily with Colleen.* "Want to help me with lettuce for a salad? Yes? Bring over your step stool."

Rabbit in one hand, Aubrey dragged the stool with the other. Another rumble of thunder made her pause momentarily, but then she scrambled up the steps to the sink, plopping the stuffed animal on the counter. "Rabbit will watch us, but we better keep a eye on him. He *loves* lettuce."

"I suppose he does." Maureen frowned at the grimy stuffed animal's presence on the counter, but she reminded herself that distracting Aubrey from the storm was the higher priority. "All rabbits like lettuce and carrots, don't they?" She broke off a small section of lettuce for Aubrey to wash.

Over the sounds of the approaching storm, neither had noticed the grind of the garage door and Bill's entering the kitchen until they were greeted with his usual "I'm home."

"Daddy!" Aubrey squealed in delight. "I'm helping Mommy."

"I can see that." Bill reached down to pet Bobo, who greeted him with a wiggling body and his imitation of barking: high-pitched yips. "How's it goin', ole boy? Survive another day in this female-dominated household?"

Tall with an athletic build, smooth olive skin, dark eyes, and a full head of nearly jet black hair—not counting a distinguished dusting of white at the temples—Bill's coloring was totally opposite Maureen's, a stark difference that had initially caught his interest. He moved like the athlete he was, gracefully, but with economy. Bill rarely wasted time, never sauntered anywhere, and approached life with a mix of good instincts.

Fifty years old, a family doctor at a thriving practice, Bill was a natural leader—not only at his office, but also at church, in the community, the girls' school organizations, even events like a neighborhood pick-up basketball game. His easy assurance, commanding demeanor, and tone of voice made him stand out. People felt safe with Bill and trusted him. They came to him for advice.

"Look, Daddy." Aubrey grinned up at him now, offering her cheek for a kiss. "I'm helping Mommy get the lettuce clean." She proudly held out her well-handled—and therefore, rather wilted— piece of lettuce. "Colleen's mad again but Rabbit and I don't care. This is more fun."

Bill turned to study his wife's profile. He gave Maureen a peck on the cheek. "Hey. So what's the deal with Colleen?"

Maureen waved off any concern, gesturing with the carrot she was peeling. "Nothing, really. Just the usual teenage stuff. How are things at the office?"

But Bill wasn't fooled, taking note of the deflection and the telltale set of Maureen's neck and shoulders. He reached up to loosen his tie, unbuttoning the collar. "Busy. Had several more inexperienced new mothers in today. I'm spending way too much of my time teaching them basics they should already know."

"Isn't that why you hired Carrie?"

"Had to let her go today, unfortunately. She just wasn't getting the job done." Bill reached out to tug on Aubrey's ear, distracting her while he snatched a carrot.

"Oh, Bill. So Hailey's back to picking up all the slack?"

"We all pick up the slack, Mo. And it's my responsibility to make sure we're all contributing as needed. Getting the job done."

An edge had crept into his voice, and once again Maureen was eager to change the subject. "Would you start the grill, please? Once you get your clothes changed?"

"No problem." He reached out to tug Aubrey's ear again, eliciting another giggle before he headed down the hall, pausing momentarily at his other daughter's door. Closed and *locked* door, as he discovered by attempting to give the handle a turn.

Dinner was strained, echoing the feel of the storm that mostly passed them by, skirting off to the north. It left the evening feeling bereft, the earth wanting what the skies flaunted but denied to give. Except for Aubrey's chatter, conversations didn't flow easily, thanks in part to the pointed one-word answers and grunts from Colleen. She ate little, mostly rearranged food on her plate, and asked to be excused as soon as Maureen began clearing the table.

Later, when Bill summoned Colleen for family devotions, she begrudgingly joined them. She'd not been an active participant for weeks, uttering only a word or two when directly questioned. But tonight Colleen amped the protest even higher, for her entire posture was in revolt; she sat rigidly with crossed arms, head pointed down as she stared at her lap. Maureen felt relieved when it was finally time to end with prayer.

Maureen had just tucked Aubrey into bed and closed her bedroom door when she heard Bill calling.

"Mo?"

Maureen leaned heavily against the door, closing her eyes and sighing. She'd hoped to escape it all—Bill included—by heading directly to bed. She wanted to fade into oblivion by watching some mindless television show until she fell asleep. It all felt so overwhelming at this hour. *Certainly I can get a better perspective in the morning*, she thought, convincing herself that checking in on Colleen wasn't a good idea and hoping Bill's call wasn't regarding anything more difficult than helping him find a mismatched sock.

She reached for toothbrush and paste as Bill leaned against the sink, his back to the mirror, arms crossed over his chest. He didn't turn to face her, but she noted the disconcerted frown, the telling twitch along the line of his jaw as he clenched his teeth.

She inched away from him before she asked, "What did you need?"

He turned to face her, inserting his face into her line of vision. "Pretty obvious things aren't good between you and Colleen. I take it you upset her again?"

"I upset *her?*" she said in shock, spraying toothpaste across the mirror, which of course further inflamed her frustration.

"Please keep your voice down, Mo. Okay, bad choice of words. But I need to know you've got a plan to handle this."

"She was rude to *me.*" Maureen jammed her toothbrush back into its designated slot. "Can't you ever try to see things from *my* perspective?" She could feel tears of frustration threatening, but she blinked them back.

"I'm just trying to help you view all the angles, Maureen. As a doctor, that's what I do. Help people. I'm just trying to help you, too." Spoken in controlled, soothing tones. His doctor's voice.

Maureen yanked open a drawer, rummaging through neatly folded nightgowns until she spotted the oldest one she could find. She began pulling off clothes, tugging the gown over her head with such jerking, magnified movements that she tore off a button. "Aubrey put her Rabbit in Colleen's room. Colleen had a fit about it. I tried to help *both* see they were wrong. Does that make me such a terrible mother?" She paused a moment. "And the bluebirds have rejected my bird house … *again.*" Crumpling onto the bed, Maureen allowed a few tears to spill over. "I ought to just take the stupid thing down."

"Good land, Mo, what do bluebirds have to do with anything? You and Colleen aren't speaking and *that's* what you're crying about?" He stared at her in disbelief, taking in her red, runny nose, disheveled hair, nightgown askew because of the missing button. He shook his head in amazement, sudden pity dousing all irritation, and eased down onto the bed beside her.

"I was just trying to help you, honey." Pulling her against his chest, Bill tucked her head under his chin. Maureen continued to weep silently, tears spilling down her cheeks. "Evidently this is some girl thing between you two that has to play out. Have you been praying about it?"

"Of course I have." He could feel her stiffen.

"Then what's the main issue here? What has you so upset, for cryin' out loud?"

"She … she accused me of being a hypocrite."

"A hypocrite? Why on earth?" He pulled his arms from her, shifting his body so he could watch her reaction.

"I have no idea. Something about a conversation she says she overheard. On the phone." Maureen got up to grab a tissue from the bathroom, blew her nose. "I'll try to talk with her more about it tomorrow, Bill, but right now I have to go to bed." She began pitching decorative pillows onto the floor, pulling back covers.

"What's on for tomorrow?"

"Vacation Bible School meeting and a lunch." Maureen stopped a moment, considering. "My sense is that I can't … I can't rush this. And you can't push a teenager either—especially not Colleen. You know that. Not until she's good and ready." She climbed into bed, anxious for the oblivion of sleep to come. To escape from the pressing worries, if only for one night.

Bill reached for the TV remote, started pressing buttons, flipping through channels at near lightning speed. Maureen pinched her eyes shut tightly; Bill's nightly ritual annoyed her (*How can he tell what's on when he sees each channel for only a millisecond?*), but she kept her opinion to herself.

"This hypocrite thing? You really need to find out what Colleen's thinking in relation to that."

Maureen moved to the far edge of the king-sized bed, curled up into a ball. Her back to Bill. She tugged the blanket up to her chin, finding childish solace in the soft, satin edging.

"Maureen?"

"What?" Distanced, as though she were far, far away.

"For the family's sake, make it a priority to spend time with Colleen tomorrow if you can, okay? I'll be praying for you." Bill flicked off the television and turned his back to her, settling in. "It's that important, don't you agree?"

"Yes, Bill."

"Oh, and hey, I'm really sorry about the bluebirds, too."

Maureen unblinkingly stared out their bedroom window, following the light glow from the moon. It illuminated the lines of the windowpanes against the wall, framing the waving silhouetted fronds of a palm tree. She stared at the graceful, bowing dips of the shadows of the leaves until, out of her peripheral vision, she noticed a single star twinkling. When she tried to look at it directly, it appeared to vanish, eluding her. Looking away, she noted that it was indeed there, just out of her line of direct vision. And then Maureen closed her eyes, seeking the escape of sleep.

Maureen groggily woke to the sound of the shower running. She lifted her head up, glanced at the clock, and groaned. *Doesn't it just figure?* she fumed to herself as she scurried out of tangled covers. *I toss and turn half the night, only to finally fall asleep about an hour before it's time to wake up.* She'd been sleeping so soundly that she hadn't heard the alarm, and Bill—*what was he thinking?*—hadn't awakened her.

She quickly made the bed, replacing the numerous scattered pillows in their proper places. After a trip to the bathroom and a hastily mumbled "good morning" to Bill, Maureen hurried toward the kitchen where she was soothed by the aroma coming from the pre-timed coffee pot. She poured herself a cup and walked over to the same window she looked out every morning—to view the bluebird house. Running late or not, she would still indulge in her daily ritual: a few sips of coffee and a check on the box. *Still, nothing.*

Bobo rose from his bed in the family room and scampered to her feet, cocking his head up at her. She slid open the door and once again pushed out the reluctant dog. *Isn't it appropriate that we have a dog who doesn't even know what it wants to do?* she thought to herself, shaking her head.

The combination of oversleeping and the need for an earlier departure felt like a guarantee that this morning would be especially hectic. Soon enough, Colleen woke with her attitude still firmly pronounced, and even Aubrey, normally a morning-loving child, was whiny and petulant. After Maureen offered her several outfits, which Aubrey summarily dismissed, mom and daughter finally agreed on a totally inappropriate shorts set. White top, white shorts. It was a disaster waiting to happen, but Maureen was not up to form for battles this morning.

Then Aubrey decided her booster seat was too sticky. Yesterday Maureen had made blueberry pancakes. Naturally, the syrup had flowed—pretty much everywhere. "Since when do you mind being sticky? It certainly wasn't an issue yesterday," Maureen reasoned with her. Then she discovered yet another disaster: The milk had turned sour.

Maureen's one consolation was that the "Gang of Four," as they called themselves, was going out to lunch. And yes, as Sherry would be sure to point out, they were quite aware of the origins of their namesake: the infamous Madam Mao and the three other senior leaders during the Chinese Cultural Revolution. Sherry had majored in Chinese history (she had earned a master's and a doctorate, the only one of the group to do so; Sherry was also the only one unmarried, having divorced several years ago), and it was she who had given them the moniker while in college. For whatever reason, it stuck.

Fast friends ever since those college years, they all still lived within an hour's drive of each other. Though two members of the group were on the opposite side of town from Community Fellowship Church, they hadn't ever considered attending elsewhere. They craved being together, laughing, chatting, sharing, commiserating when needed, and giggling like school girls. When Maureen first thought about working part-time at the Beadazzled jewelry shop, it was these three friends who prodded and encouraged her to apply. And then they had successfully plied her with numerous arguments why she should give the job a try when the position was offered to her—knowing Bill would oppose the idea. Turned out the two-mornings-a-week job was a mixed blessing—she enjoyed the creative outlet but was growing weary with the hours—but she still credited her friends for pushing her to try something new. For believing in her, even when she struggled to believe in herself. Now, as Maureen focused on the events of the day, she sighed audibly for the unconditional love and acceptance that the gang—Emilie Esteban, Vanessa Clarkson, and Sherry Mann—so willingly gave, providing the one place she could simply be herself.

But the feel-good moment was only that—a moment. For then Maureen felt a familiar tightness shoot through her shoulders and into her neck. Worry wrapped itself around her heart as she recalled her interaction with Colleen. *Am I a hypocrite?* She couldn't begin to understand her own thoughts and feelings these days, let alone make sense of Colleen's motivations. Hurrying to clean up breakfast dishes and then finish getting ready, she mentally decided on a plan of action. *Bill's right. I do need to spend time in prayer about this. But I'm probably overreacting to Colleen, too. The gang will make me feel better in no time, and we'll be laughing about all this over lunch.*

"*Mom.* You're gonna make me late for my meeting before school."

Colleen stood at the door to the garage, one hand on the doorknob, the other gripping the strap of her backpack. She added the classic foot thumping, an impatient *tap, tap.* Colleen had felt the power of having the upper hand, and she wasn't about to relinquish it.

Maureen came into the kitchen, Aubrey in tow, just in time to catch Colleen rolling her eyes. "We're coming right now, Colleen. No need to get upset."

Colleen flounced down the steps to the car and was heard slamming a door when Maureen discovered that Aubrey not only had Rabbit, but was clutching another stuffed animal, a particularly dirty one that had been left outside in the rain. It was still damp and now smelled of mildew.

"Oh, Aubrey. No. We're not taking Jonesy Giraffe today."

Out came the lower lip.

"I don't have time to argue! Go put it away." She could hear yet another car door being slammed.

Tears formed and Aubrey pleaded, "But Gramma wants to see him. She wants to see Jonesy going *zing, zing, zing.*"

The once bright yellow and white giraffe used to move its head in a slow circle to the tune "You Are My Sunshine." Unfortunately, wear and tear—and the rain, undoubtedly—had taken their toll. The giraffe now played at such a frenetic speed that it sounded like "*zing, zing, zing,*" and its neck jerked at an equally spastic pace, making him look quite comical. The moldy smell, however, was anything but.

Is it ultimately worth the fight? Maureen asked herself, and then sighed in resignation. "All right. But this is *the last time* it goes out the door. Agreed?"

Aubrey, mollified, nodded.

Their first stop was Colleen's middle school, which was fairly well maintained but still had that typical public school look of frugal budgets, too little money for upkeep, and occupation by kids who weren't into caring for their school. When Maureen pulled over to the curb to drop off Colleen, she called out "Have a good day," but not too loudly. Maureen had been tolerantly instructed on the proper etiquette for Dropping off Middle Schoolers by Moms. There were several all-important, inviolate *Rules,* and she wasn't about to break one of those this morning.

No answer from Colleen, of course, and none was expected. Maureen pulled out, determined to focus on the other events of the day. Aubrey, however, was not to be deterred, yelling "Bye, Collie!" while cheerfully waving Jonesy (doing his *zing* routine) out the open window. Oblivious to her sister's retreating back and what it communicated, Aubrey generally ignored all of the *Rules.*

Next stop was Bill's parents' house. They fortunately lived close by and were delighted to watch Aubrey whenever needed—Maureen's two mornings per week at the shop—plus any other circumstances, like this morning's VBS meeting. While unbuckling Aubrey from her car seat, Maureen winced again at the giraffe. "You sure you can't leave Jonesy in the car? Just think—he could ride around with me all day on a road trip. He'd love it."

Aubrey gave her a withering look that conveyed her mom's suggestion didn't even merit a response. Giving her curls a flounce, she climbed down from the car, tucking Rabbit under one arm and Jonesy Giraffe firmly under the other.

Maureen was about to ring the doorbell when the door flew open, her mother-in-law's attention fully focused on one of the two granddaughters who were the objects of her wholehearted devotion.

"There's my precious sweetheart," Kate Roberts exclaimed, gathering Aubrey into her arms. Aubrey erupted into delighted giggles.

Where has the whining, demanding three-year-old that I had to deal with this morning vanished to? Kate glanced over, and Maureen pointedly flashed her a pasted-on smile.

"And what have we here with Rabbit? Did Rabbit bring a friend?" Kate asked.

Aubrey vigorously nodded her head, intentionally giving Maureen a "told you so" look of triumph.

"Mom, I really need to …" But Kate's attention was fixated on Aubrey, unmistakably communicating that Maureen was to wait. How she wished she could simply announce *Gotta run,* and exit gracefully. But after all these years, Kate still intimidated her. Maureen read her cues and stood by, physically patient if not emotionally so.

A guessing game developed over the animal's name. Maureen glanced helplessly at her watch while Kate offered several silly suggestions until finally Aubrey quipped, "No. But you're close, Gramma. It's *Jonesy* Giraffe."

An unintended early rescue by Aubrey, and Maureen jumped at it. "I'll be back to pick her up around three, Kate. Is that too late?"

"'Course not. Little precious here and I have lots to do today, don't we, sweetheart? Well, Aubrey and I and Rabbit and Jennifer Giraffe, right?"

Aubrey burst into laughter again, barely getting out "Gramma, no!" before Maureen took her chance to escape.

She gave daughter and mother-in-law quick pecks on their cheeks and hurried down the sidewalk, calling out, "Thanks, Kate," over her shoulder.

"Wave bye to your Mommy," was followed by a cursory wave and the firm *click* of the closed door.

Again Maureen imagined herself telling the gang and soaking up empathy about in-laws. Consolation for out-of-control children. Understanding about husbands who came home from work too tired to deal with families. Laughter would erupt and then all frustrations would be forgotten, if only temporarily. By the time Maureen turned into the church parking lot, she was smiling to herself, eager to get the meeting going and then enjoy lunch.

"Good morning, Kath!" she cheerily called out to the pastor's wife. Maureen beamed at Kathy; Kathy waved and beamed back. Maureen asked herself, *Wonder if a pastor's wife ever needs to put on an act, hiding hurt feelings? Arguments at home?* She shook her head. *I can't picture Kathy ever dealing with irritable kids.*

After a hectic but productive morning, Vanessa wandered into Maureen's room, greeting her friend with an enthusiastic hug. With three active boys and a good deal of her own energy, Vanessa was the perfect choice for VBS games director. For she was the eternal tomboy. Most women—the gang included—openly envied her exuberance and still athletically slim figure, though Vanessa herself appeared oblivious to it.

"Didn't see Emilie anywhere, did you?"

Vanessa shook her head. "Was she supposed to be here?"

"Yeah, she was. I just talked with her yesterday. She said she'd be here."

"Hope she's not sick or anything."

"Yeah, me too." Maureen glanced around, making sure no one was close enough to overhear as they walked out of the church. "You're not going to believe this. But Emilie and Ed are talking about having another baby."

"You're not *serious?*"

"Better not mention it, okay?" They climbed into Vanessa's sports car, the concession to her love of speed and daring. "I shouldn't have said anything. But Emilie really *is* serious about this." A slight pause. "And so is Ed, evidently. They think it's what God wants."

"Oh, good heavens, Mo. Don't tell me you're falling for that?"

"Nessa, honestly—"

"Honestly *nothing*, Maureen. Between you and me? If Ed is saying he heard God's voice telling him to have another little E-kid, then he needs to be on meds."

Maureen tried, but failed to stifle a chuckle. "Ed didn't say that. And he's not hearing voices, silly. He just thinks the number *seven* is biblical." She shrugged her shoulders.

"So is 666, but you don't hear about couples shooting for that." They both laughed, releasing some of the unease they were feeling as they'd plunged into touchy subjects. "I'm not saying anything more. It's just that, well, my intuition—oh shoot, my common sense—tells me that having another child is a bad idea. Can't put my finger on why, but Ed's been hitting my buttons lately. And that's it. Only my humble opinion." She glanced over at Maureen and crossed her eyes. Which brought the desired smile from her friend. "Movin' on to another topic. How are things with Colleen?"

Maureen groaned, then slumped down a little farther into the seat.

"Not so great, eh? How does it compare to a home with three boys who all think the greatest competition in the world is to win 'the most foul-smelling sneakers' contest by the end of the day?"

Maureen offered a weak smile.

"Caught 'em passing their athletic shoes around last night, voting on the winner. And would you believe Greg was in on it too? I swear he was enjoying it as much as they were, egging them on."

"Did he enter his sneakers too?"

"Oh absolutely. But here's the really big news: Greg and I just declared that, beginning as freshmen in high school, Clarkson boys do their own wash. Greg Junior's already had his lesson in operating the washer and dryer."

"Wow. That's gutsy. Going okay?"

"Hmm, not so much. Instead of piles of just dirty clothes on Greg Junior's floor, now there are piles of dirty *and* clean clothes." Vanessa turned to look at Maureen, noted the mock-horrified look on her face. "He had to literally clear a path through the mess just to get from the door to his bed."

Maureen offered an empathetic grimace. "How does he tell what's clean and what's dirty? And more importantly, how can you stand it?" She laughed.

"I made the mistake of asking him if he could distinguish from dirty and clean, and mind you ... there's underwear in those piles too."

"So what'd he say?"

"Smell check."

Maureen burst into laughter. "Oh, Nessa, you're the best medicine. I needed this lunch *so* badly."

They rode in companionable silence for a few moments until Vanessa reached over and squeezed her friend's hand. "Do you think it's anything serious with Colleen?" Maureen felt her countenance change immediately, and the lightheartedness that had lifted her spirit vanished. She knew that Vanessa could put on an act of irreverence in her humorous response to life. But Maureen also knew that underneath that flippant exterior was a heart full of sensitivity and tender love. When needed, Vanessa wasn't afraid to let that side of her show. The sudden appearance of that very quality had undone Maureen a number of times before.

"Not really. It's just—"

"Colleen's being a typical mouthy teen and Bill's ... shall we say, pushing your buttons?"

Maureen stared at Vanessa's profile, embarrassed by her friend's insight. "And how did you gather all that?"

"Immutable signs." Flatly stated.

"Immutable, eh? You into big words today?"

"Been reading a book on theology. Impressed?"

"Definitely. But don't dodge, Nessa. Get back to my *'immutable signs.'*"

Vanessa drew a deep breath, prepared to tread softly. "Know how they say skin on a scar will always be thinner and more sensitive?"

"Sure. I have enough scars to prove that theory."

"Well, you're … *thin*. Does that even make any sense?" she laughed at herself.

Maureen kept her gaze straight ahead, staring out with unfocused eyes at the car in front of them. "Bill has always told me that I register every single emotion on my face. I hate that."

"So … want to talk about it? Or, maybe … not?"

Maureen leaned her head against the window. Deciding she just didn't have the emotional energy to go through it all now and then again with Sherry and Emilie, she said, "I think I'll wait, Vanessa. It's just too much—"

"To plow through twice?" To Maureen's nod, Vanessa replied, "I understand. And besides," she gestured toward their destination, "conveniently, we've arrived."

As they pulled into the restaurant, Maureen pointed out, "Look—there's Sherry. And Emilie's car is already here too." She opened her door, calling out, "Hey, Sherry."

Sherry waited, hands on hips. In her typical tailored business suit, Sherry looked very much the professional she was. She kept her light blonde hair neatly bobbed, and the intelligent eyes that peered at them through tortoiseshell-framed glasses were without makeup. What softened Sherry's entire look, however, was her wide grin and outstretched arms. "Been looking forward to this since we set it up. Give me some hugs, you two."

The three linked arms as they walked up the sidewalk. Vanessa conspiratorially winked at Maureen. "The Clarkson family is into decrees these days—more on that topic later, Sherry," (eliciting another laugh from Maureen) "so I'm gonna propose yet another one: Today, no salads allowed. Only glorious, fatty entrées for us. And dessert. Something tells me we're all gonna need the happiness that only fat can bring."

"Sounds like a divine idea," Sherry agreed, and all three were laughing together as a smiling host held the door for them.

The cozy, intimate restaurant was a converted home from the late 1800s, and was one of their favorites. As the three walked in, they noticed the intermingling smells of spices and freshly baked bread, at once enticing and soothing. An assortment of brightly colored flowers—large baskets of pansies—looked welcoming on windowsills and tables scattered throughout the gracious interior. They glanced at each other and grinned in anticipation, hugging each other closer within their locked arms.

The host, mirroring their happiness, gushed, "Welcome to The Cottage, ladies."

"Thank you. We're meeting one more, Emilie Esteban. I think she's arrived?" Vanessa inquired.

"Yes, I believe she has. Follow me right this way, please."

Leading them to a corner table, he motioned to a secluded niche where they would have a good deal of privacy. There was still much bustling about as they distractedly greeted Emilie, decided who would sit where and settled in, at last giving Emilie their total attention. And then simultaneously, as though choreographed, all gaiety came to an abrupt end.

Emilie appeared stricken, shrunken, weak. Her shoulders were slumped over, head tilted down, hands clenched together in her lap. When she did glance up, they saw that her eyes were red and swollen, her face raw and chapped, every flaw of her deathly pale skin—wrinkles, sags, lines—highlighted. Emilie looked like an old woman.

Maureen reached over and clutched Emilie's hands. "What is it? What's happened, Em?"

Emilie lifted her chin, but closed her eyes as she slowly shook her head. The silence was unbearable. And so they filled it, voices overlapping with peppered questions.

"Is it one of the kids?"

"Is it Ed? Is his business in trouble somehow?"

"Has someone been in an accident?"

"Oh, Em … is it *you*? Have you been to a doctor? Is that why you missed the meeting this morning?"

"Let us help."

"Tell us what to do."

"Emilie?"

When she finally spoke, the flatness of Emilie's voice was like a generated recording, devoid of personality and emotion. "Ed's met another woman. He's moving out." She glanced down at her wrist, checked the time on her watch. "Right now, as a matter of fact."

They stared at her, mouths open. And though they didn't realize it, each one held her breath, features frozen in disbelief.

"He told me just as I was about to go out the door this morning. Oh, sorry I wasn't there today, Maureen." An aside, eerie in its calm. "Says he's in love—for the first time in his life. And so he knows this is what God wants him to do. Go to be with *her*, of course." Emilie began to speak faster, slurring one word into the next. "After all these years … he was living for me and the kids, he says … sacrificing his own personal happiness … and finally it's *his* turn in life to be happy. So he says now … with *God's blessing*, he says … that …"

Emilie stopped then, allowing the words to slip away as though she were a music box that gradually wound down. Silenced now, she was smaller still.

The three friends exchanged quick, horrified glances and then Maureen, still holding Emilie's hand in her own, squeezed tighter. One thought raced frenetically through her mind: *Say the right thing. Whatever you do, Say the right thing.* "I don't believe Ed would follow through with this, Emilie. He'll come to his senses." Maureen looked around the table for affirmation from the others. "I bet he'll be back before you know it. *Certainly* he'll change his mind."

Vanessa started to add something, but hesitated and stopped, flustered.

And then Sherry whispered under her breath, "Maybe it would be better for Em if he *didn't*."

That drew an astonished look from Maureen, but a shrill, staccato laugh from Emilie. It was nothing like her usual beloved, boisterous laugh, and that sarcastic sound—more than anything that Emilie had said so far—brought a stab of pain to Maureen's heart.

"Funny, I was thinking some of those same things when Ed was first telling me his '*news*,' shall we say. My mind was racing, thinking surely he'd change his mind, he'd come to his senses, blah, blah, blah. And then he'd beg my forgiveness for this … this temporary *insanity*." She reached for a crumpled, much-used tissue from her lap, dabbed at her eyes.

"And then he put his briefcase on the counter, pulled out papers. Turns out my efficient husband has already contacted an attorney." She blew her nose and then closed her eyes. "It's been going on *that long*. And here I was …"—she glanced over at Maureen with a look on her face like she'd just been slapped—"so *blind* that I was actually considering having another baby."

Maureen rehearsed their conversation of the night before, trying to remember Emilie's exact words. "Em, it … this makes no sense. Didn't you and Ed just discuss this? *Recently?* Did I misunderstand?"

"Oh, no, you didn't misunderstand a thing." Emilie grabbed the edge of the table with both hands, gripping it so tightly that her knuckles turned white. "He was falling all over himself with apologies about that 'small but well-meaning indiscretion,' he called it, this morning. A lapse in judgment. But he was only trying to 'pacify you, dear Emilie,' as he so *thoughtfully* put it."

Maureen felt sick to her stomach and leaned down to find a tissue in her purse. Anything to break eye contact with Emilie—and those piercing, accusing eyes. She had no idea what to say now … how to respond. All she could do was glance up from her search to meet Emilie's gaze momentarily before looking down again. Like a puppet on a string, Emilie followed Maureen's lead, looking down at her purse too. It was like a bizarre, synchronized dance. And in the midst of that ballet, Maureen could only think, *Why is she so intently focusing on* me? *What am I supposed to say? What does she want me to say?*

"That is just … *disgusting.*" Sherry had been married to an apparent charmer who turned out to be a total fraud. He had

cheated—not once, but repeatedly. Once she discovered his infideli-
ties, she divorced him without a backward glance and often pointed
out that she'd never trust another man again. Not in *that* way. With
narrowed eyes and grim line of her mouth, she slowly shook her head
in disdain.

"It's also pathetic." From Vanessa.

Emilie turned again to Maureen, eyebrows raised.

"I just don't know what to … Ed's always been such a godly …
he's an elder at church. And he's the head of your home, Emilie,
and …"

"*Maureen.*" Sherry gave Maureen a piercing glare, cutting her
off. And then, before anyone could say anything more, a server
arrived at their table.

"Welcome, ladies. I hope you're all having a *great* day." Not waiting for an answer, she chirped, "My name's Becky and I'll be your
server. What drinks can I get you to start with? May I suggest a nice
merlot or maybe a margarita? We've got a special going on mango
margaritas today, if anyone's interested?" She appeared totally oblivious to the tension that sat like a grey cloud over the table.

"I'd like water with a lemon, please," Sherry answered succinctly.

"Sparkling water? We have—"

"Tap water will do fine."

"The same for me, please," from Vanessa.

"I think I'd like iced tea." Maureen looked over to Emilie. "Em,
isn't this where we got the peach tea that we both liked so much?"
Without waiting for an answer, she continued, "Would you like
that too then?" Still no response from Emilie. "Two of those for us,
please. Thanks."

"Any appetizers today? We have avocado and crab dips with one of our specialty breads?" Her cheerfulness was like a laugh at a funeral.

Several responses of *no* before she continued, "Okay then. I'll be right back with these and then we'll get your order." She turned and bounced away, four sets of eyes following.

"Better look at the menu now," Sherry suggested.

Vanessa and Maureen glanced over at Emilie, who merely stared at the closed menu before her. Making no move to open it, she sat completely still.

After a few moments of awkward silence, Maureen pushed the menu aside and quietly asked, "Emilie, are you going to feel up to eating anything at all? I mean …"

"Of course she is." Sherry responded with authority like the professor that she was. "She's got to eat. And we're going to make sure she does."

"But maybe that's not what Emilie needs. I mean, we could just leave and—"

"*No,*" Emilie emphatically interrupted, surprising them all. "I want to stay here. I don't want to go home! I can't walk back into the house just yet …" She caught her breath, stopped. And then the tears came.

As if on cue, everyone reached for Emilie's hands, arms, anything to touch her, reassure her. Emilie began openly weeping, the other three tearing up also, feeling the heartache along with her.

But then, as suddenly as the tears had arrived, Emilie pleaded, "Um, we've got to get ourselves together." Flustered, she grabbed for the rumpled tissue again. "I don't want anyone else to know about this yet. It's been hard enough telling you all, and …" she paused, swallowing, "well, I'm not ready for this to get out. And then there's the kids. Oh, God, *how am I ever going to tell the kids?*" Despite her resolve, she had to wipe away more tears.

"Em, are you positive this isn't just some huge misunderstanding?" Maureen asked. "Or maybe … maybe we need to look at this from God's perspective, like Joseph. You know, he meant it for evil, but God meant if for good?"

Sherry's intensity pulled her toward Maureen, and though she whispered, her words came out like a snarled hiss, "Maureen, listen to me. *Shut up.* It doesn't work that way in the real world, and you know that." Seeing Maureen's hurt response, Sherry purposefully eased herself backward, resettled, closed her eyes a moment, and then took a deep breath. "Look, Maureen, I think I understand what you're trying to say. But the idea that if we can only figure it all out, then God will simply make it vanish—"

"I'm so sorry." Maureen's eyes darted from Sherry to Emilie. "I didn't mean … I'm only trying to help Em see, to help us all see, that sometimes there's a blessing underneath. That good can come of the worst. Isn't that right?" She searched Emilie's face for answers, but it was Sherry who spoke into the tense atmosphere again.

"Quite frankly, I don't think it's time yet to search for the good in this mess. Because there's not one thing good about this!" A pained look covered Sherry's features, telltale remnants of her own past. "And if God really is *God*, then I wish he would skip the heartbreaking life lessons for the children's sake, and stop Ed in his tracks right now."

Maureen instinctively jerked backward. And then she looked to Emilie, fully expecting her to vehemently disagree. Yet Maureen watched in absolute amazement as Emilie nodded her head, and then added, "Oh, Sherry. That's exactly what my heart has been crying out. That God would … be God. And do something!"

Never before had Maureen heard any of these friends express such caustic cynicism, such blatant anger at God. *Wasn't that blasphemy?* she asked herself, realizing that she was nearly frozen in fear, waiting for … *What? Am I expecting God to strike us dead?*

"I think we need to let go of … I don't know … searching for reasonable answers for any of it," Vanessa said. "This is horrible, Em. And no amount of fanciful rationalizing of God's part in this will ever make one bit of it acceptable. And it won't make sense simply because we interpret this as 'God's will,' the wonderful catchall that every one of us"—Vanessa looked from Maureen to Sherry and then to Emilie again as she emphasized her words—"has used way too often in the past."

Vanessa had spoken in such a rush that she had to pause to catch her breath. "Emilie's hurting, and you know what? I think we should just … hurt with her." Her eyes filled with tears as she stared into Emilie's equally tear-filled eyes. "No explanations or answers. Just love. Loving her the best we can, in the way that she needs us most."

Sherry took charge then, as she usually did whenever a decision for the entire group needed to be made. "I'm guessing that no one feels much like eating, am I right? But Emilie, you don't want to leave yet, either." Emilie firmly shook her head, and Sherry continued, "Then how about if we order just soup and some of their breads? Good idea?" Relieved nods all around. "Okay. That solves the dilemma of eating versus not eating."

The server returned then, delivering drinks and taking their orders. Once she'd left again, Vanessa, Sherry, and Maureen turned their attention back to their friend.

"Do you want to tell us more details about what Ed said?" Sherry asked, gently probing.

Emilie stared down at the table rather than meet anyone's eyes. "I think I need to tell you. Get some … perspective, I guess. I keep thinking this can't be happening to me. It can't be real and I'll wake up." She sniffed and wiped at her nose with the pathetic-looking tissue.

"I heard the garage door opening, heard him coming in, felt surprise and yet delight that he was there. Assumed he'd forgotten something." She shook her head slightly, chagrined at her eagerness to see him. "Then when I saw his face, at first he scared me." She looked up momentarily, the emotions of genuine concern and fear reflected still, mirroring the past. "I thought something was wrong, so I went to run into his arms and—" Emilie's voice faltered. "He put out his hand to stop me." Again she paused, struggling to regain her composure. "I was really bewildered at that point. Started asking him if he was okay, if he was sick, maybe had the flu or something and didn't want me near him to catch it. And suddenly something about the look on his face—the fact that he wouldn't or couldn't look at me." Emilie put her head in her hands. "As blind as I've been for … weeks now … in that moment I just knew." She looked up, and a single tear ran down each cheek. "What a naive idiot I've been."

Sherry spat out, "Emilie, you trusted him. It's ingrained to trust our husbands."

"How did you find out who she is?" From Vanessa. There was no need to explain the who.

"I knew instantly. Put it all together. Ed's talked nonstop about a woman—she's in marketing, working with their new ad campaign—who's been visiting his office. 'This Denise, she's something else' and 'Denise really knows her stuff' and 'we invited Denise to join us for lunch today.'" Emilie's unfocused gaze looked off into the past, remembering. "And then suddenly he stopped talking about her. I bet you anything that's when the relationship changed." She laughed, but once again it was a deformed imitation of her true laugh. Maureen cringed. "After that, I imagine she continued to be invited to lunch, all right. But with only one person in particular. I swear I don't know whether to cry or scream. And the worst part?" She gave them a beseeching, apologetic look. "I still love him."

"A part of you always will." Sherry's voice was filled with a longing that caught Maureen off guard, and then Sherry met and held Maureen's gaze. The marks of naked pain were still there, residing in deep shadows around Sherry's eyes, defined in lines and valleys that would never fully go away. Maureen noted the offering and accepted it, nodding.

The server brought their meals at that point, placing cheery, bright-colored crocks of steaming soups before them and adding a large basket of assorted warm rolls and muffins. As enticing as the array of food looked and smelled, the scene was out of sync with reality.

Once their server was gone, a palpable awkwardness descended over them. Maureen looked around the table, seeking an answer to the unspoken question, *Who would volunteer to pray?* Emilie certainly wouldn't be expected to—she was the one they needed to pray for. Maureen took in Vanessa's fussing with her napkin, signaling that she had no intention of venturing into that abyss. And Sherry nonchalantly picked up her spoon and ladled the hot soup, indicating her desire to skip the ritual.

"I suppose we ought to pray," Maureen offered. Emilie and Sherry avoided her eyes, but Vanessa shot her a look of relieved gratefulness. Maureen closed her eyes and bowed her head, acquiescing. "Lord, I pray now for our friend, Emilie. We love her so much and we ... we hurt with our dear friend. Please comfort her, God. And please bring Ed back to you. Back to Emilie and the children. In your name, amen."

By evading questions or giving barely perceptible, one-word answers, Emilie communicated that she was ready to change the subject. So the three labored to talk about the everyday events of their lives. What was safe. What mattered not at all.

Most uncharacteristically, they soon ran out of things to say. *Everything else seems so trivial in comparison,* thought Maureen—and so they picked at their food, tearing small bites of bread, sipping a little soup. The food grew cold in their lack of hunger and interest, the soup turning bland, the bread growing stale. And then a sense of unspoken agreement guided their friendship as they nearly simultaneously pushed plates aside; it was the signal that they—all but one—needed to be on their separate ways. To the routines that made up their lives. After all the times they had sought distance and escape from the duties they faced, by eating in a quaint little café such as this one, it suddenly struck Vanessa, Sherry, and Maureen that it was the routine itself that made up the very essence of life. Ironically, it was that sameness they all unknowingly craved and clung to for one reason: security. And Emilie, they knew, had been brutally stripped of every bit.

The three of them looked at her, seeking her permission, it appeared, to be dismissed. But Emilie remained lost in her own thoughts, looking stricken as she suddenly took in the reality that never again would look the same for her.

They hugged one another in the parking lot. Emilie responded as if by rote, her senses dulled and her face blank. More than anything else, Emilie's joyless spirit broke her friends' hearts. Rarely did they share a time with each other when Emilie's laugh didn't ring out through a restaurant or park or the other places they'd gathered. In the past, the loud honking might have embarrassed them, but today they realized how precious it was. An essential thread that wove through their lives, binding them together—one of Emilie's unique contributions to the Gang of Four. Each felt set adrift without that symbol of joy.

They continued to cling to each other, desperately wanting to do something, anything to help Emilie. They peppered her with suggestions. *Can we bring in meals? Babysit the kids? Contact our pastor—or a lawyer?*

But despite their insistence, Emilie said at this point there was nothing she needed or wanted them to do. Besides pray. "And don't you see?" she pointed out, simply. "It's cooking, laundry, and even having the kids right there, underfoot, that I need right now. Anything to help keep me busy. Busy enough that I don't think too much. Or feel too much."

They reassured her repeatedly of their love and prayers, their desire that Emilie call them tomorrow, emphasizing to call whenever

she needed them. Each took a turn pulling her into a firm hug—
all but Maureen making a point to look into Emilie's eyes before
parting—and then they sent her on her way.

Vanessa and Maureen spoke little at first as they drove back to
the church, both overwhelmed with Emilie's news, lost in the enor-
mity of it all. Finally Maureen was so uncomfortable with the void
that she spoke up, confessing.

"I've been so selfish, Vanessa, thinking about my own silly
problems when Emilie has this. Did you suspect ... did you see it
coming?"

"Oh, Maureen. No, not at all, though like I told you—Ed
had been bugging me lately. But I doubt that anyone saw this
coming."

"I feel bad about the way we talked about Emilie ..."

Vanessa turned to Maureen, shaking her head. "Look, we're
not gonna wallow in guilt, because we didn't know, did we?"

Maureen agreed, reluctantly. "There's just one more thing.
Yesterday, when I was on the phone with Emilie. I think she was
about to tell me ... to admit there was dissension or distance or
discord ... something she was feeling between her and Ed. And I
cut her off, Vanessa. I was so caught up in my own problems that
I—"

"Maureen, again: You didn't know. I bet anything yesterday you
had no idea what Emilie was going to say on the phone when that
happened, did you?" When Maureen didn't immediately respond,
Vanessa pressed her, "Did you?"

"I guess not. Not really."

"And what did you mean by 'cut her off'?"

"Oh, the kids were arguing."

"So you weren't cutting off Emilie to go watch soaps and eat bon-bons?"

Maureen grinned, sheepishly.

"And I saw your face, Mo, when Emilie told us about Ed. You were just as blown away as Sherry and I."

Maureen nodded. "Yeah. Oh my gosh, Nessa. It still … I still can't believe it's real."

"You couldn't have stopped it, Maureen, if that's what you're thinking."

Vanessa turned into the church parking lot, pulled into the space next to Maureen's van. She turned to face Maureen, reached over to take her hand. "The only one who could've stopped this—how I wish I were a cussing woman at times like this—this you-know-what from happening to Emilie was Ed himself."

"Ed. How could he? Talk about making no sense. After all these years … all they've been through together. How could he just throw it all away?"

"The kids. Doesn't your heart just break for them? What does this say to them? About God?"

They reached out to each other, clasping in a hug of desperation. When they finally pulled apart, Vanessa stared off into the distance, wistfully asking, "All those years ago when we first met, could we ever have envisioned that—that any of our lives would've taken the paths that we've been down?"

Maureen thought of Sherry … and now Emilie. But she also heard Colleen's strident accusation, and the pain of it was fresh again, causing her to wince. "No, I wouldn't. Never." *Colleen.* Maureen jumped as though startled from a daydream. "What time is it? If I'm late picking up Colleen—"

"What? She'll stop speaking to you? With teens, that could be a definite plus—" Vanessa stopped, seeing the very real look of panic on Maureen's face.

"Oh no, it's two thirty already. I have to run."

"Maureen? We'll get through this. The three of us will get Emilie through this."

Maureen nodded. But the hand she used to open her door was shaking.

☆

When Bill walked in the door later, Maureen moved immediately into his arms, only able to say, "Oh, Bill. You just won't believe it."

Alarmed, he held her out from him, searching her face, asking, "What? What's happened? Are the kids—?"

Maureen quickly put a finger to her lips, gesturing toward Aubrey. "Shh. The kids are fine." With a nod toward the hallway, she beckoned for Bill to follow her.

They nearly ran right into Colleen standing in her bedroom's doorway, shooting Maureen an accusatory glare. "The Estebans are getting a divorce, aren't they," Colleen said. A statement, not a question.

Bill looked over at Maureen, his expression obviously asking if it were true. She merely shook her head slightly.

"How did you—?" Bill questioned Colleen.

"Eddie. He told me about the other woman a month ago." Noting Maureen's shocked response, Colleen added, "You mean

Mrs. Esteban didn't know this was coming before today? She didn't catch on?" Colleen rolled her eyes. "I can't believe she was dumb enough to—"

"Colleen, that's quite enough." Bill's sharp correction silenced her immediately. "Don't you have homework to do? Then get busy on it." Colleen obeyed, but as she turned to go back into her room she shot her mother an accusing look.

Bill pulled Maureen into their bedroom, shutting the door behind them. "Tell me this is just a rumor."

"It's no rumor, Bill. I saw Emilie at lunch." Her voice sounded far away to her ears, as though it were someone else speaking. "Ed's already hired a lawyer."

Bill sat on the bed, staring at the floor. When he finally looked up at Maureen, he appeared stricken. "I can't … this can't be true." Holding his arms wide, Bill pulled her into his embrace, where they clung to each other. Mumbling angrily, he choked out, "I just want to … to punch him. Beat some sense into him."

He started pulling off his tie, continuing to mutter to himself, and Maureen got up and leaned against the dresser. She wrapped her arms around her torso, as though hugging herself. She stared down at the carpet and the familiar pattern of roses and vines.

"Ed'll eventually come to his senses, Mo. I've got to believe that." He poked his head out of the closet, attempting to make eye contact. "But honestly, even if it does happen—a divorce, I mean—God will take care of Emilie and the kids. They won't be the first couple we've known to divorce. And not the first in your group of friends. Sherry's doing okay, isn't she?"

"Sherry doesn't have four children, Bill."

"But they're all believers now, aren't they? Even the youngest?" Bill disappeared back into the closet again.

Maureen was surprised by the retort that flitted across her own mind. *Like that guarantees they'll all live happily ever after?*

"Maureen?"

"I want you to tell me that we'll be okay," Maureen said softly, wistfully, as she traced the pattern of the carpet with her bare toes.

Bill hadn't heard, but she could hear the sounds of his pulling on jeans. When he came out again, he asked, "Did you speak with Colleen?"

Maureen slowly shook her head. "I couldn't bring it up in the car, with Aubrey there. And then Colleen's been busy with homework ever since we got home."

He shot her a look.

"I can't talk about Colleen now. All this with Emilie and Ed has made me feel so … insecure." Staring down at the carpet still, afraid to meet his eyes. Calmly, flatly, she stated, "I want to see a counselor." After she spoke the words, she recognized the familiar yet odd sensation of feeling detached, as though hearing her own voice from a distance.

Bill scoffed. "Where on earth did that come from? If you're feeling a little insecure then—"

"Actually, I didn't say a little. I feel … shattered, Bill. I don't understand why, but it feels like every single area of my life is falling apart into these tiny little pieces. I'm trying to grab at them and collect them up, but I can't because they're falling everywhere. They keep slipping through my fingers, away from my grasp."

"Look, just because Emilie and Ed might be getting a divorce, that doesn't have anything to do with us."

"No?" Her voice rose in inflection. "Emilie was clueless, but Eddie knew about his dad's affair? A month ago. Well, Colleen is certainly picking up something that—"

"Maureen. That's enough. If you're insinuating that I'm having an affair, then you do need to see a counselor because you're—"

"Hallucinating and probably losing my mind. I know that. And I know you're not having an affair, Bill." She chuckled. "It's me. I admit it. I'm clueless. I don't know who Ed Esteban is, obviously. I clearly don't know my own daughter either."

Maureen paused, caught the motion of Bill's clenching and unclenching jaw. He stood before the window and stared out, back perfectly straight, hands on hips.

"Most of all," she whispered, "I don't know who I am anymore. Maybe I never knew. But I think it's time I found out."

Maureen stood up and reached for the door, but Bill grabbed her arm, restraining her. "Look, we'll talk about this later, okay?" His tone was soothing, patronizing. "No one in my family has ever seen a counselor. We're not going to start that sort of thing now. Maureen, there's nothing here that the two of us can't work out together."

She looked up into his eyes. Noted the firm set of his chin. His unblinking stare. But she said nothing.

"Okay, how about this? How about if you talk with Pastor Johnson? I bet he could tell you how to help Emilie—tell you how to organize meals or something. Whatever. And that would make you feel better, wouldn't it?"

"You think making food is going to solve this for Emilie? And what about Colleen? You and me? What about my feelings, Bill?"

"Aren't we being just a tad overdramatic? Good grief, I'll talk with Colleen. We'll work this out, for cryin' out loud." He pulled her into his arms again, rubbed her back. "Look, honey. We're going through a tough time. We've got a—I'll admit it—a teen with a capital *A* attitude. Our friends are in crisis. And it's putting you and me on edge." Once again he pushed her away from him so he could look into her eyes. "But we'll get through this, okay? I promise you. We don't need a stranger meddling in our … our lives. Okay?"

Maureen sighed. Nodded her head, acquiescing.

"Also, since I'm an elder at church and—"

"Ironically, so is Ed."

He ignored the comment, continued, "If you were to go see a counselor, well, can't you see how this would play out before the community? On the heels of Ed and Emilie? You know how that would look."

"My understanding is that a professional counselor would never reveal confidences. Isn't that a legal requirement?"

Bill sighed, shifted his gaze away before admitting, "Yes. But you know this area of town, Mo. Someone might see you going and then—"

"So now we get to the issue."

"Maureen, that's not fair."

"It's just like Colleen said. She accused me of fretting about my image, and now it's come back to me full circle, hasn't it? Guess I deserved this."

"I'm just asking you to consider how this will affect all four of us. Isn't this a rather selfish desire on your part? You're already gone two mornings a week in the shop. You're busy with church. When do you have time for sessions with a counselor?"

Maureen rubbed her eyes, pushed away from him. "I need to get dinner going."

"I thought we were making a decision here?"

Her eyes bored into his for only a split second. "You're right that I just don't have the time, Bill."

"So we'll work this out—just us, together?"

"We'll work it out."

It was yet another evening of Colleen's self-imposed silence, but in a strange way, Maureen welcomed it. Reading and praying with both girls took the last bit of energy she had at her disposal, and she fell asleep minutes after she'd collapsed into bed, not even hearing the annoying click of the remote.

Only to awaken at 1:17 a.m. Instantly, wide awake.

One thought after another bullied for priority in her mind. She worried about Colleen, and what they were to do. How to handle her in a way that wouldn't push her further away from them. *And where is she spiritually?* Maureen's heart wondered. Her worries then turned to Emilie. In their bed—by herself. Maureen was tempted to cuddle up to Bill's back for the sense of security he would instantly provide, but she couldn't lie still long, was afraid she'd only awaken him also. There was certainly no sense in both of them worrying needlessly at this hour.

When she was convinced a good amount of time had passed, she looked up at the clock. 1:35. Sighing, she knew there was no hope of drifting back to sleep.

Maureen gently lifted the covers and eased out of bed. She was slipping into her robe when Bill's voice startled her.

"What're you doing?" he mumbled.

"Can't sleep. Sorry I woke you. Go back to sleep, okay?" She padded out of the room, barefoot, and closed the door gently behind her. For a moment, Maureen stood at the door and listened. Not hearing any further movement from Bill, she assumed he'd drifted off again.

Typical man, she fumed to herself. *No matter what worrisome events are happening, he can sleep like the dead.*

Maureen paused at Aubrey's door. It was wide open, the night-light in the corner casting a soft glow against the light lavender walls. She couldn't resist the urge to stand there a moment, watching. One arm was thrown casually up over the pillow, the dimpled fingers open, relaxed. Her other hand held Rabbit, tucking the worn toy under her chin.

Walking farther down the hallway to Colleen's room, Maureen stopped at the closed door and put her hand on the doorknob. She hesitated, debating. Finally she turned it, hoping to find it wasn't locked against her. The knob easily moved in her hand.

While Aubrey's positioning had conveyed peaceful sleep, Colleen's was the exact opposite. Feeling heartache for her daughter, Maureen took in how the covers had been completely tossed aside, the arms that were tensed, both fists clenched. Knees drawn up to her chin in fetal position. A frown drew Colleen's mouth downward, a deep line creased between her delicate brows. Unhappiness was sleeping there with her.

Maureen pushed the door open a bit farther, and slipped into the room. Knelt by Colleen's bed where she poured out her heart to God—silently moving her lips, but sometimes falling into whispers in her urgency. She pleaded with God for her daughter's heart, begging him to forgive her for how she'd failed Colleen. For her hypocrisy and weaknesses and how she hadn't been the example she desired to be.

Tears had wet her cheeks when she felt a faint touch on her arm. Opening her eyes, it took a moment of adjusting to the dim light from the moon before she saw her daughter staring back at her. Colleen bit her lip, and then blurted out, "*Mom?*"

"Oh, Colleen, I'm sorry. I didn't mean to wake you."

"No, it's okay. I'm glad you did, 'cause I was having a night-mare." She wiped at her nose and then rubbed her eyes. "I can't even remember what it was. But I know I was really afraid and then—then I heard you." Colleen paused a moment, and noticeably shivered. "Mom, I've felt so *awful* lately."

"You're cold. We'd better get you back under the covers, sweetie." Colleen allowed Maureen to tuck her in, easing her back onto her pillow and pulling up rumpled sheets and bedspread. Maureen took her time, relishing the moment of peace between them, and then she sat next to her daughter, leaning forward with a hand on either side of Colleen. "Now. You've felt awful, how? Are you sick?" Maureen reached toward her forehead to check for a temperature, but Colleen shook her head, dodging.

"No … no, it's not that. It's other stuff." She hesitated and then blurted out, "Mr. and Mrs. Esteban. Are they … are they gonna be okay?"

Maureen leaned back, and sighed. How she wished she could tell her daughter everything would be fine. And that the "good" she hoped to come from all this would protect Colleen from the tentacles of pain that were reaching out, threatening all who knew Emilie. "I don't know, sweetie. I just don't know. I do know this, though. That God is still God. He wasn't surprised by this—like we all were. And he's still in control, even though it might not seem like it right now."

"When I heard you talking with Miss Mann—"

"What on earth *did* you overhear, Colleen? I have no idea what—"

Colleen rushed on, anxious to get it all out now, under the protection of the dark room. "It was a verse from Matthew something, the one about 'denying yourself and following me.' You know how it goes."

"Yeah, I remember discussing that."

"Miss Mann was talking loud enough for me to hear."

Maureen smiled. "I remember she was a bit intense. She'd heard a preacher, someone on the radio, I think. Sherry can get pretty excited."

"She was saying that verse didn't mean you have to be a doormat." Colleen bit her lip again. "Mom, don't take this bad. But sometimes you—"

"What?" Maureen leaned away from Colleen, instinctively braced herself.

"You started using this tone." She grimaced. "It's like you're that icky computerized voice the doctor's office uses. You know, the one they put on your answering machine to remind you about an appointment? It's so totally fake."

Maureen could feel the tension creeping back to claim her again. "Colleen, that's not—"

"And then you said … you said something like 'a wife should be a servant,' and 'we're supposed to deny ourselves for our family.'" She frowned again. "In that *voice*."

Unsure of what Colleen was accusing, Maureen offered, "Well, that's true."

Colleen's eyes flew wide open. "*That's it*—that's the voice, Mom."

Maureen's head flinched as though she'd been splashed with ice water, and she felt a stab of pain in her neck from the reflexive action. Irritably, she returned, "But that's what the Bible says, Colleen. And well, that's the way it should be." She reached up to rub the base of her neck.

"But Mom. There's gotta be a difference between serving. And being a doormat. 'Cause Eddie and I think his mom—"

"Colleen. You and Eddie have no right to … Eddie especially, nor you … you're not being respectful. And Miss Mann wasn't saying that … she wasn't even talking about Mrs. Esteban." Maureen stood suddenly, fussing with the covers, retucking the sheet into hospital corners. "You need to get back to sleep or … or you'll be sick tomorrow."

"I knew it."

"What?"

"I knew you wouldn't listen." Colleen pulled the bedspread up over her eyes and flipped over toward the wall.

"That's not fair, Colleen. I did so listen. I just disagree."

From beneath the covers, a mumbled, "Whatever."

Maureen started to reach forward, longing to touch the top of her daughter's head, but then hesitated. And decided not to. She stared down at Colleen for a few more moments and turned to go, softly closing the door behind her. Another quick peek into Aubrey's room proved they hadn't awakened her; she was still sleeping soundly. Then Maureen jumped at the sudden press of soft fur at her feet.

"Oh, Bobo. You up too?" She reached down to pick him up, felt him squirm in her arms, the telltale sign that he was happily wagging his tail. "Okay, we'll cheat this one time. But don't you dare let Daddy know what we've done or you'll get me into trouble."

Once more she walked softly toward Aubrey's doorway. She tiptoed into the room, depositing Bobo on the bed where he immediately padded around in three circles and curled up in the bend of the back of Aubrey's knees. Besides a lap, his favorite place to cuddle.

Maureen smiled, thinking how delighted Aubrey would be to discover him there when she woke. *At least maybe one of my daughters will be happy with me tomorrow morning,* she thought.

Back in bed, Maureen finally drifted off to sleep, but she still tossed and turned, waking nearly every hour to stare at the bedside clock that had become an enemy. And each time Maureen woke, she would turn to face the window and—stubbornly, even compulsively—search for another of those elusive stars.

May 2009

In the intervening weeks, Maureen's very spirit felt as though it were slowly draining away. Every area of her life shouted that she had failed—as a wife, a mother, a friend. Her routine forced her to get up every morning and go through her day. Household chores that kept the Roberts family functioning adequately, volunteering at church

and school, and her work at the beads shop all had lists of "to-dos"
that at least provided form and purpose. Mentally crossing another
thing off the list, she knew these tasks had no more meaning than
buying a loaf of bread. But they kept her moving. Doing something.

Other events had also become routine, despite Maureen's
desperate (*pathetic?* she asked and subsequently convicted herself)
efforts to prevent their reoccurrence: her own frequent bouts with
insomnia (and staring out the window at stars), Colleen's either silent
treatment or open disdain for her *mo-ther,* Emilie's steady decline
toward depression, the gang's ineffectual and listless get-togethers,
and Maureen's continued strained relationship with Bill. No matter
what she did, it seemed Maureen couldn't help any of those who
appeared to need it most.

Only Aubrey's usual delight with a day—any day, no matter how
ordinary—provided occasions for Maureen to catch her breath. To
get up and think *Maybe this will be the day that life changes. A turn
to better days is inevitable, isn't it? Just like the night watchman waits
for the morning in the book of Psalms. He trusts the morning will come,
eventually.*

Unfortunately, this *is not the day that will happen,* Maureen
thought miserably, staring out at the car bumpers that stretched
into the distance for miles. The drive to the shop was, for whatever
reason, even worse than usual. Traffic was so backed up that she was
creeping forward by mere inches, from block to block, traffic light to
traffic light. Tempers flared, horns honked in aggravation and hand
motions were in plentiful supply. Feeling short-tempered herself,
Maureen's thoughts drifted back to the heated discussion she and
Bill had months ago when she first brought up the subject of "The

Job." How she'd mentioned it mostly on a whim, assuming it would be a fun distraction. Not thinking about the consequences of shuttling Aubrey around, that she'd have considerably less free time. Or that she'd be in the teeth of morning rush hour every time she drove to the shop. Bill had responded skeptically, insinuating it was more than she could handle. And with that gauntlet thrown, suddenly Maureen desperately wanted the job to prove that she could handle it quite well, thank you. Armed with the support and arguments the gang had supplied, Maureen had worn Bill down until he'd given in. But he'd made it abundantly clear he expected it to be a short-lived venture.

Maureen sighed and her shoulders dropped. With the passing weeks—especially the last few—the novelty of the job had worn off. *But how do I quit now without looking like a failure this way also?* she asked herself. *I refuse to give Bill a reason to be smug. I've got to stick it out, no matter how much Jennifer grates on me.*

Jennifer. Her coworker had been a sarcastic nemesis from the moment Maureen admitted she was a Christian. Openly skeptical and even critical, Jennifer never missed an opportunity to point out and gloat over the latest scandals, from the pastor caught at the adult-video store to the wealthy member at First Church who admitted to tax fraud. Jennifer rooted out hypocrisy with a devotion verging on addiction; the more she found, the happier she became. And the more intent she was to root out the next public revelation. It put Maureen constantly on edge, defensive. Carefully choosing every word she uttered, she had vowed to live beyond reproach.

Finally past the worst of the traffic and onto the short stretch of open road a couple miles from the shop, Maureen granted her building irritation full reign by ignoring the speed limit—which proved disastrous. The second she saw the flashing red and blue lights in her rearview mirror she knew it was too late to hit the brakes. *One hundred dollars. Bill's going to have a fit.* Reasoning, pleading, even tears hadn't guilted the officer into giving her a mere warning. And that meant she was even later getting to work.

By the time she used her key to open the shop's door, Jennifer greeted her by quipping, "So you decided to come in today after all?"

"Sorry. I got stopped by a police officer." The honest admission was out of her mouth before she could stop it. *Big mistake, Maureen.*

Jennifer's eyes lit up. "You got a ticket? Miss Goody Two-Shoes who never does anything illegal got a real ticket?"

Maureen stooped to put her purse behind the counter, decided to let most of the dig pass. "Yes. Happy?"

"Just surprised, that's all." She leaned forward on the counter, resting her head on the palms of her hands like a child eagerly waiting to be told a story. "What'd you do, anyway?"

Maureen sighed, responded as though she were already bored with the topic. "I was speeding."

"By how much?"

"Is this inquisition really necessary? Fifteen miles over, if you must know."

"Ouch. Bet the ticket's a doozy." Jennifer raised her brows in curiosity, waiting for Maureen to reveal the price for her indiscretion.

"Don't we have a group coming in first thing this morning?"

"Yup." Jennifer glanced up at the clock. "In about ten minutes. That's plenty of time."

"We'd better get busy." Maureen went into the back room to do setup. Used her finger to count chairs around the table. "Only eight. Bring a couple more chairs from the closet, will you?" She began cleaning up leftover beads and wire from the night before, wanting the room to look neat for this morning's party.

"Had a dental appointment yesterday to get my teeth cleaned," Jennifer shouted from the other room. "This morning my mouth is *so* sore."

Maureen ignored her. She wasn't in the mood for chitchat.

"You know why?"

Maureen jumped in surprise, for Jennifer was now right behind her.

"Because I got one of those Christian hygienists with serious repressed anger issues."

Maureen stopped working long enough to give Jennifer a dramatic frown.

"So what do we do? We put a dangerously sharp metal instrument in her hands—purportedly to clean the tartar off teeth—and essentially give her permission to—"

"Jennifer."

"Bet she's sexually repressed too."

"That's quite—"

The jingle of the bell over the door and laughing, excited voices interrupted them. Maureen immediately clicked into working mode. "I'm going to welcome them. Give them the instructions. You finish getting everything set up in here, okay?" Without waiting for an answer, she turned and went to greet the party of women.

They were an amiable group, ten neighbors from a nearby subdivision on a creative break from their weekly bunco game. Maureen gave them the usual tour of the shop, pointing out the various types of beads, patterns they could follow, the jewelry possibilities of necklaces, earrings, bracelets, or other options like bookmarks and key chains. Excited to start, the women weren't especially attentive, but that was to be expected. Maureen knew they'd have more questions once they were actually making their projects; she'd be available and willing to help however she could.

Discovering she had a knack for putting together pretty jewelry came as a surprise to Maureen. Women always noticed when she wore one of her own creations, exclaiming over its uniqueness and coordinated colors. Working with the beads and the constant possibility of new designs fueled Maureen's desire to be at the shop regularly. What she hadn't accounted for was the tedium of the job itself: keeping the shop clean, including the monotony of putting hundreds of beads into the correct storage areas. Dealing with customers with limited or no talent at creating something remotely pretty or wearable. Dealing with … Jennifer.

Most of the women were seated around the table, quietly working when one of them snickered. "Some juicy news. Many of you know Ed Esteban, don't you?"

Maureen immediately stiffened and held her breath. She could feel her face flushing, so she busied herself with a project, looking down.

"I heard. Appears Ed's found himself … well, a newer model, shall we say?"

Titters of laughter followed. Maureen's flush deepened, her heart noticeably pounding in her chest.

"Divorcing?"

"In the works, I hear. Wonder if he'll marry this woman and have four more kids?"

"He's leaving her with four kids? The louse."

"Oh, yeah. Four little Estebans—all with names beginning with an *E,* after Ed and Emilie. Dedicated father. Upstanding church member and leader." The speaker looked up, and Maureen caught a spark of delight in her eyes. Maureen noticed Jennifer was now hanging on every word too. "Only this time he's backed up the alphabet by one letter. Any more kiddos gotta have names beginning with a *D* this time around."

Laughter erupted, with several exclamations of "Oh, Jan. You're terrible."

Maureen had been threading beads onto a wire, but her movements were so unsteady that, after three unsuccessful tries at threading a single turquoise bead, she was intensely aware of those near her, worried they might notice. She put the bead and thread down and rising from her stool, leaned over to whisper in Jennifer's ear, "I'm not feeling well. Think you can handle this?" Without giving Jennifer a chance to respond, she went on, "Call Mrs. Sandler if you have any problems. And please tell her that I got ill. That I had to leave."

Jennifer looked puzzled, opened her mouth to respond, but Maureen immediately turned on her heel. After grabbing her purse, she was out the door before Jennifer could get out more than, "Maureen? Can't you—?" Jennifer turned to the group of women and shrugged her shoulders.

Not until Maureen had turned the keys in the ignition and pulled out of her parking place did she let the dam break. She allowed the pent-up tears to flow, and her heart pounded even harder, though she wouldn't have thought that possible. Her hands were shaking so badly that she gripped the steering wheel as hard as she could, hoping that would make the involuntary movements stop. Instead, when she lifted one hand off the wheel to test it, the entire hand shook as if she were elderly and frail.

She quickly donned sunglasses to hide her tears and turned the air conditioning on high to drown out the accentuated hiccups that accompanied her staggered breathing. Though traffic had thinned considerably, the drive home felt interminable, mostly because she was alone with her thoughts. *There was nothing you could do,* she told herself. *You work there; it wasn't appropriate to interrupt.* But the more she attempted to reassure herself, the faster the tears came.

Once inside the relative safety of her kitchen, Maureen leaned against the door—appreciating the solidness of it—that she could symbolically shut out the world. She finally calmed her breathing and tears simply because she was emotionally and physically spent. Immediately searching for the new bag of coffee in the pantry, she went through the mindless motions of making a pot. Then, gratefully plopping into the soft cushioned chair at the kitchen bar, she clutched a mug in her hands, breathing in its rich aroma before sipping. The soothing quiet of the house was a rare gift, and Maureen knew she needed to make the most of it while she could. Too soon she'd need to go pick up Aubrey. And Colleen.

Mechanically, she reached for her Bible and the devotional book she'd been dutifully reading, turning to the selected passage for the day, 2 Peter 1:19–21:

"And we have the word of the prophets made more certain, and you will do well to pay attention to it, as to a light shining in a dark place, until the day dawns and the morning star rises in your hearts."

Maureen's thoughts immediately flew to the display of stars she stared at each night as sleep eluded her. The scene had become almost a painted picture in her mind's eye—the stars framed by the casing around her window. She recalled the brightest stars and the dim ones, those she could only catch glimpses of in her peripheral vision.

"Above all, you must understand that no prophecy of Scripture came about by the prophet's own interpretation. For prophecy never had its origin in the will of man, but men spoke from God as they were carried along by the Holy Spirit."

She skimmed through the offered commentary. The notes about the inspiration of Scripture, how both God and man were actively involved in the process. Knowing the phrase *morning star* was not the central thrust of the passage, Maureen still kept coming back to it, couldn't let go of the nagging feeling that there was something more here. Something waiting to be uncovered. Until finally, she gave in to her curiosity and headed for their home office.

Sitting before the computer, she mused, "Okay ... Google ... what shall I type in? Think I'll try 'information about stars.' That's a start."

She skimmed through the list, chose "Basic Facts about Star Gazing," and clicked.

She read about an anomaly called averted vision. According to the website, the term explained why some particularly distant stars vanished in your direct gaze. *That's it.* She read out loud: "'The star seems to disappear when you look straight at it, but if you avert your vision—when you look to one side or the other—then you're able to see the star again. The anomaly happens because the faint light of the star reaches a more sensitive part of the retina, allowing you to detect it.'"

Maureen sat back, absentmindedly chewing on a cuticle, pondering the significance of her discovery. Then Bobo brought her attention back to the mundane, stretching himself up to scratch her bare foot. "Need to go outside? As always, great timing, little one." She unlocked and opened the back door, depositing Bobo outside. And caught a flash of blue.

Maureen turned toward the birdhouse and discovered a male bluebird perched on top. Mesmerized, she took in the entire scene. Noted bits of lint in his beak, remnants from a dryer vent. And then, to Maureen's ultimate delight, he fluttered into the birdhouse. Was out of sight for only a few seconds before he flew out of the small round hole—and was off again. Obviously in search of more materials for building a nest.

The female soon followed, carrying a twig that Maureen doubted would fit through the hole. But as she watched, enchanted by every move the bird made and smiling in her delight, the female skillfully maneuvered the twig into her home.

"Bobo," she cried out, sweeping the startled dog up into the air. "The bluebirds are moving in! They're making our little house a home."

Maybe now ... maybe this is the turn I've been hoping for, she excitedly thought to herself, the ringing of the phone intruding into her raised hopes. Running inside to catch it in time, panting in her excitement, Maureen grabbed the receiver from its cradle. And then—she couldn't help herself—she moved to the window so she could continue watching the busy papa and mama.

"Hello?"

"Maureen? It's me. Emilie. Surprised I got you. Thought I'd have to leave a message, that you'd still be at work."

"No, um, long story." Maureen felt instantly uncomfortable, as if Emilie could see into her memories of the morning, read her thoughts. She felt herself blush in shame all over again. "What's up?"

"You won't believe it. God's answered our prayers. Mo—he's come home. Ed came home for good last night, can you believe it? I just can't wait to tell everyone about it tomorrow. Won't it be fun?—I can hardly wait." Emilie was nearly babbling, giddy in her excitement.

"Em, that's … wow, that's wonderful news."

"He says he realized what a horrible mistake it all was. Missed the kids. Hated the motel room and being away from us."

Maureen gathered her thoughts, seeking the best way to obtain delicate information. "You mean he's moved back into the house? Clothes and everything?"

"Yes, he has. His razor's back where it belongs. I even tripped over his sneakers this morning and it made me cry out of happiness."

"But do you mean … I mean … did he?"

"If you mean"—she coyly giggled—"did he move back into our bedroom? Oh yes. And we are really serious about having another baby now. Isn't that great news too?"

Maureen slumped against the wall, mouth dropping open, struggling to find words that Emilie would want to hear. "Um, sure, Emilie, what an answer to so many prayers."

"I've got to run. Just couldn't wait another moment to tell someone. What luck that I found you home. Oh, and don't call Sherry—she's been so critical of Ed—or breathe a word to Vanessa yet either. I want to tell them myself—see their faces. What fun. We're meeting at that fish place near St. John's pass, right?" Without waiting for an answer, Emilie trilled on. She was nearly babbling again. "That reminds me. I want to fix something special for dinner. What do you think? Steaks? Or should I make lasagna? Ed loves that recipe his mom passed along to me."

Emilie didn't give Maureen a chance to answer. "I probably won't have time to do lasagna or the Spanish dish. Better stick with the steaks. I made an appointment to get a manicure. And a hair cut. Can you tell I plan on looking good when Ed gets home?"

Emilie finally stopped to catch her breath—granting Maureen the opportunity to jump into the void. "Em, this is wonderful news, it really is. So, did you and Ed talk about counseling? I know you told me you didn't want to go by yourself. But shouldn't both of you go now?"

There was an awkward pause. When Emilie finally did speak her tone was noticeably more subdued. "Ed and I discussed it. And we don't think that's necessary now, Maureen. I thought that would be pretty obvious, given the circumstances."

Maureen clamped her jaw shut, willing herself not to react hastily.

"God's worked a miracle in Ed's heart, and he's said he's sorry. As a Christian, I'm to forgive him. Simple as that."

"But how can you *not* ...?" Emilie cleared her throat loudly, and Maureen, sensing the indication of unwanted advice, immediately stopped. She'd overstepped her bounds.

Emilie's voice was icy now. "I would've thought you'd only be happy for me, Maureen."

"Oh, I am, Emilie. I'm really sorry, I was just …" she groped for the right words to say, anything that would heal the ugly break she'd caused in the midst of her friend's joy. "Oh, Em. I'm just worried for you—that you could get hurt again. Please forgive me if I've offended you."

"I know you want to help, Mo, I really do." The tension in Emilie's voice eased, but it was replaced by weariness. "It's just that everyone has advice for me. And everyone's way is the right way, you know? The Christian way. Ed and I need to do what's best for us. Can you understand that?"

"I guess Sherry, Vanessa, and I can be a bit overbearing, huh?"

"You all mean well."

"Then can you believe I mean well about you and Ed talking with someone? Tell you what." Some nagging stubbornness pushed her to persist. "Could you just think about it?"

"I'll tell you why it's not necessary, Maureen, if you really need to know." Emilie's voice broke, her emotions were so close to the surface. "I don't need a counselor or anyone else to tell me it was my fault, okay? Is that what you wanted to hear? That everything was my fault because … because I wasn't the wife that Ed needed me to be. I failed him."

Maureen started to disagree, but the words caught in her throat, for her own heart convicted her of the same guilt. *Aren't you failing as a mom? As a wife? And only moments ago … you let Emilie down too.*

Emilie took in Maureen's silence. "I knew you thought that. All along I knew you blamed me."

Too late, Maureen found her voice. "No. I didn't mean … honestly, you misunderstood, Emilie! I was too busy thinking about my own issues. It's about … about Colleen and Bill and me … and I couldn't—I can't share that."

"Can't share what? Why?"

"Because it's too … it's just too—"

"Oh, please. You're embarrassed? While my life is displayed like a tawdry soap opera and everyone's busy gossiping about me?"

Again Maureen was reminded of the women at the shop and she closed her eyes, attempting to shut out the ugly statements. The cruel laughter. But more so—the void of what she didn't say in defense of her friend.

"What on earth do you have to be embarrassed about, Maureen? And why couldn't you confide in *me*—your closest friend—or at least, I thought so?"

"Emilie, you are my best friend. And I was—"

But Emilie hammered on as though Maureen hadn't uttered a word. "Let me guess: It would've unmasked you, right? Couldn't have Maureen looking bad, now could we? Besides, whatever you were dealing with, it sure didn't look as nasty compared to poor ole Emilie, huh? I'm sure you were too busy helping me too, judging me and mine. Even you."

"Oh, Emilie, no. I wasn't … I didn't mean that."

"I think I'd better go, Maureen. I've already said far too much. And tell you what. How 'bout you try to find a smidgen of happiness for me before we meet for lunch tomorrow. Could you do that for me? Bye."

"Emilie, wait—please let me try to explain." But she heard only the harsh finality of the dial tone.

She had just sat down in the kitchen, morosely putting head in hands when the phone rang again. Eagerly she grabbed it, hoping it might be Emilie calling back to patch things up.

"Em?"

"No, sorry to disappoint you." Bill's voice fortunately revealed only humor.

"Oh, hi, honey. I had a ... well, a strained conversation with Emilie a few minutes ago. I was hoping it was her again ... that we could ... well, fix things."

"Sorry to hear that."

"She called to share her good news: Ed moved back home last night."

"Wow. That is great news. So what on earth were you arguing about?"

"I never said it was an argument!"

"O-kay," Bill said, clearly changing his tone. "Then what were you discussing?"

"That she's taken him back without any ... with nothing, no consequences. He said he's sorry and they're carrying on like nothing's happened now. Bill, they're even talking again about having another baby."

"Sounds a bit premature."

"A bit—? Bill, there should be consequences for what Ed's done. And they both need to see a counselor."

Bill's silence stunned her. With an unsteady voice, she defensively offered, "I can't believe you'd think Emilie should've immediately welcomed Ed back into their home, literally with open arms. And I take it you don't agree they need counseling?"

88

Another pause, long enough to make Maureen wonder again what Bill was thinking. "Let's just say I don't think counseling's the miracle answer to everything," he said.

"Bill, I never said that—" She stopped, rubbed the base of her neck. Took a moment to gather her thoughts. "You know how it feels we're relating lately? Like how your beard feels against my cheek when you haven't shaved." A lump formed in her throat, reaction to the intrusion of the sudden intimacy. Maureen swallowed, and when she spoke next her words were softer. "We've been grating against each other, Bill. And I just don't know … I'm so tired … and …" She let her voice fade away and subconsciously held her breath.

The silence became a living force.

When Bill finally broke into it, he spoke in a near monotone. "I called to tell you that I'll be home late tonight. A nasty virus is going around. The waiting room's packed. And after office hours, I've got a boatload of paperwork waiting."

Maureen was tempted to echo the flatness, but chose otherwise. "Can I drop by your office later? Bring you something to eat?"

"Don't bother. I've got some leftovers here I can heat up. I need to go, the staff's waiting."

Once again she heard the abrupt sound of the dial tone. Mechanically reaching for her coffee, she made a face as she discovered it was tepid. And when she took the mug to pour the ruined coffee into the sink, the salt of a few tears mixed with it.

After a dinner with little acknowledgment from Colleen that her mom and sister existed—and the complete opposite from Aubrey, who assumed they wanted to hear her chatter on about every aspect of her day—Maureen decided it was time to be more forceful with her elder daughter. "Colleen, how about if you load the dishes into the dishwasher while I give Aubrey a bath?"

"I don't wanna bath. I don't wanna go to bed."

Maureen ignored Aubrey's outburst.

"Mom, I have like a ton of homework to do. I need to get seriously busy, right now."

"Weren't you on the Internet when you came home? You had time for that."

Colleen glared at her mother, but Maureen ignored her as she rinsed a washcloth to clean up Aubrey.

"I don't believe this. This isn't fair—I have stuff to do."

"So do I. I need to give your sister a bath."

Aubrey, her own battle temporarily forgotten, centered her total attention on the conflict between mother and sister. She was so focused on Colleen's next move that she sat uncharacteristically still while Maureen wiped her hands and face, only squirming when Maureen's head blocked a clear view of her sister.

Out of the corner of her eye, Maureen caught a glimpse of Colleen, who'd added full-scale bodily revolt to the earlier steely glare. She stood ramrod straight, arms crossed in front of her chest, muscles twitching.

"But that's what you're supposed to do—make dinner, clean up, stuff like that. What else do you have to do all day besides that stuff? How come you're making me do your job? Don't you want me to get good grades?"

Maureen hesitated only a second, and in that gap, Colleen seized the upper hand. "I have to get busy now, Mom, or there's no way I'm gonna get my homework done." She held up her hands, ticking off the list: "I have a test in math, a quiz in history, and a book report due for English. And I haven't finished the dumb book yet either." She waited, boldly meeting her mother's gaze, and when Maureen closed her eyes, Colleen quickly turned on her heels. Threw over her shoulder, "It's not my fault my teachers are so mean."

Maureen's gaze followed Colleen's retreating back until she disappeared; then, shoulders slumped, she walked to the window to look at the birdhouse. Leaning heavily against the window, crossing her arms over her chest, Maureen searched for the beloved bright blue.

"Want me to help you wash dishes, Mommy?" Aubrey asked. "I'll help you." Mimicking her mother, she cupped small hands around her eyes to peer outside just beneath Maureen. "Hey, whatcha lookin' at?"

Maureen reached down to twist a soft red curl around her finger. "Just looking for the bluebirds, little one." She sighed and scanned the backyard again. "I don't see them anywhere, do you?"

"Nope." Aubrey pulled her eyebrows together in a puzzled frown. "Do mommy and daddy birds get married?"

"Not like people do." Maureen smiled down at her. "But maybe God marries them?"

The frown remained. "Will they stay together for always?"

"Yes," she said very firmly, and nodded emphatically at Aubrey's concern. "They will." Maureen reached out to take a dimpled hand. "Now, let's get you in the bath, shall we?"

"Aren't we gonna wash the dishes?"

"How about if we just throw them into the bathtub with you?"

Aubrey giggled. "Oh, Mommy, no."

Later, putting an ear to Colleen's door, Maureen asked, "Colleen? Are you heading to bed soon? It's getting late, sweetie." She could hear books being slammed on top of one another, papers shuffled. To Maureen's slight pressure, the door cracked open.

"Mom. I've got a lot more stuff to do."

Maureen pushed the door open farther so she could peer in, saw Colleen stuffing tiny headphones and iPod into her desk drawer. Although plainly caught in the act, she gave her mother a mutinous look.

"Apparently not that much. Or you wouldn't be listening to music, hmm?" To Colleen's continued unblinking stare, "Just wanted you to know I'm making French toast in the morning, ready at six thirty sharp. So whatever you decide about staying up late, I don't think you'll want to miss out on breakfast."

"Whatever."

Maureen looked at Colleen a few more seconds, waiting. "Well then. Good night." She closed the door, feeling the familiar weariness settle over her like she'd pulled a heavy coat over her head and shoulders. *A drenched wool coat,* she thought to herself. *Scratchy and weighing roughly the size of a petulant thirteen-year-old girl.* Despite the too-real imagery, Maureen smiled.

Surprisingly, she slept so soundly that she was only vaguely aware of Bill's climbing into bed with her later, a mumbled exchange of *You okay? Sure. Love you. You too.* Breakfast felt like an extension of that unsatisfying connection: muttered conversations, hazy encounters with one other, and a dreamlike quality to all she viewed and did. Turned out that only Aubrey enjoyed the French toast; Bill slept in as late as he could, which meant he only had time to grab a breakfast bar in his rush out the door, and Colleen was obviously still on strike. *The only accessory she's lacking is a placard,* Maureen observed.

After dropping Colleen off at school and Aubrey at Bill's folks', Maureen drove along the shoreline toward the restaurant where the gang had agreed to meet. Her first glimpse of the dark greenish-blue gulf waters prompted her to open the van's front windows. She wanted to breathe in the salty air. Listen to the sounds of rippled laughter from the beach. Concentrating, Maureen hoped to hear the soothing heartbeat of the waves hitting the shore, the familiar rhythm that calmed her like nothing else.

The seafood restaurant was adjacent to the boardwalk, and as she turned her car into the parking lot, the smell of fish was heavy on the air. Though a majority of boats had left early in the morning and were out fishing for the day—they wouldn't be back until dinner time, many displaying their catch for the tourists to admire—a few remained docked.

Maureen stood on the boardwalk for a few moments and watched the men hosing down equipment, curiosity enticing her toward the railing. Those who went about their tasks were a class unto themselves: skin tanned and wrinkled from the sun, nonfussy clothes for ease of movement, hair tied back or tucked into stained hats faded to indistinguishable colors. They were all pleasant looking in their weathering, blending in with their boats, their livelihoods. The camouflage attire of the people of the sea.

Maureen turned toward the restaurant, but she just stood there, staring intently but not reaching for the door handle. She smoothed her hair, checked that her blouse was neatly tucked in, opened her purse to make sure she'd put the keys in the side pocket. Finally she took a deep breath and opened the door, the cool air hitting her face and bare arms like the icy blast from an opened freezer. She blinked her eyes, attempting to adjust to the dimmer lighting, and retreated a step, taken aback by the noise from within. Glasses and dishes clinking, voices attempting to be heard above the background din, elevator music all competed and joined together to create a raucous cacophony.

In response to a questioning look from the hostess, Maureen replied, "I'm looking for a party of three women?"

"Oh, yes. Follow me, please."

The place was packed, and Maureen could barely keep up with the agile guide. She squeezed in between chairs at filled tables, dodged other customers, and cautiously passed servers with huge round trays mounded with salads, all types of steaming seafood, hush puppies—and all the pleasing smells associated with those dishes.

Just as Maureen warily passed a server with a particularly full-to-overflowing tray, she looked up to see a large window overlooking St. John's Bay—the churning, white-capped waves, the blue sky beyond, the ocean itself. No matter how many times she'd gazed out over the gulf, Maureen still caught her breath at the initial glimpse of the panorama. She gave homage to that tableau before shifting her gaze to the three women who sat at the table beneath it.

Before she could say anything, Emilie jumped up and came around the table to her. Immediately hugged Maureen and then pulled back so they were face-to-face, giving her friend a reassuring look while whispering, "It's okay." And then Emilie announced to the other two, "Now. We're all here so I can tell you what I told Maureen yesterday. You've probably guessed already ... but here it is: Ed's home. He's moved back. Isn't that the most wonderful news ever?"

Sherry's jaw dropped in a round silent *O,* but Vanessa was gushing. "Oh, Em. I've prayed for this very thing to happen, and now I'm surprised that it has. That's a lack of faith, isn't it? I wasn't really praying that he'd come straight home like this, but that's simply wonderful and ..." Vanessa's voice dropped off when she noticed Emilie staring expectantly at Sherry.

"And you, Sherry?" Emilie asked, leaving the question open. Like bait in a trap.

"Well, I'm pleased for you, of course. Elated for the kids. But did I understand correctly? That he moved back in with you already?"

"Oh, yes. And I've forgiven him. Completely, just like Scripture tells us to do."

Sherry's eyes narrowed. Maureen felt sick to her stomach, the once-tempting smells around her now overbearingly strong.

"I think the Bible teaches forgiveness, absolutely," Sherry calmly replied. "But it also talks about consequences—consequences for sin. Do you think Ed sinned, Emilie?"

Emilie and Sherry were directly across from one another, and their words had the effect of swordplay—attack, parry, jab, attack again. When Vanessa caught Maureen's eye, they both had the look of frightened, unwilling bystanders.

"Yes, he did, Sherry. But just like the prodigal son was welcomed home, I've totally forgiven Ed."

What Sherry did next took them all by surprise. She sat back in her chair, crossing her legs as though she were getting comfortable for a long session. It appeared that she was about to tell them a story, and when she began, Sherry's tone was that of a teacher to students.

"I've been reading in Genesis lately, and just yesterday I studied the chapter about the fall. I noticed something that I'd never thought about before. Funny, isn't it? You've read a passage so many times. And suddenly you see something new."

Vanessa fidgeted with her wedding ring, staring at it as she turned it back and forth; Maureen sat as rigid as a statue and rather than look at Sherry, she too gazed elsewhere—out toward the view of St. John's Bay again. Only Emilie stared warily into Sherry's eyes.

"You know how it goes … God tells them the curse, he makes clothes for them out of animals' skins, the first blood sacrifice."

Maureen balled her hands into fists so tight that her fingernails stabbed her palms.

"In the past, I've always skimmed right by that." Sherry shook her head. "But this is what struck me yesterday." She stopped, leaning forward over the table. The dramatic pause drew Maureen's and Vanessa's eyes to her face now, joining Emilie's. "The skins didn't just magically appear on Adam and Eve. God had to kill those animals. And then this possibility hit me: We don't really know for sure since Scripture doesn't say, but I doubt that God shielded them from having to watch what he had to do. Think about it. Would he take the animals elsewhere, protecting Adam and Eve from the horrible thing he had to do? Would he have gone to a different part of the garden, killed the animals there and then brought those skins back to Adam and Eve?"

Each question drove home her point. Maureen flinched at the reality Sherry so graphically painted for them.

"Do you suppose he simply put the skins on them, ones all cleaned up and minus any hint of the blood that had been shed? Like the coats and purses and shoes that we buy, you suppose?" She smirked then, adding a small laugh. "Considering the immense gravity of what they'd done—the grievous sin they'd committed—would he actually have desired they not make the connection of their sin to the actual *killing* of an animal?"

Maureen glanced at Emilie and Vanessa; their gazes remained fixed on Sherry, eyes widened. Vanessa's lips were slightly open, but Emilie's mouth was set in a grim, hard line.

"And then it dawned on me: Adam had named those animals. Naming had major significance in biblical times. Surely Adam felt honored to be given that task as God brought them before him, one by one. How he must've loved it—and loved those animals, too. And now ... now one or more of them had to die ... because of him. Because of what he'd done."

Sherry shivered as if she'd felt a chill. "Can you feel the foreshadowing of Christ there? Adam knew his beloved animals were innocent. They hadn't done anything wrong. Yet they died. When it was his fault."

Tears filled Sherry's eyes and she bowed her head, embarrassed by the naked display of feelings. Maureen blinked back tears also, but noticed a rustle of activity next to her. It was Emilie. Gathering purse and keys, pushing her chair away from the table. Maureen reached out for her, questioning, "Emilie?"

From Vanessa, "Where ... why are you—?"

The only response was a slight shake of her head, a clear warning. Before any of them could say another word she had snaked through the crowded restaurant. And was out of sight.

The abrupt and unexpected exit jolted the remaining three. Sherry folded her napkin and put it on the table, stuttered out, "It's—it's completely my fault. I don't know what I was thinking— clearly I wasn't thinking at all."

"No." Maureen interrupted, her voice shaky. "It's my fault, Sherry. Emilie and I had a difficult conversation yesterday. It was about blame … it came out all wrong and I never got the chance to set it right."

"I need to go. I shouldn't have come with all the grading I have … I'm behind and …" Sherry's voice trailed off. She looked up at Vanessa and then Maureen. "I've made a mess of things, haven't I? I hope … I hope our friendship can survive this." She bit her lip, rose, and walked away.

When Maureen and Vanessa reached the parking lot, they turned to each other, suddenly awkward, uncomfortable.

"We'll work this through, Mo. It may take some time, time away to heal." She gripped Maureen's arm so tightly that Maureen nearly flinched. Vanessa glanced down, then back up into her friend's intent face. "But we'll find each other again, I know we will."

"Sure." Maureen nodded, went through the motions of hugging Vanessa. And then drove home—though when she walked into the kitchen, she barely remembered how she actually got there. The ticking of the family room clock and Bobo's pattering feet on the tile were the only sounds that greeted her. Until she heard a fairly loud *thump*. Curious about the source, Maureen picked up the dog and went to investigate where the sound might have come from.

Stepping out into the hot sunshine, she put Bobo down. Glanced around the yard. Totally out of character, Bobo immediately raced off to the left and then halted, tail wagging furiously. Walking toward him, Maureen froze when she spotted a patch of blue.

That blue. Lying in the grass, and absolutely still.

"Bobo, no." Frantically, she ran the short distance toward the object that, incongruously, she dreaded reaching. Pushed Bobo away. Knew now the thump was the sound of the mama bluebird's hitting the window, suffering a fatal blow—against the window of *her* house. *She* was the cause of its death. Maureen immediately felt hot tears overflow and spill down her cheeks. There was not the slightest movement from the little body, the tiny head hanging at an awkward angle. Picking up the bluebird to gently cradle it in her hands, Maureen fell to her knees. And slumped there, sobbing.

Maureen had no idea how long she'd been there, miserable, weeping. But when she finally looked up, she spied the brighter male, sitting atop the bluebird house. The sight of the female's mate, now alone, sent another stab of pain to her heart.

Eventually she got up and buried the tiny bird under a tree in the backyard. The male bluebird continued to hover, causing Maureen a fresh jab every time she saw him. And then she made a decision. Reaching into her pocket, she pulled out her cell phone and hit Bill's number. Expecting his recording, she was surprised when Bill picked up.

"Hey, honey. Whew. Been a circus here, but you caught me at a good time." She could hear the sounds of his leaning back in his squeaky chair, putting feet up onto his desk. "What's up?"

"I've had …" Maureen realized she hadn't prepared herself well, hadn't given herself enough time. She swallowed, took a deep breath, seeking composure. "It's been a rough day, Bill. Any chance at all you could get off early and pick up the girls?"

"You okay?"

The instant concern in his voice brought the threat of fresh tears. She blinked them back and swallowed again, feeling the uncomfortable lump in her throat like a pill was stuck there. "Um, sure. I was just hoping to take the afternoon to get some things done."

"Well, ironically, I was going to call you and offer just that. I've had so many late nights lately that … well, I miss my girls. Thought I'd better make it up to them." Maureen could hear his moving around in the chair again, pushing it away from his desk so he could open a drawer. "I'll get Aubrey from my folks' and then pick up Colleen. Maybe we'll grab dinner out? Want me to get something for you, too?"

"No. Thanks." Clipped words, hiding emotion. "I'll be fine. And Bill. Thank you."

"Glad to when it works out, honey. Like I said, I was planning to anyway. Guess we're on the same page today, eh? Isn't that nice for a change?"

Maureen pictured the smile she knew had eased onto his face, the familiar crinkling at the corners of his eyes, the slight dimple that would appear in his right cheek. She closed her eyes at the wave of feeling that threatened to erupt.

"Sure. Love you."

"Love you, too. And have a good afternoon, okay?"

Maureen hurriedly clicked off the phone. Taking a deep breath, she picked up Bobo, depositing him in his bed. After changing into casual clothes and walking shoes, she headed out toward the beach. It was five blocks away, and Maureen set a brisk pace.

Once she reached the sand, she removed her sneakers. Couldn't wait to dig her bare toes into the soft whiteness, luxuriating in the sand's caress. The breeze off the water produced its usual magic: The tightness in her neck eased a bit, she visibly lowered her shoulders, the muscles in her face relaxed. And then Maureen waded into the water, allowing the surf to rise nearly to her knees before she backed away. Watching the retreating water pull at her ankles, seeing the curve of the eroding sand around her feet, finding the pea-sized holes created by tiny clams and shells rolling back into the surf from the wake of the wave—all the familiar sights welcomed her. Helped to soothe her inner turmoil.

And then she walked. Attempting to shut out all but the smell and feel of the sea breeze and the touch of sand and water on her feet, Maureen sought solace from her God.

Hours later, the beach was emptying when she noted how much lower the sun had sunk out over the gulf, producing a glorious pink-tinted sky. Families had gathered up kids and belongings, abandoning brightly colored plastic shovels and buckets, various piles of gathered shells. The cries of laughing children were replaced by the insistent cawing of the gulls. A gnawing in her stomach reminded Maureen she'd missed lunch and dinner. Reluctantly, she turned toward home.

Dusk. Maureen's favorite time of day. As she hurried home, she stole glimpses into front windows to spy on families together.

Often she'd be so intent on looking into a picture window that she'd miss the unevenness of the sidewalk and trip. Maureen smiled at herself, thinking how Bill would have accused her of *kravatzing*—their family's made-up word for snooping. Finally spotting the welcoming lights of her own home, Maureen hurried through the back gate, eagerly reached to open the door. It was locked against her. She froze—one hand still clutching the handle, the other pathetically poised to push back the screen—as she took in the highlighted scene in the kitchen.

They were all laughing together—Bill, Aubrey. Even Colleen. Leaning eagerly toward one another, conspiratorially, their heads nearly touching. The ease and comfort of their banter was near idyllic. Exhibiting none of the tension that had revolved around them lately like a swirling tornado, making family life ... miserable.

Bill had just finished scooping ice cream into their bowls, and was in the process of adding the colorful candy sprinkles on top of their mounds of whipped cream. Aubrey clearly gestured for more and Bill obliged, shaking the canister so hard the top came off—dumping a huge pile that covered her bowl. Colleen erupted with such a burst of laughter that she nearly fell off her chair, Aubrey's shoulders bounced with delighted giggles, and even Bill laughed so hard that Maureen could hear his hearty roar outside.

The glow of the lights put a hazy, warm aura around each of their profiles. And as Colleen reached out to touch her dad's arm ... to playfully steal a scoop of the sprinkles from Aubrey ... as Bill reached out to caress a raven ponytail, and then an auburn-colored cap of curls, the individual glows molded and melted into one. The three of them, deliciously happy, content. Complete.

Without her.

Immobilized, at first Maureen could only blink ... and feel the pounding of her heart. And then it felt as though it wrenched painfully inside her chest, and instinctively, she reached one hand toward the source of the pain. The other pulled at the door again. As intense desire moved her to action, she tapped lightly on the door, trying to get her family's attention. But they were laughing so hard, they didn't hear her. *Don't want to hear me?* she asked herself, realizing she didn't want an answer.

Mere seconds went by, but to Maureen, they felt like hours. Heartbroken and unable to move, she watched. A bystander.

Until Bill happened to glance up and see her. Standing there, arms hanging limply at her sides. Startled, concerned, he jumped from his chair and rushed to the door. "Why didn't you knock, Mo? Good gracious, you gave me a scare." When she didn't answer—didn't move a muscle, but merely stood there, gawking up at him—he grabbed her arm roughly and pulled her into the bright light of the kitchen. "*Maureen?* Are you all right, for God's sake?"

Maureen nodded, mumbled, "Yes. Sorry, I was just—" She saw Colleen and Aubrey both staring at her, mouths open, as though she were a stranger. "I'm going to get ready for bed." And then she abruptly turned away from them, walked down the hallway.

Bill momentarily stopped himself from following her, gripped the back of his chair for a moment and then, decision clearly made, he said, "Colleen, can you—" He waved a hand vaguely toward Aubrey and the scattered remnants of their ice cream party. "Can you clean up Aubrey and ... everything?"

Colleen nodded. She looked up at him with eyebrows drawn together, questioning.

Bill shrugged his shoulders, glanced over at Aubrey and managed a half smile, and then walked resolutely toward the bedroom.

He found Maureen standing in front of her dresser, staring with unfocused eyes at her reflection in the mirror.

"What on earth is the matter with you?" he threw at her, whispering, but his voice seething with frustration.

Maureen looked at him vacantly. "What?"

Bill grabbed her arms, shaking her to get her attention. "Where have you been? What's the matter with you, Maureen?"

She narrowed her eyes at him, pupils becoming smaller and focused now. And then she reached down to angrily pry his fingers off her arms. "I was walking on the beach."

"The beach? For cryin' … I thought you said you needed time to get things done?"

"I did. I needed time to … to *think*. To be alone, to pray. Is that a crime?"

"When it means selfish time away from your family—yes. It *is* a crime. What on earth?" He began pacing from one side of their bedroom to the other. "I don't know what's up with you, Mo. But this has to stop. Now." He stopped in front of her, positioning his face only inches from hers. "You will quit this frivolous job of yours. Tomorrow. And then you'll call Emilie and apologize. For whatever insensitive nonsense you said to her. Obviously you're not capable of handling anything right now, so I want you to call Pastor Johnson and tell him—"

"How dare you."

Startled, he took a step back from her. From the completely unexpected force behind her words. "Excuse me?"

"Who are you to order me to do … anything?"

Bill stepped forward again. Glaring at her, he spit out through gritted teeth, "I … am … your … husband. I know my role as your husband; do you remember yours—as my wife? Think about the verse Pastor Johnson spoke on just last Sunday. Deny yourself, Maureen. 'Deny yourself, pick up your cross, and follow me,' Christ said."

Maureen grabbed her antique silver-plated hairbrush and threw it with all her might at the dresser mirror, shattering it. Turned then to face Bill, tears filling her hazel eyes and spilling over, her voice pleading with him, "There. The facade that represents Maureen Roberts never existed anyway. Tell me, Bill, how do I deny myself when I've never had a self to deny?"

Her anger instantly vanished, released with the power of her emotion, and she dropped her arms limply to her sides. Only the sound of her soft weeping filled the room. And then Maureen crumpled to the floor, breaking into heaving sobs, hugging her knees and rocking back and forth.

Bill dropped down beside her and instantly pulled her into his arms. "Oh, Maureen, I'm so sorry," he whispered. "What place have we traveled to?"

He rocked her like a baby, combing a hand gently through her hair.

Minutes later, when her breathing had calmed, she whispered, "I can't go on like this any longer, Bill." She felt him stiffen, almost become rigid beneath her. "What? What's wrong?"

"Are you saying …" his voice was hoarse, rough, "… are you leaving me?"

Maureen twisted around in his arms so that she could look into his eyes, and she put a hand on either side of his face. The hazel-flecked eyes sparkled with lingering tears. "Oh Bill, *no.*" She slumped back away from him, adding, "But I think I need … I think I do need some time away to think."

Suddenly it was vitally important that Bill understand. "Do you … can you understand at all what I'm feeling? Because it's like … like I thought I offered myself to God years ago. But I never thought I was worth anything, really." She searched his face for understanding. "It wasn't an offering at all, Bill, because I judged I never had anything to give. I want to find … somewhere within me … some worth that means I really am giving God something. That's sacrifice. That's a denial." She shook her head. "Am I making any sense at all?"

He nodded. "Yeah, a little."

"Could I—?"

Bill raised his eyebrows, fear still clouding his eyes.

"If I could just go to the beach for a few days. To get some per-spective." Maureen ran fingers through her hair and then closed her eyes. "I learned something recently." She chuckled and then shook her head. "You're probably going to think this is just weird but, well, it's about this phenomenon called averted vision. It's when you try to look at a star and—"

"You can't see it, looking at it directly. I read about it, years ago when I was into astronomy and had that telescope. Some stars you can see only when you look away, and then use your peripheral vision, right?"

She hesitated.

"What, Mo?"

"You'll think it's silly."

Bill reached for her hand. Squeezed it gently. "So give me a try."

Maureen took a deep breath. "That's a perfect illustration of how I've viewed God and me—like I'm that star. Not worthy of being seen in God's direct vision. I'm just in his peripheral vision ... and that's all I'm ..." Her voice trailed off and Bill watched silent tears fall down freckled cheeks. He reached up to wipe one away.

"You're not, Mo. Never were. But no one can convince you of that but you, yourself, with God's help."

She nodded, and then, heart pounding, turned away from his steady gaze, avoiding meeting his eyes. "When I got to the back door tonight, I saw you three laughing together, having such a good time. I thought ... I realized how happy you were without me." Her voice broke then and she could hardly breathe, needed to take a gulp of air before continuing, "And that you wouldn't ... that you didn't want—"

Bill gently put his hand over her mouth, silencing her. "I love you so much, Mo. So do the girls. And we need you. You have to believe that. Please say you believe me."

"I'll try."

"Where do you want to go? To get away?"

"Sanibel Island? It's away, but not too far. I'm thinking a long weekend. Colleen has school on Friday and Monday, of course, so she'd better stay here with you. But if I take Aubrey with me, then you don't have the problem of a sitter for those days—and it gives you some father-daughter time for just you and Colleen. Think you two would enjoy that?"

"I can't speak for Colleen, considering how … *special* she's been lately. But I think it might be fun. What weekend are you thinking about?"

"How about if we leave this Friday morning? We'd be home by Monday afternoon." She could feel his body stiffen again. "What is it?—something's wrong. Bill?"

"I just need to hear you say … once more. That you'll come back to me."

She put a finger against his cheek. "I promise you—" A memory suddenly came to mind, and she smiled up at him. "Long ago you said that what you first noticed about me was my eyes—that they sparkled. That I dazzled you."

Bill grinned back at her. "One of my best lines ever."

"Those sparkles will come home to you. I promise."

He took her in his arms, relishing the feel of her body against his. "Got another good line for you," Bill began, chuckling. "You know the banker's terminology *bridge loan?* Maybe God's love is like that while we're on earth. His love is the bridge loan before we get to heaven."

Maureen pulled back to look Bill in the eyes. "Bill, that's not a line; it's a beautiful analogy."

"Think so? Well, I guess it dawned on me—thinking about you leaving—that there's a difference between being alone. And being lonely. And being left isn't as frightening when I know I'm in the bridge of God's love."

Maureen smiled up at him and moved into Bill's waiting arms again. They held onto each other for a few moments more, finding the beginnings of healing. And then Bill went to tell Aubrey of the plans, Maureen to explain to Colleen.

Maureen knocked softly on Colleen's door.

"Yeah?"

"Colleen, it's me. I need to speak with you a minute." She opened the door and peeked in. "Can I come in? I wanted to let you know I'm going away for a few days, to the beach. Just to have some time to think and pray."

"Oh? Where?" Colleen refused to look at her mom. She concentrated on her doodling efforts as if they were intensely important.

"Sanibel Island. I'd leave on Friday. Come home on Monday."

Putting her hand up in such a way that it hid her face, Colleen hunched down over her desk. "It won't be longer than that? You're sure?"

"Oh, no. It's just a long weekend. Actually, I'll take Aubrey with me and you'll stay here with Daddy. We thought you might enjoy having Daddy all to yourself for a while. Do some fun things together?" Colleen still avoided her mother's gaze, even though Maureen intentionally leaned down to search her daughter's face. "Is something the matter, Colleen? Tell me what you're thinking because—"

In a monotone, Colleen asked, "Are you and Daddy separating?"

"Oh, no ... no, Colleen. It's nothing like that, I promise you." She reached out to put her fingers under her daughter's chin and lifted it so she was forced to look up at her.

Colleen's dark eyes glistened.

"You're thinking ... that what happened to the Estebans ... it's not, sweetie. You believe me, don't you?"

"Yeah." Her voice very small and frail, "I guess so."

"Actually, I need you to take care of your dad while I'm gone. Will you do that?"

She rolled her eyes, any signs of tenuousness now deliberately hidden. "Like I'm gonna cook stuff," she scoffed. "We'll get burgers or pizza every night."

"If that's what you two want, then I say go for it." Maureen hesitated, uncertain, and then deciding not to press, turned to go.

"Mom?"

Maureen leaned against the door, waiting, giving Colleen her full attention. She could hear her breathing erratically.

"Then what were you doing when you were gone tonight?" Her words had come out in a rush, and again she studied her paper under hooded eyes.

Maureen took a deep breath. Fleetingly thought, *How honest should I be?* "I was walking on the beach, taking some time to just … think. And I was wondering, actually, if—" her voice broke and she stopped to swallow and try to calm her emotions, "—if it would make any difference if I just … didn't exist anymore."

Colleen lifted her head, mouth hanging open and pupils dilated in alarm.

"No, it's not what you're thinking. I never considered … that … no, Colleen, I didn't. I shouldn't have put it that way. But my life seems so," she closed her eyes, concentrating, struggling to find the right words, "meaningless? No, that's not the right word. It's more like I'm in a vacuum. I don't … I'm not connecting. Yes, that's closer. I'm not really connecting to your dad. To you. To Aubrey or to God. At least, not in the way I want to."

Maureen was quiet a moment, pondering. "You know, the more I think about it, the better that describes it. A connector. I realize that's what I've always wanted to be: the one who connects you and Aubrey to the past—your grandparents, and dad and me—and to the future, so you'll understand what it means to live for Christ. And *want* to live for Christ.

"Colleen, I've struggled so much with my worth that—and I can't go into … any of that—well, let's just say I know I haven't been that connector for you and Aubrey because of how I see myself. My time at the beach this weekend? I intend to figure out how to do that. The way God wants me to. For this family. For you and Aubrey. And I will do whatever I need to do to make that happen.

"You know, it just dawned on me … there's another way to describe what I'm feeling: It's like I want to be a bridge—a bridge to each member of this family. And a bridge that connects us all to God." Maureen looked into Colleen's eyes, and was encouraged to see no rejection or anger there; instead, her eyes looked intently into Maureen's. "Just one more thing. About self-worth. We can only find it in relationship with God, Colleen. I don't know why I haven't really understood that way down deep in my heart. But I've got to discover how to do that, too. Let that deep understanding move from my brain to my heart."

They were both silent for a few moments. The only sounds in the room were their quiet breathing and the steady ticking of Colleen's bedside clock.

"Does that help?" Maureen asked, searching her daughter's face again.

A barely perceptible nod of her head, and then, "I love you, Mom."

Maureen could barely see as she leaned over and kissed the top of Colleen's head, her hand caressing the ponytail. "I love you too, sweetie."

Though it had been bright and sunny the entire week before, Friday dawned miserably; they awakened to a dense fog with drizzly rain. Bill expressed some concern about Maureen's driving in such awful weather, but she was optimistic the sun would be out by noon. "That's what all the forecasters are saying," she calmly pointed out. "Sunshine by noon. So I figure this has got to clear up soon."

As Bill buckled Aubrey into her car seat, he tugged on an ear and then kissed her.

"Will you miss me, Daddy?"

"Better believe it."

"And Rabbit, too?"

"Even more than you."

Aubrey frowned, then burst into a big smile. "You're just teasing, Daddy. I know you'll miss me most!"

"You're just too smart—like your Mommy, huh?"

He pulled Maureen into his arms, a touch of insecurity and tenderness still apparent in the look he gave her. She felt a sudden surge of love, realizing how much she was still *in love* with him. "You'll be all right? Colleen promised me she'd take good care of you."

"She mentioned pizza. Burgers and tacos. That what you mean?"

Maureen smiled. "To a teenager, that's probably as good as it gets."

Colleen came down the steps into the garage and they both turned to look at her. "I, um … I hope you have a good time." She moved toward Maureen, reaching out to offer a hug. The unexpected gift brought the uncomfortable lump back to Maureen's throat. Peering over the top of her daughter's head, she looked into Bill's face and smiled contentedly. She kissed the top of Colleen's head before Colleen pushed away, muttering, "I gotta finish getting ready for school. Bye, little squirt," she called to Aubrey, throwing her a quick kiss with a wave of one hand.

Maureen watched Colleen's every move until she was out of sight and then turned her attention back to Bill. "As soon as I get to the hotel, I'll call you. Then I need to ring Emilie. Ask her to forgive me."

Bill nodded. "Good idea. And if Ed leaves her again?"

"Then Sherry, Nessa, and I will be there for her. I'm calling Sherry and Nessa also, by the way. To tell them what amazing friends they've been—how much they've given me all these years."

"Sounds like you'll be spending all your time on the phone," Bill teased.

She sighed. "Oh, not so much. 'Cause after that, I'm spending time with Aubrey. And God. I plan to spend most of my weekend talking with him."

Bill pulled her to him again, murmuring, "Gonna miss you. I love you, honey."

"Oh, Bill. I love you too. You know that, right?"

His answer was a tender kiss, and it was with some regret that Maureen let go, climbed into the van, and backed out into the waiting murkiness. Flicking on the windshield wipers, Maureen watched while her view of Bill misted over, cleared, and misted again in the steady rhythm of the blades. She waved at him one last time. Took a deep breath and turned to wink at Aubrey.

"Okay, Lolly Pops. Ready to go?"

"Me and Rabbit, too."

Out of the corner of her eye, Maureen caught a glimpse of bright blue in the front magnolia tree. "Oh, Aubrey, look!" she cried out delightedly, pointing toward the pair. "It's ... it's the bluebirds, and there are *two*—a papa *and* a mama."

Aubrey squirmed around in her seat, trying to see. "Will they still be here when we get home, Mommy?"

"Oh, I hope so." Maureen reached toward the backseat and patted Aubrey on the knee. "I sure hope so."

She smiled to herself—thanking God for the gift of hope, even in little things—and confidently turned into the rain.

Despite her early optimism about the weather, Maureen's spirits began to sag as the rain continued in a steady beat against the windshield. The fog, instead of dissipating, grew thicker. The combination of the two made drivers skittish and panicky, which turned normally tricky rush-hour traffic into a nightmare. What should have been an hour's drive to the Sunshine Skyway Bridge stretched into two, and by then Maureen's shoulders were knotted with tension. Even her hands ached from gripping the steering wheel so tightly.

Just as they arrived at the entrance to the bridge, the weather took a turn for the worse. The rain came down in a deluge, developing into a full-fledged storm, complete with lightning and thunder. Immediate concern for Aubrey caused Maureen to quickly check the backseat. But to her surprise, Aubrey appeared totally unaffected by the storm. She was chatting merrily away in an animated conversation with Rabbit. Now and then she'd gesture emphatically with a raised finger, causing Maureen to grin, despite her fears of driving conditions in the nasty weather.

The sound of the rain beating against the windshield was nearly deafening, and even the highest wiper speed couldn't clear the windshield fast enough. Maureen slowed down even more, checking the rearview mirror—there were no car headlights blinding her from behind, for which she was thankful—and then peered cautiously at the car in front. She could barely make out that it was a dark-colored Mercedes, and was grateful she could focus on its bright taillights, using them to guide her safely across the bridge.

She'd just told herself, *You can do this. You're perfectly safe,* when a jagged arm of lightning flashed across the sky, eerily highlighting the grace and beauty of the Skyway's arched cables. The dazzling light show was still sending out sparks when it was joined by a crack of thunder. Maureen was momentarily startled. She felt the car move but wasn't overly concerned. Dismissing it as a vibration from the thunder, Maureen focused more intently on the car in front of her.

But suddenly all reality of sky above and solid road below evaporated into thin air. She felt the car launch out into—nothing.

The last thing Maureen clearly saw was her headlights shining into the Mercedes, the beams acting like a spotlight on a beautiful woman's face staring out from the back window. Reacting instinctively, Maureen reached back toward Aubrey with one hand ... and toward the woman with the other. Just before the car hit the surging black waters, Maureen asked herself a puzzling question.

Why is the woman's mouth open, her face full of wonder?

Book Two

PICK UP YOUR CROSS

March 2009
Glen Ellyn, Illinois

It was the semifinal soccer game, and the stakes were high. The score: one to zero. Only three minutes remained.

To the Glen Ellyn Flames, the team in the lead, those three minutes loomed like an eternity. Coach Paul Henry had lectured his twelve- and thirteen-year-old players to never stop attacking, never subconsciously shift to "protecting the lead." But with the championship game within sight, the Flames succumbed to temptation. Their lack of aggressive play in the last ten minutes was obvious: They were merely trying to hold on to the one-point lead.

However, from their opponents'—the Raptors—perspective, those three minutes meant remaining opportunities. They played like a team possessed: heading, dribbling, passing, attacking. The ball lived on the Flames' end of the field, the threat of a goal imminent.

Fans from both teams had risen to their feet when there were ten minutes left to play. Nearly as much adrenaline coursing through them as the players, the spectators stood shouting in support, urging their favored team on.

One of the most notable voices on the Flames' sidelines belonged to Charles Edgar Thomason, the father of the team's scoring star, Charles Junior, or as everyone called him, Charlie. The imposing man's autocratic instructions were accented with a force that made him heard above all others—causing the consternation of the coach, but not likely to draw censure. For the team's shirts, shorts, and socks—including the goalie's, whose uniform was the envy of every goalie in the league—were donated yearly by Charles Senior's law firm. It was a quid pro quo that benefited everyone, especially the players. During a game, they kept one ear attuned to Coach Paul Henry's instructions. And the other to Mr. Charles Thomason.

The ball still hovering dangerously at the Flames' end of the field, Charles Senior focused his attention on Erik—sweeper, a player who needed lightning-fast reflexes because his job was to defend the critical area between the goal line and fullbacks. "Stay on the ball, Erik! Be *sharp*. Watch for the breakaway pass."

Next to Charles stood Charlie's mother, Francine, hands clasped in front of her, every muscle tense as she leaned slightly toward the field. She didn't yell, gesture, or command attention in any way. Not one to be demonstrative, Fran exhibited absorption in the game by more subtle means: Her eyes rarely left her only child. No matter where the ball was, she focused on one thing only. Charlie.

The fullback—Charlie's closest friend, Grant—stole the ball from a Raptor and controlled it with ease, confidently kicking it back to his fellow player, Bryce, the goalie. The Flames' fans breathed a temporary sigh of relief, knowing Bryce would kick the ball a good ways down the field. Assuming the ball would move in that direction, the Flames positioned themselves to run that way.

Bryce took his time, using more seconds off the clock. When he reached down for the ball, he scanned the entire field to locate his fellow teammates. Decided to give it to Charlie, their best ball handler. Odds were the ball was safest at Charlie's feet.

But for whatever reason, the kick was not the direct shot he'd intended. Nor was Charlie as quick to react as Bryce expected. At the last moment, a Raptor cut in front of Charlie; the ball hit him in the chest and the Raptor allowed it to fall toward his feet, expertly trapping it. Charlie had been taken off guard, and the Raptors took advantage of his lack of movement to seize the opportunity. They passed the ball to their star center forward, a blond with nimble feet.

The Raptors had maneuvered a breakaway.

The fans could sense optimism in the Raptors' movements. The quick shift of power.

Parents, siblings, friends, all the fans on the sidelines felt the mounting tension as they pressed forward to watch the footrace. Though Erik ran neck and neck with the potential scorer, everyone knew the outcome likely depended on one person: Bryce. At that point, it was as though the charging Raptor and the goalie were the only two competitors on the field.

These few seconds seemed like an eternity to the Flames' fans. Even more so, to Charlie. His body—which usually responded with abnormally fast reflexes, making him an exceptional soccer player— seemed to react in slow motion. He couldn't get enough air in his lungs, couldn't breathe right. And then as he turned to his left, an annoying dull ache in his right shin became a stabbing pain. In that moment, no matter how hard Charlie *willed* it to happen, he simply couldn't move his body as quickly as he desired. Rather than running alongside the opposing team's forward and giving his own fullback and sweeper the defensive support they needed, Charlie was a full stride behind.

You should've been the first defender, he told himself, panicking. *Catch up. Get there.*

But Charlie couldn't catch up. And one step was all that was needed.

For though Bryce placed his body in the best position possible, the Raptor expertly used the inside of his foot to kick the ball wide to the left. At the last moment, Bryce sensed he'd guessed wrong. In one final, futile effort, he leaned the opposite way, his splayed hand reaching out as far as possible. But the blur of the ball merely brushed his fingertips.

It sailed into the net. And the opposing team—along with their fans—went wild.

Bryce lay on the ground a moment, angry with himself. But even more so—bewildered. *How had they let that happen?* Looking accusingly at Charlie, he saw him leaning over, winded, grabbing the front of his shorts. *What's up with him anyway?* Bryce wondered.

But the Flames didn't have time to lament the tying goal, nor the Raptors to celebrate. With only one minute remaining, Charlie called his team to get ready for the kickoff. Sloughing off any signs of insecurity or fear, Charlie determined one thing: As leader, he would make sure they saw nothing but confidence in him. "Execute!" Charlie yelled out, pumping his fist and making eye contact with his forwards.

They all knew what he meant. As did most well-coached teams, the Flames had practiced a set play for just such an occasion. The Flames realized they now had to give it their best effort to score. It was a long shot, but they set their jaws with determination and sprinted to their positions on the field.

Charlie provided one last encouragement. "We can do this!" he yelled at them, repeating it again. "We *can* do this!"

The referee placed the ball on the center mark of the field. Blew the whistle. Signaled for time to start.

With calm aplomb, Charlie put his foot on top of the ball. Barely nudged it toward his right midfielder, Austin, who immediately burst into a sprint and passed it to the right wing, Riley. Taken somewhat off guard, the Raptors tried to adjust defensively. But the Flames had gained a step on them by maneuvering the ball toward the sideline.

The ball passed from Riley to Austin to Jason, who performed the move they'd practiced over and over—a deceptive flick pass, using the outside of his foot to send the ball to Charlie. Setting it up so Charlie could execute yet another flick pass to punch the ball toward the goal. It sailed past the duped goalie into the waiting net, and as the last seconds ticked away, the timing couldn't have been more perfect.

End of game.

As a roar broke out in the stands, the Flames swarmed around Charlie, lifting him onto their shoulders. Though Charlie grimaced at first, the look of joy on his face won out, and he pumped his fists in the air, shouting, *"Flames! Flames! Flames!"*

Fans ran onto the field too, gathering around the players, joining in the jubilation. But Charles Senior had moved next to Coach Henry. "Seems to me they ought to be thinking more about the *next* game," he pointed out. "They pull off that one, *then* they've earned the right to celebrate."

"Agreed," was all Coach Henry replied, nodding his head.

The Flames met the Raptors on the halfway line, ready for the end-of-game ritual of shaking hands. The Raptors' heads were down, mostly, with the exception of the blond center forward who had scored their lone goal. Noticeably holding his chin high, he didn't merely slide through extended hands, but took time to firmly shake each one. When he came to Charlie, he looked him squarely in the eyes.

"Good game," he offered. He nodded down toward Charlie's lower right leg. "Better take care of that."

Charlie gave him a quizzical look in return. "What?"

"Better have your leg looked at. You're favoring it, you know."

And with that, he moved on to the next Flames player in line.

When Charlie walked over to the sideline, his dad was waiting for him. "What was that about?"

"What?"

"The exchange with their star player. What's his problem?"

Charlie shrugged. "Nothin'. He just said it was a good game."

"Darn right it was. Good job, sport, although you did look winded out there. You and I need to start jogging." He put his arm around Charlie's shoulder as they walked toward the gathering of Flames players.

The boys flopped down onto the grass, suddenly spent. The adrenaline rush had calmed, leaving them drained physically and emotionally. But they were still active boys with energy in reserve, poking at one another in their happiness. High-fived each other until Coach Henry demanded their full attention.

"Listen up. Great game today, guys. I'm proud of you."

Amid the resulting voices and chaos, Charlie raised his hand, like in class.

Some of the players pointed it out and laughed, always amazed at his squeaky-clean image. Popular as Charlie was—due to his athletic ability, sense of humor, and striking good looks—his unfailingly polite demeanor stood in sharp contrast to most boys his age. His affability wasn't an act but simply who he was, a genuinely nice kid. A good person who had good things happen to him. Even those who were envious had to admit Charlie earned the rewards that came his way. Honor roll for top grades. Adulation from girls. Captain of the soccer team.

Coach nodded his head toward his star player. "Yes, Charlie?"

"I just wanted to say thanks to Jason for that fantastic pass."

Cheers broke out again, and several reached over to punch Jason in the arms. He grinned shyly, ducking from the pounding he was taking.

Charlie continued, "I would never've scored without his assist. I think we all oughta thank Jason. 'Cause on account of *him,* we won."

They clapped and whooped a bit more, Coach Henry joining in. He reiterated how Jason's pass was a perfect example of playing as a team—and how the entire team benefited from his unselfish play. "But as great a win as this was, I need you to put it aside.

Focus on the next one. This game," he glanced from boy to boy, attempting to capture their attention, "this game was a *means* to an end. Like a pregame. It's the next one we need to set our sights on now."

Several heads nodded and shouts of "Yeah. *Bring it on*" echoed through the ranks.

"Well, we'll find out who our opponent is—either the Comets or the Apaches—in the very next game." The coach glanced at his watch. "Starts in about fifteen minutes. If any of you can, I'd like you to stay to scout the players. See who their big scorers are, see what trick moves they've got. Who can stay?"

Several hands went up. Charlie glanced over at his dad, saw him nod in agreement. Charlie's hand went up too.

"Okay. Listen up. The game's tomorrow at ten. I want you here for practice by eight sharp. We'll do some warm-ups, stretch. By then we'll know who we're facing and we'll talk strategy." The boys began standing up, chatting excitedly. "Charlie? I want to see you a minute."

Coach waved a hand at Charlie, motioning him to follow as he walked toward his car. Charlie had to run to catch up with him, and once again he felt the now familiar ache in his right leg, in and just below the knee. Charlie concentrated on his gait rather than the pain, determined that Coach wouldn't notice.

"Give it to me straight up, son. You sure you haven't pulled a muscle? I can't take the risk of you seriously hurting yourself, Charlie. How bad is it?"

"It's nothin', Coach. *Honest.*"

"Well, I want you to go on home now."

"But I—"

"No, I mean it, son. Go home and ice that leg. Make sure you rest it good before the game tomorrow, okay?"

"Yes, sir."

Charlie hung his head, but Coach Henry put his arm around his shoulders. Gave him a reassuring pat. "Son, we need you tomorrow, at a hundred percent. Now, off you go. And don't forget to ice that leg."

"Sure. See you tomorrow, Coach," Charlie called over his shoulder as he jogged over to his dad. Too late, he remembered to not favor the hurting leg.

"Hey, why aren't you heading over to watch the game?" Charles leaned casually against his bright red convertible, arms folded across his chest. "And what's with the limp?"

Charlie imitated his dad subconsciously, mirroring his posture, leaning against the car next to him. "That's why Coach is sending me home. Wants me to ice my leg."

Charles reached down to touch Charlie's shin pad. "Did you get kicked?"

"Yeah, their fullback got me good once." He shrugged it off as insignificant. "It's a little sore. Coach is just being extra careful." Scanning the crowd of parents still hovering around the field, Charlie asked, "Where's Mom?"

"She's been talking with Mrs. Benson. Looks like she's coming this way now." Skeptically, he eyed Charlie's right shin again. "Charlie, you let that Raptor take the ball away from you like you weren't even trying. Gotta keep your head in the game, sport. Especially in the last few minutes."

The disappointment in his father's voice hit Charlie like a blow. He absentmindedly nudged a discarded gum wrapper at his feet.

"I know you got kicked, but with only a minor injury like that?" Charles shook his head. "You could've cost us the game."

Barely above a whisper, Charlie said, "Yeah. Guess my mind wandered for a minute or somethin'."

"It's like you were in slow motion." Charles rubbed his chin, deliberating. "You know, the weather's nice enough now that we could start jogging together. Time I got off the treadmill. Treadmills are for sissies anyway, eh?" He scoffed, reached out and gave Charlie a quick punch in the arm. "When this tournament's over tomorrow—and you boys take home the trophy—how 'bout we hit the road together?"

"Sure thing, Dad."

"We'll do some celebrating first, of course. No doubt about it: You'll be on your game tomorrow, right? The Flames *are* going to win."

Charlie's mom arrived, giving him a quick hug. "How's my favorite player?" Francine was fully cognizant that any obvious display of affection by a mom in front of peers wasn't considered cool, so a brief hug would have to do. Charlie usually didn't appear to be bothered by his mom's hugs—he had even been known to hug her in front of his friends—but she wasn't about to abuse that privilege. "That last-minute goal was fantastic, Charlie. Boy, what an exciting game."

"Jason set me up, Mom. His pass was awesome."

"I'm sure it was. Your goal was awesome too."

Charlie opened the back door of the car, feeling a sharp pain in his knee when he bent it to climb in, but he controlled his reaction. Bit his lip to keep from the yelp that threatened. After his mom had settled in and buckled her seatbelt, she turned to him.

"Hungry?" she asked, and then looked at her husband's profile. "What about you, Charles? Shall we stop at the drive-in? It opened for the season a couple days ago."

In answer, Charles peeled out of the parking place, squealing the tires. Turned to Fran and grinned. She couldn't help but smile back, noticing the look on his face was that of a mischievous youngster.

Fran hadn't met Charles until they were in college, but she could imagine what he had looked like at age twelve. All she had to do was look at their son; Charlie was the spitting image of his dad. The promise of the equally broad shoulders, long legs, coloring, the same unruly curls, square jaw, and broad forehead. Only their eyes were different, for Charlie had inherited his mom's hazel tones with unusual dark flecks. In relation to temperaments, however, father and son greatly diverged; Charlie wasn't driven like Charles, causing the father to question his son's desire and fire.

It became an endless source of contention between the two parents. Charles accusing Fran of coddling their only child. Fran's response that Charles pushed Charlie too hard, pressuring him, no matter what sport or activity or even pastime he undertook. It was the point-counterpoint rhythm of their lives.

Fran knew Charles was the constant instigator, the one most likely to throw out the challenge, "*Bet you can't ...*" Which turned everything father and son did into a contest. Riding bikes became a question of who could beat the other up the hill. And who was the fastest down it. Snow and water skiing became daredevil games. Even a family hike could turn into a race in a heartbeat. She also recognized that, as the parent, it was Charles's job to stop working out his ego issues through their son. The tension felt endless to Fran. And sometimes, hopeless.

"The drive-in sounds great to me. How about you, sport?" Charles glanced at Charlie in the rearview mirror, raising his eyebrows questioningly.

"A cheeseburger and fries. And a milkshake."

"Think he's earned a milkshake, Mom?" Charles teased.

"After how hard he played on that field today? You bet he has."

"As a matter of fact, I thought Charlie played a little too laid-back. We're going to hit the road jogging after this tournament's over."

Fran stared straight ahead, opening her mouth to speak. Closed it. Repeated the movement once more before calmly venturing, "Charles, I think Charlie's going to need to rest after the tournament. It's clear to me his body's trying to tell him that—"

"Nonsense. Already asked him about the leg. Both him and Coach Henry think it's just a deep bruise. Isn't that right, son?" Once again he met Charlie's eyes in the rearview mirror, but this time there was no question in his piercing stare.

"Right, Dad," Charlie answered eagerly, ever seeking his father's approval.

Fran turned around, her face registering concern. Purposefully didn't say anything—wanting to avoid the inevitable argument with Charles. But she promised herself she'd corner Charlie later to learn the truth about how he felt.

In the backseat, Charlie was restless, constantly switching positions in an attempt to find relief from his throbbing leg. But nothing eased the now-unremitting pain. He wanted to ask for pain relievers, but his dad would frown on it and his mom would only worry more. Dynamics that could ignite yet another argument between the two. So Charlie decided he would bear the pain. In silence.

Later, when they turned into their neighborhood, Charles was still in his element; he enjoyed waving at friends and took great pleasure in the elegance of the neighborhood that seemed to greet him personally. Huge oaks, elms, and cottonwoods bordered the street; though the trees were not yet waving leaves from their graceful limbs, the buds were there. Stately homes lined the winding sidewalks, well-built brick and stone edifices that provided security, status. Charles unconsciously nodded his head, reassured. He breathed a sigh of relief as he scanned the neighborhood one more time and then allowed his gaze to rest on his own home.

An opulent mansion greeted them. Artistically designed landscaping framed the stone house, while stained glass—sparkling, catching the light of the sun—arched above the imposing front door. The graceful lines of the turrets and gables tempted the eye to study its roofline, the rod-iron balconies, rich fabrics of draperies peeking through windows. Inside, a spacious two-story foyer held a winding staircase, pink marble floor, artwork on the walls along with the most recent family portrait. The stunning oil had been painted by a nationally known artist, and he had captured not merely their physical likenesses, but a sense of the three individual personalities.

Charles had leaned toward the painter, chin on hand, elbow on knee, appearing to take on any onlookers. Driving home his point—whatever that might be—on any given subject. By contrast, Fran lightly draped one slender hand on her husband's knee, while the other rested on Charlie's shoulder. Appearing as fragile as exquisite bone china, she was clearly a bridge between father and son, negotiating a connection between their starkly differing personalities by the sheer force of her intense love for each of them. And then Charlie, the young physical replica of his father. But the resemblance ended with his visage, for Charlie's face was an open invitation, reaching out for life—naïveté, eagerness, and vulnerability stamped on his features.

Climbing the steps from the garage, Charlie had to concentrate on not limping. He was simply hoping to get to his room, lie on his bed, and read—resting under the pretense of finishing a book assigned over spring break. But when their rambunctious yellow lab Bradley came racing around the corner and jumped on him, Charlie nearly lost his balance. Had to jerk backward, shifting all his weight to his right leg. This time, he couldn't hide his immediate reaction. "*Ouch.* Bradley, cut it out."

Instantly, Fran was next to him, her face a picture of worry.

Noting that his dad was still out in the garage, Charlie decided the timing—if he were going to admit anything—was as good as it was going to get. "I'm a little sore, Mom. That's all. Coach Henry said to ice it."

"A little sore? Get your shoes and shin guards off. Socks, too." All business now, Fran opened the freezer to hunt for the gel pack they'd used countless times before to cool swollen ankles, bruised thighs, a tired throwing arm. "How about if you stretch out on the couch in the family room? Grab the remote first." She momentarily turned her back to him, searching through the vast reaches of the freezer. "I'll just get you something to drink and then I'll be right there."

Charlie limped toward the family room, Bradley glued to his side. Once Charlie had plopped down and turned on the television, he reached toward the lab, feeling remorseful, rubbing behind the dog's ear. "Sorry I yelled at you, Brad, ole boy. Forgive me?"

Bradley sniffed his hand, then licked the entire right side of his face before Charlie could jerk away. "Guess that means I'm forgiven. Don't hold grudges, do you, buddy?"

"Bradley taking good care of you?" his mom asked, gently placing the frozen gel pack on Charlie's leg, moving it to the spot he gestured to. She handed him a glass of sports water and two pain relievers.

"I guess you could say he's taking care of me. If that means covering my face with slobber."

Fran laughed and sat on the coffee table. She moved the gel pack less than an inch, up toward Charlie's knee. Contemplated it for a moment and moved it an inch again, the opposite way. When she finally looked up at Charlie, he lay grinning at her.

"I'm going to be okay, Mom. Really."

"But you were hurting last week. And the week before. I've seen you limping, Charlie. Don't you think it's about time we had Dr. Seldon take a look at it?"

"He'll just tell me to use ice. Rest and stay off it. Mom, I'm not doin' that till the tournament is over."

"So you'll go see Dr. Seldon on Monday?"

"I've got school on Monday. It's not like it's an emergency or anything."

"Well, let's see what the doctor's office says. Could be they'll want to see you right away."

"What's this?" Charles walked into the family room, reaching down to pat Bradley's head before shooting a puzzled look toward Fran. "You're calling the doctor about a bruised leg?"

Charlie started to open his mouth to answer when his mom cut in, "Charles, he's been sore for weeks now."

"That's what happens when you play tough, eh, Charlie?" Charles noted the mindless conversation on a television show in the background and nonchalantly reached for the remote. "Any good games on today? Sox're playing, aren't they?" His eyes remained glued to the TV as he flipped through channels and—in a tone of forced casualness—asked, "Francine, could I speak to you for a moment? In our bedroom?" Not giving Fran a glance until he found the desired game. "Sox versus Indians. That's a guaranteed win. Find out the score, okay?"

Charles gave his wife a pointed look and tossed Charlie the remote.

Fran leaned over and kissed Charlie on the forehead. "We'll just be a few minutes. I'll be right back, promise."

Silently she followed Charles out of the room, into the foyer, and up the winding stairs. She mentally counted the steps, just as she did every time. All twenty-four. Her efforts toward finding some order in her world, comfort that the planes and angles of her home remained the same. Day after day … months leading to years. At least these things would not change, shaking the fragility of her tenuous hold on what she loved.

Charles led Fran into the spacious master bedroom, closing the French doors behind them. He walked to the curved bench at the foot of their bed, sat down and began removing sneakers. "I thought we had an agreement, Francine. No coddling."

"*I* thought we had agreed, Charles. No more pressuring him."

He pitched a sneaker in the direction of the closet. Began unlacing the other.

Fran sat on the chaise lounge and put up her feet. It was as near to plopping down as her naturally elegant movements would allow. "Charles, even Paul told him to rest the leg and ice it, for crying out loud. It's a wise precaution to have it checked by the doctor. Why are you being this way?"

"If he's going to start center forward for Northwestern, he needs to stop babying himself. Time he toughened up, Francine."

"I can't believe this. Charles, he's not even thirteen years old yet."

"That means there's five years left. Five years to prove he's recruitment material. He's not going to get the interest of a coach if—"

"Stop." Fran leaned toward Charles in her frustration, pulling her hands into fists. "Stop right this instant. We don't even know where he wants to go to college yet. Maybe he'll be interested in Harvard. Or Wheaton. Charles, we're going to—*you* are going to allow Charlie to decide this. So help me, I will stand my ground on this one. You will not pressure him already about college and a soccer career. He's a boy! And we will allow him to remain a boy until the time comes when he needs to make grown-up decisions."

The intense look on Charles's face slowly evolved ... relaxed ... into a wide grin.

Charles would never forget the first time he noticed Francine. He was a junior, the star quarterback on the college team. Somehow he'd missed completing a requirement for graduation, a science course—either geology or biology. For that reason alone he'd registered for Biology 101 and was dreading it, until he glimpsed the gorgeous brunette sitting in the first row.

In the first five minutes he'd learned her name: Francine Dupre. Yes, she'd patiently answered, her father was French, her mother, American. She'd gone to France every summer to visit relatives and spoke French like a native. Amazing eyes, her body tall and slim and poised—she looked like a model and carried herself that way. The aura around Francine tended to set every male within twenty feet on edge; she was that noticeable.

Still, those attractions alone wouldn't have provided enough impetus for Charles to pursue her. He'd eventually learned of a deeper quality. Though she appeared as delicate as the English teacups and saucers his aunt kept in the curio cabinet of his adopted childhood home, there was a side to Francine not readily apparent—a flint-like will. And like flint, when struck with steel, she sparked. Charles Edgar Thomason soon realized the delicate bone china was the perfect match for his steel.

As he watched Fran's eyes flash and spark now, Charles couldn't help but think back to the girl who first caught his attention in Biology 101.

"What are you grinning at?" His smirk and raised eyebrows made her anger even more intense.

"Always did like a spark of fire in your eyes," he said, his own eyes glowing.

"You're absolutely despicable, Charles." She charged up off the chaise, her feet barely skimming the floor as she covered the distance to the door. She flung back over her shoulder, "I'll take this to mean we are in agreement now. You will stop pressuring Charlie. And I will make an appointment with the doctor once this tournament is over."

"Hey. I never agreed to that. He's got a bruise, Francine!" Charles moved to the landing outside their room, leaned over and called down, "We are not in agreement on this." He scowled at her retreating back, disgusted with himself for the momentary distraction.

But she had moved on. Was already checking on Charlie. "Okay, love?"

Apparently engrossed in the ballgame, Charlie merely glanced her way and barely nodded. "Sure. Doin' great."

Charlie's eyes were on the game, but his attention had roamed elsewhere. From the moment his parents started bickering, he'd begun fretting. More and more frequently, their disagreements focused on him—his schedule, which was a constant rush to varied activities; any physical issues, from mere sniffles to the broken arm he'd suffered last year; and his emotional makeup, whether he was happy or merely out of sorts. The need to be constantly upbeat dogged Charlie; the slightest sign of weariness or negativity caused his mom to worry. And then his dad lectured them both. *No matter what, it's my fault when they fight about me,* Charlie lectured himself. *I gotta be more careful about what I do. What I say.*

"My fault," Charlie mumbled to himself.

"You say something, Charlie?" his mom asked, poking her head around the corner to check on him.

"Nothin', Mom." He shrugged his shoulders, grinning now. "I'm great."

When Charlie woke the next morning, his thoughts immediately went to the game. And then to his leg. Gingerly, he moved it a little. Reaching down to feel it, he noted the area of swelling just below his knee. *Not nearly as sore as yesterday,* he thought. He swung his legs over the edge of the bed and heard a slight rap on the door.

"Awake, Charlie?" His mom eased the door open a fraction, peeking in.

"Hey. Just woke up."

Fran was tying the belt of her robe as she pushed open the door with her elbows. "How you feeling this morning, love?"

"Fine." He stretched out his leg. Testing. "It's better, Mom. The ice must've helped."

"It feels good enough to play?"

"Mom."

"Okay, I get the point." She grinned at him, holding her hands up in surrender. "So, eggs, bacon, and toast this morning?"

"Sounds great."

"Charlie, if at any point you're hurting and need to stop playing," she hesitated, cautiously weighing her words, "well, I know Coach Henry would agree with me. It's okay. Will you please remember that for me?"

"Sure, Mom."

She leaned down to rest her cheek on top of his head for a few moments while she whispered, "I love you, Charlie. Whether you play and don't do well. If you score and win the game for the team. Or if you don't play at all. Every bit of that has nothing to do with how much I love you." Then she tilted his head up to her so she could look into his eyes again. "Okay?"

Charlie nodded. "Okay."

Silently, she turned and left his room, closing the door behind her.

What would Dad say if I came off the field? Charlie had not spoken the question out loud, but he might as well have. The words were just as concrete and real in his mind.

He stood up, feeling a stab of pain as he put all his weight on the right leg. But as he stretched and walked around his room, the pain seemed to ease. *It was just stiff from sleeping,* Charlie reassured himself. *It's better. I'm sure of it.*

Donning his uniform, Charlie's mind and heart began racing. He smiled to himself, anticipating the excitement of being on the field. Feeling the ball at his feet. Sensing—knowing when to pass. And when to shoot for the goal. It was his own pep session, his way to psyche himself for the game—mentally, physically, emotionally. By the time he was dressed, he'd mentally run through several drills. Lastly, Charlie stood before his mirror. Ran a comb through his hair, but decided it was a waste of time to wet down the untamed curls. He knew girls liked his hair, but the curls were his nemesis.

He trotted down the stairs, enjoying the aroma of frying bacon wafting its way to him, ignoring any twinges in his leg. *It will only bother me if I allow it to,* he'd decided.

Bradley had been sitting at Fran's feet, eagerly awaiting any bits of food that might fall his way. But as soon as he heard Charlie, he came running, wagging his tail, demanding his morning ear rub. "Hey, Brad. Mom drop any treats for you yet?"

"Mornin', sport," from his dad. He was buried behind the paper at the kitchen table, but he peered around it to look Charlie over. "Your mom says your knee's doing great, eh?"

"I did not say great." Fran pivoted to give Charles a glare before turning back to the stove to retrieve bacon and eggs for the three of them. After taking her place at the table, she asked, "Charles? Could you pray for us, please?"

Charles neatly folded the paper, putting it beside him. "Big day, huh, Charlie? It's gonna be a great day, I just know it." He bowed his head, Fran and Charlie following suit. "Lord, I ask for protection for all the boys today, especially Charlie, for his sore leg. Help them to play hard, to do their best, to play fair. Thanks for this food and all you give to us. In Jesus' name, amen."

Father and son both gulped down the meal, despite frequent disparaging looks from Fran. She eventually gave up, realizing they both were far too excited—and anxious to get out the door—to attempt even a pretext of proper manners this morning.

Wiping her hands on her napkin, Fran asked Charlie, "Is there anything else you want or need before you go?"

Charlie thought a moment. "Just wish me luck, Mom."

Fran reached out to hug him, pulling him tightly against her chest.

"Always remember what I told you this morning, okay?"

"Sure, Mom."

"Charlie, I—"

He waited, gripping the doorknob, impatient.

"Never mind. I'll be there as soon as I can. Have fun, okay? Promise me—you'll have fun?"

"Aw, Mom." Charlie laughed. He opened the door and rushed down the steps, calling over his shoulder, "No way I hafta promise that!"

Fran stood by the door, tension making her shoulders and back ache. She heard the car start and seconds later, the garage door close. Still she stood there, instinct telling her to call them back. Resigned, Fran turned back to the empty kitchen. And trudged upstairs to get dressed.

Charlie and his dad were lost in their own thoughts as they drove to the field. Charles was second-guessing himself, wondering, *Have I been too hard on Charlie? This is your doing, Fran—making me doubt.*

Shooting pains were traveling up Charlie's right leg. He fidgeted, stretched it out again and again. Glanced up to his dad to see if he'd noticed, but Charles's eyes remained focused on the road. Charlie turned his head away, willing the pain to stop.

By the time they'd pulled into the parking lot, Charlie's adrenaline was pumping so much he was able to ignore most of the discomfort. He nearly bounced out of the car in his excitement, shouting, "Later, Dad. Wish me luck." As he jogged away, he turned back to give his dad a quick wave and then hurried over to the group of boys who were huddled near Coach Henry.

"Go get 'em, son." Charles leaned against the car a moment, savored watching his son high-five his teammates. Noted how they gathered around as he joined them, their leader, many addressing him as *The Toe Thomason*. He felt a flush of pleasure, intense pride.

Coach Henry motioned for Charlie to join him for a private conversation. He looked worried, concern making a deep groove between his brows. "Seems like you're still favoring your leg, Charlie. How is it this morning?"

"I iced and rested it like you said," Charlie offered, eager to emphasize the positive first. There was no sense trying to fool his coach; he knew their movements and skills better than anyone, including themselves. Knowing he'd be asked about his leg, Charlie had already prepared an answer, determined to soften his response yet still be truthful.

"It's still a little sore, but honest, Coach," Charlie stretched the leg out before him, tilting it left and right, demonstrating his flexibility, "it's *better*. It won't stop me from doing what I need to do. *Promise*." He looked up at Coach Henry, his face an open plea for permission to play.

Torn between his responsibility to protect Charlie, his desire to acquiesce to him, and the team's need for their leader, Paul Henry weighed the options. Charlie had no idea what his coach was think-ing, but he watched conflicting emotions move across his face. Noted how his eyes softened. Saw a twitch of tightening muscles about his jaw, and feared the decision as his mouth remained in a grim, straight line. But Charlie knew to keep quiet. More pleading would only come across as overkill. So he waited, sensing more than a game waited in the balance.

Coach looked down at Charlie's leg once more and began slowly nodding his head. "Okay. You're in. But if I notice you limping more, Charlie …"

"I know, I know. You'll pull me. But it won't happen, Coach." Charlie had kept the practice ball at his feet, and he toed it up onto his knee, bounced it from one knee to the other and back down to his feet. "See? I'm good!"

Coach grinned at him. Reached out to squeeze his shoulder and then called out, "Okay, Flames. Out on the field. Drill time."

Charles had been intently observing the interaction between the two. He followed Paul's every move until Charlie ran away from him, laughing and dribbling the ball onto the field. Only then did Charles breathe a sigh of relief and casually stroll to the sidelines where he joined the other parents. All were exhibiting either excitement or tension, most demonstrating both. He was exchanging greetings and shaking hands when he felt a firm pat on his back. It was Pastor Greg, Charlie's youth pastor, offering his hand and a cheery, "Good morning, Mr. Thomason. What a great day to win a soccer game."

Charles shook his hand firmly, appreciating his appearance on this busy Saturday. "Hey, thanks for coming, Greg. Charlie will be so excited when he sees you here."

"Wouldn't have missed it. Several of my guys are playing today. Figured I needed to see the game myself to keep 'em honest. When they start bragging about their moves tomorrow in Sunday school—to impress the girls, of course—I'll know who's exaggerating just a tad."

When it was nearly time for the game to begin, Coach Henry stepped to the center of the swirling mass of motion and emotion—the squirming, energetic players. They were like thoroughbred racehorses in the starting gate.

He offered a short pep talk, reminding them of their fundamentals, and then said, "I'm proud of you, each and every one of you." Barely getting out the word *you,* he had to take a deep breath to regain his composure. "Whether you win or lose, I want all of you to remember that. It's been a great year. And it's been a privilege to be your coach."

Coach Henry smiled at them, a spark of his competitive nature escaping from his taunting grin. "Now, get out there and let's show 'em how the game of soccer is played."

Led by Charlie, the boys shouted their ritual chant. "On *three.* One, two, three … *Flames. Make 'em feel the burn!*" And Charlie repeated his ritual tribute—locating his parents in the crowd, waving to them, and finally, positioning into a handstand. Walking on his hands to the center of the field. It never failed to make Fran chuckle and shake her head, Charles to glow with pride, and the entire crowd—Flames fans *and* opponents—to respond with laughter.

Charlie's stunt broke the tension somewhat, but the electricity was palpable in the stands and on the field.

The referee placed the ball on the center mark, showing Charlie and the opposing center fielder the coin he would toss into the air. Since it was the Flames' home field, the Des Moines Comets were allowed to choose heads or tails. The center fielder called out "Heads," and when the coin landed faceup, the referee pointed to the Comets as winning the toss. Charlie motioned for his teammates to take their positions outside the center circle.

Charlie watched the center midfielder and forward move together and immediately began shouting out instructions, "Trevor, Austin, heads up. They're coming your way." In his total concentration and excitement, at first Charlie noticed little discomfort in his leg. Whether that resulted from a conscious putting aside or an actual absence of pain even Charlie didn't know. But he was able to run, dribble, and steal without the continuous ache he'd had to deal with yesterday.

The only problem was the other players: They were by far the most talented team the Flames had faced. For the first time that season, the Flames began to wonder, *Maybe we're not as good as these guys.* Despair and capitulation to that dangerous belief were not far behind.

When Charlie had a breakaway run at a goal—the goalie's fingertips just brushed the ball, causing it to hit the goalpost—the Flames' spirits were lifted considerably by the near miss. Charlie built on the excitement from their fans, pumping his fists and yelling out, "We can do this. Next time it's in!"

But by halftime, the game remained scoreless. And Charlie's leg had begun to hurt. He didn't really notice it until they jogged off the field, but the throbbing pain was back with a vengeance. It was all he could do to keep his gait even, knowing that if Coach Henry noticed, he wouldn't be going in for the second half.

As the Flames huddled up at the sideline, Charlie could hear his dad call out, "You're doing great, sport. This half is ours!"

Glancing over his shoulder, Charlie acknowledged his dad with a quick wave before centering his attention on Coach Henry, who worked through a list of suggestions and corrections. The boys sat at his feet, resting tired legs and feet, drinking bottles of sports water. But though their bodies conveyed a lackadaisical attitude, they were listening intently. Only one player found it nearly impossible to concentrate: Charlie. The pain had not only returned, it was worse than ever before.

"Charlie? I want to talk with you for a minute." He hadn't even noticed Coach was wrapping it up, reminding them to hydrate again.

"Coach?" Charlie looked up to him. Concern he was about to be yanked tightened his gut, but he inwardly vowed to hide his fears.

"You seem hesitant to go head-to-head with their center forward. Don't be intimidated by him."

"He's pretty quick, Coach."

"So are you, Charlie. You're just as fast—or faster." His eyes flickered down to Charlie's leg. "You didn't appear to be hindered by your leg in the first half. Not that I noticed, at least. And I was watching. But are you hesitating because it hurts, son?"

"No, Coach, I wasn't. It really was fine." The truth, technically. Charlie held his breath, hoping that he wouldn't ask how it was right now.

"Okay, but if it—"

"It won't. It can't," Charlie interrupted, not allowing the conversation to go in an unwanted direction. "We're gonna win this one, Coach. And I'm not gonna miss out on being a part of that."

Coach Henry nodded, his apprehension lingering still.

The players gathered on the field again. Having lost the coin toss at the beginning of the game, it was now the Flames' turn to kick off. They spread out, eyes fixed on Charlie.

The two teams were so evenly matched they spent virtually equal time on each end of the field, but the Comets connected successfully first. A wobbly, weak pass caught everyone, even Bryce, off guard.

The Comets and their fans went wild in celebration, but it wasn't to be the only score.

A momentary lapse by Charlie—his leg was commanding attention—led to a breakaway. Charlie recovered quickly enough to run with the center forward, but their right wing was especially quick. A last-minute pass left Bryce too vulnerable. And this time the ball bounced sharply against the net.

That was a goal with an exclamation point.

The Flames hung their heads. Their fans, suddenly subdued. Coach Henry, however, was immediately active on the sidelines, gesturing and shouting. Trying to get Charlie's attention. "Charlie," he shouted frantically, finally getting the boy's attention. "Get 'em refocused."

Charlie waved his arms, motioning for his teammates to join him. "We've been practicing the give 'n go. But this time, let's do it in reverse." He looked at Trevor. "*You're* gonna take the shot when we can set it up." Charlie made sure his gaze at Trevor was steady, communicating he believed without a doubt that his friend could pull it off. "Be ready, Trev. Okay, everybody? One, two, three … *Flames.*"

They lined up for the kickoff again. The referee blew the whistle, and the game was on. Amazingly, it ran like clockwork. For a moment, Charlie could tell Trevor was locked into the play they'd practiced over and over; he was setting up to assist Charlie rather than take the shot himself. But then it was as though Trevor physically switched gears, his feet performing what his brain was telling them. Then a defender tripped and their luck held: Trevor had a breakaway.

The crowd could already taste the goal; the fans immediately jumped to their feet. The Comets' sweeper was frantic, knowing he'd been outmaneuvered. And the goalie, in his sudden indecision, committed himself way too early, going left. Trevor sensed the advantage. Kicked right. And the ball sailed into the net.

Charlie was noticeably limping as the boys celebrated. Though his body recognized the pain, his spirit did not—would not. Coach Henry was waving him over, but Charlie ignored him. When he glanced toward the sideline, Coach gestured again, clearly signaling him to come out. Charlie shook his head no, waving him off. Finally held up his hand and fingers in the "okay" sign and leaned over, grabbing his shorts for a momentary rest.

Just before the referee blew the whistle for the kickoff, Charlie raised his arms over his head—as though celebrating a victory already—and gave a thumbs-up sign.

It was as if the boys had been injected with new energy and hope. When the ball was put into play, their skills raised to a new level. Coach Henry shouted encouragement from the sidelines. And the fans stayed on their feet—there would be no more sitting in this game. The hope had moved from the team to the stands like an infectious energy, and the fans were eager for another goal.

In a brilliant move, Grant stripped the ball from a Comet and streaked down the sideline with the ball until he passed it to Austin. The sweeper charged at Austin at full steam. And tripped him. When Austin looked down, he gleefully noted the sweeper had made a crucial mistake: He was inside the penalty box.

The Flames were awarded a direct free kick, and the boys were nearly beside themselves with excitement.

Charlie was always the designated kicker for these fouls, and as he paced back and forth in front of the goal, he began a mind game with the goalie. He leaned over, staring intently into the goalie's face, narrowing his eyes. The pain in Charlie's leg seemed to spike at just that moment, but once again he treated it like an insignificant distraction. The referee signaled for play to begin; Charlie leaned slightly to the right, and then left. Maneuvered so he'd kick the ball with the outside of his foot, deceptively sending it in the opposite direction in which he would run.

The scene appeared to unfold in slow motion. A few steps. Connection, foot against ball. At the last moment, even while recognizing it was fruitless, the goalie threw his body toward the arc of the ball. But he didn't even get near it as the ball sailed through, touching nothing but net.

Goal.

All eyes had followed Charlie until he made contact with the ball. Then the center of attention was transferred to the goalie and finally, to the ball itself. The Flames' fans erupted into delirious celebration once again: jumping, hugging, high-fiving one another.

A few seconds ticked by before anyone looked back at Charlie, who lay on the ground. His fellow teammates, assuming he had fallen in joyful exhaustion, rushed to him, many joining him on the ground in a party of rejoicing. But their happiness turned to horror when they realized Charlie wasn't jerking from side to side in spontaneous joy.

He was writhing in pain.

Charlie instinctively reached toward his leg, but immediately drew back in terror. He was in agony, and when he rolled toward the stands, teammates and fans saw why. Bone—broken bone, stark white next to the black socks through which it protruded— jaggedly bulged from Charlie's right leg, just above his shin guard.

There was a collective intake of breath from the crowd and then a woman's piercing shriek of "*No.*" Charles began pushing through the fans, working his way down the bleachers at a furious pace. Fran, frozen for a moment in shock, attempted to follow right behind him. But she found herself weak-kneed, ungainly, and tripping in her haste.

As loud as the fans had been when the goal was made, an eerie silence now descended over the entire area—on both sides of the playing field. Hushed voices were the background to the agonized cries from the boy on the field that wrenched every parent's heart.

The coaches reached Charlie first, but Charles soon joined them, dropping immediately to the ground. He gathered Charlie into his arms, his steady voice reassuring, "You'll be okay, son. The paramedics are on their way. We'll take care of you."

Charlie had stopped screaming, but he moaned now. When Fran crouched beside him, she took his head gently between her hands and whispered, "I'm here, love. You'll be all right, I promise. I'm here."

His look of pain nearly crushed her.

"It hurts, Mom." He grimaced again, bit his lip. "It hurts so bad."

"It's okay, love," she said. "The ambulance will be here soon."

"We called immediately after you fell, Charlie," Coach Henry offered. "You know how close the fire station is. As a matter of fact, I think I hear the siren now."

Fran tore her eyes from her son's face to search for the ambulance, and instead met her husband's stare. Only the two of them understood all that Fran communicated in that brief moment—the damning accusation, the depth of resentment, and overall, the pain that flickered across her eyes. Fran made sure Charles knew their son's pain was her pain. And that Charles was responsible for it.

The siren grew louder as the ambulance turned into the park, made its way onto the field. The crew—a man and woman—was quick without rushing, taking charge by speaking calmly. The man leaned over Charlie, intent on making direct eye contact with him. "My name's Rich, and my partner and I are going to take care of you until we get you to the hospital." Both knelt on the ground and began pulling out equipment, setting to work. "What's your name, son?"

Charles started to answer for Charlie, but the paramedic cut him off with a stern look.

Charlie slowly opened his eyes, noted the friendly face of the man working above him. "I'm … Charlie." He gasped, and held his breath.

"Can't you see he's—?" But Fran was also silenced.

"Okay, Charlie. I need you to do something for me. I need you to try and take regular, even breaths if you can. Think you can do that?"

"I'll … try."

"Super. We're gonna get you some help with oxygen. Can you tell me what you're feeling? Besides your leg, does anything else hurt?"

"No. Just … my leg."

"My partner's name is Liz. Say 'hi' to Charlie, Liz."

Liz smiled at Charlie. Eyes full of compassion, she also made sure Charlie could see her face as she leaned over him. "Hi, Charlie. I'm checking your pulse and heart rate. We'll get some meds going real soon here to help with the pain."

Though she'd been frustrated earlier, Fran shot her a look of appreciation. She reached up to smooth the hair back from Charlie's forehead and caress his face. Desperately wanting to smooth away the pain etched into his features.

"Your mom and dad here, I assume?" Rich asked.

"Yeah, my dad's right here." Charlie said, concentrating on breathing in and out. "And that's my mom," pointing toward Fran.

"Great job on the breathing, son." Rich squeezed Charlie's shoulder.

"Pulse is one hundred twenty. Thready. Respiratory rate, twenty-two. Looking pretty pale," Liz said.

"You cold, Charlie?"

He nodded, and yawned. The paramedics exchanged a quick look. One neither Charles nor Fran missed.

"Stay awake with us, Charlie. Are we boring you already? Usually we don't have that effect on people until they've been with us for, oh … at least fifteen minutes. Right, Liz?"

Liz smiled broadly again, patted Charlie's arm. "I've got a couple questions for you, Mom and Dad. Your names, please?"

"I'm Charles Thomason Senior. My wife is Francine."

Both paramedics continued calmly working, administering treatment with skill, inspiring confidence with every move they made.

"So, Charles and Francine, any other medical conditions we need to know about? Diabetes? Seizure disorder? Anything at all like that?" Liz inquired.

"No, nothing." Fran answered for both of them.

"Any allergies to medicines? Penicillin? Anything we should be aware of?"

"No, not that we know of. He's always been so healthy—" Fran's voice faltered. "But he has been complaining recently about his leg."

"Obviously you're a soccer player," Rich said to Charlie.

Liz placed an oxygen mask over Charlie's face, so he merely nodded.

"My number-one scorer," Coach Henry said, speaking in hushed tones. It was as though the circle of people were in a sacred place. "Anything we coaches can do to help?"

Rich glanced around at the boys. Noted the worry on their faces, many close to tears. "Well, my partner and I could use your help to lift Charlie onto the stretcher. Then I'd say he's in the best possible hands until we hand him over to the emergency-room crew." He gestured toward the group of boys anxiously milling about. "It's your other players who will be needing you then, Coach."

Coach Henry glanced the boys' way, giving them an encouraging thumbs-up sign.

"Okay, Mom and Dad, one of you may ride with us. Decide who that'll be." Rich gave both of them a serious look, his voice a distinct command. He began organizing the men around Charlie, giving precise instructions to lift as gently as possible. "On the count of three: one, two, *three.*"

Charlie cried out in pain again and clutched his mom's hand.

As the paramedics wrapped a blanket around Charlie, Fran gave her husband a steely look. In a tone that broached no argument, she firmly stated, "I'm going with him."

Charles merely nodded back, followed Charlie with his eyes as they lifted him into the ambulance. As Fran climbed in, she didn't glance back once at Charles. It was Liz, finally, who looked at him with a reassuring smile. "We'll take good care of him." And then Rich shut the doors.

Charles stood there, mute, seemingly paralyzed, until Pastor Greg squeezed his arm just above the elbow. "I sure don't want to interfere, Mr. Thomason. But can I take you to the hospital? Would that be of help?"

Still unresponsive, Charles stared at him dumbly for a moment, as though not recognizing Greg. "Um, I have my car. I can drive myself."

"Are you sure? We could get someone else to drive your car. To the hospital, I mean." Greg still had a hand on Charles's arm, was carefully choosing his words. "I just thought you might want someone with you right now."

Greg watched Charles hesitate again, noted how the usually commanding man appeared incapable of making a decision. He forged ahead, taking charge of the situation. "Come on, my car's right over here." Greg steered him toward the parking lot, waving over Dave, Erik's dad. "Hey, Dave. I'm going to drive Mr. Thomason to the hospital. Would you drive his car over later? Great. Oh, and Dave," Greg said, glancing at Charles. He still appeared to be mute in his shock. "If you all would say a prayer for Charlie, I know Mr. and Mrs. Thomason would appreciate that."

Charles forcibly blinked his eyes, rousing himself. "Oh, yes. We would. Thanks, Dave."

Dave reached out to give Charles a quick hug before taking the keys from him. "Let us know if there's anything else we can do, okay?" Motioning behind him to include the other parents, he added, "I know I speak for all of us. We'll want to check on Charlie later at the hospital. And ... do anything we can to help. Anything at all. Just let us know, okay?"

Charles nodded, mumbling his thanks and then, head down and shoulders hunched, followed Greg. For a man virtually always in the lead, Charles was nearly unrecognizable.

As they settled into Greg's car, Charles seemed to collect himself a bit. Shaking off his lassitude, he ran a hand through his hair and rubbed his eyes. He cleared his throat before saying, "I do appreciate this, Greg. For a minute there, I couldn't ... think clearly. I've seen plenty of broken bones in my day. But never have I seen a break like that before. And for the life of me, I can't figure out why."

"Why it broke? Or why it broke that badly?"

"Both. He didn't hit anybody. The goal post. Nothing. I can't imagine why it would break from Charlie simply kicking the ball."

"Doesn't make much sense, does it?"

They drifted to other topics: church and the latest talk about expanding. Charles seemed eager to shift their discussion to safer subjects—anything but Charlie—and Greg understood his need to do so.

As they were turning into the hospital parking lot, however, Greg offered, "I want to tell you, Mr. Thomason—"

"Why don't you call me Charles?"

"Thanks, I'd like that. Just so you know, Charlie's one of the main leaders in the junior high youth group. He's a great kid, all the way around. Really looks up to you. Wants to be just like you."

Not meeting Greg's gaze. "I would think he'd talk more about his mother."

"Hmm. Nope. It's you he's generally focused on. Oh, it's clear he loves his mom. The handstand routine? Says he does that just to make his mom laugh. Cracks me up. But it's also no secret, Mr. Thomason—sorry, Charles—that you're his hero."

Charles's head snapped around at that point, and he gave Greg a skeptical look.

When Greg turned off the ignition, he asked, "May I come in for a few minutes? Pray for all of you?"

"I'd appreciate that. So would Fran."

They walked into the emergency room together, both immediately struck with the blatant need before them. Two small children, held by worried parents, cried pitifully, a weakened elderly gentleman sat slumped over in a wheelchair, several had bandages from wounds, others were ill with coughs or the flu. Charlie was nowhere in sight, admitted immediately due to his more serious injury.

At the receptionist's station, Charles stopped to ask, "Charlie Thomason? I'm his father."

"He's just down this hallway, the fourth cubicle on your right."

When the automatic doors swung wide, they could see Fran pacing in the stark bright light of the hallway, arms hugged tightly against her chest. She didn't notice them until Charles put his hand on her arm. "What are they—?"

She jumped, startled. "Oh. Charles. Charlie's had an X-ray already. I thought it was patently obvious the leg was broken. Wondered why they had to put him through that, but I guess they need to check everything. I had to sign permission forms for other tests too. A CT scan. Some kind of bone scan—can't remember what. But Charles, they're going to put a small amount of radioactive material in him for that one. What on earth? And of course they wouldn't let me go with him ..."

Charles turned white instantly, as though the blood had drained from his face. He reached toward her but was distracted by the approach of several doctors, their faces grave as they conferred quietly among themselves. And then they stopped before Charles and Fran. Suddenly, unnervingly silent.

One of the specialists cleared her throat and glanced from Charles to Fran to Greg, her face a mask. "Charlie's parents?"

Charles reached out to shake her hand. "I'm Charlie's father. Charles. And this is Francine, his mother. This is Greg Trent, one of our pastors at Oak Hills Chapel."

They were shaking hands, practicing the proper etiquette, when Fran blurted out, "Where's Charlie?"

And Charles demanded, "What's going on, doctor?"

The doctor's kind eyes settled on Fran's direct look. In a calm yet authoritative tone, she offered, "I'm Dr. Lois Owens, the orthopedic specialist here. Charlie's still undergoing some tests. We're scheduling him for an MRI also."

"But why—?" from Charles and Fran, nearly at the same moment.

"Let's go into a consultation room, shall we? Pastor Trent, is it?" the doctor asked.

"Yes. I'll just go out into the waiting room."

"Actually, I think it might be good for you to join us." She glanced toward Fran and Charles, seeking their approval. "With your permission, of course."

Charles nodded. "Yes, that's fine." His voice sounded remote, devoid of emotion, as though his body and its responses were not acting in tandem. Leaving Charles awkwardly disjointed, disconnected from the situation.

"Right this way, please." Dr. Owens directed them into a small room just off the corridor. She flicked on the switch, pouring the harsh fluorescent light into the white-walled room. Their senses were assaulted by the stale smell from a room with no windows and little ventilation plus the lingering remnants of antiseptic and various medications. The telltale pungent scent of nearly all doctors' offices and hospitals. The room was anything but inviting with its scuffed linoleum floor and worn furniture, but Charles and Fran were grateful to escape the exposure of the busy hallway.

Dr. Owens clasped her hands together, inclined her head toward Charles and Fran. Her features noticeably softened, conveying compassion.

"First, I want you to have the peace of mind that we've given Charlie pain medication. He's not suffering physically right now and he's resting comfortably." She gave them the briefest of smiles before continuing, "But I want to get right to the point. It's most unusual for a bone to break like Charlie's has, so we were concerned about what we'd find."

She took a quick breath and plunged on, "I'm so sorry to have to tell you we've discovered Charlie has a sizeable tumor connected to and just above his tibia, involving the knee also."

Fran gasped, and Charles reflexively put an arm around her. Neither could take their eyes off Dr. Owens's face.

"We've called our pediatric oncologist, and we need to do more tests. Our resident oncologist, Dr. Joel Lee, is overseeing those procedures. Nothing is certain until a biopsy is done. But it appears to be osteosarcoma."

"Oh, God," Fran cried.

"That's a type of cancer." Charles's voice was flat. Still removed from him. More so, his emotions.

Dr. Owens never let her eyes wander, her gaze intently shifting back and forth between Charles and Fran. "Yes. It is. We don't know what causes it, and I want to relieve any guilt you might be feeling. I assume Charlie's been complaining about his leg?"

Fran physically jerked away from Charles's touch. She faced him with an accusatory glare, spitting out, "I knew something was wrong, Charles. I knew it. And yet you—" The charge was left incomplete. She closed her eyes, slumping in her seat.

"Fran, be reasonable. We had no idea," Charles pleaded. "None at all."

Dr. Owens reached out to put one hand on Fran's clasped hands, the other on Charles's arm. "Please … may I finish? I brought it up for that very reason. Parents almost always feel overwhelming guilt when osteosarcoma is first found. Especially in this manner, with a severe break. But it's not your fault that you didn't rush him to a doctor or the emergency room beforehand, since it's very typical that symptoms are present for months before the diagnosis is made. You couldn't have known. So please, please don't carry that burden of guilt—and especially don't … Let me put it this way: Charlie's going to desperately need you—both of you."

Fran began weeping softly, but Charles made no move to comfort her.

"What happens next? What kind of tests are you running?" Charles asked, calmly assessing the situation.

"We've sent some blood to be evaluated, and eventually, we'll want to do a CT scan and radionuclide bone scan."

"When will he go into surgery? Certainly you can't leave him like this much longer." Charles's voice rose slightly in intensity. "I mean, you are going to fix his leg, aren't you? Take out the tumor and then put pins in the bone, or whatever it is you do?"

"We won't do surgery until Dr. Mia Chang gets here."

"And she is?"

"The pediatric oncologist. She and I will make the determination about how we recommend to proceed."

Charles leaned back in his chair, a defensive movement. He narrowed his eyes at her. "The determination of what, exactly?" The icy tension in his voice increased dramatically, appearing to fill every space in the small room.

"Mr. Thomason, it's premature to speculate." Dr. Owens's voice was calm in contrast, almost patronizing. "We're not even positive yet this is osteosarcoma. We'd do the biopsy first and then—"

Charles's eyes suddenly grew wide and his body jerked reflexively as though he'd been slapped. "My God, *no*. You will not. I absolutely forbid it!"

Fran blew her nose, looked up at Charles with confusion. "What? What are you talking about?"

Dr. Owens and Charles stared at each other until Dr. Owens eventually looked away. Fran appealed for an explanation, glancing from one to the other, even to Greg. All three avoided meeting her gaze.

"Tell me what you're talking about," Fran ordered, her intensity causing any tears to temporarily subside.

Dr. Owens finally—and boldly—turned to Fran, though her voice was incongruously soft. "The possibility that Charlie's leg may need to be amputated."

Fran could feel the blood draining from her face. She felt light-headed, struggled to clear her thoughts.

Someone knocked, then stuck his head in the door. "Sorry to interrupt, but you're needed out here for a moment, Dr. Owens."

She turned back to Charles and Fran, and then to Greg. "Pastor Trent, maybe you could lead the Thomasons in prayer while I step out?" Greg barely had time to respond before she stood and seemed to add as an afterthought, "I'm a believer in the great power of prayer." She slipped quietly out the door.

Greg twitched uncomfortably, the awkwardness and intimacy of the moment making him feel like an invading stranger. Recognizing Fran and Charles hadn't had one moment by themselves to absorb the horrific news, he looked anywhere but at them; it was as though he were observing them naked—emotionally, spiritually. His pastor's heart longed to provide comfort and encouragement. Give them a sense of hope and help them feel God's love. But Greg was suddenly paralyzed, struck dumb. *What could I possibly say to them,* he wondered, *that wouldn't sound cli-chéd or trite?*

Through clipped words, Charles spoke up, interrupting Greg's ambivalent thoughts. "Well, I suppose you should pray, Greg. Before these supposed doctors come back."

Fran fixed a reproachful glare on him. "Charles. How can you not appreciate—?"

"*Just stop it,* Francine." Charles winced with apparent disgust as her nose dripped and she reached to dab at it. "*Yes,* I'm angry. That these doctors would even consider … *amputation?* I mean, how anti-quated can you get? Certainly no respectable doctor does that sort of barbaric thing anymore. And no son of mine is going to be a … a *cripple.* I'll threaten to sue if she mentions it again."

"And if Charlie's *life* is at stake, Charles? Think about the rami-fications of what you're saying." Fran turned toward Greg, saw that he sat leaning over with his head down, staring at the floor, hands clasped in front of him. "Greg," her voice hoarse with entreaty, "please pray for us now. We desperately need …" She let the words trail away.

When Greg straightened up, Fran saw tears spilling from his eyes too. His display of compassion touched her deeply, and she blinked back a flood of new tears. Greg coughed. Wiped unashamedly at the tears as he frantically thought, *God, I don't have the faintest idea what to say. Help me, please, Lord.* Aloud, Greg replied, "It would be my privilege."

The suffocating room felt like a cavern to all three of them. Every sound—the irritating background buzz of the overhead fluorescent light, the squeak of Charles's sneakers on the linoleum floor when he drew his feet beneath him, the crisp rustle of Greg's windbreaker jacket as he switched positions in his chair, and Fran's sniffs—all appeared magnified. For a few seconds, those sounds so occupied Greg's thoughts he could concentrate on nothing else.

With trepidation, he began, and after several long moments of prayer in which Greg simply admitted their desperate need for God, he fell silent, and the room remained still until Dr. Mia Chang entered—a tiny, demure woman, but obviously well respected by the manner in which the other doctors deferred to her. All attention turned to the oncologist. And the ominous sheaf of papers she held.

Charles and Fran appeared to be holding their breath, their faces glued to Dr. Chang's, seeking any sign of hope. Their unmasked vulnerability was uncomfortable for Greg to witness, but unlike Greg, the doctors had observed it many times before. They weren't inured to its effects; blatant suffering still pricked their hearts, especially in relation to children. But they had learned to function in spite of it; the success of their jobs depended upon that ability.

"I'm sure you have questions for us. We can't answer them all yet." Dr. Chang glanced at her watch. "We need to wait for the results of the bone scan."

Charles's impatience made him terse. "We'd like to know. Is it cancer?"

Dr. Chang lifted her chin, answering him directly, voice unwavering. "We won't know for sure until we get the results of the biopsy. But unfortunately, everything points to a diagnosis of osteosarcoma. And it appears to have metastasized to Charlie's lungs. I am so sorry."

For the moment, Fran had no more tears. *This can't be happening,* she heard her mind repeat, over and over. *It's not real. This can't be happening to us.*

Charles's denial came in another form; he became an automaton. Facts—black and white responses devoid of emotion—would serve to delay making this information personal. Pertaining to *his* son. *His* pain. He clenched his jaw, sat more upright. Leaned toward Dr. Chang as though he were about to threaten her.

"How do we cure it?" More of a demand than a question.

"We treat it"—substitution of the word *treat* lost on Fran, but not Charles—"by first of all, surgery. We'll remove the mass and the affected bone. Then, we'll start a course of chemotherapy. We may also need to use radiation therapy."

Charles's eyes bored into the doctor's. The shift from nonfeeling, robotic responses to seething anger was so abrupt that Charles himself was taken by surprise. But he'd been thrust back into his childhood, was once again the insecure eleven-year-old. His vision was filled with hazy memories of his father—the sight of his emaciated, pallid arm next to his robust one. His inability to do more than barely squeeze Charles's hand. Sounds ... moans and pitiful cries that he heard through the wall of his bedroom. He remembered breakfasts of cold cereal, sitting alone at a Formica table. Bleakness. Hopelessness that somehow resided still in the memories of all his senses.

"How can you be so sure about all of this? Have you seen it?" Charles shouted at Dr. Chang.

"Charles, please," Fran whispered under her breath.

"The pictures were very clear, Mr. Thomason, showing a spot on one of Charlie's lungs. But it appears to be a limited stage cancer,

which is good news. That means his prognosis is more encouraging."
She paused to let that information sink in, then continued, "I don't
want to rule out surgery on Charlie's lung, as that's the direction we
may choose to go—followed by chemotherapy. For now, the tumor
on his leg is our first priority. We don't want to put him through
any more trauma than is absolutely necessary. Besides a biopsy on
the lung, the only surgery we'll be doing at this point is his leg." Dr.
Chang's demeanor changed from informational to compassionate,
and her tone softened. "I know this is hard. I'm so sorry. So very
sorry."

The muscle in Charles's jaw tensed. "And what's the … the survival rate for …?"

"Please, Mr. Thomason," she immediately interrupted. "We
don't have enough information yet. After Charlie's surgery, after we
get the tests back from biopsies, then we'll discuss treatment. And
Charlie's future. Fair enough?"

"This is intolerable, doctor." Charles's eyes bored into hers, testing. Threatening again.

The doctor seemed unfazed. "The bone scan will tell us that and
help us decide—once we're in surgery, and can judge better—whether
we can do the limb-salvage surgery. Or, if necessary, to amputate. We
need you to sign some forms, give us permission to make that call
while we're in surgery."

Charles's stare intensified, an overt attempt to intimidate. His
tone was eerily calm as he said, "Let me state this clearly: You will not
take off my son's leg. I will never give you permission to do that. And
I demand you do everything possible to save his leg."

"Charles—" Fran began, but Dr. Chang broke in.

"Please understand. Limb-salvage surgery could leave his leg severely deformed, and artificial limbs are now so advanced that Charlie might actually be more active with a prosthesis than with a disfigured leg. But more importantly, because we believe the cancer has metastasized, and depending on how adversely Charlie's tibia and knee are affected, you could very well be risking your son's life to not give us permission to amputate."

Silence. Charles's body was frozen, rigid in his anger.

And then Fran's weak, hushed voice broke into the vacuum. "Where do I need to sign?"

Charles looked at her in disbelief, his eyes wide, mouth gaping. "You're going to agree to this? Just like that?"

She pursed her lips—an attempt at a measure of control—but then a sob escaped as she cried out, "I want …" Fran swallowed, choked out the words, "I want … my son. I want my precious son." Her voice broke completely then, and she let out a haunting wail. "I don't care if he's missing a leg. I don't care if he's deformed or without hair or whatever they must do to save him." She waved a hand toward the doctors, an admission of their presence. "Don't you get it, Charles? I want him alive. I want to hold him in my arms. I want to feel his heart beating. I want to watch him grow up. I want … I want *Charlie*."

The room was deathly quiet except for the sound of her sobbing.

Charles dropped his head a moment, and then looked up, his face a picture of brokenness. The skin on his face went suddenly slack, eyes dilated, mouth hanging awkwardly open. He nodded meekly, the fight in him—for now, at least—dissipated. He watched Fran sign the papers, and then reached for the pen himself. "Is there

a possibility …? Could Charlie—could he die during this surgery?"
The pen shook in his hand.

Dr. Owens answered, "With any major surgery, that's always
a possibility. But Charlie's vitals are stable. There's no reason that
should happen." Compassion bathed her voice. "We intend to take
the very best care of your son, Mr. Thomason." She deliberately
looked over to include Fran, too. "Mrs. Thomason. We know he's
your most treasured possession."

"You mentioned Charlie possibly being more active? What could
Charlie do with this … prosthesis?"

"One of our patients had his leg amputated two years ago," Dr.
Owens began, sensing an opening for encouragement. "He jogs,
rides a bike, plays in the baseball league. He's fourteen now, still
growing. He needs to have the prosthetic device refitted often, but
it's amazing what he can do."

"And what name do all the kids call him?" Charles's voice was
thick with cynicism, but pain veiled his eyes.

Dr. Chang spoke up. "Actually, you might be surprised by that.
When our patient's hair fell out from chemotherapy, every boy on his
baseball team volunteered to shave his head too. And when the idea
spread to his class at school, every male teacher and boy in his class
also shaved off his hair. *Every single one,* Mr. Thomason. Does that
sound like ridicule to you?"

Chastised, feeling awkward, Charles mumbled, "I'd … I'd like
to see Charlie now."

The doctors nodded, and they all filed out silently—but not
before Dr. Chang reached over to squeeze Fran's hands. For a fleeting
moment, through that vulnerable gaze, Fran caught a glimpse into

the doctor's soul—the hallowed ground of the suffering of other children. The horrors of chemotherapy and radiation and amputation. Hope accompanied by setbacks and heartbreak. And death, despite all her valiant efforts. Dr. Chang sighed deeply, and then Fran stared at the doctor's back as she hurried down the long hallway.

Greg lightly touched Charles's arm. "I need to give my wife a ring, and then I'd like to call Pastor Perkins—if that's all right with you, so that he can be praying?" Greg gave both Charles and Fran a firm hug before he watched them walk away from him.

Instinctively, they reached for each other's hands.

Charlie's room contained various medical machines with paraphernalia spaced all around the walls. But the area where the bed should be was starkly bare.

The emptiness was a stab to Fran's heart, and she picked up Charlie's soccer shirt. Putting it to her face, she breathed in her son's smell. Without consciously realizing it, she swayed, humming a nursery song.

Charles stood beside her and whispered, "I can't believe this. *Why Charlie?* Out of all of those boys, why *our* son? He should be out there playing soccer right now. Not here in this … this …" He glanced around the room, grimacing. "Certainly not here in this pathetic, ugly hospital. Waiting to have his leg …" He let his voice trail off, and then put his head in his hands.

"Maybe … maybe he'll still be able to do those things," Fran whispered. A wistful statement, not given with much hope. In her mind's eye, Fran saw Charlie with an ugly, awkward metal leg that stuck out at an odd angle from his shorts. Pictured his sitting on the sidelines, reduced to merely cheering on his teammates. The image nearly broke her heart.

Head still buried, Charles took a deep breath. Exhaled. "I want my son too, Francine. I want him to live."

"I know that, Charles. I know." And she then willingly brought back the imagined picture of Charlie. Recognizing that at least he was alive in that vision.

Charles moved to the other side of the room, observing her. With his feet spaced wide apart, arms folded across his chest, he said through gritted teeth, "I will fight this, Francine." His entire body went rigid. But his eyes were nearly burning with intensity. "Whatever we face, we will not give in to it. Not ever. *And Charlie will fight this too.*"

"Fight what, Dad?" Charlie's voice sounded groggy, weak. "Did we win the game?" As orderlies rolled Charlie's bed back into its place, Charles and Fran moved to either side of him. Fran gently took Charlie's hand in hers—it was bruised from the IV, and Fran frowned at the tender spot—while Charles gripped the bed's railing. The paraphernalia of IVs hooked up to a tall, gangly pole, various monitors beeping and humming, and several nurses tending to the positioning of each line distracted Charles. His eyes took in every machine, every line attached to his son. He blinked rapidly and then gripped the bed rail so tightly his knuckles turned white.

Charles leaned in close, deliberately attempting to keep his voice steady and calm. "We were just talking about your recovery, son. How we're all going to fight to get you well. Your mom. Me. You, too." He cleared his throat, coughing lightly. "Get you back out on that field before you know it. Running and ... and ..."

Fran reached across Charlie, putting her other hand on Charles's arm.

"How long they sayin' before I'm outta here, Dad?" Each word getting a bit more slurred.

"We don't know for sure yet, Charlie. But your mom and I will be helping you every single step. Deal?"

"Yeah, sure. Deal." He yawned, and asked in barely distinguishable words, "Did we win?"

"I don't know, son. I'm convinced we did, though. Momentum had switched back to us for sure."

Charlie smiled, his only acknowledgment. Eyelids heavy, he drifted back to sleep.

Personnel were bustling around them, prepping Charlie for surgery, an unwanted reminder to Fran that they'd soon be taking him away again. "Charles. Maybe we'd better pray now?"

In case Charlie could hear, he thought carefully about what he would say—more so, would not. "Take care of our son, Lord, please. We're so grateful for—" His voice faltered, and Charles waited until he could speak calmly again. "Thank you for Charlie, and for all he means to us. We know he's in your hands. In your name, amen."

When Charles opened his eyes, he discovered Charlie staring up at him. "It'll be okay, Dad. Don't worry. I'll be okay."

An orderly moved to the head of Charlie's bed. When Fran finally tore her eyes from her son's peaceful face, she reluctantly saw it was time to release him. She placed her palm on his cheek, putting her lips right next to his ear. Whispered, "I love you, Charlie. With all my heart."

The nurse gave Fran a reassuring pat before they wheeled Charlie down the hallway.

Charles and Fran watched until they disappeared around a corner. She and Charles simultaneously reached out again, holding hands as they walked silently to the waiting room. But that slight physical touch was the only connection made, for each heart was an entity to itself. Two islands surrounded by a sea of pain.

Charles and Fran sat in a back corner of the waiting room, oblivious to the low lighting from several lamps, the shadows created by the softened hues in the twilight of the day. The window blinds were still open, allowing some outdoor lamps from the hospital's parking lot to pour in more light. But the result was a contrast of bright and subdued, illumination and gloominess, a chiaroscuro painting. A television, tuned to a twenty-four-hours news station, was turned down to its lowest setting. Next to them was a coffee station—clearly in need of a cleaning—a profusion of used, stained cups, rumpled napkins, and opened sugar packets, sugar sprinkled everywhere. Charles slumped in a chair; Fran stretched out on a couch. Neither spoke. The only sounds were the low voices of the newscasters, Fran's occasional sighs, and the hiss of the coffeemaker.

Earlier, Charlie's entire soccer team, along with the parents, had come to visit. The usually boisterous boys were subdued as they waited to hear about Charlie's condition. When informed about the seriousness of the injury—though not of the cancer or possible amputation—they were even quieter in their shock. Above all, Charles didn't want their sympathy—didn't want that for his son. So he thanked them for their concern and asked them to continue praying, encouraging the sober boys by insisting Charlie would come through surgery just fine.

At the sound of the door opening, both Charles and Fran instantly stood—Fran's body rigid, attention focused on the two people who possessed information that would shape the remainder of their lives. Charles, towering over the two diminutive doctors, leaned toward them in a way that appeared to fill all the air around them.

Dr. Chang took a step backward. "First let me reassure you that Charlie's doing just fine. All his vitals are good."

"And his leg?" From Charles.

"I'm so sorry. We did everything possible to try and save it, but Charlie's leg had to be amputated above the knee."

Fran began sobbing hysterically and Charles groped toward her, taking her hands in his. Soothing, hushing, imploring, "Francine, *Francine*. Please, Francine." She wouldn't look up at him, only stared down into her lap, crying despondently. Her grief had become a vortex, despair feeding upon itself.

Charles attempted to reach her again. "*Lennie.*"

She quieted then. Looked up at her husband, a shadow of recognition mixing with sorrow. Fran hadn't heard the endearing name in years.

When they were dating, Charles said she reminded him of his grandmother's tea set—Lenox bone china. Fragile, delicate, beautiful.

So he'd given her the pet name, calling her Lennie in moments of tenderness, and then later when she'd suffered her first miscarriage. After that, Charles discarded the name, deciding it only encouraged her to fight less. To surrender far too easily, giving in to defeat and failure. And miscarriage after miscarriage.

"You're not keeping anything from us, are you? I mean, is Charlie *really*—?" Fran asked, fearfully.

Dr. Chang reached over and took Fran's hands between her own. "He's fine, Mrs. Thomason. We wouldn't withhold vital information about a patient's health, so you can be assured that Charlie's doing well. He truly is."

Charles blurted out, "How long for the recuperation? Before he can have a prosthesis fitted?"

Dr. Lee brought his hands up as though holding off a rambunctious child. "Mr. Thomason, Charlie's going to need time to heal. And with chemotherapy, well, you have to give this process adequate time. Give *Charlie* time."

Dr. Chang was nodding her head in agreement. "The stump must fully heal. The sutures, the inevitable swelling. And this is based on the assumption that we'll have no problems like an infection along the way. We'll get to a fitting as soon as possible, Mr. Thomason. Dr. Owens will help us determine when the time's right."

"Listen to me." Jaw set, Charles's tone was intense, nearly threatening. And although he was looking at Fran, his comments were also directed toward both doctors. "We're going to fight. And we will beat this … this cancer. Next year at this time, I promise you Charlie will be playing soccer again." Charles pointed his index finger into the air. "One year from this day"—with each word, he stabbed out again for emphasis—"Charlie will be out on that field." Point made, he leaned back, crossing arms over his chest.

The doctors exchanged knowing looks, but they refrained from responding and instead directed their comments toward Charlie's recovery in ICU and how long before he'd be released to a room. "Charlie could be in the ICU for two to several hours," Dr. Chang said.

"Yes, so we encourage you to take a break. Get something to eat. You need to keep up your strength—for Charlie's sake," Dr. Lee implored. And then after reassuring them once more, the doctors left Charles and Fran alone again.

Neither spoke. The silence was such that anyone passing by would've thought the room empty—except for the two frozen forms and the vestiges of temporary residence scattered about: newspapers, a coat and sweater, lipstick-smudged coffee cups and reading glasses.

A nurse finally directed them to Charlie's room around midnight, when they made the decision that Charles would drive home and settle things there, bringing back a change of clothes for Fran. He trudged out to the dimly lit parking lot with a list of things to do, people to call, and various items to bring to the hospital. He hated the thought of not being there when Charlie was brought to his room, but nurses assured him Charlie would be so groggy that he'd be barely conscious.

Fran was sipping a cup of coffee when she heard voices just down the hall. She rubbed sleep-deprived eyes and ran a hand through disheveled hair, prepared herself as best she could. Aides and nurses pushed open the door. Wheeled in a tiny, pitiful form enveloped in a huge bed, swathed in bandages, hooked up to even more lines, wires, and machines than earlier. The shock of it all caused Fran to draw a quick breath.

Standing back, Fran could only peek at Charlie as she anxiously waited for the nurses to get the IV adjusted, blood pressure pump and heart monitor readouts set up, and begin preparing to elevate Charlie's leg. *The stump,* Fran thought to herself. Tears threatened again but she willed them away.

The nurses were so busy at first they largely ignored her. Finally acknowledging Fran's presence, they began coaching her. "His IV bag is nearly empty," the nurse pointed out. Her words were clipped, movements efficient. "When it's empty, it will start beeping, this button flashing. Here's Charlie's call button to the nurses' station. Let us know when that happens by pressing it. Got it?"

In Fran's grogginess, she concentrated hard to take it all in. "I think so."

"Normally we'd be teaching Charlie about this, but he's pretty much out of it still. I'm hoping he'll sleep fairly well till morning, though we'll need to keep taking his vitals throughout the night."

The nurse continued adjusting various lines, a catheter bag, and the sling system which held up his stump.

"Before I leave tomorrow morning, I'll show you the pressure garment. You'll need to know how to remove it yourself before Charlie can leave the hospital. Then you'll have to clean the wound and reapply the wrapping."

Fran nodded at her, suddenly overwhelmed by it all. *I haven't yet absorbed the fact that my son's had an amputation,* she thought frantically. *How can I remember all these steps?*

"If he should wake and complain about pain, call us right away. Okay, I think that's it for now." Her pocket's contents—pens, hemostat scissors, other unknown small items—made a unique clicking sound as she hurriedly walked back down the hall toward the nurses' station.

Fran looked down and saw Charlie's eyes staring into hers.

"Mom?" His pupils were dilated, hazy. She watched them grow smaller as he focused on her face.

She searched for his hand, taking it gently between her own, mindful of the attached IV. Forced a reassuring smile. "Oh, love. How are you?"

"Leg hurts."

"The nurse just left, but I'll get her back here immediately."

His eyelids were already getting heavy, closing slowly. Fluttering back open as he struggled to stay awake before closing again. "Nah, don't bother. I think I'm gonna …" he yawned, slurring his words now, "just go back to sleep." He smiled, mumbling just before he nodded off, "Whatever. They're givin' me. Good stuff."

Fran reached up to smooth back the curls from his forehead, luxuriating in the very feel of him … his skin, hair, hands. She traced the small scar on the back of his hand with her thumb—a reminder of Bradley's puppyhood and his razor-sharp teeth. Noted the cowlick on the right side of his forehead—which he'd had from birth, and that she recalled tenderly tracing her fingers over the very first time she'd held him. She allowed her gaze to roam over every inch of her son, taking in and cherishing all the boyish angles and bruises and scars, still-present baby fat amid the muscle.

She still felt stabs of pain when she recalled the miscarriages—a total of three, before Charlie was born. Two babies were far enough along to be identified as girls—a daughter had been the longing of her heart. After Charlie arrived and she could no longer get pregnant, Fran remembered wondering if she'd regret having only a boy. Her eyes welled with tears. *Regret?* she thought, and then smiled. *Never. Not once.*

And then, *And he's still with us. With me,* she reassured herself. She realized anew that Charlie's birth had been a miraculous gift after the miscarriages. And his presence with her tonight was a gift from God again. A tear dropped onto Charlie's arm as she whispered, "Thank you, God. Thank you for my son."

Charlie's eyes flitted back open. "Mom?"

"Oh, love. Sorry I woke you."

He yawned. "Nah, not you. It was the sky."

"What's that?"

"I saw the sky—all these stars. It was so bright because the sky was full of them."

Taken back by his nonsensical explanation, Fran gave him a puzzled look.

"They were all so clear. Usually most're hard to see."

"How so?"

"You know, Mom. The dimmest ones. When you try to see them, they just kinda … disappear." His voice sounded raspy. His reasoning was drug-affected. But it was evident that he'd seen and experienced *some*thing.

Sensing it was important to Charlie, Fran wanted to understand. "I think I know what you mean. You're talking about how stars seem to twinkle—an effect from their being so far away? Is that it?"

Charlie yawned. "Not like that … in my dream. Really … cool."

"Oh?"

"I could look right at them, Mom, and *really* see them. So clear, I wanted to touch ... almost could." He blinked a couple times, an attempt to keep himself awake. "Wish you could've seen them too." His voice grew softer, his words further apart again.

"Funny, I have this vague memory of your grandmother talking about that. It was something about those who look at stars and see them clearly are more able to—what was it? I think she said it meant you were more sensitive. To God."

"How old were you?" Charlie asked.

"Oh, I think around ten or so. I do clearly recall that we were on the back porch, looking up on this amazingly clear night. I think it was cold. Must've been winter, I imagine? Or fall. But I stared and stared at those stars, trying to see them like Mother said."

Charlie yawned again, closed his eyes, conceding to sleep. "Could you?"

"No, I couldn't. At least, not the way she described it. And I remember feeling disappointed." Charlie's breathing was steady and even. She doubted he'd heard her. "Go back to sleep now, okay? Get some rest."

"Yeah. Maybe I'll see ... more stars."

Fran kissed him tenderly on the forehead. "I hope so, love. I really do."

The next two days were a blur for Fran. Her whole world had shrunk to the confines of the hospital walls. It was where she slept, showered, ate, and cared for Charlie however she could, day and night. Her bed was a couch she made up every evening, falling onto it totally spent—yet still listening for Charlie's every move. Ready to jump up and run to his side at the slightest sigh or groan or whisper of "*Mom?*"

Charles went to the hospital as much as he could, between putting in hours at work and caring for the necessities at home. He disliked not being there all the time, but his practical side knew it wasn't feasible. There simply wasn't enough space for three of them in the hospital room; he couldn't justify being there twenty-four hours and there wasn't the need. But though he wasn't there physically, his heart and thoughts constantly were.

He attempted to time his morning visit with the doctors' rounds, judging it important to hear firsthand how Charlie was progressing, how the stump was healing. They hadn't yet offered information on Charlie's future treatment or his prognosis—and he and Fran hadn't asked. Charles knew instinctively that Fran wasn't ready. She appeared too tenuous for that discussion, and he was afraid more bad news would push her past what she could endure. He'd tried to catch Dr. Chang alone for a one-on-one discussion but hadn't succeeded.

The first two days after surgery, Charlie had been asleep more than he was awake. When he was conscious, he was barely communicable—due to high doses of pain medicine. The doctors explained it was best for Charlie to get through those first few days in a semiconscious state. Though Charles was intent on telling Charlie about his amputation and was frustrated with the delay, the doctors and nurses insisted the discussion could wait.

But it was torture for Charles. For many reasons.

"He's got to know. Now," Charles had told Fran the morning after surgery.

"For heaven's sake, why, Charles? Why the urgency?"

"Because he can't mentally or emotionally defeat the cancer if he doesn't know it's there."

Fran moved to her son's bedside, stared at his peacefully sleeping face. "The time will come, Charles. But not yet. He's not even coherent, for crying out loud."

Charles whispered through gritted teeth, "You're being overly protective, Fran. Let him be a man for once, will you? Let go so Charlie can do what he needs to do."

"He's *not* a man, Charles. He's a *boy*," Fran hissed back. She groped for Charlie's hand, threatening to disturb his sleep. She moved unconsciously, only cognizant of the battle that had seemingly raged between her and Charles since the first miscarriage.

She turned deliberately toward Charlie, away from her husband. "We're setting up Charlie to be in the middle of this impasse between us. We can't be on opposite sides for this … this *fight* … as you're so prone to term it, Charles. Don't you see? Charlie will lose if we're not both on the *same* side. And if Charlie loses, that means—that means—"

A nurse pushed against the door, giving it a desultory *knock, knock* as she breezed in. "Time to check Charlie's bandage. I'll just be a minute." Efficient, operating from a checklist including far too many duties, the nurse hadn't noticed the tension in the room, the conversation she'd interrupted.

And once interrupted, it was easier to put aside. To delay the inevitable battle … until the next day or the next.

Until the third morning after his surgery, when Charlie awoke early. Before Fran was even out of her makeshift bed, she heard, spoken with a noticeably clearer voice, "Mornin', Mom."

Fran lifted a groggy head from the pillow, trying to assess if she'd heard correctly. "Charlie?" Hoping to clear her vision, she rubbed sleep-deprived eyes. "Are you awake?"

"Yeah, I think so. I mean, I still feel kinda loopy. But I'm *starved*, Mom. My tummy's growling." With effort, Charlie lifted his head to watch his mom climb out of bed, reach for her robe. "How much longer till I get some breakfast around here anyway?"

Fran moved to him as fast as she could, leaning over to kiss his forehead, caress his hair. "Just as soon as I can get them to bring you something. I'm thrilled to hear you're hungry."

Charlie grinned up at her. "French toast sounds good. And eggs. Bacon, too. Gosh, it seems like years since I've eaten."

She chuckled at him, but shook her head. Dreading the disappointment she'd cause as the messenger of bad news. "Don't you remember? You're on a restricted diet." Seeing the immediate dismay that came over Charlie's features, she hurried to add, "But maybe you can eat a little more today." He brightened a bit, confident in his mom's ability to bend the rules for him.

Fran glanced into the mirror, ran a hand through her hair, and tightened the belt of her robe. She winked at Charlie. "Armed for battle. I'll be right back."

By now, Fran knew all the nurses, what shifts they worked. She made a beeline for the head nurse who'd demonstrated a soft spot for her son.

"Andrea? Good news: Charlie's got an appetite this morning. I think that's an encouraging sign."

Built like an athlete, tall, lean, and wiry, Andrea had been working through stacks of reports, but she pushed them aside to share in
Fran's joy. "Oh, that's great news."

"He'd like French toast, bacon, and eggs. And grape juice. Can
he have grape juice and some milk, too?"

"Let me make a couple calls, but I think I can make most of that
happen. Let me warn you ahead of time, though: Don't be surprised
when he doesn't eat more than a few small bites. That's just typical.
Eyes bigger … you know the drill." She jotted some notes and asked,
"Anything else?"

Fran looked away, chewing on her lower lip. As much as she
dreaded it, Andrea was the one to ask. "Since he's so lucid. Obviously
not in as much pain this morning. Should Charles and I … should
we …?"

"Yes. Now's the time to talk about his leg. But let Charlie … how
shall I put this?" She leaned back in her chair and tapped a pen against
the armrest, pausing a moment. "Let Charlie give you the clues about
how much he wants to know. Listen for what he says—and more
importantly, *doesn't* say. That's how he'll tell you how much he wants
to hear." Andrea tossed the pen onto the counter and then clasped her
hands in front of her. "My guess is he'll also tell you what he already
knows. Which I'm bettin' is quite a lot."

Fran nodded. "Thanks, Andrea." She hurried back to Charlie's
room, wondering if maybe he'd drifted back to sleep. *Hoping so?* she
asked herself. *Coward.* As she pushed the door open, however, she
was surprised to hear the television.

"Figured out the remote, huh? It's great to see you more alert,
Charlie. And before I forget—all the guys have been here. Grant, at

least three different times. Riley and Erik and Bryce. Connor. Every single member of the team, actually. Everyone's pulling for you, Charlie. And they miss you, a lot."

Charlie clicked off the television. Turned to his mom, his eyes instantly filling with tears.

"Charlie. What is it?"

He pushed his head back against the pillows. Shook his head.

"Are you in pain, love? Should I call the nurse? What can I do?"

He started to say something. Closed his mouth, lips pursed, and then began again. "Why, Mom? Why did they hafta cut off my leg?"

He knew. She felt a stab to her heart once again. "Your leg broke because there was a tumor, Charlie. And it's—"

"It was cancer," Charlie completed the sentence matter-of-factly. "But what exactly does that mean? Will I have to have other stuff done?"

"Yes, Charlie. I'm so sorry."

"Like what?"

"We don't know for sure yet. But Dr. Chang thinks chemotherapy will wipe it out. The cancer."

"There's more?"

Fran swallowed, feeling the blood draining from her head. *Get yourself together,* she berated herself. *Charlie needs you.* She took a deep breath. "Yes, Charlie."

"It's in my lungs, isn't it?"

Fran's eyes flew wide open. "How did you—"

"Been having trouble breathing." He sighed. "Sometimes I couldn't catch my breath when I was running."

"Charlie, why didn't you tell your dad and me?"

"I just thought it was ... I don't know. Allergies or something. Thought I needed to get in better shape."

Fran gently stroked his arm. Fought the pressure of tears pushing at the back of her eyes. "It's in only one lung—that's good news."

He was quiet and pensive a few moments. Fran waited patiently, allowing Charlie to set the agenda. "I, um ... saw a show a while back. About a kid who got cancer. Lu ... something?"

"Leukemia?"

"Yeah, that was it. She had to have chemo. Lost all her hair."

"Yes. That usually happens with chemotherapy." Willed herself not to look at Charlie's hair ... his adorable curls.

"She was really sick a lot too."

"Dad and I already asked about that. They promised to work really hard at moderating those side effects with some new drugs. Hopefully, you won't have too many problems, and it's even possible you won't be sick at all, love."

"How will I ..." his eyes instantly filling with tears, "will I be able to walk at all? Or will I be in a ... wheelchair?"

"Oh, Charlie, from what Dad and I hear, you'll not only be walking, you could run someday."

His eyes narrowed, brows drawn together. "How's that possible?"

"Technology for prosthetic limbs is just ... just *incredible*. Dr. Owens was telling us how amputees ride bikes and ski and play sports—all kinds of sports, Charlie. But it's going to take time. You'll need fittings. Therapy. We all have to be patient with this process ... your healing."

Fran was already nodding affirmatively, anticipating Charlie's question of "Soccer? You think I might be able to play soccer again?"

"Possibly. Someday." She studied his face, the wide open and vulnerable expression. The depth of hope that only a child can possess. And the faith to fuel that hope.

A firm knock at the door interrupted them, plus Charles's greeting of "Hey, how are my two favorite people in the whole world?" He leaned down to meet Fran's upraised face with a kiss, reached out to ruffle Charlie's hair. Taking in the scene before him, Charles commented, "You look much better today, son." Giving Fran a quizzical look, he added, "You two … talking over some things, I take it?"

Charlie was suddenly subdued, serious. "I knew, Dad."

Probing, Charles asked, "You knew what, son?"

"I knew they were gonna cut off my leg." He sounded older, far more mature than his years. "I've known the whole time."

Fran and Charles exchanged dubious looks. "The whole time? What do you mean, son?"

Charlie frowned, avoided their searching faces by turning toward the window.

"In the emergency room, after the tests. The way everyone reacted. Kind of tiptoeing around me. I figured it out then."

Charles fidgeted with the keys in his pocket. "Son, we're going to get you the absolute best. The latest technology. We hear it's astonishing what these prosthetic limbs will let you do."

"Yeah?"

"I was talking with Pastor Greg. He knows a guy who has a prosthetic leg—one that fits just above the knee like yours will. Runs in *marathons*, Charlie." Charles moved closer so that he was right next to Charlie, inclining his head toward him. "As a matter of fact, this guy ran in the Chicago marathon last October. Plans to run in it again this fall." He paused for effect—gauging Charlie's reaction—and noted that Charlie hung on his every word. "Remember I was talking about us starting to jog together? How 'bout if we start training for the marathon? We'll do it together. Deal?"

Intuitively wary of Charles's overwrought enthusiasm, Fran had been observing the give-and-take between the two. She no longer existed; father and son were so absorbed in each other it was as though they were the only two people in the world. Alert, defensive, and scrutinizing Charlie's every reaction, Fran searched for any sign he was feeling overwhelmed. Her reflexes—physical and emotional—were timed to coordinate with the smallest hint of fear on Charlie's part. When she caught a subtle shift, a slight widening of Charlie's eyes and a quick intake of breath, Fran found she had to tightly clasp her hands together to keep from pushing Charles back.

At the same time, Fran watched how Charles pulled Charlie into his fierce vortex, eyes glowing, intense, and focused on his target.

"You can do it all, son. I know you can." Charles had positioned both his hands on Charlie's shoulders, looking him squarely in the eyes. "You're going to work hard, aren't you?"

Tears slipped from Charlie's eyes as fear and alarm blanketed his features. He appeared to face an inner battle, shifting his eyes downward and away from his dad's unrelenting stare, finally resting his gaze on his elevated leg.

Charles gripped Charlie's arm, momentarily forgetting the IV only inches away. And then his face slowly morphed into a mirrored image of his son's; panic moved across and possessed Charles's own glistening eyes, and his mouth fell slack. He mechanically followed Charlie's line of vision and stared at all that remained of his son's leg.

Though only seconds had passed in the poignant exchange between father and son, it played out in slow motion to Fran. Her response felt equally delayed and lethargic, like she was underwater or her limbs tied down with weights. Finally, she reached out toward Charles's hand, gripping his wrist as tightly as Charles held onto Charlie.

"Charles," she whispered urgently. "Let go."

He gave Fran a vacant look. Eyebrows raised, questioning. Then, suddenly aware, he glanced down at his fist as though he'd just recognized it as his own. Mumbled, "Oh, sorry, son. I forgot about your ... the IV." He brusquely swiped at his eyes and backed stiffly away from the bed. Putting both hands in his pockets, he shot Fran a venomous glare before walking toward the window, where he stood, staring.

Fran tenderly cradled Charlie's cheek in her palm. "It's all right, love," she soothed. And then she turned to confront her husband, fully expecting to meet his disapproval. She set her jaw, felt her stomach muscles tighten.

There'd been numerous times Fran had intentionally avoided her husband's intimidating anger. For Charles's wrath, she'd discovered, was a life force in itself—a daunting mountain to climb that often defeated her in its fury before she could take one step. But whenever she judged Charlie's health—emotional or physical—was at stake, she called upon a hidden strength enabling her to stand up to him.

As she slowly turned her head toward Charles, she understood this fleeting moment would not be the final battle. From the piercing challenge Charles had fixed on her with his gaze—any hint of tears now gone, his pupils narrowed to two jet black dots—Fran recognized the full consequences of her actions. The gauntlet she'd thrown.

"Enough, Francine." His voice nearly stripped of emotion, he stated, "We can't do this anymore. We need to find ... resolution. But now's not the time."

"No, it's not."

"We'll talk about this later. Soon."

Attempting to compose herself, Fran sat down in a chair. Folded her hands in her lap. She took a deep breath. "Charlie, love, can you forgive both of us? Obviously we're ... a bit frayed at the edges, I guess you could say." She gave him a wan smile.

Charles walked back over to Fran, placing his hands on her shoulders. Squared his own, and raised his chin. The two arranged in perfect positions for a posed portrait. "Son, the bottom line is, we're going to get the job done. Whatever it takes to get you walking again. Your mom and I promise you that, don't we?" He squeezed Fran's shoulders, a nonverbal signal for a temporary truce. "We're going to meet this challenge. All three of us together."

Fran reached up to lightly pat one of her husband's hands. "Yes. Absolutely." She kept patting him, mechanically. "Everything's going to be just fine. Before we know it, things will be back to normal and ... and ..."

Looking into her son's eyes, Fran saw he was wrestling to hold back tears. "No. Don't hold it in. Go ahead and cry, Charlie," she entreated, jumping up to enfold him in her arms. "You need to cry. Grieve for your lost leg. You have every right to!"

As Charlie began to cry and soon sob, Fran wept with him.

She'd been so focused on her son, Fran had temporarily forgotten Charles. When she looked up at him, her heart broke to see deep pain transforming the handsome features into a caricature of despair. In the next moment, however, she caught Charles's eye and was surprised to see a look of panic alongside the torment. And then, instantly, it was as though Charles had put on a mask—one that hid everything he was feeling, shutting her out as effectively as if a locked door had been slammed in her face.

"Charles? You need to grieve too. Please, Charles." The imploring look she gave him blatantly, vulnerably begged him to reveal tenderness. To be vulnerable in return.

But Charles merely flinched and turned his back; once again he stared out at the city below.

Fran closed her eyes, feeling more tears of disappointment form. Tears she blinked away as she consciously focused on Charlie and his needs. His sobs had diminished to soft whimpers. She tightened her embrace, kissing him on the beloved curls.

"It's okay, Mom," Charlie said softly. "I'm better now."

How can I feel so alone, so disconnected, Fran asked herself, *when I'm holding my son in my arms? And my husband is hardly more than an arm's length away?*

A short while later, a noise in the hallway was followed by an aide calling out cheerily, "Breakfast." She propped the door open and carried in the food. "Enjoy," she said, disappearing as quickly as she'd come.

Fran lifted the metal lids to reveal the eggs and French toast she'd ordered. "Hungry?"

Expecting an enthusiastic appetite from Charlie, Fran was surprised to see him push away from the food, closing his eyes and grimacing. "You're gonna think I'm crazy," he said through gritted teeth. "But it … it *hurts*."

"Oh, Charlie. I'll get a nurse in here right away."

"Stop fussing over him, Fran. What hurts, son?"

Dr. Owens, on her morning rounds, rapped lightly on the door. "Good morning. Looks like I've come at the perfect time to mooch some breakfast. That smells good."

Charlie managed a strained smile, but she immediately noted his distress. "What is it, Charlie? Having some phantom pain? Does the amputated leg hurt?"

Wide-eyed, he asked, "How did you … and how can it …?"

"How can an amputated limb hurt?" She put her chart down, placed her hands gently around Charlie's bandaged stump. "I need to check your incision, Charlie, but I'll be as gentle as possible, okay? If you aren't ready to see just yet—and that's understandable—then avert your eyes. Check the weather outside … or look at your mom. She'd like that. Okay, I'm removing the pressure garment now … the bandage … takes a while. Let's see here … oh, it looks great, Charlie." Dr. Owens was efficient and swift, and Charlie began to breathe easier. "It's healing well. The incision itself looks super. Swelling's down. Yes, this is looking so much better already."

Andrea had followed Dr. Owens into the room, ready to assist. She smiled at Fran, nodded at Charles. "Hey, buddy. I hear you're hungry this morning, huh? That's great."

Andrea set to work dressing the wound and refitting the pressure garment as Dr. Owens watched. Charlie cried out and Fran flinched. She took Charlie's hand and squeezed gently.

"Hangin' in there?" Dr. Owens asked.

Charlie nodded, but he was biting his lower lip.

"Almost done, brave young man. Know what? We need to get you up and around today." She picked up Charlie's chart again, began making notes. "So what do you think, Andrea? Think we can get him out on a walk later?"

"I'd love to take this handsome young man for a stroll." Winking at Charlie, she rushed out of the room, moving with her usual sense of urgency.

Dr. Owens put a hand on Charlie's shoulder. "That's done. Now, tell me about your discomfort, Charlie."

"It's like … like my leg is still there, and it's *burning*."

She looked up at Charles and Fran before beginning to explain, "Despite what you might be thinking, phantom pain is absolutely real. Every amputee patient I've ever had has experienced it." Dr. Owens turned toward Charlie again, emphasizing her point. "You're not imagining it, Charlie." She scribbled some notes on Charlie's chart. "We can help relieve the pain with meds, Charlie, which I'm going to order right now. Experiencing any other symptoms?"

Charlie shrugged. "It's prob'ly nothing."

"Everything's important, Charlie. Even things that may seem small to you, I want to know about."

"Well, I'm hot. All the time. Wish it could be cooler in here."

"As a matter of fact …" she paused as she wrote again, "I was expecting you to tell me that very thing because circulation is very much affected by an amputation." Dr. Owens put down the chart to give all three of them her full attention. "Here's the problem: The body controls its temperature by cycling blood through your limbs. It distributes heat when your heart pumps the warm blood outward throughout your limbs. Then the returning blood— which has lost some of its heat—cools the rest of your body, your upper torso. Since you've lost your leg, Charlie, you can't do that the same way you used to. So most amputees complain of feeling hot."

"So how do we fix that?" Charles asked.

"Once Charlie's home, keep that air conditioner running. I'll ask Andrea to speak with maintenance about a cooler temp in here, but the way everything's regulated by computers …" she trailed off, sighed. "We'll give it our best shot. Any questions, Charlie?"

Charlie chewed his lip a moment. Shrugged his shoulders.

"Another issue we need to discuss is rehabilitation." She glanced toward Fran and Charles, adding, "Mom and Dad, you need to take good mental notes. Be a part of Charlie's team—his rehabilitation team. I'm going to have the therapist visit Charlie later today to begin teaching him exercises to strengthen his limb. Start the process to get him ready for a prosthesis.

"I'll be honest with you, Charlie: You have a lot of work ahead. But from what I've learned about you already, I absolutely don't doubt your ability to do this." She waited a few seconds, allowing the compliment to sink in.

"How long before I get my leg?"

"Depends. On how quickly you heal. Hey, go ahead and eat—I would, if I were you!"

Charlie picked up a fork, began gingerly picking at his food.

"Did your mom and dad tell you about the chemotherapy?"

"Uh-huh. What will that be like?"

"Dr. Chang can give you more details, but you'll most likely come in for treatment for a couple weeks, then you'll have a week or two off. Depends on how your body responds."

Charlie put down his fork as though about to ask another question. But he avoided Dr. Owens's eyes, staring down at his food.

"Anything else, Charlie?" Dr. Owens waited patiently.

A few seconds ticked by before Charlie asked, in a barely audible voice, "Am I gonna die?"

The question struck at Fran's heart like a knife, and she felt the all-too-familiar tightening in her throat. Glancing toward Charles to gauge his reaction, she saw that he remained as closed to her—to them all—as though they were strangers.

Dr. Owens's voice was straightforward yet gentle at the same time, the tightrope walk of balancing hope with reality. "Charlie, we don't know how you're going to respond to chemotherapy. But we have every reason to believe you'll do very well. And if so, then you should have an abundance of time to run around on that high tech leg of yours."

Charlie's shoulders visibly relaxed. He nodded at Dr. Owens and then picked up his fork, sampling a small bite of eggs.

"Okay. See you next time, my friend. I want to hear you've taken a stroll around the joint, okay? Check out the nurses. See if any are good-looking."

Charlie grinned at her, shyly ducking his head.

"I heard that." Andrea scurried in just then, handing Charlie his pain pills. Hands on hips, she quipped, "Some nerve these doctors have. They know who really does all the work around here."

"We sure do." Dr. Owens laughed and waved as she walked out. "No way I'm denying that."

Charles also walked toward the door, jingling the coins and keys in his pocket again. He cleared his throat. "I'd best be going too, son. See you later this afternoon."

"Sure, Dad." Charlie was picking at his French toast, mostly pushing it around on his plate.

"French toast not so great?"

Charlie shrugged. "Not nearly as good as Mom's."

Charles laughed, and playfully punched Charlie's shoulder. "Hey, that's one politically correct answer." He turned to go and then added, "I hope your walk goes great. Give it your best effort, okay?"

"Yeah, sure."

"Great. Well … I'll see you two later." Though Fran sought to make eye contact with him, he avoided her, leaving the room without even a backward glance.

Later, nurses helped get Charlie out of bed and onto crutches. Every slight movement required a significant amount of time—plus physical and emotional energy. When removing his leg from the sling that kept the limb elevated, Charlie had to grit his teeth. Swipe at irritating, unwanted tears. Tackle whatever small movement he had to accomplish next to simply reach a standing position.

Throughout the interminable process, Fran took in Charlie's every grimace, any utterance of pain. She had to clamp her jaw shut to keep from crying out herself. From physically stopping what she considered torture. In contrast, the nurses offered nothing but encouragements: "You're doing great, Charlie. Hang in there. We're just about done with this part. You can do this."

Once he finally leaned on the crutches—the severed limb dangling oddly—Charlie barely had enough strength remaining to hobble out of his room. He took only a dozen steps down the hall before exhaustion overpowered his will.

Even so, the staff had nothing but lavish praise for Charlie, which produced a huge smile of pride, paleness suddenly replaced by the flush of exertion and the glow of accomplishment. Once the star on his soccer team. Highest scoring player. Captain. Held in esteem by all his teammates. Now reduced to these few faltering steps.

Though her heart knew a painful ambivalence, this time Fran joined the cheering section. "I've never been more proud of you, Charlie," she told him.

Charlie's hospital days were filled with time-consuming routines and exercises; every movement tended to be laborious and pain-filled—from slowly raising the angle of his bed to a sitting position, to using the breathing machine that helped clear his lungs. Even hosting visitors sapped his strength. One afternoon the entire soccer team visited, although—per Andrea's strict orders—only four boys were allowed in Charlie's room at a time. They were all noticeably uncomfortable at first, but Charlie quickly put them at ease. As expected, they were curious concerning how long Charlie would be in the hospital, the treatments he'd get, and especially, about the artificial leg. By the time they left, Charlie was thoroughly exhausted.

Fran noted his weariness and smoothed back the hair that hung over his forehead. "Seemed like that went well. You have a good time with everyone?"

"Yup. I really did." Charlie yawned, suddenly so sleepy that he could barely keep his eyes open. "It was cool they brought the championship trophy for me to see."

"Uh-huh. And now I think you need a nap. You've had quite the day and—" But Charlie was already drifting off to sleep; there was no need to convince him. Fran pulled a chair next to his bed and settled in, kicking off her shoes, tucking one foot up underneath her. She leaned back and rested her head against the back of the chair.

Contentedly, she simply watched him sleep until Dr. Chang slipped in, motioning for Fran to join her in the hallway. "Charlie getting some needed rest?"

Fran smiled. "Friends from his soccer team visited. They wore him out. And then he walked earlier today too—down to the end of the hallway and back this time."

"Wonderful. He's working so hard, making great progress." Dr. Chang's smile suddenly dissipated and she gave Fran a straightforward look. "That's why we think it's a good time to operate on Charlie's lung."

Fran felt the blood drain from her face. "So soon? I mean ... I knew you planned to do that eventually. But is Charlie ready?"

"We want to be as aggressive as possible with Charlie's treatment," she explained. "Since he's doing so well physically—Dr.

Owens tells me she's never had a patient heal so quickly—Dr. Owens and I think it's the right time to do the surgery."

Charles arrived then, overhearing Dr. Chang's comments concerning surgery. He noticeably raised his chin as he thrust out his hand to shake the doctor's. "That's my boy! Good afternoon, doctor. Absolutely, Charlie's ready."

Dr. Chang smiled, nodding her head. "Our other concern is his emotional healing, however. How do you think he's doing in that respect?"

Simultaneously—as though synchronized, yet slightly off-beat—Charles and Fran replied:

"He's great."

"He's struggling."

Both had been looking at Dr. Chang, but turned to stare into each other's eyes. With reproach.

"Charles, you don't see him every day, all day, like I do. How could you possibly make that determination? That snap judgment?"

"And how could you say he's doing less than great?" Charles, immediately exasperated, pointed toward the nurses' station. "They're all saying Charlie's doing fantastic. The nurses, the people who bring his meals, other patients even. You told me about his walk today, and how everyone he saw was amazed. Down to the end of the hall and back. Everyone notices how well he's doing but you, Fran."

"I think we're both too focused on Charlie's physical healing, Charles. I don't know that either of us really knows how to judge his emotional response to the amputation. The cancer. I just don't know—"

Dr. Chang broke into their exchange. "I haven't noted any clinical signs of depression," she interjected. "But that doesn't mean he won't get depressed later. I'm looking for more specifics. Say, uncontrolled weeping. Or the opposite—withdrawal of any display of feelings. As though Charlie's shut down emotionally." She raised her eyebrows, looking from Charles to Fran, expectantly.

Charles was vehemently shaking his head *no*. Fran replied, "No, he's not … not doing either of those."

"Any major changes in his personality—from before the surgery? I'm not ruling out any changes. Charlie's been asked to deal with a monumental change of direction in his life. That's a significant adjustment for anyone, let alone a child. So it's more a matter of how *well* he's dealing with that."

"He's still Charlie, now isn't he, Francine? Still the same Charlie."

Fran had to agree. "He's such a trooper. Sometimes I think he's doing better with this than we are."

"If that's the case, then I think we should proceed with the surgery. We try to balance pushing Charlie's body too far physically with the need for the urgency of treatment. We feel Charlie has the best chance if we surgically remove the metastases from his lung. Followed by aggressive chemo."

"What does that mean? Aggressive?" Fran crossed her arms across her chest.

"We want to use multiple drugs. We'll try several, in different combinations. It's trial and error until we get the right combination."

"How often?"

"Again, that's dependent upon how Charlie responds. But probably two or three weeks of treatment followed by a week off."

Feeling numb, Fran could only nod, but Charles doggedly pursued the doctor's reasoning. He had obviously been doing his own research, and though clearly somewhat annoyed, Dr. Chang answered his questions calmly and with grace.

"Let's focus on what's most important," Dr. Chang insisted, pulling the conversation back where she wanted it. "Charlie's healing and treatment and getting a prosthesis … all of that will be affected by a positive attitude," she continued. "That's what is key here, what makes a tremendous difference. But he still has a long way to go." She momentarily fumbled for an explanation. "It's like he has to climb Mt. Everest. And yes, we're all here to help him—you two especially bear that responsibility. But in many respects? He has to climb it alone."

"Ultimately, it's just him and God, isn't it?" Fran said. "Charlie needs to trust God, to rest in his strength even more than his own." Fran's voice was small, seeing the reality of Charlie's difficult journey from a new perspective.

Charles's reaction, however, was the polar opposite: His face suddenly flushed bright red, and he balled his fingers into tight fists. With emotions tightly held in check and voice controlled, he still seethed, "No, it's absolutely *not* just him and God. Charlie's got all of us to support him. Me, you, the doctors, his teammates, other friends. Pastor Greg and his teachers. We'll all prod him on however we need to. Because he's certainly not going to merely sit back and rest—in God. In any way."

Embarrassed, eager to diffuse Charles and the awkward situation, Fran smiled nervously. Placed a slightly trembling hand on Charles's arm. "Yes, I … I obviously misspoke." She turned to direct attention away from Charles toward Dr. Chang. "When do you want to do surgery?"

"Tomorrow morning."

Not a sound from Charles, but Fran gasped, "That soon?"

"There's no infection in the leg. The sooner we get this done, the quicker his body can completely heal. And the sooner we can begin the chemo." Dr. Chang eyed the two of them for a moment, obviously debating. Then began, weighing her words as she did so, "Has Dr. Owens spoken to you about our observations of children who have cancer?"

Charles and Fran exchanged a tentative glance. "No."

Dr. Chang pursed her lips, tucked her hair behind an ear. "They often exhibit this unnerving … sensitivity. It appears that, because they're forced into experiences far beyond their years, they develop an uncanny appreciation for what's truly important in life. And the children who are Christians—believers—demonstrate an amazing sensitivity to God that's …" She stopped abruptly, taking in Fran's openmouthed response. "What is it, Mrs. Thomason?"

"This is uncanny. Charlie and I just talked about that very thing."

Charles raised an eyebrow in irritation. "When? You didn't tell me this."

"It was just after surgery; I simply forgot to tell you, Charles. I discounted it as … I don't know … maybe an odd effect from the anesthesia. He'd had a dream about stars and was babbling on about being able to see them all so clearly. And I told him something my mother had said years ago—that people who see stars clearly can see God's will more clearly too."

Dr. Chang smiled. "That is amazing. But here's my reason for bringing this up: Charlie's a bright child, obviously. I have the impression he was pretty intuitive even before he got cancer. But he's going to be even more so now ... have this 'sixth sense' ... whatever you want to call it. Bottom line is that he's going to pick up on things." She paused, looking from Fran to Charles. "Lots of things. And *anything* that might interfere with our patient's recovery, Dr. Owens and I are concerned about."

Charles stared back at her, returning her steady gaze. Finally, breaking the tension, he stated matter-of-factly, "Fran and I will take that into consideration, Dr. Chang."

They started toward the room, but Charles reached out to stop Fran. "Let's agree on something before we go in. Charlie's to only hear positives—that the surgery will get rid of all the cancer."

Dr. Chang broke in. "I can't promise that, Mr. Thomason."

"Are the odds good you'll get it all?"

"Tests show we have an excellent chance, but—"

"Then you can tell Charlie exactly that, can't you?"

She smiled, solicitously. "That's what I had planned to tell him."

Fran reddened; she closed her eyes and sighed. But Charles, either oblivious to or ignoring Dr. Chang's gracious nuance, had already charged into Charlie's room.

After Dr. Chang told Charlie about the surgery, she waited patiently, granting him time to absorb the news. Then she gently asked, "Are you worried about the pain, Charlie? Because we can help you with that."

"Yeah. Some." He swallowed, as though deliberately ingesting his fears. Charlie looked from Fran to Charles, his parents flanking the sides of his bed. "But I can do this, I know I can. Right, Dad?"

Charles gave his son a thumbs-up sign, his face glowing with approval. "Of course you can, son. Of course you can."

The hospital room sizzled with the exchange between the two, the hidden expectations. Stripped to its core, the connection between father and son was palpable in its vulnerability and cry for the most basic of needs. *Survival. Acceptance. Love.*

Then Charles's voice knifed into the void and Fran visibly started. "So, tell them again, Charlie. Tell Dr. Chang the surgery tomorrow is a go." His dark eyes bored into his son's hazel ones.

Charlie obeyed. "Let's do it. I want to get it over with, I really do. It's that much faster I'll get the chemo started and done. And that much sooner I'll get my leg."

"That's my boy."

According to Dr. Chang, the surgery the next morning went extremely well. She reassured Charles and Fran the doctors were hopeful they'd gotten all the cancer and that Charlie's prognosis looked excellent.

Fran thanked God for his goodness.

Charles praised Charlie for his courage to go ahead with the surgery, and then charged him to work even harder to recover.

Point.

Counterpoint.

With Charlie wedged squarely in the middle.

The next few weeks presented Charlie with one seemingly insur-mountable challenge after another. He sailed through the lung surgery only to learn that infection had settled into his stump. It was a devastating blow. After the infection healed, he began chemotherapy—which sent him reeling from its considerable side effects. It appeared to be two steps forward, three back, until Charlie hit the fifth week after his initial diagnosis and surgery. His youth and overall excellent health kicked in and he began winning small battles. Charlie was released from the hospital, and from then on, progress was amazingly steady.

Though rehabilitation was a grueling process, Charlie attacked it like he would have charged for a goal on the soccer field. His rehabilitation team insisted he was their best patient ever—way beyond his years in maturity, determination, courage, focus. So that Charlie would gain the greatest possible mobility with his prosthesis, they put him through a punishing workout of various exercises—stretching, water and resistance therapy, weight train-ing. Any increase in how far Charlie could stretch his severed limb brought a grin of victory. Each quarter pound more he could lift produced an exuberant fist-jab. Efforts by Dr. Owens to properly shape his limb as it shrunk to its more permanent size—to ensure the prosthesis would fit well—evoked stoic decisions on Charlie's part to simply endure. That was all anyone could ask of him during that particularly painful part of his therapy.

Every advance was not without price. Each was bought with intense pain. And then mined by Charlie as a resource for more progress.

Chemo, however, was a different challenge. Try as he might, Charlie could not face it with a positive attitude; it succeeded in defeating him every time. Though he took drugs to alleviate the nausea, vomiting routinely followed his treatments. As a result, he lost his appetite. Then he lost weight. Soon afterward, he lost his hair—all of it. His face looked flat without eyelashes or eyebrows to give it dimension and definition.

In Charlie's estimation, he looked like a freak. So he avoided mirrors at all costs, ducking beneath the one in their home's entranceway. Keeping his eyes averted when standing over a sink in a bathroom. On the rare occasions he did catch a glimpse of himself, he would frown and smirk, vowing never to cut his hair once he was done with chemo. And though the members of his soccer team wanted to shave their heads in support, Charlie vigorously opposed the idea. They were actually disappointed when he'd argued that he didn't want to look at any more bald heads. "Mine's enough to deal with," he insisted. "I'll think I'm looking in a mirror everywhere I go if I have to see you guys hairless too. Thanks—but no thanks, guys."

Another side effect was susceptibility to infection. Though Fran was like a drill sergeant in protecting Charlie from anyone with infectious potential, he still caught colds and viruses. Which put him into a vicious cycle, for once he became ill, his treatment would be delayed. The longer he went without the treatment, the longer his chemotherapy would need to last, making him susceptible to infection for that much longer.

Charlie also discovered his rehabilitation exercises and determination to get around independently meant constant accidents. Bumps into table edges, intense pressure on his limb while using the weights, even falls were inevitable, according to Charlie and his dad. According to Fran, these mishaps were to be avoided at all costs. Due to Charlie's shortage of blood platelets from chemo, he bruised easily. And bled profusely even from minor cuts. The combination of rehabilitation and chemo was Murphy's Law waiting to happen.

And every struggle of Charlie's was profoundly telling on Fran.

Fran and Charles had made a bargain to put aside their differences for Charlie's sake, and for the most part, they had kept it. Putting him in the middle—causing Charlie even more hurt—was enough of a deterrent that they swallowed back words. Kept raging emotions in check. And generally avoided direct confrontation. It was taking a mounting toll on both parents, the damage internal. Neither was consciously aware of the explosive force that lay hidden, waiting to erupt. Ultimately threatening to destroy the fragile ties that bound the three together.

One particular bout of postchemo nausea ravaged Charlie's body even more than usual. Though his stomach contained nothing more to expel, the convulsive heaves continued to engulf his entire body, hour after hour, until Fran could stand it no longer. She simply held him to her, and cried. When Charles stayed away, completely avoiding Charlie's bedroom and bath, she was appalled by his lack of empathy.

Once Charlie was so exhausted that he finally fell asleep and she could leave him for a while, Fran stormed into Charles's office, where she found him filling out reports. Calmly, methodically working as though he hadn't a care in the world.

She attacked him with words. "How can you possibly be so uncaring? Don't you feel an ounce of compassion for your son when he's suffering like that?" she threw at him. "I swear you have about as much ability to feel as a sociopath."

Charles pointedly put down his pen, faced his irate wife. Trying to keep from reacting, striking out with anger, he calmly responded, "Francine, evidence of love is not merely through tears."

She crossed her arms, a subconscious barrier between them. "But just once … just once I wish you could let Charlie see that you feel … *something*, for God's sake."

"You have no idea what—" and then, knowing that he was failing at his resolve to remain calm and detached, he stopped. "Know why I came in here? To pray for Charlie. You were holding him; praying felt like the only thing I *could* do. And maybe I … let's just say there are things you don't know, Fran."

"Like what? What is it that I don't know, Charles? Enlighten me, will you?"

Charles picked up his pen, returned his attention to his work. She could see the familiar muscle tensing in the firm line of his jaw. "I really don't think details are necessary." He shrugged his shoulders. "You do what's necessary, that's all."

"Like your father did?"

He jerked his head up to spit back, "Don't *ever* throw his actions back at me again. I am *not* like him. When you lose both your parents, you become what you have to. To survive."

Stung, remorseful, Fran instantly softened. "I guess I really don't … you've never told me much about your dad's death, Charles. I know your mom died in childbirth when she had you, but your dad?" Probing gently, she said, "I don't know anything, really. But I'd really like to hear more. Please, Charles?"

He lifted his pen into the air, casually waving off the suggestion. "Water over the dam. No sense revisiting any of it. He got cancer and died. End of story."

"What kind of cancer? How old were you then? And can you tell me how that made you feel?"

Slowly, Charles lifted his gaze to meet her eyes, frowning.

"Okay, so you don't want to talk about that. But what about your aunt and uncle? The ones who raised you?"

"They were wonderful—you know that. You've met them. Fran, this is going nowhere …"

She sat down, taking a deep breath and willing herself to not react defensively. "Charles, so many times in the past I've attempted to get you to talk about this. There was no compelling reason before—besides the fact that I just wanted to get to know *you* better. What's affected you … made you who you are today. It feels like … like we have this huge barrier between us, and I want so much to *know*. And now—now there is a compelling reason: Charlie. For his good—and because you love him—won't you tell me more about your dad? Please, Charles? For Charlie's sake?"

Charles put down his pen and pushed away from the handsome cherry desk, leaning back in his leather chair. He narrowed his eyes as he gazed out the large picture window that overlooked their front yard. "Dad got cancer of the kidney. Pretty devastating today even—but back then? It was a death sentence, effective almost immediately. He died after only three months."

Understanding flooded Fran's mind. "Oh, Charles. I'm so sorry."

Charles chuckled. "A tad late."

"Charles, I—"

"Not fair. I'm sorry." He ran a hand through his hair. "See why I don't like to talk about it? Brings out the best in me, huh?"

"How did you …?"

"Feel? I was just a kid, Fran; heck if I know."

"But Charles … children have feelings too. I mean, just watch Charlie. Listen to him." Fran stood and walked to where she could be in Charles's line of vision, look him in the eyes. "He's oozing fear and insecurity and frustration and sometimes anger and—"

"And what difference does it make?" he snapped. Charles leaned in, coming within inches of Fran's face. "Ultimately, Charlie still has to suck it up, Fran. To get well, to fight anything, you gotta just do what needs to be done. Life is hard. Life is hard and it's tough and it certainly isn't fair. So you deal with it." He turned, scooting his chair back beneath the desk. Picked up his pen and immediately went back to work.

Fran shook her head at him. Sighed disappointedly. Knowing she'd been dismissed and the subject was closed, she walked out of his office, closing the door firmly behind her.

By the last week in April, Charlie was ready for his big test, the biggest in his life, in Charlie's estimation. He was to visit the prosthesis facility for the first time. In his mind, he'd earned this day. The dedicated exercising, correctly using his pressure bandage (though in the warmer, humid days of spring he'd ached to rip it off and leave it off), constant care of his suture line—keeping it clean, applying ointments and moisturizers—and elevating his stump at the slightest sign of swelling had all combined to a successful outcome. Finally, Dr. Owens had pronounced him ready for this next step. Charlie couldn't wait to visit the company that produced the "technological marvels"—as Dr. Owens put it—that would get him upright again. At the same time, he was cautiously skeptical, attempting to restrain expectations to protect his hopes. Protect himself.

Located in a suburb of Chicago—not far from home—the offices and plant that made the prostheses proved far beyond what Charlie could have imagined. When the clinicians walked Charles, Fran, and Charlie through the facility, the technology appeared to be right out of the future.

One technician handed Charlie an ankle-foot prosthesis that was partly made of silicone. "Go ahead, *feel* it," he encouraged. "It's designed to be as lifelike as possible. Comfortable. And its natural give—due to the silicone—keeps you from tripping. I get more speed with less effort."

"Excuse me," Charles interjected. "*You* do? How could you actually try out this foot?"

The man grinned. Stood up, and walked to the opposite side of the room and back. Still smiling broadly, he asked, "Care to see it?" He lifted his pant leg to show them the ankle of the same prosthetic foot, attached to his lower shin. "Want me to take off my shoe and sock for further proof?"

Charlie's eyes were wide with wonder. Charles appeared taken aback, and Fran, also amazed, laughed out loud. "No, that won't be necessary. We'll take your word for it!"

They later discovered the company employed several amputee victims to learn firsthand how to continually improve their products.

Naturally, it was the prosthetic legs that most attracted Charlie's interest. "You actually put computers in these knees?" Charlie marveled, staring at the inner workings of a leg designed to attach at the hip. Another technician, a woman, smiled at Charlie's fascination. She'd witnessed the enthralled reaction many times, but introducing an amputee—especially a child—to the technology was always fulfilling.

"And you program them? How?"

"To mimic the amputee's gait—and for all different movements and speeds, such as walking, jogging, running. Even biking," she explained. "You'll get to do all that, but here's a brief description of what's in store for you. Technicians will analyze your residual limb strength first. Been doing your exercises?"

Charlie was proud to vigorously nod yes.

"Great. Next they'll study your particular gait. How you walk. Whether you tend to lean forward, put the weight on the balls of your feet, maybe have a slight hitch in your stride. All kinds of things like that. And finally, they look at your posture—if you stand perfectly upright. Maybe slouch a little. Then they duplicate those measurements to mimic your particular gait for running. Biking adds yet another dimension of evaluations."

Giving her a skeptical look, Charlie asked, "How can they do that when I'm on crutches?"

She reached out to pat him on the shoulder. "Leave that to them. They'll figure it out, I assure you." She grinned, raising an eyebrow. "Trust me?"

Charlie pointed at the prosthesis. "If you'll let me have one of those, absolutely. Just tell me what to do."

When they began the custom fitting, the step prosthetists, as those specialists were called, literally walked Charlie through the detailed process. They took measurements and evaluated Charlie from every possible angle. Next, after fitting him with a temporary prosthetic leg, the specialists filmed his gait from all directions. Walking without crutches—even though he was tightly clutching bars on either side of him—brought such a huge smile to Charlie's face that Charles laughed out loud and Fran cried with joy.

As the prosthetists fed all the gathered information about Charlie's limb strength, gait, measurements, and posture into a special software program, the family watched in amazement as they saw a figure—mimicking Charlie's gait exactly—walk across the computer screen.

The part of the prosthesis that would actually fit to Charlie was formed in generally the same way a cast was—except using clear materials. That way, the technicians could observe how it fit to Charlie's skin and if the cast needed any adjustments. Charlie's age and the need for the limb to grow with him were also taken into consideration.

After all the preparations were finished and they left the facility, Charlie allowed his imagination free rein, indulging in constant daydreams about how wonderful this new leg would be. So when the much-anticipated call came informing Charlie his leg was ready, he was nearly beside himself with excitement. Charles took the morning off, almost as eager as his son.

Fran, however, felt a nagging anxiety. She worried Charlie might expect too much, too soon. Fully cognizant that she'd likely provoke an argument with Charles, she still elected to caution Charlie as they drove to the facility.

"Charlie, love, remember this is only the first fitting. It might be too painful for you to wear for very long. Or it might need more work—to make it fit right. Could be we'll need to come back at a later date."

Charles kept his view straight ahead, but Fran observed the set of his mouth and telltale lines fanning out from the corner of his eye. "It's also equally probable it will fit him like a glove. And Charlie will take to it right away."

"I can't wait to lose these crutches," Charlie gushed. "I'm so sick of chapped and sore armpits."

"But you're still going to need them for some time yet, probably. And—"

"Could you just let him be excited about this, Fran? Can't we assume that things will go well? Could you do that just this *once,* for cryin' out loud?" Charles snapped.

"I'm only trying to prepare him in case … in case it's God's will that we need to be patient. For a while yet, maybe."

"And what if it's God's will that the leg fits perfectly? And it works like … like a real leg? Then all that worry was wasted energy, wasn't it?"

Fran thought to herself, *God's will doesn't seem to bring many good things lately. I pray so hard. But bad things still happen.*

"Fran?"

"Sure." She stared out her passenger window, hugging the armrest. "We'll face whatever we need to. When the time comes."

"Could be we'll need to *celebrate*—by ordering a burger and milkshake at the drive-in. Right, Charlie?"

Charlie could see his dad's eyes in the rearview mirror, drawing him in. "Yeah, that sounds great, Dad."

"Whatever happens, you'll do your ole dad proud, won't you, son? No pain, no gain, right? Hey. This afternoon we'll get out the soccer ball, eh, Charlie? Try dribbling and passing it a little."

When Fran shot Charles an astonished, pleading look, Charles interjected, "I was just kidding." He lifted his hands from the steering wheel, feigning innocence, staring into the rearview mirror to get Charlie's attention. "You knew I was teasing, didn't you, Charlie? Just your dad's way of letting you know I'm on your team. *Always* on your team, right son?"

"Uh-huh."

"And hey, this part I wasn't teasing about. I know you'll make me proud, Charlie. Because you're going to do your best, aren't you?"

"Yeah. Sure, Dad."

But the lilt of excitement in Charlie's voice had diminished. Replaced with an edge that pressed against Fran's heart and caused her to search her son for signs of stress. She took in the line of worry creasing between his brows. The slumped shoulders—a posture Charlie had never exhibited before his surgery. The tension revealed in his clenched fists. She bit her lip to keep from lashing out at Charles right then, but resolved: *This has got to stop. For Charlie's sake, Charles and I will have this out.* She leaned back into her seat.

And begged God to help Charlie today, no matter what challenges he faced. Whether it be physical pain … or his father's unrelenting pressure.

Once they'd stepped into the office, the lead prosthetist welcomed them, reaching out to shake Charlie's hand first. "I wasn't here the last time you came in. Sorry to have missed you," he said with a strong British accent. "Name's George Beckham." To Charlie's immediate spark of interest, he responded, "No, sorry to say that I'm no relation to that Beckham. The famous David. You a fan of his, Charlie?"

"Oh, yeah. He's the best."

"Maybe someday Beckham himself will come watch the famous Charlie Thomason play—on the world's first bionic leg."

Fran cringed inwardly; out of the corner of her eye she noted Charles's smug look.

"Cool."

From the table behind him, George produced the prosthetic leg, complete with special ankle and computerized knee. Presented it to Charlie as though he were a doctor placing a newborn into its mother's arms for the first time. "Here it is, Charlie. State-of-the-art. Made especially for you.

"Now, understand our first priority is getting the inner workings to fit and work perfectly. That's just a temporary covering on the outside. The cosmesis component will come later. Did they teach you that word from your last visit here—cosmesis?"

Charlie nodded. "It's like the skin, right?"

"Exactly. We'll do our best to make it look like your other leg. But that comes later. For now, let's see how this gizmo's gonna work. You up to that?"

Before Charlie could answer, Charles interjected, "Of course he is. Charlie's never been one to back off a challenge."

It was all Fran could do to bite back a reprimand, but she realized it wasn't necessary; Charlie's complete attention was on the marvel in his arms. Like others had done during their last visit, George explained how the leg would allow Charlie to walk nearly effortlessly and with stability, due to the computer sensors taking measurements and making adjustments fifty times per second.

"Wow. Fifty times a *second?*" Charlie asked, to George's enthusiastic nod.

"The knee's got a hydraulic piston. Which means you can do complicated movements like stepping off a curb. Go up and down stairs. Climb in and out of a car.

"See this battery? That provides your power. You'll have to charge it every single day, so when you get ready for bed, just pop the battery in its charger for the night." Demonstrating the charger and where the battery fit, he said, "Easy as that." George paused a moment, assessing Charlie's mental and emotional readiness. Deciding in the affirmative, he asked, "I'll have you practice doing that later. For now ... think you're ready to give this high-tech leg a go?"

Charlie's eyes flicked to his dad, communicating a desperate need for approval. A belief that he, Charlie, could do this.

But instead, Charles—compelled by a voice deep within his soul—kept his face blank, deciding at this critical moment to communicate *nothing* to Charlie. *Now's the right time, son. Time for you alone to pick up your cross,* Charles's own inner voice insisted. *I will not allow you to become dependent on your mother. Be a mama's boy. Or to depend on me, either. Fight, son—fight for whatever you need to survive.*

Charles's eyes bored into his son's. Probing. And demanding.

The gap between question and answer appeared inordinately long to Fran. Again she forced herself to hold back a caustic comment.

Charlie appeared to search within himself for motivation to take this leap of faith. For a moment, his eyes seemed unfocused. His shoulders rose noticeably as he took a deep breath. "I'm ready." Sitting up straighter in his chair, he repeated with more enthusiasm, "Yeah. I'm ready. *Let's do it.*"

George motioned for Charlie to accompany him and then raised a flat, upright palm toward Charles and Fran, signaling he didn't want them to follow. "Mom and Dad, I'm going to ask you to remain here for just a bit while Charlie and I work together in the rehabilitation room. I want to give Charlie a chance to try this leg on his own first. Once he's getting the hang of it—has gathered some confidence—I'll send my assistant Roberta to get you." George looked over his glasses from Fran to Charles. "We find that's best."

Though he caught the looks of disappointment from Charles and Fran, George exited with Charlie before either could utter an objection. And then they immediately turned to each other, irate.

"Well, thanks to you for that, Fran." Charles glared at her, his voice coated with disgust. "Obviously he saw how you smother Charlie. Which meant Charlie would likely fail if you were watching, coddling him."

Fran glowered right back. "I was thinking it was your fault, actually. How could George have failed to notice your ... either your overbearing pressure or utter lack of compassion for Charlie. That you didn't even—"

"Keep your voice down," he ordered, between clenched teeth.

"You couldn't even encourage him, Charles. You couldn't even …" Fran shook her head, too exasperated and flustered to find the words she sought. She purposefully strode toward the back of the room and then reversed her direction, turning abruptly on her heels. "I've got to get out of here. There's a bench just outside." She opened the door and walked out, her voice trailing behind her. "We'll just let the receptionist know …"

Charles followed behind, begrudgingly. Yet as angry as they both were, he agreed it was imperative that they go outside. Away from people. Out of earshot.

They both knew instinctively the time had come. They would have it out.

Momentarily performing for the receptionist, Fran smiled sweetly, explaining where they'd be. Without showing if she'd noticed the tension, the receptionist simply smiled and agreed to come get them when George summoned.

Fran proceeded immediately to the bench, leaning back and closing her eyes. Charles paced. Hands in his pockets, he fumed, ranting incoherently to himself.

She took a deep breath. Plunged in. "Charles, you've simply got to stop this. I can't take it anymore," she spit out. "Don't you get it?" Tears filled her eyes, and in that instant, she finally gave full vent to the rage nearly exploding from within. "I can't sit back and watch you do this to Charlie one moment longer. You're going to destroy our son!"

"Me? You actually think it's me that's destroying him?" As he pointed an accusing finger at her, he trembled in his fury. "You're the one, telling him to just trust God. Don't you understand that's the same as telling him to quit and give up?"

She jerked upright, defending herself, "No, it's not—it's not that at all." But she wasn't prepared for Charles's next move.

Charles stood towering over her, his body intimidating—intentionally positioning himself that way—as he never had before. Fran felt a shiver go through her as she looked up, taking in the full blast of his anger.

"That's exactly what that sick cliché means, Fran. Of all the idiotic, lame things to lay on Charlie. You're telling him to give up every time you say that. You might as well just tell him to go ahead and ... and *die*."

And then the tears formed. Slowly at first, as they collected in his eyes. But then spilling over, gushing out. Coursing down his cheeks. Fran's mouth dropped open. She'd rarely seen Charles shed a single tear, let alone witness this kind of weeping. He hadn't really cried once since this entire nightmare began. A great, heaving sob erupted from deep within, and in his sudden embarrassment, he turned his back to her, hunching his shoulders as he moved away. Moaning now, sounds of utter devastation. Fran's anger instantly dissipated, converting to compassion for her husband, and she instinctively rose to reach for him—only to be pushed away.

"Charles, what is it? Tell me, please."

Barely above a whisper, he choked out between sobs, "I'm so ... so scared. Scared we'll lose him. I can't—I just can't lose anyone else. It was too much ... as a child. I can't ..."

"Your mother and father."

Charles struggled to talk still. "He kept saying, *'Just trust God. Rest in God's will. Everything will be … fine.'* But he left me. And then she did too." The words ended in a whimper. From Charles, the intimidator.

"Your father said that, right? But who else—who left you, Charles?"

He buried his head in his hands. "Her name was Sarah, but I called her mom. She was the only mom I knew, really. And then she left me too."

"Who? Why? Charles, I'm so sorry. Are you saying your dad had remarried?"

Charles slumped down onto the bench, and he stared at the ground. Finally quieting some, he took a deep breath and continued, letting his words come out in a rush. "Yes, he did. I don't even know what her maiden name was, but she was … wonderful." He swallowed, and continued on. "They were so happy—we all were—just like a regular family. And then Dad got the cancer diagnosis. He promised me she would always be there. That I just needed to trust God and everything would be okay. But then Dad died … and she left." He was silent, bereft.

Fran reached out tentatively, softly touching his arm. "You must've felt … rejected? And so alone."

Tears continued to slip from Charles's eyes. She watched them fall onto the ground at his feet and reached out a palm to tenderly wipe his cheek.

"I *was* alone. Everyone was gone—my mom, who I never knew, of course. My dad. And then Sarah, too."

"Do you know where she went? What happened to her?"

Charles shook his head. "I went to live with my aunt and uncle. Never heard from Sarah again. And I vowed ..." he struggled to keep from losing control again, "... I vowed that I'd never allow anyone to tell me—or anyone I loved—to just trust God or anything like that because I would never willingly be a victim again."

She put her arm around him. Rested her cheek against his shoulder.

"It wasn't long after I went to live with Uncle Richard and Aunt Lynn that I heard this preacher—they pretty much always had Christian radio blaring, their not-so-subtle way of preaching at me—and he was preaching on the verse where Christ says to 'Deny yourself, pick up your cross, and follow me.'"

Charles turned to her, his eyes blazing. "It was like I heard that verse for the very first time." He held up a tightened fist as though he had just captured the concept once more. "That was the answer. You fight for ... for everything. Whenever life throws something at you, you don't just sit back. You do something about it. Rest in simplistic trust? By God, no. You pick up your cross—whatever it is—and you fight! You fight with every inch of your being. And I will fight for my son, Fran, I will."

Fran cautiously put her arms around her husband and pulled him to her, praying for acceptance, steeling herself for rejection. But she felt him subtly give way as he relaxed against her, no longer holding her at arm's length—pushing her away physically. More importantly, emotionally. They molded to each other's bodies as they had not done in months. And wept together.

Charles, suddenly embarrassed, muttered, "That verse? I think it's become like a mantra in my head, you know?"

Fran pulled back so that she could look into his eyes again. "I imagine it was like a recording in your subconscious that played over and over. You didn't even need to start it up, it was so ingrained."

"I'm trying to remember. We've studied that passage in Sunday school. Pastor preached on it too." Charles was reflective a moment. "I suppose it doesn't mean all I've wanted it to all these years."

Fran shrugged. "I've always assumed 'pick up your cross' was more of a reminder that I should be willing to go that far for him—to suffer as he did." She chose her words carefully, conscious of the vulnerable path between them. "And to be willing to suffer—maybe to the point of actually *dying* for him. If that's what he wants me to do. Kind of a 'if you want to become my follower then you'd better count the cost' kind of warning."

Charles pulled out a handkerchief and blew his nose. "I guess so." He cleared his throat, stalling for time. Struggling to control his emotions once again and find the right words. They were like fencers, dueling with parries, if not thrusts. Neither wanting to hurt the other, but defending themselves still, remembering too many wounds in the past. "It's a stark image, isn't it? The cost of being a Christian. Symbolically carrying the crossbeam to the place of crucifixion."

He turned toward Fran, his face reflecting a mixture of pain and peace that would force him to look further inward. "I guess I've never really wanted to accept that kind of pain in a believer's life. Not the concept of it. Certainly not the reality of it in my life—but more so, not in those I love." His voice broke, and he stopped a moment. "My coping method," he laughed cynically, shaking his head, "my way to cope—or deny, I suppose—was putting all my energies into my will to fight. And so I've fought, all right. Fought you. Memories. My dad and Sarah. My own son."

Fran reached up to put her palm against his cheek again. This type of duel between them was new and untried, hesitant and unsure. Yet as she listened to the silence between them, she found it safe. And so she whispered, "I can picture that vulnerable little boy." Her heart breaking at the scene in her mind's eye, the child an exact replica of Charlie, she continued, "You were all alone. And you did what was needed to survive a devastating situation, Charles—one that might've broken a weaker man who *hadn't* fought back. You thought you were doing the best thing for Charlie too—pushing him to do what would help him, all the while reliving your painful past through him. It's no wonder you were so desperate, Charles."

"I was afraid of being left alone again, Francine." He pulled her into his arms. "Oh, Lennie," he whispered against her hair. "I need you so much. I need you *both* so much. I'm afraid, Lennie. I'm so very afraid."

"I'm afraid too, Charles. But even in the leaving, God's there. Maybe it's like the cross is the bridge between death and resurrection. Doesn't God become the bridge between our fears and our ability to trust in him?" Fran stared off into the distance as though attempting to bring something unrecognized into focus. "I want to believe that being alone is different than being lonely. And being left isn't as frightening when I know I'm in the bridge of God's love."

"I do too. But I'm thinking that's merely my coping and denial tendencies again. Fact is: Sarah left."

"She must've been in horrible pain, Charles. And afraid. I wonder if the responsibility of you weighing on her was just more than she could handle."

"As a young boy, I was so angry at her. But now? Well, now I just feel … sad. Sad for her *and* me. We both missed out, didn't we?"

They had no conscious realization of time passing. Of how long it was before the receptionist came to beckon them back inside. The two apprehensive parents who stood to walk back into the building had ventured onto new paths: revelation of a past that had bound and chained them in covert ways. A present that offered glimpses of hope for the future.

The young man who looked up to greet his parents glowed, proudly standing on two legs again. Completely oblivious of the painful journey to the past Charles and Fran had just been on, Charlie stared only straight ahead. Focused on the length of the floor below the beams at his sides. And though his first steps were slow and awkward—he clung to the chest-high supports on either side of him—Charles and Fran were as proud as though he'd scored the winning goal in the World Cup.

Fran stopped before him, pressed both hands to her heart. Began weeping for joy through a smile not incongruent with her tears. She turned to look over at Charles, reveling in his reaction.

"That's my son," he choked out, emotion tightening his throat, tears filling his eyes, unashamedly. "Oh, Charlie. I'm so proud of you."

If not for the crutches, a stranger observing the family leaving the building that day wouldn't have guessed which one walked on a newly christened prosthetic leg. For they moved forward as one, leaning toward a center together, supporting one another.

After they'd pulled into their driveway, Charles uncharacteristically sat silently a moment, fidgeting with the keys, passing them from one hand to the other. Turning to look back at Charlie. Finally, he offered, "We can do this. Together—all three of us, I mean—with God's help. We will do this." Then, almost an afterthought, "You know I love you, son."

Later that evening, as Charles and Fran stood on the patio— Charlie was fast asleep, his leg reverently placed so he would see it first thing in the morning—they stood apart from one another. Gazing up at a cloudy sky, only a few stars peeking out from the haze.

"It seems like only yesterday, and yet so long ago at the same time, when Charlie first woke from surgery. Chattering away about stars."

Charles took a sip of his drink. "Tell me more about that. What all did he say?"

"Just that he could see stars so clearly. They weren't—you know, hazy at all. But incredibly clear to him." She sighed, hugging her arms to herself as she continued to look upward. "I can almost imagine it, you know?"

He scoffed. "Not tonight. Typical Chicago gloom. We'd have to get far away from this weather and all the city lights to see stars clearly."

Fran ventured, "Charles, what if we went away this weekend? A long weekend, to the beach? We could take the Thursday night red-eye, get to Tampa by Friday morning. Drive down … we'd have three whole days together." Her voice rose in excitement as she shared the strategy for their escape. "Wouldn't that be wonderful? For all of us?"

He twirled the stem of the glass between his fingers. "Where you thinking? Marco Island?"

She didn't reach out to him, though her arms ached to do so. Instead, she allowed her words to convey the longing. "Oh, Charles. I think it's just what we need. Charlie's in between chemo treatments right now, so it's perfect timing for him. Could you get away, last minute like this?"

"It's a slow time. Definitely a possibility." Charles put the glass down and gently took her hand, pulling her to him. He reached up to caress her hair. "Can you … can you forgive me?"

"Oh, Charles. There's nothing to forgive."

"And Charlie? Think he can forgive me?"

She traced the line of his jaw to his lips with a finger. "Why don't you ask him? I think he'll say the same thing I just did. There's nothing to forgive."

Charles kissed her gently, and turned her so she was in front of him, leaning against his chest, his arms around her. He pointed out a star newly emerged from behind a passing cloud. "There's a fairly bright one for you."

Fran smiled. "I see it. Must be one of Charlie's."

"We'd better get to bed. Busy day tomorrow. I'll call about a flight. How about if you try to get reservations at that hotel we liked so much, okay?"

"Umm. Absolutely."

Neither moved. Fran contentedly snuggled even closer.

"You'll need to take Bradley to the kennel. Cancel the paper and the mail." As they regretfully pulled apart and Charles locked the door behind them, he asked, "Would you mind packing for me too?"

"Oh, I suppose I could do that." Fran grinned playfully up at him. "Besides some clothes, I just might tuck in a star or two."

Preparations and departure went amazingly smoothly, but their plane was late arriving in Tampa; a front of steady rain had moved in, causing delays. Refusing to allow the gloomy weather to dampen their spirits, however, they were all bubbling over with excitement as they climbed into the rental car they'd drive to the beach.

"A Mercedes, Charles? Really?" Fran asked skeptically, though she was grinning at him as he loaded their suitcases into the trunk.

"Absolutely. Only the best for our trip. Charlie, how about if you sit up front with me? You can be my navigator."

If possible, Charlie's smile widened even farther. "Sure thing, Dad."

Charles held the door for Fran as she climbed into the back. He put a hand to his mouth, whispering conspiratorially to Charlie, "You know your mom. She could get us lost in our subdivision."

"I heard that. But this seat is fine with me. Now I can be a backseat driver."

They laughed and teased each other as they drove south, relaxed and without a hint of stress or tension—a direct contrast to the unsettling weather. When Charles suddenly became quiet, however, Fran sensed the change. And immediately felt herself go on guard.

"Charlie. I've been wanting to say something to you," Charles began. "When … when I was a child you know that I lost both my mother and father."

Charlie watched his father intently. Became rigid in his intense concentration.

"And then … then I lost someone else that I dearly loved. And so I've been … I've been way too hard on you, son. My fears got transferred to you, and that wasn't fair." Charles didn't look at Charlie, but continued to stare out to the road ahead—partly because the weather was so poor. But mostly because of his insecurity and fear of how Charlie would respond.

He swallowed, and with effort, continued, "I am so sorry, Charlie. Will you forgive me for that, son?"

"Sure, Dad," Charlie replied, as he smiled shyly up at him. "But there's really nothing to forgive."

Fran closed her eyes and breathed a prayer of joy as tears slipped down her cheeks.

A huge rumble of thunder shook the car, and Fran jumped, startled. Looking out the window, she searched for a road sign; she'd been so focused on Charles and Charlie that she'd not even noticed—until just then—how bad the weather had become. The rain pounded on the windshield and lightning flashed almost continuously. "Where are we now, Charles?"

Immediately, as though on cue, lightning highlighted the vast beams of the Sunshine Skyway Bridge. The simultaneous thunder proved they were thrust into the very heart of the storm—the thunder and the car's sudden responding jolt sideways. Then, just as quickly, it jerked forward, almost as though a huge, unseen hand had taken control.

"What on earth?" Charles said.

Frustrated that she couldn't see much of anything out front, Fran turned around to look out the back window. She felt the sensation of launching into nothingness pull her out and away from the road below. Gazing upward, Fran stared off into the distance. Another attempt to bring that same unrecognized something into focus.

Until they plunged into the raging waters beneath them.

Book Three

FOLLOW ME

Mid-March 2009
McMaster's Bible College, Tennessee

The all-too-familiar feelings assaulted Michal again, bullying her mind back to the rolling hills of Ethiopia. She was six years old then—tall for her age and therefore gangly and awkward, freckled, with long blonde hair pulled back into a ponytail. It was the type of fine hair that would not be contained neatly; wispy locks escaped around her face and neck. Tendrils which tickled and exasperated.

The nauseating fear had attacked first. Creeping over her like an aggressive fog, causing her to break out in a cold sweat and her stomach to feel like it was being turned inside out. Panic was its accomplice, robbing Michal of any capacity for rational thought; she felt paralyzed.

Images flashed like a spastic slide show. The battered brown suitcase, her grip on the handle so intense that she watched her knuckles turn white. The hem of her dress, the tiny stitches of thread. The toes of her worn tennis shoes. Her dad's deep-set dark brown eyes, filled with weariness and disappointment. Her mom's light grey eyes, stern, reproachful. Attempting to control Michal with the sheer force of their intensity.

She could smell the dew of the morning mingled with the pungent exhaust from the idling old station wagon. Feel the heat of the sun on her head and shoulders, the scratchy upholstery against the tender skin of her thighs, the irritating wetness above her lip, evidence of a runny nose, her emotions barely held in check. She heard the irregular rattle of the car's aging engine, her own sniffs and hiccups.

Snatches of dialogue came in an onslaught against her ears. They erupted like gunfire, and she cringed.

"Please, Daddy. I could have school right here. Mommy can teach me."

"You have to go—it's what's best. Most importantly, it's what God wants."

"But maybe … maybe God's wrong this time." As soon as she let the words slip out, she knew she'd committed a grave mistake.

Her father leaned down on one knee, looking her right in the eyes. Narrowed his gaze. "Never say that again, Michal. You know God reveals his will to us. After we've prayed and sought him through Scripture. He's never wrong, never. God will take care of you, don't you believe that? Your mom and I are trusting God. Now it's your turn to trust him too, Michal."

"But what if I get sick? Who will put a cool cloth to my fore-head?" In her rising anxiety, her questions came faster, her words staccato and sharp: "What if my tummy doesn't want food again? Who will make a special broth and feed it to me?" The tears formed suddenly, pushing out of her eyes and running down her cheeks. "Who will—?"

Her mother's voice now. "Michal, enough. We've been through all this. I would come if you got really ill, but you're not going to. You're going to be fine. This is God's will, Michal, and you will stop this right now. Be brave like all the others before you—like your grandpa when he was your age. And your dad and his brothers and sisters. Are you going to be the first McHenry not to accept the importance of our work here in Ethiopia? And that this is the only way we can stay, doing what God's called us to do? Don't you care about the unbelievers here who need Jesus?"

And then she felt the good-bye, the closing scene. The obligatory hug that merely left her feeling vacant. Longing for more, for … something. Never the melding that Michal ached for from her parents, when the contours of two flow one into the other. Instead, this hug was instruction, correction in euphemistic form.

The recurrent dream changed at this point, switching venues, and she shivered violently. She was underwater; it was pitch black and she was gasping for air, grasping for what taunted and teased just beyond her reach. And then she woke, bolting upright in bed.

Michal's heart pounded and she panted as if she'd been running. Blinking her eyes and attempting to orient herself, she stared at the curtain, watching it flap softly against the sill. A motor idled from a car outside her room. She took a deep breath and reassured herself, *Calm down. It's okay. You're not in Ethiopia. You're in your dorm room, at school, in the States.*

"Michal, you okay? That's the second nightmare you've had this week." Beth, Michal's roommate, peered at her curiously from the other twin bed.

Michal flopped back onto her pillow. Stared up at the ceiling, faintly visible in the early morning light. "Bad memories. But yeah, I'm okay." She turned to view the alarm clock on her desk, then flipped over and groaned, complaining, "Except for the fact that I've got to get up. I don't know. I'm just not getting much out of chapel lately."

"Me neither. I really don't want to go this morning." Beth frowned, making a face like she'd sucked on a lemon. "It's a missionary today."

"Oh, yeah. Where's he from?"

"Don't remember. Don't want to."

"Wasn't it Chile? You're not interested?"

Beth's face registered near horror. "Nope."

Since Beth had grown up in Brazil, where her parents were still missionaries, Michal assumed she'd be curious.

"So use one of your cuts."

"Can't. I've used 'em all."

Michal's eyes opened wider at that. "For the whole semester? Already?"

Beth pulled the covers up over her head, so all Michal heard was a slightly muffled, "Yup."

Michal raised herself up on one elbow to have a better view of the lump that was Beth. Confused, she asked, "But you've been walking over to chapel with me almost every morning. Haven't you been going in?"

McMaster's Bible College required daily chapel attendance, except for a number of approved "cuts." A small, nondenominational evangelical school that awarded degrees in Bible for ministers, missionaries, and laypersons, McMaster's stressed living a Christian lifestyle—pretty much demanded it. In the administrators' minds, learning how to live a holy life began in daily chapel. Attendance was required; actual participation—as every student knew—was optional.

No response from Beth but a noticeable shaking back and forth under the faded maroon bedspread. It was an inexpensive quilt, the kind sewn by machine in big, looping stitches that easily snagged and snapped. Leaving threads hanging and the resulting smooth patches without additional quilting.

In contrast, Michal's bed was covered with a bright blue and yellow quilt, a genuine one. It was completely handmade, pieced together square by square, the tiny stitches perfectly spaced in a beautiful pattern called Starry Nights. Michal's quilt was the one cheerful accent in the otherwise unadorned room—a very atypical college dorm room in many ways.

Most of the other women in Peterson Dormitory—after advance notification of assigned roommates—had been proactive about contacting one another. They'd developed elaborate plans to decorate their rooms with matching bedspreads, study pillows, rugs, sheets, and towels. Some even purchased curtains to replace the drab and worn navy ones provided. Rooms with the plainest raw materials— beige-colored cement block walls, metal desks and beds, scuffed tan linoleum floors—were effectively disguised to effects almost worthy of ads in home-makeover magazines.

Michal and Beth's room was a notable exception.

Though they'd been assigned as roommates—both were missionary kids (MKs) who hadn't lived in the States for years (the administration thought it a perfect match to help with adjustment problems)—Michal and Beth never bothered to contact each other. So there was no prior coordination of decor. No assigning of who was to bring or buy what. Bed coverings, towels, rugs, and pillows were hodgepodge at best. Whatever was worn-out and could be spared from home at worst. The quilt, which Michal's Aunt Sarah had made—and which she treasured—was the one bright spot in the entire room.

Neither Michal nor Beth appeared to care that their room was teasingly yet affectionately known as the "Barrel Room." After school began, the dorm had an open house—an opportunity to browse through each others' rooms, admiring the coordinated decoration. For the special evening, Michal sketched a picture of a barrel on brown poster board. After tacking it to the door, she laughingly explained that the contents of their room had come from the bottoms of missionary barrels. Which were described as containing books of matches missing half the sticks. Socks with holes. Towels with frayed edges. Blouses without buttons. And patchwork quilts.

As Michal held the quilt up to her chin, she gave Beth a look of astonishment. "What have you been doing, Beth? Where do you go during chapel?"

"Oh, I just kinda … hang out."

A sudden worry struck Michal. "Hey, you're not getting sick again like you were back in September, are you? I thought you were never gonna get over that stomach flu, Beth."

"No. It's not that—not anything physical. I feel great, really."

Michal glanced over at the clock again, and at that exact moment, the alarm came on. At the sudden harsh, irritating sound, she reached over to smack the button with her palm.

"I hate that alarm. If I'm not waking up with my heart pounding because of a stupid nightmare, this dumb clock has the same effect."

Beth rolled toward the wall, grousing as she did so, "Then why don't you set it to music?"

Michal jerked the covers down, climbed out of bed. She ran her fingers lightly through her hair, trying to judge if it needed washing. Noticing Beth's inactivity, she urged, "Beth. You need to get up."

"Why? I'm already gonna get detention for too many cuts. What's one more?"

Michal padded over to her roommate's bed. "Beth, are you okay? I mean … really. Are you all right?" The pause worried Michal, and she reached out to lightly touch Beth's shoulder.

Still electing to remain beneath the bedspread, Beth finally responded, "I'm just sleepy. I was up late studying. Stupid English exam."

"Well, if you're sure then. I'd better get going." Michal began tugging up her sheet, straightening the pillow and quilt. "You just going to stay in bed a while?"

"Uh-huh."

When Michal entered the bathroom the six women in her suite shared, she discovered Ruth and Jenny were there, one at a sink and the other in the shower. Since Michal and Ruth were the only ones who were somewhat personable in the early morning hours, Jenny merely grunted when Michal entered. Michal simply said "Morning" back. But when Ruth began singing in the shower—prompting Jenny to frown and roll her eyes—Michal laughed.

Deciding her hair could go another day without washing, Michal showered quickly. She wet her shoulder-length hair and pulled it into a casual ponytail with a simple rubber band. Her blonde hair had darkened considerably and was now a light brown with blonde highlights. But it hadn't lost its wispy tendency, nor the natural curls; both qualities meant that tendrils still escaped the confines of the rubber band. Rarely, on special occasions, Michal would blow-dry her hair—but even then, she'd merely tuck it behind her ears. No fancy styling, no bows or barrettes, no fuss.

The other girls were amazed when Michal arrived at school with absolutely no makeup. No blush, mascara, lipstick, powder. Definitely no eyelash curler (she'd responded with amazement when shown the "contraption," as she called it), eyeliner, or eye shadow.

As Michal stood at the sink brushing her teeth, she took note of the spattering of freckles across her nose and cheeks, a remnant from her childhood Michal considered an ongoing aggravation. After rinsing her mouth, she impulsively stuck out her tongue at the offending spots. Otherwise, her skin was perfectly clear, emitting a peaches-and-cream glow. As a rare fair-skinned person in remote sections of Africa, she'd learned to apply moisturizer with sunscreen every day, and did that still. Smoothing the cream around her eyes, she took for granted the long, naturally curly lashes (she had no need of the contraption) framing her almond-shaped light grey eyes, the slightly turned-up nose, the full and well-shaped lips. Samantha, another of her suitemates, liberally used makeup, and quickly recognized what a skillful application could do for Michal's cheekbones and eyes. But

Michal had remained adamant she hadn't the time or desire to "mess with all that stuff."

Michal's one indulgence was a pair of pierced earrings, small gold hoops she'd received as a young child. Rarely removed, the earrings were such a part of her image she scarcely took notice of them anymore.

At five feet nine inches, she was no longer gangly, having grown into her long legs. A natural athlete, Michal moved with grace and coordination, but preferred to run only as a personal discipline, declining to participate in competitive track and other organized sports. Sometimes she'd join an impromptu pick-up game of soccer, basketball, or volleyball, her skills quickly making her a desired team member. Intramural team players begged her to play, but she'd refused, insisting she needed more time to "hit the books." When needing a stress reliever or a break from study, however, she'd run. Sometimes for several miles, as she had in Ethiopia.

Michal indiscriminately pulled clothes out of the closet—a plain white blouse and jeans. Years of coming to the States on furlough and discovering her clothes were woefully outdated had led to a firm resolve: She disregarded being in style almost entirely. Attempting to rotate her outfits (she had a total of about ten, as she switched blouses with differing skirts, slacks, and jeans), Michal didn't fret much over that either. In her opinion, hassling over clothes, hair, and makeup wasn't worth the time or effort.

She rummaged through a drawer, debated putting on socks, but quickly vetoed that idea and tossed them aside. Slipped on worn but comfortable sandals. Took one last glance at herself in the mirror and nodded, satisfied.

After shoving books and notebooks into her backpack, Michal wondered if she should say something to Beth. The sound of regular breathing proved Beth had drifted back to sleep. Afraid her roommate might be irritated if awakened again, Michal thought better of that idea. Feeling a mixture of guilt and frustration, she closed the door softly behind her.

As Michal hurried to chapel, her thoughts shifted toward Florida, to her Aunt Sarah. Spring break was only a few days away, and she'd already purchased a bus ticket to Fort Myers—how good it had felt to finally hold that small piece of paper in her hand—the confirmation she really was going. Now it was safely stored away, tucked into the book of Psalms in the Bible she kept in her room.

"Hey. You're walkin' like a woman on a mission. Some sort of special entertainment going on that I don't know about? That the reason for the huge smile on your face?"

Michal had been so focused on her trip to Florida that she'd taken no notice of others around her—not even Allistair Fuller, a McMaster's student who wasn't just anybody. This was *the* Allistair Fuller, number-one guy of interest to all her suitemates (and possibly every other woman in Peterson Dorm) for numerous reasons: He was a senior, star on the soccer team, baritone in a men's quartet, and student body president. Michal's suitemates had also listed off everything that made him "easy on the eyes," as they described it: a noticeably square jaw (with the prerequisite dimpled chin); an unremarkable nose (no extra large or hooked ones accepted); wavy, dark brown hair (they were convinced he'd never go bald); deep-set, light blue eyes rimmed with dark, thick lashes (you could "get lost in them," they'd insisted); and a wide, inviting smile (a definite plus).

Whether Allistair was aware he was exceptionally handsome was open for debate. Some insisted he was oblivious to it, and was actually very likeable. Others read conceit into everything he did: how he played the game of soccer, the way he spoke up and voiced opinions in class, how he conducted himself simply walking around the campus. When he was friendly to underclassmen, some would say, "Look, he's not beneath talking to anyone." While at the exact same time, detractors would cynically comment, "Look how condescending he is." No matter what Allistair did, though, it was almost always noticed.

Beth and Michal hadn't overlooked Allistair either. He was, admittedly, hard to miss. But in their equally offbeat, characteristically cavalier way of dismissing attitudes and desires the other girls wallowed in, the two MKs banished swooning over guys, pretty much completely. And Allistair in particular.

From Michal's observation, if you gave most college women a mere five minutes of free time, their thoughts and discussions inherently drifted toward men. She and Beth were amazed by this constant infatuation; they were puzzled by the mesmerized spell their friends seemed to fall under. And frankly, they were irritated by the distraction the entire gender caused.

At the same time, and not so surprisingly, Michal hadn't gone unnoticed by the men on campus—sans makeup and fussed-over hair. Even sweaty and covered with mud on the soccer field. Her infectious laugh, sunny disposition, and evident good looks (despite the lack of any attempts toward enhancement) had attracted a good deal of unwanted interest.

Up to this point, Michal had remained detached because she was singularly focused on completing her education. And ultimately, upon reaching her final goal: returning to the mission field in Ethiopia. *What else are these years about?* she'd asked herself, grilling her suitemates with that very question. They'd given her blank looks in response, proceeding to argue that making friends, competing in sports, and learning about life and love were equally important pursuits. Michal's caveat was that none of those sounded especially spiritual. Anything that distracted from her goal, in Michal's opinion, was a waste of time. More importantly, the time God held her accountable for.

Michal also failed to notice that before Allistair approached her, another young man—a nervous one with a dark green ski cap pulled so low it covered his ears and nearly his eyes—was about to call out to her and had just raised a spindly arm to attract her attention. When Stephen Jones noticed Allistair in such close proximity to Michal, however, he jerked the arm down to his side. Hunching his shoulders—which pulled his entire body into a posture resembling a huge comma—he scurried away.

The retreating Stephen Jones was the ultimate antithesis of Allistair. A lowly sophomore, shy and reticent and skinny, studious and therefore given to holing up in the library (hunched over a desk in yet another comma posture), studying for hours. Earning the straight As he'd received on every test and paper in every class— he was a most aggravating fellow student who elicited a disgusted "There goes the grading curve" from others whenever he walked into class on the first day.

Stephen had delayed joining any ministries in order to establish good study habits, was not confident about his athletic abilities, not on any sports teams, and generally—except for the grading curve consequences—not noticed. It was as though he were invisible, not actually taking up space in his environs. Even Stephen's roommate knew very little about him except that he was exceptionally smart.

Besides his propensity for earning top grades, Stephen had three other notably positive traits. However, for whatever reason, he appeared to consciously hide these attractive qualities. One was his height, for he was tall enough to be center on the basketball team, should he seek the position. But Stephen's slouch was such that few noticed he towered nearly a foot above them.

And then there was the dark green ski cap—the pilly, stretched-out, dirty dark green ski cap. Though Stephen didn't wear it to bed, he kept it right next to his pillow; after the alarm went off, he reached for the ratty cap, which he immediately jerked back onto his head. Some speculated he wore it even in the shower, but the cap's filthiness seemed to negate that rumor. The fact was that underneath grew luxurious, wavy blond hair; when exposed to the sun, his hair glistened with golden highlights.

Lastly, very few at McMaster's had ever glimpsed what could be considered Stephen's greatest asset: his dimples. Deep ones most women fervently wished they possessed themselves. These also were rarely revealed since Stephen simply didn't find many reasons to smile. Had he done so, a number of women would've been intent upon enticing that smile to show itself more often.

If Stephen had added a personable nature to his intelligence, height, hair, and dimpled smile, he could have been a viable competitor to Allistair. But by embracing the labels of reclusive, nerdy, shy, and nearly mute, he rendered that nearly impossible. Still, a serious observer of people would have to arrive at this conclusion concerning Stephen: He was a diamond in the rough.

Stephen had finally gathered the courage to attempt a conversation with one he'd admired for her serious attitude about learning. Out of all the women on campus, Michal alone stood out as worthy of his time. But the moment Allistair stepped in front of him and claimed Michal's attention, Stephen fled. In his panic, he plowed into an upperclassman who angrily chided, "Hey. Watch where you're goin', will ya?"

Muttering a quick "Sorry," Stephen attempted to make himself invisible as he hurried toward chapel. Hoped Michal hadn't noticed. And berated himself for his blundering attempt.

Lost in her own thoughts, Michal hadn't noticed Stephen, and was caught off guard by Allistair. "Oh, hi. Guess I was already … well, out of here."

Allistair's hand flew to his chest and he dramatically stopped in his tracks. "Not Miss Studious. She of the 'I've got to study all evening. I don't have time to go get pizza. I can't take Saturday off to go to the lake.' Surely not that Michal McHenry? I'm appalled."

She laughed. "Okay, I confess: I was thinking about spring break—not classes or studying. Not the paper I have due tomorrow or the quiz in Epistles. Stuff I should be thinking about." Michal glanced up at Allistair, smiling. "I'm going to Florida to visit my aunt. And honestly, I can't wait to get there."

He grinned back at her. "Gotta ask you something. Your name. Michal?"

It was the usual question, and she was used to it. But aggravation at her mother's choice of names still coursed through her every time someone inquired. Again. "Have you seen how it's spelled?"

"Don't think so. Why?"

She spelled it for him. Raised her eyebrows and waited. "Well? Come on, Bible major. Certainly you recall the story of a certain biblical character named David?"

Allistair's face lit up. "Oh. Saul's daughter—who became David's wife. That Michal. But why—?"

"Why name me that? Because when my mom was pregnant with me, she was convinced I was going to be a boy. And that God wanted her to name him Michael, after my dad. So she did. Sort of."

He laughed. "Well, I think that's pretty cool. Not everybody gets to have unusual names like we do. Allistair's certainly not your common, everyday name either—and wouldn't have been my first choice. So … on another topic. Where in Florida you going anyway?"

"Fort Myers." Michal closed her eyes, the pleasure of daydreaming apparent on her face. "I intend to spend every possible moment at the beach. Doing nothing but sleeping and swimming. Maybe try out a boogie board, since everyone tells me they're a blast. How about you?"

"Traveling with a ministry team and my quartet to North Carolina."

"Oh, yeah, of course. I heard."

"We're doing concerts near Atlanta, Greenville. Columbia, too, I think? Rumor has it we'll spend at least a day somewhere around Myrtle Beach."

"That would be neat." Michal felt embarrassed, realizing how self-serving her time at the beach appeared compared with Allistair's Christian service work.

"You're on one of the ministry teams, aren't you?"

Michal glanced up to meet his eyes again, giving him an appreciative smile for pointing that out. "Yeah, I am. But freshmen don't get to travel overnight."

"Sure. I remember. I didn't go on an overnight trip till I was a junior. Didn't qualify until then because of my soccer games."

"You're an amazing goalie." Michal blushed, realizing what a groupie she must've sounded like. "I mean … um, in Ethiopia, just about every kid plays soccer. We didn't have many real soccer balls there, though. At least not where I lived. So we'd use just about anything as a substitute."

"Really? Like what?"

"I guess the strangest was a really big taro." She laughed as Allistair gave her a questioning look. "Oh, a taro's like a potato. Thicker skin, kind of hairylike." Michal laughed again. "We kicked that nasty thing around until it literally fell apart—in chunks, all over the road."

"We? You mean you played with it too?"

"Yeah, me and my brothers. Boarding school was the only place where we had a real soccer ball." She brightened at a sudden memory. "Once one of our supporting churches sent us a rubber ball—it was actually for playing volleyball, I suppose. But we didn't have a net or anything for that. So instead we kicked it around, played soccer with it as long as it lasted."

Reaching up to tuck a lock of hair behind an ear, Michal shook her head, smiling at the picture in her mind. "Which wasn't for very long. I think it hit a rock and deflated pretty quickly. Then we kicked that pathetic-looking lump of rubber around. Looked pretty funny too."

Michal stared down at her feet, avoiding Allistair's steady gaze. Students going into chapel pushed around them and they moved with the rush, trying to get out of others' way. "Well, better get to our seats before chapel starts. Before we're late." She glanced up at him, then quickly looked away. For whatever reason—and it was puzzling and annoying to her—she felt embarrassed. Again.

"Yeah, guess so." They went inside, where Allistair offered—as though passing someone in a hallway, never to be spoken to again, Michal assumed—"Well, see you later."

"Yeah. You too."

Allistair started toward the seniors' assigned seats, but abruptly stopped. Turned back to Michal. "There's a home basketball game tomorrow night. Would you like to go?"

Totally caught off guard, Michal was speechless, unable to think clearly. Neither the tenor of his voice nor the look on his face betrayed anything—whether it was purely a spur-of-the-moment idea, something he'd regret later. Or if he'd actually considered asking her somewhere. She couldn't even tell if this was a genuine invitation or a "be kind to the MK" scenario. Realizing he was still staring at her—that time had passed—she stammered, "I … um, hadn't thought about it. I've got an exam in New Testament on Friday I need to study for."

He tucked his Bible at his side, thrust both hands down into his pockets. They could hear strains coming from the chapel's huge pipe organ. "Gotta take a break sometime. But hey … if you really need to study …"

Michal could feel a sense of import: It was one of those defining moments, an impression that something significant weighed

in the balance. Her intuition whispered this was more than choosing between a date and the need to study. And it was beyond
the well-defined box dividing what it took "to accomplish my
goal of graduating" and any activities that were "a waste of time."
A choice that defied the comfortable lines she drew to separate
sacred from secular. Christian and biblical from unspiritual and
sinful. Some sense of nagging exigency demanded, *Don't miss this
opportunity.*

"I won't. I mean—" she laughed again, an awkward staccato
sound. "I would like that. To go to the game. With you." She couldn't
believe she was actually hearing herself accept the invitation. "You're
right; I could use a break."

"Awesome. Pick you up at seven? Peterson Dorm, right?"

"Yeah … um, that would be great."

"Okay. See you then."

Allistair was quickly engulfed in the press of students. But
Michal was momentarily paralyzed, the second time that morning
she'd felt like her limbs couldn't move as her mind instructed. But
someone rubbed against her arm—she realized she was standing in
the middle of the aisle—and the sensation brought her awake for the
second time that day.

Almost like a blind person, Michal felt her way toward her
seat. Friends around her mumbled greetings, most expecting no
response. Any "hellos" were immediately drowned out by the
deep, pulsating chords of the organ as it surged from pianissimo
to forte. The worship leader stood, raising his arms, the signal to
stand. And they began the familiar strains of "We've a Story to
Tell to the Nations."

Michal tried to size up the speaker who stood on the platform. She took in the limp, worn suit, the dull, striped tie, the generally disheveled look. *He's such … so obviously … a missionary.* Looking beyond the clothes—which were totally out of style, even to her usually oblivious eye, Michal quizzed herself irritably. *What is it about us missionaries that sets us apart? Is it our demeanor, too? Are we so accustomed to another culture we no longer feel comfortable in our own?* Michal shook her head, sighing out loud. And then immediately glanced around her to see if anyone had noticed.

Noting that just about everyone around her already appeared bored, she turned her attention back to the missionary. As he sang, his eyes never once looked down at the hymnal. *He knows every word,* Michal thought wryly. *Just like I do. Bet we sang it at every church we visited during furlough.*

"We're so pleased to have Reverend Gideon Coleman with us today. Reverend Coleman's a missionary to Chile, a man of God who's made tremendous sacrifices to reach the indigent peoples of the remote desert region," President Williams began. "He's been there—how many years is it now? Thirty-two? Is that right?" He turned around to acknowledge Reverend Coleman's humble affirmation. "He has amazing stories to share, so prepare to be blessed. Now, before Reverend Coleman comes, let's pray together, shall we?"

Listening to more disguised moans and sighs from the students around her, Michal wondered if the speaker had already lost his audience. *Won't keep him from preaching,* she thought, grinning to herself.

"Please turn to Matthew twenty-eight, verses eighteen through twenty."

At she opened her Bible, Michal had to remind herself not to shake her head yet again. Couldn't he come up with something original? The Great Commission?

"I know … I know. Every missionary uses this passage, right?" Coleman asked. "Well, after we read this we're going to focus on just one important word. Then I'll list some principles you'll need to jot down in a notebook. Follow along with me now. 'Then Jesus came to them and said, "All authority in heaven and on earth has been given to me. Therefore go and make disciples of all nations, baptizing them in the name of the Father and of the Son and of the Holy Spirit, and teaching them to obey everything I have commanded you. And surely I am with you always, to the very end of the age."'

"The word we're going to look at this morning? The word *go*. A small word, but it carries a big meaning: It's in present progressive tense. Grammarians will understand that means the word *go* should actually be translated as *going*. Because it assumes we'll all be doing this in our daily lives.

"But this is what I want to focus on today, young people. You are the missionaries for your generation. Behind the assumption of you going are these imperatives. Number one: If you feel a call on your heart to go, then you must put that first. Above everything else. Above current relationships, and above potential relationships."

Coleman constantly shifted his gaze all around the auditorium, attempting to meet as many students eye to eye as he could.

"You should not marry someone who isn't feeling the same call to missions that you are—that's a potential to be unequally yoked. And you shouldn't be dating someone who doesn't have the same call as you either. Young people, hear me on this important point:

It's God's will to break off any relationship unless both of you agree you'll go wherever God sends you."

There was noticeably more movement around Michal. She could hear students shifting in their seats, either slumping further or sitting up straighter; notebooks were furiously written in or pointedly closed. She caught sighs, grunts, and whispers that all seemed to announce, "I'm reacting to this. Whether positively or negatively, I definitely have an opinion."

"Secondly, I'm hearing a frightening new demand from young couples. It goes something like this: 'We won't go anywhere we can't keep our children with us, from newborn up through high school years.' Suddenly boarding schools have become the enemy—Christian boarding schools that have been in existence for decades and have proven track records of putting out well-adjusted and intellectually prepared graduates.

"Turn to Matthew ten, will you? Verses thirty-seven through thirty-eight." He snatched a pair of wire-rimmed reading glasses from his pocket and placed them on his nose. "Anyone who loves his father or mother more than me is not worthy of me." He put down his Bible. "Okay, who's speaking here?"

Several volunteered, "Jesus."

"Anyone who loves his son or daughter more than me is not worthy of me; and anyone who does not take his cross and follow me is not worthy of me." His gaze wandered around the room again, connecting with numerous students, eye to eye. "I have a tough time seeing that as anything less than a direct command. Anyone else agree?"

Several "a-mens" reverberated across the room; many came from administration and faculty members in the first two rows.

"Now, let's stop a moment. I'm going to ask for a show of hands." Coleman leaned forward over the pulpit, symbolically getting as close to his listeners as possible. Hearing a stirring again, Michal glanced around and was surprised to note how many consciously—or subconsciously?—responded by leaning toward him. "How many of you are MKs?" He raised his own right arm, holding it straight above.

Some jerked their hands up immediately, proud to be singled out. Others were more hesitant, not wanting the attention, like Michal.

"And how many of you were fortunate enough to go to a Christian boarding school so your parents could remain on the field?" Coleman's arm remained upright, and it appeared that nearly everyone who responded earlier kept their hands up also. Michal's was among those, but she could feel her heart pounding. Her face flush red.

"Now this time I don't want you to raise your hands. Instead, I want you to answer this question in your heart. I challenge you to consider it later in your prayer or journaling time, will you? But here's my question to those of you who went to boarding schools: Your parents made incredible sacrifices to go where God called them. Are you thankful for that?"

Michal stared down at her Bible, eyes unfocused, seeing only blurred words.

"Let me state that again: Your parents made sacrifices. Yes, you made sacrifices. But to what end? So the unsaved could hear the gospel. And young people, that's good reason to give up so that others may receive, is it not?"

Coleman paused dramatically. Waited patiently for the effect. He wasn't disappointed, for a lone listener was heard clapping. Cautiously, others joined in. And then it became awkward for the rest—Michal included—not to applaud, for the clapping built and grew, spreading throughout the auditorium like an infection.

Coleman continued hammering his points, going nearly ten minutes over his allotted thirty; Michal caught snatches of his voice and then sporadic applause, even laughter a couple times. But she actually heard very little of his message. Her attention kept drifting to Ethiopia, and what she heard ringing inside her head: the lilting, animated Amharic language of the people she so loved.

Rustling around her—everyone was reaching for hymnals—finally signaled chapel's end. Michal hadn't heard the page number, so she peeked over at her neighbor. "Send the Light." *But of course,* Michal thought, allowing herself a slight smile.

After the benediction, a few worked their way to the front of the auditorium, eager to speak with Reverend Coleman. Most crowded toward the doors, intent upon escape—whether to the library, a class, the snack bar, or merely to get out.

Michal had just stepped outside when she felt the slightest touch at her elbow.

"A lot of that was pure crap, huh?"

Horrified, Michal looked up to see who dared utter the words. It was Allistair.

"Allistair. What are you—?" Michal glanced around to see who was near. Who might've overheard. She whispered, "What are you talking about?"

"The chapel speaker. I'm not arguing against us going to the mission field. 'Cause I fully agree we should all become missionaries—but to wherever we are. You don't have to go to a foreign country to be a missionary. But the part that really ticked me off? Laying the guilt on some of those poor kids who went to boarding school—and had a lousy childhood because of it." Allistair's eyes sought Michal's. "I'm sure your experience was great, but others?" He shook his head, vehemently. "I have a good friend who—"

Michal interrupted, almost in a panic. "I think we'd better talk about this some other time, Allistair, since I'm running late. See you later, okay?" She nearly sprinted away from him, regretting she'd agreed to see him the next evening. *I can't go with him to the game,* she thought, berating herself for submitting simply because she'd felt flattered. *I certainly don't want to talk anymore about boarding schools. And I'm only allowing myself to be ... distracted. Gotta focus on getting back to Ethiopia. Where I belong.*

As Michal took her seat in class—it was Bible Study Methods, a requirement—she shivered, a delayed reaction to Allistair's defiant attitude, his rebellious words. It was beyond her comprehension to even think of criticizing a chapel speaker, and again she worried about who might've overheard.

Glancing quickly around the classroom, she caught a glimpse of Stephen. He was hunched over his desk, studying.

The quiz. Michal suddenly remembered. *I completely forgot to go over the material last night.*

Frantic, she turned to the assigned chapter, skimming through the sections she'd highlighted. By the time the professor walked into the room, Michal had reviewed her notations. But whether she'd recall everything was debatable.

That first class was only a preview of how the remainder of her day would play out. A feeling of being a step behind became her shadowy nemesis. When she'd finally finished her last class—in which a returned paper received a B rather than the A she'd hoped for—and was heading back to her room, inwardly grumbling, she childishly kicked stones out of her way. It felt good to take her frustrations out on something.

Once again Michal was so preoccupied she didn't notice another had joined her until he kicked a rock into her line of vision. Glancing up, she saw Stephen Jones had fallen into step with her. The sight of him hunched over, cap pulled down to cover his ears, kicking at stones in tandem, was enough to strike Michal as funny. She giggled. "I take it you've had a rotten day too?"

"And I take it you weren't at the first lunch hour?"

She gave him a lugubrious look. "I was late leaving New Testament class because … oh, forget it … too long to go into. Let's just say it wasn't good. Then I needed to ask Dr. Brown something. Things went downhill from there." Michal shook her head, frowning. "Sorry. That's my sad story. So what happened during the first lunch hour?"

"I'm surprised you didn't hear. The Nerd," Stephen stopped momentarily, comically pointing to himself, "managed to drop his lunch tray."

"Oh, no. With all your food, I suppose?"

"But of course. Why bother doing it otherwise?"

Michal giggled again. "I'm sorry. It sounds like something I'd do. Actually, I'm surprised I haven't dropped a tray already."

"I hear my faux pas may be on YouTube. Isn't that grand?"

Michal's mouth dropped open. "No. I can't believe anybody'd be that mean."

"Well, apparently somebody is."

"It's nice to talk to you, Stephen. But we've never officially met." She smiled, happy to have a conversation with the mysterious outcast. She held out her hand to him. "I'm Michal McHenry. MK. Originally from Kansas City but really from Ethiopia. Near Addis Ababa."

Stephen took her hand somewhat tentatively, but as he did so, he popped the green cap off. Inclined his head, blond hair falling over his forehead and catching glints in the bright sun, flashing her a huge smile. Dimples highlighted. "I'm Stephen Jones. Studious nerd who provides video for others' twisted humor. From Ohio. Pleased to meet you, Michal McHenry."

The effect on Michal—who was so often oblivious—was close to dazzling. She was nearly speechless at the transformation, stammering, "Um ... you've got dimples. I didn't know—" Too late, she realized she'd pointed out the obvious. Clearly something a girl should never mention. "Oh, I'm sorry. That was just stupid." She could feel the heat going up her neck, knew she was blushing. *How many times today?*

Stephen tugged the cap back on and returned to his usual scowl. Jammed his hands into his pockets and proceeded toward the dorms, taking large strides with his long legs. Michal had to scurry to catch up with him, judging an apology was a must. "Sometimes I say the dumbest things. I just talk, without thinking. Know what I want to tell people when I do that?"

He glanced up, the sulk a little less severe. When he didn't say anything, Michal took his silence as encouragement to continue.

"What I want to say, you know, is that I didn't grow up here. I don't read social cues like I should." She laughed, an abbreviated sound signaling frustration rather than happiness. "I really am clueless sometimes."

She could barely hear Stephen mumble, "I feel clueless all the time."

"Oh, no. You're not, not at all. Like in class? Some of your answers to Dr. Rosenburg? Wow."

"You're a good student." Stated simply, as fact. He kicked another stone, starting the game again.

"Not like you. I work hard. But I can tell it comes a whole lot easier for you."

Somewhat defensively, Stephen interjected, "Oh, I work hard too. It's why we're here. To learn and go on to serve God. In churches or on the mission field." His eyes lit up as he held her gaze confidently for the first time. "Wasn't the chapel speaker great today? I thought he was inspiring."

Michal hesitated a moment, taken back at the juxtaposition to Allistair's thoroughly negative appraisal. "Yeah, he was. Good." She nodded her head. "Yeah, I liked him."

"What he said about dating and missions? Boy, I absolutely agree. And about having kids?" Suddenly cognizant that he was staring at a girl, talking about having children, caused him to take a turn feeling embarrassed and he looked away. "I mean, you've got to … um … you've got to put God first. Don't you think?"

"Oh, yes. Absolutely."

"I mean … you're going back to the mission field, right?"

Michal nodded vigorously. "As soon as I graduate. I'll need to raise support first. But afterward, as soon as I can."

"If you got married and had kids? You'd send them to boarding school, wouldn't you?"

"If God called me to. I mean, I'd have to trust God to take care of them. And if that's the only way we could reach the unbelievers there in Ethiopia, sure." She knew all the phrases to say, the right responses. "I mean, after all, my grandpa did it. My dad and then me and my sister and brothers." Michal held out her arms, palms up. A pantomime of surrender. "So my kids—if I ever have kids—well, they could … would need to probably … go too."

Stephen turned to her with a look of awe. "It must've been an incredible experience to be at a boarding school. Every single day … such … such closeness with each other. Fellowship and studying God's Word, growing closer to each other because of your parents' commitment." He reached out to lightly touch her arm, a movement resembling a fan fawning the object of his devotion. "I just can't … can't imagine what a blessing that must've been."

Uncomfortable, noticing a strange prickly feeling on the back of her arms, Michal stammered, "Oh, don't. Really. You know … we all do what God's called us to, right?" They'd arrived at Michal's dorm. She looked up at the window of her room, wondering if anyone were watching.

Stephen stared earnestly into her eyes, intensity animating his features. "I just thought it was great Reverend Coleman reminded us about the seriousness of what we're doing. The reason we're here, you know? That we're preparing for service in the church or on the mission field—and we're not here for silly games. Like sports or other stupid stuff. Dating games. I think we students need to get our priorities straight, don't you?"

"Yeah, that's true." Suddenly more serious, Michal's nod became adamant. But then the silence between them—the awareness they were simply standing there, staring into each other's eyes—made them uncomfortable, shy. They both looked away, Michal to poke at a buried rock with the toe of her sandal while Stephen reached up to pull the cap down lower on his forehead.

Michal was startled when Stephen blurted out, "Can I ask you a question?"

"What's that?"

"How'd you get a name like Michal?"

She laughed. "That's the second time today …" and caught herself, just in time. Remembering who had asked earlier, someone she didn't want to talk about. "My mom thought I was going to be a boy, and she liked the name Michael. So, she changed the spelling a little."

"Like Saul's daughter. Destined to become David's wife."

Michal grinned up at him, appreciating his height and the quick recognition. "You're good. Not everyone remembers that."

Blushing, he refused to meet her eyes, taking his turn at kicking a rock.

"Well, I'd better go," Michal said. "Speaking of getting our priorities right, I've got plenty of work to do."

Stephen hunched over even more, if that were possible. He continued to concentrate on the rock, an excuse to keep his gaze downward. "Yeah, me too. Nice to talk with you." He ventured a quick glance, caught her eye for a split second. "Um, see you around. Bye."

And then he did an abrupt about-face, hustling down the walk like he was running from a fire. Never venturing a glance behind.

Michal smiled at his retreating back, amazed at what had just transpired.

A waste basket was wedged in the door of the suite to capture the cross-breeze as several of the girls gathered in the suite's lounge. They were stretched out on the chairs and couch, a couple on the floor with backs against the tired-looking furniture. Laughter broke out as Michal walked in, just as Jessica demanded, "Pass the popcorn, will you? Geez, you guys are hogging it all."

Michal noted all but one of her suitemates were there—Jenny, Samantha (Sam, as they generally called her), Jessica, and Ruth—plus two from the adjacent suite, Lauren and Amy. Beth was noticeably absent.

"Hey, Michal. What's with you?" Ruth asked, narrowing her eyes at Michal's expression. "You're lit up like the stoplight at Main Street. So what's up?"

"You won't believe it. Do I have a story to tell you."

Jessica—her mouth full of popcorn—simply patted the couch, motioning for Michal to sit next to her. She held out the bag of popcorn.

"No chips?" Michal complained, grimacing. "Beth and I haven't had anything but popcorn for ages. I can't stand another kernel."

"That's all we've got left too," Ruth groused. "What can I say? It's time for spring break. Time to go home, raid some cupboards, replenish the supplies."

"And speaking of Beth, does anybody know where she is?" Michal asked. Frowning, resigned, she reached for a handful of popcorn, unable to resist the smell after all.

Everyone's head was shaking. "She wasn't in our Romans class," Sam offered. "Second time she's missed this week. Dr. Shaw didn't look happy about it either."

"I'm getting worried about her," Michal said. "Seems like she just wants to stay in bed all the time. She's skipping chapel too—has a ton of cuts, she told me."

"She's puttin' on the pounds. Definitely added the freshman fifteen," from Samantha.

"Samantha." Michal shot her a glare, determined to be loyal, defensive of her roommate.

"That's not kind, Sam," Jessica lectured, and then laughed, as Samantha took that moment to stuff her mouth with a large fistful of popcorn. And then watched a good portion fall all over the floor.

"Frankly, I want to hear Michal's news before I get back to studying." Jenny glanced at her watch, sucking in her breath. "Two thirty. Geez, how did it get that late already? Can you give us the condensed version, Michal?"

"Well, Allistair asked me to go to the basketball game with him tomorrow night." Gasps and exclamations all around. "And when Stephen Jones takes off that wretched stocking cap and smiles …" she drew out her words in dramatic fashion, holding everyone's attention, "he's got really nice blond hair. And dimples."

Comments and questions came in a bombardment.

"Allistair asked you out? No way."

"I'll tell you what's no way—no way I'm believin' that about Jones."

"Jones gives me the willies. Seriously." Samantha formed an L shape with her fingers, held it to her forehead. "Loo-ser. Jones is a big time loser."

"He actually smiled? Stephen Jones smiled? Didn't know he had it in 'im."

"Oh, Michal. Allistair?"

"You've got to wear some of my clothes, Michal. Something really cool. Do your hair. And makeup. Let me do it." Samantha, who'd been sitting on the floor, was now up on her knees and had inched forward so she was at Michal's feet.

"I'm not going." Michal's voice was calm. Nonchalant. She shrugged her shoulders, crossed her arms over her chest, and relaxed back against the couch.

Again they all talked in unison, still in disbelief. But arguing now, incensed.

"What? Who in their right mind would turn down …?"

"Michal would—that's who."

"You've got to go out with him, you idiot."

"She's not serious. You're teasing, right? You are teasing us, aren't you?"

Michal chewed on a nail, thoroughly enjoying their exclamations of displeasure, taking her time to answer. "Actually, no. I'm being serious. Allistair is … well, not as spiritually mature as I thought he'd be. In comparison? Stephen seems so much more mature."

Stunned silence.

Michal started to inch forward, pushing herself up from the couch. "You know, I'd better get busy studying—"

Jessica grabbed her on the one side; Samantha and Lauren moved to hold Michal down on the other. "No way you're leaving until you explain yourself. You think you're dropping a bomb like that and then disappearing on us?" Lauren exclaimed.

"What bomb?" Beth stood in the doorway, appearing disheveled and worn-out.

All eyes turned to look at her, taking in the noticeable change in Beth over the last few months. Her hair looked wild. Bright red, it generally had a wiry, refusal-to-be-tamed unkemptness, but it appeared she hadn't even attempted to calm the unruly curls that day. And it was dull, mostly devoid of the luster they'd all been envious of last fall.

Like Michal, Beth usually didn't use makeup. But the dark shadows under her eyes and the hollows under her cheekbones—if Beth had gained weight, her face certainly belied it—cried out for concealment. Otherwise, her complexion was an unhealthy, pasty white.

Usually more meticulous about her clothes than Michal, today Beth was wearing a wrinkled, blousy top several sizes too big, and she hadn't bothered to tuck it in. Instead, it hung out over a pair of jeans that were also ill-fitting, bunching awkwardly around her hips. The bottoms of the jeans dragged on the ground—getting frayed and filthy from the red clay of the area—completely hiding her shoes. If she had any on.

The word *wretched* popped into Michal's mind, and she immediately felt ashamed.

"Are you okay? Beth, you look awful," Samantha burst out. Michal shot her an angry look, silencing any further comments.

"What're you talking about? What bomb?" Beth sounded defensive.

"I was telling them about my conversations with Allistair. And Stephen Jones," Michal explained, searching Beth's face. She stood up, taking her roommate's hand. "Come on, Beth. I think you look plain worn-out." Michal guided Beth tenderly, opening the door to their room and gently pushing her through. Over her shoulder, she offered, "We'll talk more later at dinner." To their loud protests, she reasoned, "Hey, I needed to study anyway. I'm sure you all do too?"

Michal received an assortment of groans and grumbles in response. A pillow was launched in her direction, though she easily dodged it. But they all got up and reluctantly filed into their respective rooms.

Only Samantha seemed to intentionally delay, waiting until everyone else had gone before whispering to Michal, "Hey, I'm sorry I said that. To Beth." She lowered her eyes. "Will you tell Beth I'm sorry? That I didn't mean anything by it?"

Michal squeezed her friend's arm. "Beth knows that, Sam." She lowered her voice. "I think we're all concerned about her. I know I've been …" she let it trail off, unfinished, shaking her head. "See you when we go to dinner?"

"Later."

Michal watched her go into her room and then turned to look at Beth. She was stretched out on her bed, facing the wall again.

"Did you want to talk?" Michal ventured. "Or just sleep?" Beth took in a deep breath, let it out slowly.

"I'm just tired. I think I have some kind of flu thing again."

"Want me to call the nurse?"

"No." Beth rolled over to face Michal, her face a mask of alarm. Realizing she was overreacting, she intentionally calmed. "I just don't want to bother anybody when it's nothing at all, really. I'll feel better after a good night's sleep." She suddenly brightened, sat up. "Know what I really need?"

This was the Beth Michal had instantly taken to when they'd first met, the roommate who was full of mischief, a prankster. One who always found something to laugh about—even in the worst of situations.

When Michal had been devastated by a C on her first paper for Dr. Brown, Beth had thrown her into stitches with a perfect imitation of the professor. The way he sucked in his bottom lip when making a point. How he'd rub his bald head, smoothing the few strands that still grew on an otherwise barren landscape. The way he used his index finger to push up wire-rimmed glasses on his long bony nose.

By the time Beth had finished her comedy routine, the paper seemed much less important. Because Dr. Brown was less important, less intimidating. Michal attributed the A- she got on her next paper to Beth's "magic." From then on, she realized how fiercely she'd come to love Beth. And vowed to be her friend forever.

Lately, though, it seemed like Beth had moved away from Michal. Not physically, obviously; she was there every morning when they woke to the dreaded alarm; they marched off to chapel together (though where Beth disappeared to once they arrived was anyone's guess); they shared lunch and a couple classes, and dinner was always a "community event" for all the suitemates. (Unless one temporarily snagged an interested male. Which Michal and Beth vowed was "so not on our agenda.")

When they came back to their suite after dinner, both would socialize, teasing about who was seen with whom, discussing gospel teams, sharing a gripe session about professors and tedious assignments and tricky exams. But usually Michal and Beth were the first ones to excuse themselves to study.

Lately, though, Beth studied only a short time until her head would begin to droop. Then it was only a matter of minutes before she'd announce, "I'm too tired to study," or "This is a waste of time," and get ready for bed. Sometimes she didn't even bother to brush her teeth, change out of her clothes, or put on pajamas. She'd pull down the sheet and ratty quilt and climb in. Fully dressed.

The worst change of all, however, was how Beth's laughter had faded like the tide slipping away from the beach. As Michal fretted over her beloved friend, she realized she hadn't actually ever seen the tide recede; it was too gradual, too furtive. And it was the same with Beth. *Was it that I couldn't notice, the changes so slow, so slight?* Michal quizzed herself. *Or that I didn't want to notice?*

But now Michal was encouraged by Beth's animation, wondering, *Maybe I've been imagining it all?* Aloud she offered, "No. What do you really need, roommate? Your wish is my command."

"Chocolate."

The glistening sparkle in Beth's eyes was so wicked Michal erupted with laughter. Between giggles, she lamented, "But we don't have any more chocolate, remember? We polished it off over two weeks ago."

Beth stood, imitating Dr. Brown's gait (eliciting more laughter from Michal) as she stiffly walked over to their "stash"—the drawer where they kept a popcorn popper and snacks. At the start of the semester, they'd enjoyed assorted candy bars, bags of chips, cookies, and granola bars. But the drawer had sadly dwindled in supplies, and was now empty except for the dreaded popcorn.

Michal watched curiously as Beth rummaged around, making an exaggerated show of her search. Dramatically drawing out a scarf like a magician pulling one from a sleeve (from Michal: "How did that get in there?"), Samantha's stuffed teddy bear ("Beth, Sam's been looking for him for days … she's going to strangle you when she finds out you're the one who snitched him"), and finally, the objects of their desire: two candy bars.

Beth held them up, one in each hand. "A-ha. Once again Beth the Magnificent has shocked the world with her brilliant powers."

Michal laughed delightedly as Beth tossed one to her. "Yum. Where did these come from?"

"Revealing my source means I'd have to shoot you." The sly look she gave Michal seemed to strongly hint the source was male.

Instantly curious, Michal raised an eyebrow. Like Michal, Beth had precious little money to spend on extravagances. Candy bars certainly weren't expensive, but just the day before Beth was complaining she was completely broke—except for the exact amount of gas money to ride with another student to her grandparents' home over spring break.

For Beth to claim a secret source was equally suspicious. She had the same circle of friends as Michal: suitemates and classmates. Michal knew them all—at least, she assumed so. And like Michal,

Beth had steadfastly avoided any relationships with guys, stating emphatically she didn't have time. And besides, both agreed guys were too immature, too simplistic, too much like … well, boys.

"Secret source? A guy maybe?" Michal probed, as she polished off the last of the chocolate, licking her fingers.

Beth shook her head and then lay down on the bed; she was taking such tiny bites she still had half of hers left. Pulling herself up onto one elbow, Beth gave Michal a hard stare. "You're one to talk. What's this about Allistair? And Stephen Jones?"

Michal sat at her desk. She spread out books and notebooks, situating them in the order needed to tackle assignments.

"You're stalling, Michal. Spill it."

Michal grinned at her, shyly. "Well … turns out Stephen's not such a nerd after all. He's really nice, actually. And without that awful hat, he's pretty good-looking, too."

Beth gave her a look of astonishment as she wadded up the wrapper and tossed it toward the trash can. "No way."

"Seriously. He's got nice blond hair."

"But he scowls all the time, Michal. And he's such a … such a hunchback. Honestly, the way he skulks around the campus. Gives me the creeps."

"I know you won't believe this."

"What?"

"Stephen is more spiritually mature than Allistair."

Beth laughed, scoffing. "Now you're really losing it. Allistair's what? President of the student body?" She scrunched her pillow, molding it just the way she liked.

Intently chewing on a nail, Michal merely nodded.

"And he's on the best ministry team?"

Michal popped the finger out of her mouth, studying the nail's ragged edge. "Told me they're off to Georgia and North Carolina over spring break. He's in the quartet. I'm pretty sure he preaches, too."

"I know he does 'cause he's taking Homiletics. All the guys in there are required to preach at least five times."

"How on earth would you know that?"

"'Cause I tried to sign up."

"For Homiletics?" Michal's mouth dropped open. "No. You never told me that. Girls aren't allowed, are they?"

"Apparently not. They wouldn't let me in, anyway." Beth yawned. "I'm getting sleepy. Hurry and tell me about your date with Allistair before I fall asleep."

"Not gonna be any date." Michal opened her notebook for New Testament, ruffled through the pages. "I'm really wondering if Allistair's a fake, Beth. You wouldn't believe what he said about today's chapel speaker." She noted Beth's eyes were closed, her mouth slightly open. "Beth?"

When there was no answer, Michal sighed, concerned that Beth wasn't studying for the exam. She chewed on the nail again—Michal reverted to the childish habit whenever feeling anxious—and studied until it was time for dinner. Noting Beth was still sound asleep, Michal tiptoed out the door, meeting her suitemates in the lounge.

Samantha gave Michal a look. "Beth not going with us?"

"She's sleeping. I think she's sick again."

No one commented, but the quick glances indicated the four of them had discussed Beth earlier.

Eager to change the mood, Ruth gave Michal a friendly shove. "So are you going to tell us now about Allistair?"

"Yup." But she stubbornly remained silent.

"Well?" from Ruth.

Samantha gave Michal a playful smack on the arm. "Michal."

She glanced around, checking out who might overhear their conversation. "Let's wait until we're seated in the dining hall, okay? I don't want anyone else to know about this."

Jenny shook her head in amazement. "Anyone else on this campus—well, maybe not Beth—but anyone else would just die to have everyone know that …"

Michal cut her off with a fierce glare.

"Okay. I'm not saying it. But you are the only one who would freak out like this."

As they entered the spacious dining hall, Michal pulled back from the group, hesitating. After all these months, she was still intimidated by the scene before her—the mass of students milling about, filling the vast room with a rush of bustling energy. In their midst were large bars offering everything one could ask for: salads, breads, sandwiches (cold deli, or a hot sandwich made to order), varied full entrées, one bar devoted entirely to pasta and pizza, and lastly, the dessert and drink bars.

Walking into that dining hall presented Michal with a multitude of choices she'd never had to face before, dozens of possibilities she couldn't even have imagined in Ethiopia. The result was almost overwhelming. As she stood in the doorway, momentarily frozen, she observed students walking in confidently, with decisive purpose. They hurried to the salad bar or were quick to peruse the entrées, choosing one easily. Others ordered sandwiches with apparent aplomb, pairing bread with meats cooked a certain way.

When Michal was a child back in Addis Ababa, she wouldn't have been able to conceive of this much food in an entire city—let alone in one room. And the variety was still nearly beyond her comprehension. Her diet in Ethiopia had been consistent and predictable: wot (a stew), yams, taro, a cabbage like kale, squash, peppers, onions—often wrapped and baked in the ensete leaf (termed "false banana" since it resembled the banana plant). Corn was a rare luxury from their family garden. There was no such thing as choice. You ate what was placed before you—gratefully. Or rather: You acted that way.

The staple bread of Ethiopia had a tough, dense texture and was made from the ensete plant. When Michal first stood before the bread bar at McMaster's, she'd sucked in her breath in amazement, eyes roaming over the display of bagels, yeast rolls, sweet breads with nuts, biscuits, cornbread, luscious sourdough loaves, and French baguettes, everything from plain white to healthy multigrains. She'd felt uncomfortable and guilty, thinking of her family and the villagers back home. Living with … so little.

But that was nothing compared to the waste she observed daily. Michal knew her views on what students flagrantly threw out wouldn't be appreciated; she kept those thoughts to herself. At the same time, she was careful to eat whatever she put on her plate—which made her selections that much more cautious and deliberate. Along with the entire dining hall experience, the process of selecting food was harrowing for Michal.

It was also the perfect setup for major teasing.

Suitemates razzed Michal mercilessly about how she came to a complete stop when she first walked into the dining hall. How she then proceeded to advance in slow motion, waiting timidly for others to move out of the way. About her tendency to choose only the familiar, to approach the least crowded bar, choosing small amounts of what she could easily get to. Michal was always the last to arrive at the table with her very predictable food. No custom-made hot sandwiches. She'd invariably have the smallest portions. And she ate every bite, leaving her plate conspicuously clean, another mine for significant unwanted attention.

By the time Michal made her way to the table, Samantha was already primed and grinning.

"Did you see the spiral-sliced ham, Michal?" She held up a forkful. "It's got that maple glaze on it—yum."

She gave Samantha a vacant look. "Ham? Where was that?"

Samantha giggled while Ruth poked her with an elbow.

"Hey. Cut it out. I'm only pointing out the obvious. It was over on the entrée bar, silly."

"Oh, so that's what everyone was hovering around."

Samantha started to make another comment, but Ruth kicked her. "Ouch. All right, already. So tell us about Allistair, Michal. You've kept us in suspense long enough."

"It's nothing. He just asked me to the basketball game."

Several looks of obvious envy—and exclamations.

"But after chapel, he said what Reverend Coleman shared was—" Michal leaned into the center of the table and whispered, "pure crap. Honest, that's a word-for-word quote."

"I took a cut today. Sounds like I missed something good. What on earth did this Reverend Coleman say?" Amy asked, amusement coloring her words.

Ruth was indignant. "He's a missionary. To Chile."

"Uh, okay. So did he show slides of a sunrise and sunset?"

Amy's sarcasm was lost on Ruth, who responded with horror at Amy's audacity to ridicule a chapel speaker, let alone a missionary. "No, he didn't."

"He said we should all be open to becoming missionaries," Michal pointed out. "That we should date only those who feel called to be missionaries too."

"You know, I gotta tell you. I'm confused. 'Cause he made it sound like all of us should go to the mission field." Jessica put her hands on her hips and tilted her head, smirking as she looked at each of them. "So … if all of us go overseas to the mission field, then who's left here? Who supports everyone?"

"Jess, you know that's not what he meant. Not technically."

"You're called to go back to Ethiopia, aren't you?" from Ruth.

"Definitely," Michal answered.

"Well, it's pretty clear to me you can't go out with Allistair." Ruth's declaration set off a firestorm of discussion.

"What? That's stupid," Samantha railed.

"Just because Allistair didn't agree with Reverend Coleman doesn't mean he's opposed to being a missionary."

"Actually, he told me he believes we're all full-time missionaries," Michal interjected.

"What on earth does that mean?" Jessica looked confused again.

"A missionary can be anyone who tells others about Jesus. We're all supposed to do that." Ruth was currently taking a class on missions and sounded a bit condescending.

"But isn't there a difference when it's vocational missions?" Jenny asked. "As opposed to having other jobs—like us, since we're ... you know ... students right now? We're not full-time vocational missionaries."

"Then Michal can still go out with Allistair."

"No, she can't."

Michal broke into the argument, stating firmly, "I told you, I'm not going out with him anyway."

Samantha's face lit up, and she whispered, "Well, speaking of you-know-who. Announcement," she trilled, in a singsong voice. "He's headed our way this very moment, eager listeners."

Before Michal had a chance to mentally prepare, Allistair was casually resting his hand on the back of her chair. "Do some studying this afternoon for your exam?" He glanced up at the girls gathered around her, nodding his head in greeting. "Hey." The twinkle in his eyes hinted he was getting a kick out of their interest.

"Yeah, I did and—"

"Great. I'll see you tomorrow night at seven. Never dated an MK before. Something tells me I've got a lot to learn." And with that, he turned and was swallowed into the crush of students milling around.

"Well, that's the way to tell him the date's off," Samantha offered, dissolving into giggles that pulled in everyone else, enjoying the joke at Michal's expense.

Chagrined, Michal attempted to defend herself. "He didn't give me a chance, did he?"

"Seems to me you didn't exactly try to find one either."

Michal held up her hands in mock surrender. "Okay, okay. So I didn't do the right thing. I should've said no first thing this morning."

"Oh, I don't know," Amy mused, shrugging her shoulders. "So Allistair didn't like the chapel speaker. Why not find out what he disagreed with? Maybe you'll find you and he don't see things so differently, after all."

"Whatever. I can't back out now. Well, I need to get back to studying. Anyone else ready to go back to the dorm?"

"I'm going back for dessert," from Jessica. "Chocolate cake."

"There's chocolate cake tonight? I didn't see that …" Samantha mumbled as she followed Jessica, leading the entire group toward the dessert bar.

Though Michal was tempted to follow, she declined, and was hurrying down the path toward the dorm when she sensed someone falling into step beside her. Stephen.

Shyly, she grinned up at him. "Hey, Stephen."

He gifted her with one of his rare smiles, the dimples making their appearance. Michal had to remind herself, *Close your mouth, dummy,* the transformation was so amazing.

"I um … I was um … was kind of wondering …"

Michal waited, thinking she should obligingly help Stephen finish the sentence, but she had absolutely no idea what he was trying to say. So she fixed on him what she hoped was an encouraging look.

"I was wondering if you'd want to study together. Tomorrow night. For the New Testament exam."

Suddenly panicked, Michal was at a loss for words. *How on earth could I possibly tell him I have a date?* She could feel her heart pounding. Sensed the awkwardness of her silence. *After we shared our similar commitment to studies.*

Taking Michal's silence to mean she wasn't interested, Stephen backtracked. Tried to save face. "Oh, um … you know. It's not … well, you probably need to study on your own."

He was already speeding up in his haste to get away. But she grabbed his shirt sleeve. "No—it's just that I can't. I would've loved to, Stephen, I really would. But someone else already asked me to—"

"Study with them," he interrupted, avoiding Michal's eyes. Briefly glancing at her once more, he bravely ventured, "I understand. Another time maybe?"

It was a lie, really, to let Stephen believe that. But she grasped the substitution Stephen had offered as a way out of a dilemma. With a measure of guilt, she answered, "Yes, I'd love to study with you, Stephen. I really mean that. After we get back from spring break?" Michal smiled, and realizing that she still held onto his shirt, let go, flustered.

Stephen nodded solemnly, apparently believing her. But he didn't utter a word as he took off at a trot toward the library.

When Michal got back to her room, Beth was busy studying, sprawled out in the middle of her bed. She glanced up at Michal, grimacing. "Hey. Come join the torture."

So the two of them dove into their study notes together, sharing points and quizzing each other until they'd covered the material. By the time Michal needed to move on to other subjects, she felt fairly confident about taking a few hours to attend the basketball game with Allistair. *Yeah, I feel confident about taking the test,* she thought to herself, *but not at all confident about being with Allistair.* "What was I thinking?" she mumbled out loud.

"What's that?" Beth didn't take her eyes from her book.

"Oh … nothing important," Michal answered, sighing. "Nothing at all."

At six thirty the next evening, Michal peeked out her door to discover every one of her suitemates waiting outside, demanding to be let in. She slammed the door shut, stubbornly insisting, "Go away. I don't need your help getting ready. I'm already dressed."

She could hear Samantha groan loudly. "That means she's wearing exactly what she wore all day long."

"I heard that, and I am not!" Michal yelled, crossing her arms, staring at the door as though facing her friends.

"So what did you change? Your socks?"

"Just as long as she didn't change her mind."

Michal could hear them tittering at each others' wit. Which drew a pantomimed laugh from Michal—and then a real one from Beth. She was having a great time observing the scene from the comfort of her bed, leaning back against the headboard, books scattered around her again.

"Come on, Michal. Open the door. We only want to help. Please."

Against her better judgment—and lamenting to Beth, "I know I'm going to regret this"—Michal opened the door about an inch and peeked out again. "What exactly is it you want anyway?"

Matter-of-factly from Ruth, "We just want to check your outfit."

"And your hair and makeup," Samantha added.

"I don't—"

Their patience exhausted, all three pushed the door open and plunged into what sounded like a military inspection.

"Oh, you're not wearing that blouse. Absolutely not."

"You don't have any makeup on at all, do you? Not even lip gloss."

"What did you do to your hair? Besides nothing?"

"Take those stinky sneakers off right now."

Beth broke out in a fit of laughter, holding her side as though it hurt.

"My sneakers do not stink. I wash them all the time." Michal gave Beth a look of deadpanned insult. "And thanks for your support, roommate."

"Hey, you're all on your own. It was your choice to go out with the most popular guy on campus."

"That's why this will be the last time I go out with Allistair Fuller."

Samantha had disappeared into her room and was gathering makeup. Jessica was literally yanking the maligned sneakers right off Michal's feet. And Jenny was holding up a blouse she'd already chosen from her own closet, singing its praises, sounding like a used car salesman.

Resigned, Michal accepted that doing what they wanted was ultimately easier than fighting. And by the time she'd "passed inspection"—she had to twirl in front of them as they nodded their heads in approval—the call came from the lounge. Another freshman, nearly breathless, voice full of wonder, proclaimed, "He's here. I mean … you know. Allistair's here."

Michal nervously walked down to the lounge, and as she rounded the corner, she saw Allistair turn toward her, smiling broadly. He gave her a quick perusal, one swift assessment from head to toe. "You look great." Politely holding open the door, he gestured with the other hand. "Shall we go?"

Michal was surprised how easily they slipped into conversation; they chatted about spring break, how excited they were to get away for a while, the churches where Allistair's team would minister, what it was like on a traveling ministry team. Despite her resolve to remain detached, Michal was interested in what he'd be preaching on, and impressed by it too. And at Allistair's urging, she talked at length about Aunt Sarah. How she also grew up in Ethiopia, but was the only sibling not to go back to Africa.

"Why was that?" Allistair asked.

"I'm embarrassed to admit I don't know because I've never asked," Michal confessed, realizing she hadn't shown much interest in Sarah's life. "I guess I've been pretty self-centered that way. Never realized it till just now."

"Hey, I didn't mean it that way. I was just being nosy, that's all."

"Oh, I know you didn't. But it's good you asked. Whenever I'm with Aunt Sarah, she always steers our discussions to be about me— what I'm learning, how I'm doing. You know, this time I'm going to ask her questions too."

"She sounds like someone who's a great listener."

Michal smiled. "Yeah, she really is."

"I think everyone needs someone like her in their life."

Michal agreed, tucking a straying curl behind her ear. Jessica had insisted Michal wear it down, the sides pulled back with a large barrette that perfectly matched the color of Jessica's blouse. But as usual, her hair wouldn't stay in place, and there were small tendrils at both sides of her face. Framing her expressive eyes (minus eye makeup—Michal had drawn a firm line on that), highlighting them.

Allistair was quiet a moment, pensive. He had a McMaster's baseball cap on and reached up to straighten the brim before putting his hands in his pockets. "My first year here, we had a chapel speaker who really convicted me." He stared straight ahead, his expression conveying a seriousness she hadn't seen in him before. "I decided right then I needed to go to the mission field."

"You did?"

"Yeah, I was convinced that's what I was supposed to do. Knew exactly where to go too." He glanced over at her and grinned shyly.

"And that was …?"

"Africa, of course. Isn't that where the most spiritual missionaries go?"

Instantly defensive, Michal stopped in her tracks. She glared at him, mouth open.

Allistair reached out with both hands, conceding. "Oh, no—I'm really sorry. What I was trying to say was that's what I thought. In my totally immature way of thinking back then."

"So what does that say about missionaries there now?"

He pointed to an empty bench. "Look, how about if we go sit down for a minute?" Putting a hand against Michal's back, he gently guided her toward the bench. To her consternation, Michal was intensely conscious of his hand. And how it felt. "I think I need to completely start over, don't I?"

She smiled, despite her firm intention not to. "You think?"

He took off the cap and ran a hand through his hair. Slumping over with his forearms on his knees, Allistair looked up at her through squinted eyes. "Gotta tell you … I don't know when I've ever started a date so badly."

Michal had to giggle at his obvious distress and disarming honesty.

"So, does that reaction mean I get another chance?"

"Oh, I always grant do-overs. Like on the playground."

Allistair grinned, eyes twinkling. "Exactly."

"My dad says since we're given grace, we have to grant it too. And do-overs are life's way of making that possible."

"I think your dad sounds like a wise man."

Michal nodded matter-of-factly. "He is. And …"—she dramatically drew out each word—"ever so spiritual, too."

She let Allistair suffer for a moment, looking into his openly vulnerable expression that almost broadcasted, *How do I take this? Is she being serious?* And then she burst into laughter again.

"Walked right into that one, didn't I?" he asked, laughing along with Michal. "Can I try to explain my way out?"

"It's a do-over."

"Well … see, back then I thought everyone was called to the mission field, not at all understanding the idea of integration." His face lit up, and he elaborated, "But here's the way I understand it now: We're all called to a lifetime of sharing the gospel. That might be in Africa, at an office, in a classroom of kids, or behind a register at a local grocery. Or it might be where I'm now convinced God wants me to go—to a church somewhere here in the States."

Allistair grew more animated, using his hands to articulate his point. "I don't think any one of those is a higher calling, Michal. The highest is wherever God wants me. And I think a person can be called to clean houses the same as someone is called to full-time vocational ministry. See, what's important is … that I'm seeking his will for my life. What he wants me to do." He looked at her intently—as though her opinion mattered to him. "Make sense?"

"I guess. I mean … I'm having a hard time with secular jobs being equal with a missionary or pastor. Isn't full-time Christian ministry more important than other mere … jobs? And what if someone was really called to the mission field? Wouldn't she be wrong not to go?"

"So are you assuming everyone's initially called to missions or to work full-time in the church? And it's only if those don't work out that he or she is free to do other things? Jobs which aren't as good or important as being a pastor or missionary?"

Michal started to shake her head no, and sat back against the bench. She chewed on a nail, peering intently at Allistair. "Well, I guess I am kind of saying that."

He leaned closer to her, his eyes alight with enthusiasm. "See, that's my point, Michal. I don't think that's true at all. I believe someone's initial and highest calling could be to work a cash register at a grocery." To her continuing doubtful look, he added, "Look at it this way. Can't a clerk who's committed to sharing the gospel reach people who come in the store every day? Why is that less of a ministry than those sharing in another country?"

"So being a grocery clerk is as high a calling as a pastor. Or a foreign missionary." Spoken as statements, but in a skeptical tone.

He glanced toward the gymnasium, noting the groups of students making their way in. "Give it some more thought. How about if we talk more the next time?"

Next time. Michal noted his assumption, feeling excitement and apprehension in the same moment.

"We'd better roll or all the good seats will be gone," Allistair continued. "And the bleachers during a game probably isn't going to be the best place for a deep theological discussion." The twinkle was back in his eyes again as he smiled down at her.

"I suppose not. Unless we're going to scream our opinions at each other." They laughed, and Michal grew more serious again. "You've given me some things to think about. Some assumptions … I guess I've always had."

"I think that's what a good class does. Makes you evaluate why you believe what you do. You throw out what's mere assumption. Keep what's right—but you know why it's worth keeping."

Michal leaned in close to him, whispering conspiratorially, "Some people would say that's dangerous."

Allistair laughed and reached out to guide her through the gym doors. "I don't doubt that. Wouldn't be the first time I've been accused of being dangerous."

Walking into the gym, they were immediately assaulted with its unique ambiance: the exuberant, raucous crowd, several calling out greetings to Allistair, cheerleaders shouting, the loud strains from the pep band. As they scanned the bleachers for a place to sit, Michal couldn't miss the comments and looks she and Allistair were attracting. Several students noticeably elbowed friends, igniting conversations and even some openmouthed stares. Her date with Allistair was eliciting a gossip frenzy. She squirmed—emotionally and physically—beneath the obvious scrutiny. Like it or not, Michal was suddenly and totally on view.

Once they'd settled into seats, Michal shouted to be heard over the roar of the crowd, "So, were your comments a sneak preview of sophomore theology classes?" Gazing at his profile, she watched a smile slowly materialize. It struck her how much she enjoyed making that happen.

He turned to face her, beaming now. "Absolutely. Might have to charge you for it, though."

"No way. Previews are always free. And besides, I'm still debating if I accept your do-over."

"You mean I'm not forgiven?"

But Michal's answer was lost in the din as the players ran onto the court, the band began playing the school's fight song, and the crowd's cheering went up yet another decibel. The students rose to their feet, and Allistair and Michal's conversation from then until halftime focused on the refereeing and the opponents—how they clearly deserved to lose, though the smattering of fans on the opposite side of the gymnasium would've violently disagreed.

By the time the players ran off the court, the score was thirty-eight to thirty-five, Wildcats. Home fans—happy to be in the lead, at least for the time being—began spilling out of the bleachers, eager to visit the snack bar and chat with friends. Only one day remained before spring break officially began, and their enthusiasm was riding high, even without the added adrenaline rush of the game.

Allistair turned to Michal. "I'm dying of thirst. Too much shouting, I suppose."

Michal nodded her head in agreement. "I can't remember the last time I yelled this much. Feels good."

"Great for stress relief, isn't it? How about a soda?"

"Sounds great."

Allistair held out a hand to help her down the bleachers, and Michal gladly accepted; the borrowed wedge sandals from Jessica were awkward to walk in, a real nuisance in her opinion. But the moment she gripped Allistair's hand, she felt what seemed like butterflies flitting around in her stomach. Her small hand seemed to nearly burn in Allistair's much larger, stronger one. Once safely on the gym floor, Allistair released her, motioning toward the snack bar. As they made their way through the throng of students, Michal could only think about how much she wished he were still holding her hand.

He steered her toward an empty table and held the chair as she sat down. "What kind of soda?"

"Hmm, grape, please."

He laughed. "Living on the wild side tonight, eh? Anything else? Pizza? A hamburger or hot dog? Chips?"

"Oh, no. Thanks, Allistair. Just a grape soda would be wonderful."

Michal stared at his back as he worked his way across the room. Others also watched his progression and pointedly turned to look at her. Feeling uncomfortably scrutinized again, she began examining one of her nails. Accompanied by a stern conversation with herself. *You won't be going out with Allistair again. So don't make too much of his attention. That unreal butterfly stuff.*

A small but insistent voice argued back. *But he's so easy to talk with. He laughs easily like I do. We could just see each other occasionally. What's wrong with that?*

The sound of Allistair's voice pulled her from the covert bickering. He was laughing with another senior, a lovely girl who was poised, golden-haired, confident, and gifted with a beautiful voice, evidenced by many solos in chapel. Michal noted that Tiffany Smith was everything she was not. "Tiffany, this is Michal McHenry. Michal, meet Tiffany Smith."

Elegantly flipping her hair over her shoulder, Tiffany graced Michal with a smile that resembled a sneer. "Allistair and I met at tryouts for singing ensembles. We were the only two freshmen to make the top McMaster's ministry team."

Tiffany stared at Michal, one eyebrow raised, silent, waiting for the compliment. Instead, Allistair spoke. "Really? I don't remember that." He handed Michal her drink and a large-sized chocolate candy bar. "Well, good to see you, Tiff. Enjoy the game." Abruptly turning his back on Tiffany, he sat down facing Michal.

But Tiffany wasn't about to be dismissed. Resting her hand on Allistair's shoulder, she added, "If I don't see you tomorrow in class, I'll see you on the bus." She met Michal's eyes, eyebrow lifted again. "Allistair and I will be road mates for the next week. Spending each and every day together, cooped up in that ratty ole bus. Giving concert after concert. At least we're going to the beach, too."

Allistair focused his attention on unwrapping his candy bar.

"Well, enjoy the game. I need to go pack." She patted Allistair's shoulder familiarly. Michal took it in, wide-eyed. "Good to meet you, Melissa."

"Michal," Allistair corrected, before Michal could utter anything. And then he looked up at Michal, eyes crossed. She stifled a laugh by coughing into her napkin.

"Oh, so sorry. Guess I'm not used to calling a girl by a boy's name. See you Saturday, Allistair." Tiffany turned on her heel and wove her way through the tables. Several guys turned their heads to follow her progress, but Allistair was not among them.

He leaned closer to Michal, whispering through clenched teeth, "She drives me insane. Honestly, I wish I hadn't made that first team. Haven't been able to get rid of her since."

"But she's—"

"Obnoxious. Stuck-up. And by the way, I took a chance you'd like a candy bar." He grinned, noting it was already devoured, that she had some chocolate on her bottom lip and one finger in her mouth. "I take it you do? Did?"

Conscious that she was caught licking her fingers like a child, Michal blushed. "Oh, yeah. Thank you, that was really thoughtful. Actually, I love any kind of chocolate."

"Never would've guessed," he teased. "Any kind? No preferences at all?"

"None. We so rarely had chocolate in Ethiopia that … well, let's just say it's the ultimate treat."

"Yeah? I'll remember that. Might need to bribe you sometime." He stood up, stretching. "Ready for the second half?"

Michal glanced enviously at the crowd milling toward the gym. "Allistair, I hope you don't mind. But I think I'd better go review again for my exam." A hint of disappointment glinted in his eyes and his smile began to disappear, so she rushed on before her resolve waned, "But I've had a wonderful time. It was a great break from studying. And I don't want you to miss any of the game. I'll walk back to the dorm by myself."

"Oh, I couldn't—"

"Please. I'd feel awful if you missed out on the best part of the game." Allistair was still shaking his head doubtfully when Michal insisted, "Please, Allistair. I'll be fine." She held out her hand to shake his, which he took, giving her a somewhat puzzled look. "And the candy bar was super. Thank you so much. That was a special treat."

Letting go of Michal's hand, Allistair pushed his hands into his pockets, peered down at her. "Okay, newbie freshman." She grinned. "Go study. I've heard rumors you're a great student, a serious one. And I respect that. I sincerely do."

Shy again, Michal looked away, muttered, "Well, thanks. My parents are sacrificing a lot for me to be here. I just have to ... you know?"

"I do."

"Well, um. Root for me too, okay? If we lose, I'll hold you personally responsible."

Allistair flashed that huge smile at her again. "Not the team? Just me, eh?"

They shared one more intimate laugh before Michal raised her hand to wave good-bye. And then she hurried away.

The next day flew by. After her exam, Michal thought she'd earned a strong B if not the A she'd hoped for. Quizzes in other classes weren't difficult either, and by the end of the day, she breathed a sigh of relief.

Michal had hugged Beth good-bye. Jessica, Ruth, Jenny, and Samantha had already headed home for spring break, leaving the suite uncharacteristically quiet. Few students remained on campus at this point besides Michal; her bus for Florida didn't leave until the next morning.

She was leisurely packing when the suite's phone rang—the resident advisor informing her she had a visitor in the lounge. For a moment, Michal was flustered. She knew Allistair was one of the few students remaining; his team also didn't leave until morning. But when she entered the lounge, she was relieved, and intrigued, to see the familiar hunched form sprawled on the couch, clicking the remote.

"What is it with men and remote controls?" she teased. "And not watching one channel for more than two seconds?"

Stephen stood, and the smile and dimples flashed again, sending a quick stab to her heart. "Hey, Michal. Someone told me you'd still be here. Hope you don't mind me bothering you?"

"Oh no, not at all. I'm glad for the company. Will you be here until tomorrow morning too?"

"No, actually, I leave in about ten minutes."

"Oh, okay."

Stephen plopped back down, his gangly legs and big feet stretched out before him. Michal sat too, making sure she was a discreet distance away.

Both were quiet, awkward—not knowing what to say. And then they both began to speak at exactly the same time ... laughed at their bungling ... and quieted again. Finally, Michal ventured, "Was there something you wanted to tell me? Ask me?"

"Um, no. Well, are you looking forward to spring break?"

"Oh, yes. I'm going to my Aunt Sarah's. In Fort Myers. Florida." She rushed to add, "Of course you knew that. That Fort Myers is in Florida, I mean."

Stephen smiled and she felt the tickle in the pit of her stomach; the butterflies were back.

"Oh. Yeah, I did. But I didn't … I mean, I didn't know you were going. Or that your aunt lived there."

"Yeah. She does live … there." *Why is this so hard,* Michal wondered, *when it was so easy to talk with Allistair last night?* "How about you?"

"What's that?"

"Where are you going for break?"

"Oh. Just home." Michal inclined her head toward him, and he caught the clue. "Ohio. Bay Village, to be exact."

"Doing anything special?"

"Nope. Don't think so." Stephen glanced at his watch, and Michal saw it was a computer type, very studious looking. She was impressed.

"Time to go?"

"Yeah, I suppose so." He stood, awkward again. "I just um … wanted to say good-bye. See you when we get back?"

"Oh, yeah. Absolutely."

Michal followed behind him, walking toward the door when suddenly Stephen stopped and turned toward her. But she never guessed what was coming, didn't anticipate his intention to put his arms around her, pulling her roughly toward him. Before she could even take a quick breath, he'd planted a wet, sloppy kiss on her lips.

Just as quickly, he was gone. Sprinting toward his dorm.

Michal put her hands to her cheeks, feeling the heat of her flushing. It wasn't her first kiss—but it nearly was. And the other hadn't been that urgent or forceful.

Her heart was pounding. But she couldn't decide: Was it out of excitement? Or shock?

On the bus to Fort Myers, Michal was still debating. *Did I somehow convey to Stephen that I wanted him to kiss me?* She shook her head, wondering, unsure of herself and the message that she'd possibly, unknowingly sent.

The other questions in her mind, however, haunted her more: *Will he do it again? And do I want him to?*

She leaned her head wearily against the window and soon went to sleep, dozing peacefully until excited exclamations awakened her, for they were approaching the Sunshine Skyway Bridge. Rubbing her eyes, Michal was mesmerized by the bold primary colors of several kite sails over the water. They floated gracefully on the breeze, bobbing now and then as those riding the sails steered them higher or lower. *What fun that would be,* she thought, envying the thrill of such a ride.

It was a sunny day in Florida; the brightness made her squint even with sunglasses on. With only a few puffy white clouds marking a light blue sky, the sun was in its glory: Reflections on the tips of the spiking waves of the Tampa Bay sparkled like diamonds. A few of the ever-present scavenger seagulls winged by, and though Michal couldn't hear them—the air-conditioned bus was closed tight—she knew they'd be spouting their typical raucous calls.

Pulling herself straight in her seat, Michal spied an overhead sign saying the North Skyway Fishing Pier was one mile ahead. The landmark held dozens of cars, with even more people positioned around its railing fishing. A couple pelicans were sitting boldly atop the piers—eager to glean offerings from generous fishermen.

The spans and massive cables of the bridge came into view next. The cables were at parallel diagonal angles so that they resembled masts from a ship and their accompanying extended sails. Painted a bright golden yellow, the result was an imposing, awe-inspiring structure. And then her gaze was pulled to the breathtaking scene before her. The bridge curved down to the left, water all around, where the South Skyway Fishing Pier extended off to the right. The city of Bradenton beckoned from the south—beckoning her personally, it seemed. She sat back contentedly and closed her eyes.

It wasn't long before the low hum of the engine and the gentle rocking of the bus soothed Michal back to sleep. The next time she was roused by commotion on the bus signaled their imminent arrival at the station. Fellow passengers were busy gathering their belongings; impatient children were hard-pressed to stay in their seats; and others were eagerly staring out windows, seeking familiar sights, pointing them out excitedly. Michal joined the latter group, eyes scanning the area for a glimpse of her aunt's bright yellow sports car.

The bus pulled to a stop, its brakes complaining about the imposition. At that moment, Michal saw her. She was wearing a wide-brimmed straw hat over her short brown hair, a pair of denim capris with a crisp white cotton blouse, sandals. And she was waving like mad. Michal beamed, waving back.

When the driver opened the door, the bus wheezed like an arthritic old man. Michal made her way slowly up the aisle, backpack hanging over one shoulder, a small purse strap over the other. Smiling, gracious, she waited for families to exit the rows in front of her. Generously volunteering to help those with small children. Since you never got anywhere quickly in Ethiopia, Michal had learned patience. To appreciate the road traveled as much as the destination. And to attend to the needs of people rather than a timetable.

When she climbed down the steps, Michal was immediately enveloped into Aunt Sarah's waiting arms. Her aunt gave the type of hug Michal had longed for all her life—one that her parents, for whatever reason, had never been able to give. Michal felt every contour of her aunt's body fit snugly to hers. There was no shyness in this hug—only vulnerability, total giving, and the physical manifestation of unconditional love. It seemed to proclaim, "I will hold onto you until you say, 'That's enough.'" Aunt Sarah graciously allowed the recipient to set the agenda; that way, her niece received all she wanted and needed. Aunt Sarah made sure of that.

When Michal pulled away, she looked into her aunt's smiling face. "Welcome, my darlin' Michal. I can't tell you how much I've looked forward to having you come back again. To come home."

It was exactly the right thing to say.

Michal took in the bright, twinkling eyes and laugh lines around the wide, smiling mouth. She knew her aunt spent little time frowning or complaining. Instead, Sarah focused on finding the joys in life, seeking any excuse to burst out with a quick "Ha!" of laughter, searching out reasons to choose contentment and happiness. That bent gave her a nearly constant look of humor, like she was savoring a joke others hadn't yet heard. Or expecting a cheerful surprise at any moment, one of mischievousness and fun. Children would follow her like a pied piper. And so would Michal.

"How are you?"

"Oh, I'm fine—now that I'm … home. Aunt Sarah, thank you for allowing me to come. I can't begin to tell you how much I've looked forward to this—ever since I left at Christmas, actually."

"Let's gather up your bags and get outta here."

Waiting for luggage to be unloaded, Sarah and Michal stood side by side, obviously kin. They were the same height, holding themselves and moving in similar ways, and though Sarah's hair was tucked beneath her straw hat, the escaping wispy curls were identical in color to Michal's—only specked with white. They watched the proceedings intently with matching light grey eyes. Smiling and laughing easily. The only minor difference was the evidence that Sarah lived and gardened in Florida: Her freckles had blossomed in the bright sun and nearly covered her face. But anyone observing the two would've assumed they were mother and daughter.

Unbeknownst to Michal, her similarity to Sarah disappointed her parents. They disapproved of Sarah for numerous reasons, so Michal's resemblance to her aunt—in physical appearance and personality—was a constant reminder of the family's "black sheep." The two shared easy laughter, outspokenness, and stubbornness in holding on to bad habits. Like chewing nails. (A closer look at the two women would show both had short, uneven nails and a raw cuticle here and there.)

So it wasn't willingly that Michal's parents sent her to Sarah's over Christmas and spring break. Rather, it was a *fait accompli* … a consequence of their being far away in Africa, while Michal was in the States. The Reverend and Mrs. Michael McHenry would be spending the week fervently praying any influence Sarah had on their daughter would be minimal and short-lived.

Suitcase finally in hand, Michal was delighted to see the convertible's top down. Sarah tossed her hat and Michal's suitcase into the trunk and asked, "Did I guess correctly you wouldn't mind your hair getting blown?"

Michal grinned back. "What do you think?"

They laughed together, ripples sounding like echoes of each other as Sarah gunned the powerful car and steered into the line of heavy traffic. *If Dad and Mom could see us now,* Michal thought as they passed others like they were mere ants, attracting attention from the males they left in their dust.

After dinner, Sarah and Michal sat contentedly in the Florida room, sipping iced tea.

Sarah reached over to put her hand on Michal's. Uncharacteristically, she had tears in her eyes. "Thank you for humoring a dried-up old woman, Michal. For keeping me company this week."

Michal put her other hand on top of her aunt's, squeezing it. "Oh, Aunt Sarah. I love being with you. And you are not an old woman."

"Ha! You're only saying that because I have a hot car. Makes you and me 'eye candy' for men."

"There is that." Michal giggled but then grew serious. "But you also teach me so much, Aunt Sarah." She felt her aunt's calico cat,

Mr. Grits—who'd been named after one of Sarah's favorite dishes—rub against her ankle. She reached down to pet him, but he ran off, meowing indignantly.

"So … you said earlier you were fine. But how are you really doin', Michal?" Sarah peered into her niece's eyes, head cocked at an angle.

"How do you do that?"

Sarah took a sip of her tea. "Do what?"

"Take one look at me. And know stuff."

Sarah watched Michal smile warily—and yawn widely.

"Oh, now there's my keen ability to know stuff, eh? Keepin' you up when you're dog tired." The thought suddenly dawned on her, "What time did you get up this morning anyway?"

Michal stretched. "Wasn't too bad. Three."

"Oh, gracious." Sarah was immediately on her feet, gathering up dishes. "Leave 'em now, just leave 'em be," to Michal's attempts to help. "We need to get you to bed."

Michal nodded, sleepily. "I think I could be asleep in seconds."

Sarah shooed Michal down the hall toward the guest bedroom in her roomy ranch home, passing a collection of family pictures in the hallway. Michal caught glimpses of her grandparents, their faces serious, almost grim. Her aunts and uncles, with their many children, and several of Michal and her brothers and sister—Paul, Peter, and Becky.

The bedroom and adjoining bath were like another welcoming hug for Michal. Their deep brown and cream tones soothed her spirit. Fluffy balloon shades, a desk with fabric skirt, and a window seat filled with pillows made the room inviting and warm. It was as though Michal's every need had been anticipated and provided for: bubble bath for the tub, terry robe and slippers waiting for her in the closet.

"Aunt Sarah, this is all so …" Michal gestured toward the room, her arm moving in a wide arc, "… so perfect."

"You have everything you need?"

"Almost—except for one thing." Sarah gave her a puzzled look as Michal reached out to give her aunt a good-night hug. "Now I have everything."

"Sleep as late as you like. No schedule tomorrow. Not a thing on the agenda—except rest. Eat a good bit. And plenty of girl talk." Sarah called out over her shoulder, "Don't be surprised if Mr. Grits joins you. He's claimed that bed as his lately and might be distressed that you're invadin' his boudoir. Night."

Michal called out, "Night, Aunt Sarah. Love you."

In response, Sarah blew a kiss.

When Michal walked over to the bed she discovered Mr. Grits was indeed curled up on one of the pillows. "Well, as long as there are two pillows, I guess I can share one with you." He raised his head to peer at her and then meowed, arched his back in a pronounced stretch, and jumped off the bed. Michal had to giggle as she watched him prance down the hall—with great drama and dignity—making it clear he'd been insulted.

Michal didn't wake until the sun shone so brightly through the eyelet curtains that it was nearly like a spotlight. She blinked, taking a moment to remember where she was, and inhaled the delicious scent of bacon and biscuits. After a quick trip to the bathroom, she slipped into the terry robe and padded down the hall.

"Well, good mornin'. Did you sleep well?" Sarah stood at the stove, tending the aromatic bacon.

"I don't remember a thing after my head hit the pillow. That smells amazing."

Michal opened the refrigerator, anticipating her aunt's next words. "Help yourself to some fresh-squeezed orange juice. Eggs sunny-side up?"

Michal nodded. "Please. Did I smell biscuits, too?"

"Check the basket on the table. No decent southern cook would ever serve breakfast without grits, of course. Not that I don't know you eat a bite only to humor me."

"Can't I get away with anything with you?"

Sarah winked at her. "Prob'ly not much. Hand me four eggs from the fridge, will you?"

When they'd both had their fill and Sarah was enjoying another cup of tea, she suggested, "It's supposed to be a beautiful day. How 'bout we go to the beach? I thought we'd pack a picnic lunch. Take a couple good books. Be lazy, irresponsible beach bums. Sound good?"

"Heavenly," Michal replied.

They packed towels, sunscreen, a huge umbrella, chairs, and a cooler stuffed with delicious food. The final two things Sarah lifted to put into the trunk brought looks of surprise and excitement from Michal. "Boogie boards?"

Sarah shrugged, acting as though she'd never seen the thick Styrofoam boards before. "How'd these get in my garage? Not sure just what they are, but we'll take 'em along."

"Have you ever ridden one?"

"Me? Dignified as I am?"

"You have. I was going ask if we could get one. And here you've already got two." They climbed into the car, Michal bouncing around like a child on Christmas Eve. "Ever since we watched those kids the last time, well … I've just been dying to try it."

"You seriously think I'd let you have all the fun? Not get myself one too?"

Michal shook her head, laughing. "I should've known, shouldn't I?"

As they drove to the causeway the traffic was fairly heavy. Tourists were bustling along the sidewalks, going in and out of shops and restaurants. After finding a parking space and hiking a few minutes, they discovered a perfect spot: an area with a gracefully curving palm tree, providing just a bit of shade in addition to the umbrella they planted in the white sand.

They nested a bit, shaking out a large blanket, anchoring its corners with towels and sandals, placing the cooler in the shade. And then they peeled off the clothes they'd worn over swimsuits, already feeling the heat of the day.

At that point, Michal took in her surroundings: the gorgeous aquamarine blue of the gulf against the bright white sand, the rhythmic sound of the waves hitting the shore mixed with the calls of the seagulls, the delighted cries of children playing in the water or making castles in the sand with bright-colored pails and shovels. She closed her eyes, concentrated on the salty smell of the breeze as it caressed her. "Oh, Aunt Sarah. Do you think heaven has beaches?"

"I do. But even prettier than this."

"I can't imagine anything prettier than this."

"Okay, a reality check: Did you take a look at the size of those waves, Michal?"

She grinned, noting the lift in her aunt's voice. "Looks like fun to me."

"Ready to boogie?"

They both laughed, excited by the thrill of a new challenge. "I'm ready if you are."

Carrying the boards to the surf, they watched as others nearby demonstrated how to ride the waves. Or attempt to—they watched boards shoot one way and riders another. Sputtering a bit afterward, the beachgoers tried to shake hitchhiking sand out of bathing suits, push back tangled hair, and generally collect their wits. But Sarah and Michal readily agreed that it looked like great fun.

The boogie boards came with ropes that attached at the wrist, so when the rider got separated from the board it was readily accessible. After fastening the Velcro, the two adventurers set off. They soon encountered the first challenge of this new sport: getting past the powerful breakers that continually knocked them back toward the beach.

For the next hour, Sarah and Michal were thrown from their boards, pounded by waves of water, and completely upended in the surf. Yet in spite of all that, they laughed hysterically at how much fun boogie boarding was. After examining various scrapes and bruises (declaring none serious enough to keep them from going again), they realized they were also ravenous. Back on the beach, they set out a veritable feast, thanks to Sarah's generous provision. And once satiated, they stretched out on the blanket, indulging feelings of laziness.

"It's what you do at the beach," Aunt Sarah assured Michal. "After what we boogie boarding broads just did, we've earned it."

Michal giggled in response as they lay on their backs; the sea breeze soothed tired bodies. Nonchalantly, Michal broached the subject weighing on her mind, "So we had this chapel speaker last week. A missionary."

"Bet he was exciting and original."

Michal muffled a laugh by putting her hand over her mouth, feeling guilty, as if her dad or mom might be listening. She raised her eyebrows at her aunt.

"Don't give me that wide-eyed look. I've heard more than my share of 'em. How some of them could make living in a foreign country sound so boring is beyond me, when it's anything but that—as you well know. But all that's neither here nor there. What was it this chapel speaker said, anyway?"

"Well, one of the things was I should only date guys who are also definitely going to the mission field."

"Have you settled that call in your mind and heart?"

"Oh, sure." After squirming under her aunt's unwavering gaze, however, she admitted, "At least, well, I'm pretty sure I have. Settled that."

Sarah waited a moment, still staring at Michal, unblinking. "Doesn't sound very convincing to me. Why don't you wait until your senior year to make a major decision like that?"

"But I've just always … since I was a kid. Known. You know how it is. Didn't you?" And then, realizing her unintentional blunder, began stammering. "I mean … oh, I'm sorry, Aunt Sarah."

"No need to apologize. Long story … but it wasn't meant to be." She waved a hand in the air, casually dismissing the discussion of herself. "But let's get back to you. Rather than a distinct call from the Lord, sounds more like a case of osmosis."

"Osmosis? How does it—?"

"Relate to being an MK? Well, I'm under the belief that the call to the mission field shouldn't be simply absorbed from your parents. I just think that kind of huge life decision should be made independent of them." She shook her head as though clearing her thoughts. "But let's get back to what the missionary said. How did you feel about it?"

Sounds of laughter reached their ears. A family out in the waves, jumping together when the water surged toward them. Sarah and Michal were distracted a few moments, vicariously enjoying the familial joy before them. Michal found it hard to switch from the scene of carefree laughter to the subject of constrictions placed on her by the chapel speaker. "Well, I guess I agree. I should, I think— or I need to. A friend of mine, Stephen—he's really mature and very spiritual, Aunt Sarah; you'd like him—he thought Reverend Coleman was inspiring."

"Good for him. But what did you think?"

The pleasing scene before her disappeared, and suddenly she was transported back to her home in Ethiopia, the unadorned little kitchen with plain wooden table and chairs. She stood at the sink wiping dishes while her mother washed. And she heard her mother's words, repeating them as her own. "Daddy and Mom talked about their calling first. How that had to be absolute first priority in their lives. Only when they'd settled that with each other, did they agree it was okay to date.

"Mom said she knew it would be a sin to allow herself to fall in love with someone who—" Michal looked over at Sarah then, expecting tacit agreement. But she was so startled by the haunting look on her aunt's face that she lost track of what she was saying. Michal took in the grimness about Sarah's usually broad, smiling mouth. The lack of life in those ever-animated eyes. All her features seemed to have … fallen. For the first time, Sarah looked old. "Aunt Sarah? What is it?" Michal reached over to touch her. "Are you okay?"

Slowly, Sarah turned her head to look out toward the ocean again. "Let's just say I think you should be more concerned about developing friendships with young men who are committed to seeking God's will for their lives—whatever that may be."

Allistair's words echoed in her mind, nearly exact duplicates of her aunt's. *I think what's important is that I'm seeking his will for my life,* he'd said. Momentarily, Michal was back at school, sitting on the bench with Allistair. And she felt compelled to ask another question, one that—since that night—had never been far from her conscious thoughts. "Aunt Sarah, do you think it's more spiritual to ask God to send me to the mission field? Isn't being a foreign missionary the highest calling there is?"

Sarah was quiet for so long Michal thought she hadn't heard, and was about to repeat her question when her aunt sighed, as though letting go of a great weight. Michal watched her profile—the narrowing of her eyes, the continued downward turn of her mouth. She absentmindedly ran a hand through her still-wet hair. "You'll have to find that answer on your own, dear girl." And then she turned toward Michal with a mischievous smile that caught her off guard. "We've been entirely too serious for far too long. I say we hit the boards again. You game?"

Michal grinned. "Let's do it."

For the remainder of the afternoon, they focused on the exhilaration of catching a wave at the exact right moment—just before it peaked—to experience the longest ride possible. Balancing themselves on their boards while the waves pulsed beneath them. Riding all the way to the shore, coasting up onto the sand, fists pumped up into the air. Celebrating success.

Eventually their energy waned, suits became itchy with freeloading sand, and the scrapes and bruises were too sore to ignore any longer. Gathering clouds brought a cool breeze. It was time to stop—for the day, at least. By mutual agreement, however, they declared the boogie boards a very wise investment, promising each other the "boogie board broads" would return another day.

They ordered pizza from a small Italian restaurant and downed it like rescued castaways. When asked about the possibility of ice cream for dessert, Michal was about to decline when Sarah added, "Before you make up your mind, you should know it's chocolate with chocolate chips."

Michal's face lit up. "Oh, I can't turn that down." She watched Sarah scoop a generous amount into both bowls. "Beth says chocolate's one of the main food groups."

"Your roommate is very wise."

"Aunt Sarah?" By Michal's tone of voice, Sarah could tell she was wading into a more serious topic again.

"Uh-huh?" She plopped dollops of whipped cream on top.

"About the chapel speaker."

"Yeah …"

"I've been thinking. He also mentioned that all missionaries should be willing to send their kids off to boarding school. And if we weren't willing to, we weren't putting Jesus first in our lives. I'm curious what you think about that."

"How do *you* feel about it?"

Michal spooned a big bite of ice cream into her mouth, savoring the chocolate. She could tell that Sarah seemed to be following a pattern: allowing Michal to come to her own conclusions. She was grateful for Sarah's approach—realizing it was challenging her—but Michal also felt the slightest frustration. She just wanted answers.

"Well," she tried, "boarding school's not so bad. If I needed to do it for where God's called me …"

Sarah was ready to put another spoonful in her mouth but stopped, the spoon held in midair. She gave Michal a look full of compassion. "I've heard you havin' nightmares, Michal." She put down the spoon and took Michal's hand between her own. "I know it wasn't easy for you. Does it help to know it was hard for me, too?"

Michal's eyes instantly filled with tears. "Daddy never said a word … I just assumed … and I've never told anyone about …"

"Your dad didn't have an easy time of it either. None of us did." She watched as a single tear rolled down each of Michal's cheeks. "Why haven't you told anyone of your nightmares, Michal? That's the only way to take away their power over you—to talk it out with someone. Know why I know that's true?"

Michal shook her head. She didn't trust herself to speak.

"'Cause I talked with a counselor who helped me work through some difficult times in my life." She let go of Michal's hand and reached for her spoon, encouraging Michal to do the same. "I want you to know that I begged Michael and Hannah to bring you back to them. Or to let you come live with me here in the States if they couldn't ..." She let her voice trail off, shaking her head in exasperation.

Astonished, Michal asked, "You did? You actually asked Daddy and Mom that?"

Sarah nodded. "I had to just ... let it go. Though I doubled and tripled my prayers for you."

Michal concentrated on the bowl before her, furiously stirring the ice cream and whipped cream together. "I would've loved living with you."

Sarah grinned. "Just think how much trouble we could've gotten into all those years." Serious again, Sarah added, "It clearly wasn't meant to be. And though I disagreed with your parents, please hear this—because it is the truth. Your parents love you desperately. They did what they thought was right. Which is what we all do." She shook her head. "Hindsight wisdom is way too easy. The tormenting 'I should haves' can drive you crazy. So you move on. Hopefully learning something along the way."

"So we don't make the same mistakes over again? Like me trying to decide who I should date?"

"I know you'll make the right decision, Michal." Sarah idly scraped the bottom of her bowl with a finger, getting the very last puddle of melted ice cream. Michal watched with amusement. "You know, sometimes I wonder if God cares more about our process to make a decision than he does the decision itself." She popped the finger into her mouth. "Unless you have any other deep theological topics of discussion, shall we change course and see what's on TV tonight?"

Michal grinned. "Absolutely."

Sarah pointed to Michal's bowl. "Then make sure you get every remaining drop of ice cream and let's get at it, shall we?"

The nightmare came again that evening, but it seemed to last all night long, with scenes unfolding like acts in a play. Saying goodbye. Boarding school. Administrators blaming Michal for being so miserable. The nausea flushed over her, and her eyes opened wide.

Why did I think the nightmares wouldn't follow me here? She allowed tears to come. *Until I settle this completely—either I'm going back to Ethiopia, or I'm not—I'm not going to have any peace in my heart. Or peace from these nightmares.*

By the time she joined Sarah for breakfast, Michal had washed away any evidence of tears, greeting her with a cheery, "Good morning."

"Good morning, Michal. Sleep well?"

Michal's only answer was to reach for her aunt, giving her a hug. Sarah had been holding a cup of hot tea, but she instantly put it down, giving Michal her full attention.

"Another nightmare?"

"Uh-huh."

Sarah tightened her hold on Michal.

Later, after settling in at the beach, Michal and Sarah were only slightly disappointed to find the waves quite tame. So after lunch, they happily settled in the sand to read, followed by naps. The ease of that afternoon reminded Michal of floating on a raft on a gentle creek. They returned home to shower and change for dinner at a seafood restaurant and a walk on the beach at dusk.

Upon reaching the sand, both slipped off sandals, allowing their feet to luxuriate in its cool softness.

They strolled along, Michal next to the shore, her feet almost constantly in the soothing water. Sarah beside her, an exuberant wave sometimes bathing her feet too. Every once in a while one of them would lean over to inspect a shell. If deemed worthy, it was shown to the other, shoved into a pocket for safekeeping. The next week—long after Michal had removed the collected shells—she would reach into that pocket to search for a tissue. And find grains of sand there.

Sarah spoke into the sound of the waves hitting the shore, her voice matching the calm rhythm of the sea. "I need to speak with you about something, Michal."

Instantly attuned to her aunt's serious tone, Michal stopped, cringing inwardly. "Did I do something—"

"No, no. This is about me. Something that I've never told you." Sarah took a deep breath. "Something you deserve to hear." She began walking slowly again, and Michal matched her pace.

"Your questions have … have been hard because they've struck so close to my heart." Sarah glanced over at Michal, a surprising shyness about her now. "I'd just finished a master's degree when I fell in love. Oh, my. I was so in love."

Michal looked at her with wonder. "Who was he?"

"Oh, his name doesn't matter, since it was a stuffy family name, one he was really kind of embarrassed by. But from the moment I first met him, I called him CK." Sarah smiled, wistfully.

"Was he handsome?"

"Oh, my, was he ever. Tall, head full of dark curls, one of those jaws like Kirk Douglas." To Michal's blank look, she said, "Of course

you wouldn't know him. Well … CK was incredibly handsome. Take
my word for it, okay?"

"What was he like? Did he make you laugh?"

Sarah dug a big toe into a pile of shells, drawing out the story.
Clearly enjoying Michal's intense interest. "He was … he was a man
of such integrity, an attorney. A prosecutor. I'd go to court just to
watch him." She sought Michal's eyes then, for hers were lit with
a glow—the glow of love that was still there, after all these years,
Michal realized. "And yes, how he could made me laugh. Like the
time he tripped and fell into a mud puddle. And then just sat there,
splashing like a child, saying, 'Might as well enjoy it since I'm already
a drenched mess.'" Sarah laughed out loud at the memory, and
Michal laughed right along with her.

"But I fell in love with his heart, Michal—his heart for God, for
people. For his son."

"His son?"

"CK's first wife died in childbirth. When I first met them his
son was ten, and then later, after we married … well, I'll never forget
the first time he called me mom …" Sarah's voice broke, and she
stopped.

"What happened, Aunt Sarah? Did something happen to them?"
Unconsciously, Michal's entire body tensed as they stopped walking,
and she held her breath.

Sarah cupped a hand over her eyes, shielding them from the
setting sun reflecting off the ocean. "You know how it hurts to
look at a sunset like this? And yet at the same time … you want
to look because it's so glorious? And so you do, even though it's
painful?" Sarah turned her gaze to Michal, and Michal saw that

her eyes were filling with glistening tears. Tears also reflecting the brilliant glow off the water. "That's how my memories are, Michal. They're glorious and painful in the exact same moment." She swallowed, and Michal saw tears run down her freckled cheeks.

"We'd only been married six months—six wonderfully happy months—when CK got cancer. And in three months … he was gone. I was convinced it was all my fault. Because I hadn't obeyed God and gone to Ethiopia, like your grandmother and grandfather said I should have. See … I was planning to go when I met CK. Even had my plane ticket. And then … everything changed. He had an established career. And a young boy—a boy who I couldn't even think of sending to boarding school. I had no right to inflict that on him.

"So when CK died … I thought it was God punishing me, taking him like that, and so I … I just left CK's son, thinking— irrationally—that was best for him. I wanted to get away from him, before he suffered for my sin too. And so I went to Ethiopia." She hastily wiped the tears away. Closed her eyes and then took a deep breath before looking into Michal's eyes.

"I'd never planned to tell you any of this, Michal. I guess mostly because of my foolish pride, maybe. I don't know. But from your questions these last couple of days, I realized how much you needed to hear my story. Because I went to Ethiopia out of guilt, Michal. Guilt and hurt and despair. And cowardice—I can't leave out that. Going for those reasons was—" she shook her head vehemently, "— it was all wrong. I couldn't function. I couldn't sleep or eat or do anything—not even love those dear people. Because I hated myself.

All I knew was anger in those miserable days. And you know who else I was angry at?"

Michal shook her head.

"God. Oh, yes, I was angry at him, all right. For ruining my life. How I blamed him for everything that had gone so horribly wrong."

Michal sucked in her breath. She'd never heard anyone hint at such a sin, let alone say it out loud. Unconsciously, she took a step backward. And immediately, Sarah took a step toward her.

"So I tried to run from life again, Michal. Came back home, to the States. Where a godly counselor finally helped me find forgiveness and grace from a loving God. A God who slowly put my crumbled heart back together. And I made a vow, Michal, a vow that I keep to this day." Sarah made a fist, holding it out in front of her. "If I couldn't be in Ethiopia—because I eventually came to the conviction that I never was called to live there—then I would do all I could to send support to my family."

Sarah turned away then, appearing exhausted as her shoulders slumped beneath the weight of her story. Suddenly she sat down on the wet sand, motioning for Michal to join her. They both simply sat there, staring out at the waves rolling in, listening to the calming effects of the surf.

Michal ventured into the silence, offering softly, "Daddy says you send … a lot. I can tell he's pleased about that."

Sarah drew her finger across the sand. Writing MICHAL there. Michal began doodling too, beginning with STE.

"Michal, we all bear the scars of pain. Some are more obvious than others, but none of us gets through life without collecting a fair share. Your folks included." Michal stopped writing, her finger poised. "Those things they said to you—the reasons they wanted you to stop crying about going to boarding school? They were repeating the very same lines they'd heard when they were children.

"You see, hearing you cry brought back memories of their own pain. And then they just hurt all the more, knowing your suffering personally like they did. And the more you fought going, the greater their hurt. So in desperation, they threw out whatever would hopefully just make the pain stop. They never meant to be cruel, Michal. Never." Sarah reached over to put her hand on top of Michal's, where she tenderly rubbed the soft skin.

"Don't make a decision about returning to Ethiopia out of guilt or expectation, Michal. And don't run there in an attempt to escape from life—like I did. If you seek God, he will reveal his call for you. In his time. In his way." She reached up to smooth a stray curl from Michal's cheek. Tucked it behind an ear. "Can you trust in that?"

"Uh-huh. I think so."

"We'd best get back. Going to be dark soon."

Reluctantly, Michal followed Sarah's lead as they headed back toward the car. "A friend of mine used to say that a walk on the beach is never long enough," Sarah mused. "She was so right."

Typical of holidays, the remainder of the week flew by all too quickly for Michal. She and Sarah enjoyed doing whatever struck their fancy on any particular day. They spent more time on their boogie boards, but they also shopped at quaint little stores along the beach. They visited Sanibel Island to look for better shells, and browsed the farmer's market. And they spent a couple afternoons simply going on road trips—Sarah allowing Michal to drive the Corvette.

Though Sarah had gently probed about the young men in her life, Michal evaded the topic. Just the slightest mental drifting back to school instantly brought the images of Allistair and Stephen clearly to mind, making her stomach tighten in a knot. She felt near panic when she tried to understand her feelings toward either of the two, and any memories of the kiss produced a shiver that traveled down her spine.

They were enjoying a leisurely dinner in the Florida room the evening before Michal's departure when Michal felt a sense of urgency, realizing this was her last chance to broach the subject of men.

"Aunt Sarah?"

It was that tone again, and Sarah recognized it immediately. The veiled attempt to sound casual, as if discussing something of no real significance. Michal had used it to introduce professors' comments in class, her relationships with Beth and her siblings, and their continuing discussions about Ethiopia. Sarah smiled inwardly. "Hmm?"

They'd finished the chocolate ice cream that evening, a fitting finale for the week. Michal dawdled over the small amount left in her bowl, making it last as long as she could. "I wanted … um, to ask you about something. It's just something silly." Sarah resisted the temptation to jump into the silence. "There's these two guys."

"Uh-huh?"

"One's name is Stephen."

"I think you mentioned him earlier this week."

"He's really serious about his studies. Like I am."

"That's good. Shows responsibility and maturity."

"Yeah. But there's also this other guy …"

"Ha. There's the rub."

"His name's Allistair."

"Quite a name to live up to."

"He's a senior. And student body president."

"Definitely interesting."

Michal smiled. "And he … he's not at all what I thought he'd be like, Aunt Sarah. He confuses me. For example. Stephen has one of those serious-looking computer watches. But Allistair wears one with Mickey Mouse on it."

"Oh? Well, I kind of like the sound of this guy, Michal, with that kind of sense of humor. I'm a Mickey Mouse fan myself, you know."

Michal smiled but then immediately bit her lip, sobering. "I'm not gonna need to choose between them 'cause I just plan to stay friends with both, you know? And besides, until I figure out what God wants me to do …"

Sarah got up out of her chair, motioning for Michal to follow. "Come outside a minute. I want to show you something."

The pungent smell of the night air assaulted them with a burst of fragrances: jacaranda, gardenia, honeysuckle. The slightly damp yet sweet and salty smell of an evening near the gulf coast of Florida. It was perfectly clear out, not a cloud in the sky. And though Sarah's home was in a well-populated area, where the stars weren't as clear as they might have been, they were still abundantly evident.

Sarah lovingly put an arm around Michal's shoulders and pointed upward. "Look at all those stars. Beautiful, aren't they?"

Curious where this object lesson was going, Michal mumbled, "Mmm, sure are."

"There's this fascinating phenomena called averted vision. Notice how when you try to stare directly at the more faint stars you can't really see them? It's like ... when you try to look directly at them, they disappear."

"Yeah, I've noticed that before."

"Pick one of those stars. Shift your sight back 'n' forth, looking directly at it and then away from it. What do you notice about your peripheral vision?"

"I can see it again. Just barely, but it's definitely there. That's weird."

"Sometimes, Michal, discovering God's will is like looking at a star. Instead of staring directly at him, you need to pay more attention to your peripheral vision."

"Okay. So ... explain what you mean by that."

"There are so many evidences around you to help make decisions. Like the people in your life. Like chapel speakers. Or maybe not." She grinned mischievously and Michal shook her head. "Others might be professors. Friends too—special girlfriends. And sometimes ... sometimes it's even those creatures from another planet entirely—males. Ha." Michal laughed at her. "Other evidences are what you're studying and praying about. Your gifts from the Holy Spirit. Talents and interests you have. And there are the myriad of experiences happening around you—don't overlook those either. See, all these evidences are hovering, and they can help you know God's will for your life."

"Wise aunts included in the list?"

"Possibly." Sarah winked, but was instantly serious again. "The point is, Michal, all those things in your peripheral vision, so to speak, are there to inform you too. They're like a ... like a ..." She groped for the right words to portray her meaning. "Like a mine, I guess. With veins of gold. You need to seek them out … see what their value is to help you make the major decisions of life."

"Aunt Sarah, you know something I've never told Mom and Dad? Something I would love to do?" Michal ventured.

"What's that?"

"Be a teacher. I've always wanted to teach children, ever since I can remember." Her eyes filled with tears, blurring the stars. "But in a regular classroom with bright posters all over the walls. The ABCs along the top of the blackboard." She grew more animated with each addition. "The children's desks grouped in bunches … with welcome signs on each one. Signs I made out of all colors of construction paper."

Sarah folded Michal into a tighter hug. "You know, I've often wondered when a hope becomes an expectation. Hope starts out innocent enough. And then it slides all too easily into the other. Happens to all of us, I'm afraid. But at the same time, there's another voice you must listen to—what your heart's telling you. Listen to your own mind and heart. God will speak to you there, too. He's in the business of matching passions with gifts. Desires of the heart with answers to prayer."

They turned to gaze up into the sky again.

"Those two young men you were telling me about?"

Michal knew her aunt would give her wise advice about Stephen and Allistair. Was eager to hear which one she approved of.

"Your heart will give you that answer, too."

"But which one—?"

Sarah shook her head. "Oh now, darlin' Michal. This is more exciting than reading the most exciting novel ever. My saying anything would take all the fun out of watchin' you choose."

They laughed, holding onto each other as though one couldn't stand without the other's support.

Saying good-bye the next morning was wrenchingly difficult for both. Tears filled Michal's eyes, but Sarah skillfully directed her attention away from the separation toward the excitement of finishing her second semester, pointing out she'd soon be a sophomore rather than a mere freshman. And she focused on the relationships that awaited her, a commitment to help Beth, the fun of interacting with her suitemates, the exciting challenges Allistair and Stephen both presented.

"I love you so much," Michal whispered.

"And I love you too, my darlin' Michal." Sarah looked into her eyes, noticed a vulnerability and insecurity that made her hasten to add, "Call me anytime you need to, okay? Promise me that?"

"I promise."

Regretfully, Michal broke away from her aunt's reassuring embrace. And felt the insecurity even more keenly. A voice within whispered, *You're going to need those arms again. Soon.*

The dorm felt like an airport terminal on the busiest day of the year; it was so full of energy, suitcases, conversations, people. Everyone had a story from spring break she couldn't wait to tell.

Michal patiently waited for her turn to share—gathered with Beth, Samantha, Jenny, Ruth, and Jessica in their suite's lounge—but when she did she was equally exuberant, giving a full-body demonstration of riding a boogie board.

Only Beth seemed reserved, although she also told a few stories about her grandparents. How her Grandpapa Elliott—obviously suffering from some senility—called her Sandy the entire time, no matter how often she corrected him. She described how he'd laugh in embarrassment and then explain, "'Oh, Sandy. I'm losing my mind, I truly am.'"

Beth added, giggling, "It got so I just answered to Sandy. When Grandma would call me Beth, I'd sometimes catch myself thinking, 'Beth? Who's Beth?'"

Michal noted that the hollows in Beth's cheeks were gone, which pleased her. "Is your grandma a good cook? You look … healthier, Beth. You look good," she said. The other girls chimed in, agreeing.

"Oh, yeah. She fed me, all right. Fried chicken. Mashed potatoes. Ham. Butter beans. Pinto beans. Coleslaw. Biscuits."

"Aunt Sarah made biscuits almost every morning too," Michal interjected. "I think they're addictive."

There was a brief rap on the door. "Michal? Someone for you in the lounge."

The teasing started immediately. "Wonder who's here for you already, hmm?" and "Allistair maybe?—the guy she's never going to date again." Michal reddened. Considered dashing back into her room for a quick check in the mirror, but immediately thought better of it, knowing instinctively it would increase the teasing tenfold. So, consoling herself that she didn't care anyway, she resolutely started out the door, the teasing following.

"Tell him 'hello' for us, will you?"

"Don't forget to tell Allistair this is your last date."

"Why not greet him with a holy kiss?"

Which immediately sent them all into fits of laughter. Michal could hear their carrying-on all the way to the dorm's lounge when she pulled open the door.

Where she saw Stephen, sprawled on the couch. Punching buttons on the remote, exactly like before.

"Hey, Stephen. Good to see you." The passing thought *I wish it had been Allistair* flitted across her mind, immediately producing a wave of guilt. Which then made her want to make it up to him somehow. "Have a good break?"

Stephen didn't bother standing at her approach, but he tugged off the ugly hat, presenting the more pleasing visage again. "Oh, it was awesome. It really was." Michal sat down, and he inched closer to her.

"Well then … you must've done something pretty exciting?"

His face lit up. "My parents surprised me. We visited my brother—he's a doctoral student at George Washington University. We went to all kinds of neat places in DC. The Smithsonian— the aviation building is probably my favorite. And we visited the Holocaust Museum again. You know, every time I see those pictures of the people who died, I wonder about all those people who never got to … to fulfill their destiny, you know? You've been there, right?"

"No, I—"

"Oh, you've just got to go. It's amazing. This is my third time. I'm surprised your parents haven't …"

Feeling embarrassed, Michal said, "They're in Ethiopia, you know."

"Oh, yeah. Sorry. Well, anyway … I spent some time in the Library of Congress, too. Hours, as a matter of fact." Stephen was quiet a moment. When he did start speaking again, it came out in a rush. "Oh geez, I feel bad. I mean … your family has sacrificed by going to Africa, giving up everything for God's highest calling. And here I am, going on about seeing unimportant things like museums when you haven't ever had the opportunity to—"

Michal interrupted, "No, actually, see … I've had a few experiences you haven't had, Stephen."

He appeared surprised at the novel thought. "Yeah? Like what?"

Though Michal had quickly asserted the existence of privileges, she went momentarily blank. And then the thought struck her. "Well, like you've been to zoos, I'm sure?"

"Oh, yeah. In Philadelphia, but also the National Zoo in DC. San Diego's is super. Columbus, Ohio, has a great one. They're known for the apes exhibit. So, do they have a good one in Ethiopia?"

Michal grinned. "Actually, I meant that when you're in Ethiopia, you don't have to go to a zoo. The animals are all around you."

"Oh. Cool. Like what's there?"

"Colobus monkeys. They're amazing creatures. And I've seen ostriches in the wild."

"Well. I never thought of that. Well … hey, I'd better go. Gotta get unpacked. Mom sent so many snacks with me I brought a whole separate suitcase just for food. Bags of chips, candy bars, cookies, energy bars … you name it."

"My aunt sent food with me too. But it's all homemade. Things like brownies. Chocolate chip cookies. Snickerdoodles—I just love those, don't you?" Stephen abruptly stood up and she joined him. He was almost to the door, had turned his back to her when she added, "Well, it's back to the grind tomorrow."

He stopped, his eyes darting around the room. Surveying it for other students—and finding no one else present—he reached out and grabbed Michal to him. Without warning, like the last time, came the urgent kiss.

It took Michal's breath away. There was the sudden thrill of being in a man's arms, a tall and very good-looking man's arms. The intoxicating feel of being wanted in a physically sensual way. The almost giddy sense of being overpowered by someone who was attractive to her.

"I just know God wants us to enjoy this closeness," he muttered under his breath. "I've prayed about it, our intimacy." And just as abruptly as he'd taken her into his arms, he let her go. "See you later."

Michal stood there, blinking, realizing how strange she felt. Exposed. For others had come into the lounge by then, witnessing Stephen's kiss.

Deeply embarrassed, Michal could feel herself blushing profusely. And she fled.

By the time she got back to the suite, most of the students had scattered to get ready for classes the next day. But her own suitemates peered curiously at her.

"How was it?"

"Was Allistair glad to see you?"

Determined to give only the briefest of responses, Michal replied, "It wasn't Allistair, actually. It was Stephen."

Disappointed faces and groans all around.

"No. Really, it was good to see Stephen." Michal closed the door and immediately looked into Beth's questioning eyes. "Not you, too?"

"Michal. Stephen's no Allistair."

"No, he's not. Maybe he's ... better." Michal let it go, electing to entice Beth instead. "Aunt Sarah sent chocolate, Beth. Chocolate chip cookies. Brownies. Fudge even."

Her roommate's eyes widened considerably. "Get that box over here before I drool all over the place, will you?"

They laughed, Michal hoping the trip to her grandparents had been exactly what Beth needed. She handed Beth the box of treats, feeling the worry she'd carried for her roommate ease away.

It wasn't long, however, before a new set of worries settled in. Allistair didn't call. As late afternoon wore away to evening, she ate far too much chocolate in her anxiousness. Fidgeted. Began dropping things. Until Beth, exasperated, finally said, "Okay, spill it. What's up with you?"

Michal shrugged her shoulders. "I don't know."

"Oh, yeah, you do. It's about Allistair, isn't it?" Michal gave Beth a look of amazement. "Oh good grief. Don't look so surprised. Doesn't take a genius to see right through you. You really aren't so terribly hard to figure out, sorry to inform you."

"But honestly ... I don't know which one I like better. Stephen or Allistair. Which one I *should* like better."

Beth smirked and raised one eyebrow.

"What's that mean?"

"What-ever." She grabbed her pajamas, the bucket with her toiletries, and reached for the door. "As for me, I'm pooped. Time to get ready for bed."

Michal's eyes filled with tears from pent-up frustrations and deep disappointment—disappointment in Stephen for not even asking about her spring break. In Allistair, for not contacting her at all. In herself … for wanting. And she recognized her disappointment in God, too. For not being clearer. For not making anything … easy.

Oh, Lord, she prayed, *I can't determine your will concerning Ethiopia, can't make a decision, so it seems as though I'm just kind of … drifting that way. Like I'm riding the waves at the beach again, allowing a force underneath to simply push me along. Is this the way you intended for me to go back to Africa? By drifting?*

And that decision seems tied to me seeking out Stephen—or Allistair. I don't know what to do about them either. Everything's such a mess.

She glanced at the clock. Shook her head, willing herself to accept the fact that Allistair was not going to call. But as she gathered up her texts and notebooks to stuff into her backpack, she squeezed her eyes shut. Willing the threatening tears to accept the facts also.

The next morning—the Monday of the week leading up to Easter—Michal hit the alarm clock with even more venom than usual. She stared at the ceiling, thinking through the week that stretched before her. Lectured herself about expectations concerning Stephen. Even more so, Allistair.

The various ministry teams were scheduled to share about their trips in chapel throughout the week. Since Allistair's was the most important one sent out, his team was up first. With Allistair, of course, as the main speaker.

Maybe afterward, I can approach him, casually welcoming him back? And then she jerked the covers back, forced herself to get out of bed. *Get real, Michal. Unless he seeks you out first, there's no way you'll be talking to Allistair—ever again.*

She saw Beth was already up, noting again the positive changes in Beth since they'd returned to school.

As Michal and Beth walked to chapel, Michal vacillated between hope and discouragement—alternating from one to the other with nearly every step. Until she saw Allistair and Tiffany chatting away amicably with the other members of their team. They hovered around the front of the large auditorium, laughing with an easy and familiar banter.

When Allistair stepped up into the pulpit a few minutes later, Michal could barely look up at him because she was so afraid her longing would be blatantly obvious on her face. That all who glanced at her would surely see the hurt written there much too plainly. And when throngs of students huddled around Allistair afterward, Michal quickly abandoned any lingering thoughts of approaching him. Sending one last swift look of disappointment toward the happy group—with Allistair in the middle—she hurried to class.

After that morning, Michal saw Allistair often—going into chapel. In the bleachers at basketball games Michal attended, sup-posedly to see the games. In reality, hoping to bump into Allistair. And she observed him in the dining hall at nearly every meal. But he was generally with other seniors, Tiffany included. He'd wave pleas-antly at her when they caught each other's eyes, for he frequently seemed to be present in the circle of her radar—in her peripheral vision. He'd even offer a friendly, "Hey, Michal," when they passed in the hallways. But every encounter—from the briefest glimpse at a distance to the exchange of "Heys" in the hall—brought another stab to her heart. And the recognition that God had sent her at least one answer: Allistair had moved on.

Stephen, however, seemed to pop up nearly everywhere, though with no regularity or rhyme or reason. Michal, always caught off guard when he appeared, would offer a jolted "Oh, Stephen" type of response whenever he fell into step beside her. Strangely, he didn't ask her to study with him. Or to meet at any specific times or places, except for the evenings he'd show up in the lounge.

The two of them never developed what felt like normal and easy communication patterns—at least, not from Michal's vantage point. Instead, they shared an awkward and disjointed "How's it going?" … "Got a quiz tomorrow in New Testament" … "Chapel was so amazing today" communication style. More like a DVD when there's a problem with the disk: The scene's interrupted, and the digital picture breaks up into spastic squares. Michal's attempts at communicating with Stephen left her feeling exactly the same way. Jolted and interrupted, spastic even. And frustrated.

She couldn't shake the nagging feeling that she was missing something—but not like losing an object. It was more like someone abruptly changing the subject with no transition, jumping to another topic so quickly she was left feeling puzzled, wondering, *What? What are you saying?* Or when a book's missing a page, so the storyline doesn't fit together. So she'd argue and reason with herself, trying to banish the confusing, negative feelings. Listing reasons why God had worked it out this way, seeking proof of order and logic to her life. Ultimately, that it was right to be seeing Stephen.

But always there was the problem of Stephen's kisses—the confusing feelings they aroused. Stephen assured her repeatedly that he prayed about the two of them: about his need to learn to be intimate, how Michal was helping him. That God was answering his prayers for closeness. According to Stephen, their kissing was actually spiritual in nature.

Michal's thoughts and feelings on the matter, however, were pure bedlam. *Do I really like him kissing me?* she'd ask herself, walking back to her room, reaching up to aggressively wipe away any evidence of their intimacy. *Why do I feel flattered and fluttery inside, and yet repulsed at the same time?*

When idle thoughts about Allistair clouded her mind, she'd fall into a pattern of quizzing herself. *Are you only missing Allistair because you want what you don't have—because he's the one that got away? Focus on Stephen; work harder on your relationship with him. God's showing you his will. Like Aunt Sarah said, remember those influencing your life in your peripheral vision. And Stephen's the most prominent one there right now.*

On Good Friday, Michal repeatedly asked God to forgive her. For not concentrating on her studies like she should. For not keeping her vow to be singularly focused on getting her degree so she could get back to Ethiopia as soon as possible. And finally, for her disloyalty to Beth, since they'd pledged to each other they would not get seriously involved with anyone—since that would take too much time from their studies. By Easter Sunday morning, Michal was so overwhelmed with guilt that she resolved, *Okay, no more Stephen. No more thinking about Allistair either. I'm totally done with this entire mess.*

The resolution lasted until Stephen smiled at her on Monday afternoon.

Weeks passed. Nearly every day Michal talked with Stephen— or rather, attempted to. Their conversations evolved into one-sided affairs consisting mostly of Stephen's solicitous attempts to teach her, as he would point out applications she should apply to her life. Lessons learned from chapel speakers, professors, and Stephen himself. Michal would nod. And agree, judging it was God's way of teaching her to submit.

The nighttime calls came regularly, announcing, "Someone to see you in the lounge." Her heart beating, sometimes she'd still naively hope it might be Allistair. Finding instead that it was always Stephen. They'd have another awkward, halting conversation. Another kiss combined with a "God's really blessing our intimacy, Michal" sort of comment before he'd bolt out the door, leaving her feeling a little emptier each time. With a vague longing for something she couldn't describe or put a name to.

Though Michal was puzzled why she and Stephen hadn't developed a close friendship, she assumed God's will was clear. She would simply follow Stephen's lead. Things were at least relatively settled in her heart and mind.

It was the second week in May, another night when Michal slept fitfully, the nightmare visiting her repeatedly. But it was more, too, odd noises in the night just beyond waking—a sense that things were off somehow.

The sound of a baby's cry awakened her.

She opened her eyes in the dim light of early morning, curious and confused. Looked over at Beth.

"Michal. Look what I found." Beth held out a squirming, mewling—it was too tiny and pathetic to be called a cry—baby toward her, a look of pure awe on her face.

Immediately jolted into full wakefulness, Michal sat upright and leaned over the bundle. Peered down into the pinched, red face. Took in the tiny fists that waved precariously about in the air, appearing to be looking for someone—or something—to blame for its predicament. A wispy thatch of wet hair—dark brown? It was too wet to tell—curled around its tiny head.

"What do you mean you found it?"

"Outside our window—I found it there. Didn't you hear it crying?"

Michal shook her head. As much to answer no as to shake off the sense she was still asleep and dreaming.

Beth hugged the baby against her chest, cradling it while she cooed, attempting to quiet its cries.

"We've got to call the resident advisor. What am I thinking?" Michal reached over to squeeze Beth's arm. "We've got to call 911, Beth. The baby has to be examined. Make sure it's okay. And they need to find its mother."

Beth rocked the baby, its cries subsiding somewhat.

"Beth. Are you listening to me?"

She gave Michal a glance of annoyance. "I'm trying to get her calmed down. And warm."

"Her? How do you know it's a she?"

Beth grinned. "I checked, silly. How do you normally tell?"

"But … does she have a diaper on?"

"No. Not really."

"Not really? What was she wearing when you found her? They might be able to tell who the mother is from those clues."

Beth mumbled something, holding the baby out from her, peering intently into the tiny face.

"Beth. Stop a minute and talk to me. This is serious."

Her head jerked up, the previous near ecstasy changed to irritation. "I know this is serious, Michal. But don't yell or you'll make her cry again. Can't you see I'm just trying to soothe her, make her feel loved? Where's your concern for her, anyway?"

Chastised, Michal was quiet a moment. "Sorry. But I'm going to use the phone in the lounge to call 911. And then the RA." She put on her robe, taking time to tie it securely. Assuming they'd be overrun with emergency personnel—all too quickly. "Times like this I sure wish one of us had a cell phone. Now, what do I tell them? Maybe you should call?"

"No. I'm not putting her down right now. Not after everything that—"

"Okay, okay. I'll do it. But come out in the lounge with me, just in case they ask something you need to answer, will you?"

But as Michal reached for the door, Beth still hadn't moved.

"Beth?"

"Go ahead and call. I'll be there in a sec."

Frustrated, Michal rushed to the phone and punched in 911. She was relieved to hear a calm voice on the other end.

"You've reached 911. What's the nature of your emergency?"

"My roommate—Beth Elliott's her name—just ... she just found a newborn baby outside our dorm room."

"What's your name, please?"

"Michal McHenry."

"Michal McHenry? Did I hear that correctly? Michal?"

"Yes, it's spelled M-I-C-H-A-L. But I'm a girl."

"That's fine, Michal. I just needed to get that straight. And what's your phone number there?"

She repeated it carefully and gave their address.

"That's McMaster's Bible College? Peterson Dorm. Seven three one Mill Street? Correct?"

"Yes, and we've got a newborn baby here. Someone left the poor thing outside."

"You said your roommate found the baby. Is the baby breathing normally?"

"She seems to be fine. I mean she's fussing and waving her hands around."

"What's her coloring like, Michal?"

"Her coloring? Well, she's kinda red. And pink."

"And your roommate's name is Beth Elliott?"

The dispatcher asked to speak with Beth, but when Michal beckoned for Beth to get on the phone, she shook her head, vehemently whispering, "Tell them I'm holding the baby. I can't just put her down."

Michal was relieved to finally hear sirens and—in a near panic at that point—said she had to hang up. That if she didn't call her resident advisor immediately she'd probably be in a lot of trouble.

"Okay, Michal. That's fine. I just needed to make sure we had the right address. Can you see the lights from the ambulance now?"

"Yeah. They're right here—just outside the main entrance."

"Great. Call your dorm advisor. And thank you, Michal."

"Thank you." Michal punched in the RA's number. She picked up on the first ring, alarm apparent in her voice. "Yes?"

"Miss Hamilton, I'm sorry to bother you, but—"

"What's happened? Is someone hurt?" Her questions came out in a rush, and Michal could hear her climbing out of bed. "Who is this?"

"Michal McHenry. And no, no one's hurt. But my roommate, Beth, found a newborn baby. Outside our window." By then, many of Beth's suitemates were awake. Alarmed by the sirens and lights, they began peppering Michal with questions too. Michal tried to wave them off while continuing to explain to Miss Hamilton. "No, Beth's okay. I'm sorry, Miss Hamilton, for not calling sooner—"

"Michal, what's going on?"

"You'd better just come to our suite. I've got to go let the paramedics in."

Michal hung up, frantically motioned Samantha and Jenny toward her room. "Go see Beth. Ask her. I've got to go open the outside door."

By the time she got back—followed by a burly man and an efficient-looking woman carrying various items of equipment, including a stretcher—Beth was sitting calmly on a chair in the lounge. Surrounded like a Madonna by Jenny, Samantha, Jessica, and Ruth. All were oohing and aahing at the bundle Beth still held clutched against her chest.

"Ladies, would you mind stepping back, please?" the woman asked. "My name's Sharon. This is my partner, Will." The girls moved away from the baby—hovering in the lounge so they could continue to observe the developing drama—but Beth didn't even bother looking up, she was so enraptured by the tiny life she held.

"Beth? Is that your name?"

She nodded, barely acknowledging Will's question.

"We need to take the baby in a minute here, Beth. Need to check her out."

No response from Beth this time. Michal noticed Beth had wrapped the baby in her ragged quilt. It was far too big and hung down onto the floor, bunching at Beth's feet.

They continued to pull out equipment. Graciously giving Beth a few moments to collect herself, Michal assumed. It was apparent—as the paramedics shot each other concerned looks—they didn't want a tug-of-war over their miniature patient.

Michal was about to ask why they'd brought in such a big stretcher when Sharon soothingly asked, "Beth? Will you hand me the baby now, please?"

Beth looked up at the paramedic, but her gaze was unfocused. Confused. "What?"

Sharon held out her arms, palms extended. "Please give me the baby, Beth. We need to examine her, okay?"

Finally Beth appeared to understand. Gently placed the bundle into Sharon's waiting arms. Separating the tiny body from the giant bunting, Sharon lifted the naked baby from the quilt and placed her on the stretcher. Which immediately brought forth a loud, angry cry from the little one.

Beth's arms jerked toward her reflexively, while Sharon's arm shot out in reaction to Beth, blocking her from touching the baby—both actions occurring as though rehearsed. Will and Sharon exchanged another quick look.

The team worked in tandem, quickly taking vitals. Speaking quietly, efficiently moving from one task to the other. All while the baby continued to cry, kicking its legs in protest. Waving its arms around as though attempting to push away the offending instruments.

"Is she going to be all right?" from Miss Hamilton, whom Michal was surprised to hear. She hadn't noticed she'd joined them in the lounge, already crowded with too many. "I'm Jane Hamilton, the resident advisor for this dorm. If I can help with anything, please let me know."

"It would be best if you accompanied Beth. To help … answer questions."

Miss Hamilton glanced toward Beth, assuming they'd meet eyes in agreement. But Beth's full attention was focused solely on the baby. As though nothing else in the room existed.

"Yes, of course. Beth, you should go get dressed."

No answer. Miss Hamilton caught Michal's eye then. Motioned her head toward Beth, indicating she was to get Beth's attention. When Michal reached out to put her hand on Beth's shoulder she could feel tremors moving through her roommate's body. And even at that slight touch, Beth felt unbelievably cold.

"Beth? Beth, you need to get dressed, okay?" Michal tightened her grip, shaking her just a bit. "Miss Hamilton will go with you to the police station, okay? To make a report about finding the baby."

She turned toward Michal, apparently still confused, acting as though she barely recognized her.

"Come on, Beth. I'll help you."

Beth finally stood. Instantly, Michal recoiled at the blood pooled on the chair.

"She's bleeding." Samantha gasped, pointing.

For a moment, everyone froze in position. All eyes riveted on the bright red puddle on the chair, dripping onto the floor. And then everyone's gaze shifted toward Beth. To her face. Which still focused only on the baby, who was crying more softly now. Mewling like a kitten again, her mouth working, making barely audible sucking noises.

Will and Sharon communicated through a mere glance. Responded as though a manual had prepared them for this type of emergency. Quietly, Sharon wrapped up the baby in a white blanket they'd brought in with them, scooping her up into her arms. Will reached toward Beth, gently guided her toward the stretcher, helping her to lie down.

"But what's the matter with her? Is she ... will Beth be all right?" Michal's voice rose in intensity with each question. Still unknowing. Searching for the connection between Beth, bleeding, nearly in shock. And the baby's faint cries.

Until realization dawned.

Michal exhaled, her words of not much more substance than air. "It's hers. The baby—it's Beth's baby, isn't it?"

The paramedics worked over Beth, neither bothering to look up; they were so intent upon checking the mother. Covering her with another blanket. Getting ready to insert an IV. Chatting with their dispatcher, another at the hospital, alerting them of their imminent arrival—with baby. And mother.

Time passed as Michal watched the scene unfold, but she hadn't been aware of it. She glanced over at her suitemates. Saw them staring

at Beth. Looks of shock and—was it fear? Or the stark prick of reality
causing something closer to horror?

Miss Hamilton had already changed into street clothes and was
planning to accompany Beth. It dawned on Michal she should go
too—to comfort and support her roommate. *My roommate?* The
thought rushed through her mind. *Is she really the same person I said
good night to last night?* As she tugged off pajamas and pulled on jeans
and a shirt, her thoughts continued to race. Nothing made sense.
Absolutely nothing.

When she opened her door, they were getting ready to transport
Beth. The baby was back in Beth's arms, and the paramedics had just
lifted the stretcher. Miss Hamilton held the door as they proceeded
through.

"Miss Hamilton? I want to go … I should be there. I want—"

But the paramedics were shaking their heads. "I'm sorry. Michal,
is it? But only one can come. It needs to be someone in authority.
Someone who can contact Beth's parents."

"But they're—"

Miss Hamilton waved a sheaf of papers. "I have all the information, Michal. We'll notify them. Don't worry about it—or about
Beth. I promise we'll take good care of her." Her cell phone rang,
and she grabbed it quickly. "Yes? Oh, yes, Dean Mitchell. We're on
our way to the hospital now …" her voice fading as she followed the
entourage.

It was a strange and sad procession that moved down the hallway.
Beth and baby on the stretcher, carried by the now-silent paramedics. Along the sides of the hall, students had gathered in doorways
to watch, trying to take in the bizarre scene. Whispers exchanged,

wide-eyed glances stolen, conveying curiosity and embarrassment. Others simply stared without hesitation, assessing the situation, pronouncing instant judgment. Some merely shook their heads, silent, not able to absorb the reality before them.

Michal watched for a moment from her own suite's doorway, indecisive. Exchanged vacant looks with Ruth and Jessica. Samantha and Jenny had retreated to Jenny's room, where soft crying could be heard. Girls from adjoining suites flocked to Michal, throwing questions at her. Asking and demanding answers she didn't know, could respond to only with raised shoulders and a shake of her head.

Fending them off, taking one last look at the chaos around her, Michal made a decision. They were just getting ready to go out the main doors when Michal caught up. Reached out to touch Beth's elbow, making some sort of connection with this person who suddenly felt like a stranger to her.

"Beth, I'm … I'm so sorry." Tears instantly flooded Michal's eyes. She felt wretched. "I'm so sorry I didn't know. I had no idea. But if you'd told me, I would've helped you." She walked beside the stretcher. Attempting to stay alongside Beth as the paramedics skillfully maneuvered through the doors.

Beth looked up at Michal. Haunted eyes, appallingly white skin, her mouth limply falling open. But no words came out, no explanation. She looked down at the baby in her arms, hugged her closer.

And then they were gone. Michal simply stood there, watching them load her into the ambulance and drive away, sirens blaring and lights flashing. Tears began coursing down Michal's cheeks until she erupted into sobs. Was oblivious to the other students who gathered in curiosity—many men among them. They pointed, whispered among themselves, speculated.

Michal looked up through her tears to see Allistair standing before her. He touched her lightly on the arm. Softly asked, "Michal, are you okay?"

She shook her head, covering her face with her hands. Felt Allistair pull her into his comforting arms, heard his heart beating against her cheek. He was warm and secure and comforting. For those few moments, some of the crushing pain dissolved away in his embrace.

Finally, he held her away from him so he could see into her face. "Are you okay? I was afraid you were going to pass out for a moment there."

Michal nodded, attempted to control her sobs. Wiped away the tears from her soaked cheeks. Noted that she'd left a wet spot on Allistair's shirt, where he'd held her tightly against him. "It's Beth. She—"

"I heard. You had no idea at all?"

She shook her head, feeling a new surge of tears push at her eyes. "Allistair, how could I not know? And why didn't she tell me? It's my fault—my fault it happened this way."

"Michal, no. You can't blame yourself. Beth chose to hide her pregnancy—from everyone." He ran a hand through his hair, tousled and uncombed from just getting out of bed. He'd immediately rushed to her to check how she was handling the crisis. "Cases like this, Michal? They say the pregnant woman is in such deep denial that even she doesn't admit she's expecting. So there's no way she would've told you—no matter how close you might be."

"But how?" She wrapped her arms across her chest, sobbing openly again, and stared up into the dawn of the morning sky. "I didn't want to see it. That's the real explanation here. Beth didn't trust me because I wasn't trustworthy. And I didn't want to know the truth, Allistair."

Michal gave a cynical laugh then, the obvious pain making Allistair wince. "Oh, yeah. Check out spiritual Michal, earnestly seeking God's will for her life. While my roommate—who's only inches away from me—is able to hide the fact that she's giving birth? What a picture of my pathetic life. My roommate's in agony—and I'm asleep."

She turned to go back into the dorm, but Allistair grabbed her arm. "Michal, please—please stop blaming yourself. Beth's responsible for her own choices. This has no bearing on your life … your choices. What God wants you to do."

Michal boldly turned to face him, her eyes flashing. "Oh, but you're wrong, Allistair. I think God is speaking to me through this, loud and clear. And now it's my job to listen. To finally listen." She resolutely walked away, allowing the door to slam shut behind her.

Walking past groups of women—some reaching out to pat her arm, whispering an "I'll be praying for you" type of encouragement— Michal said nothing in response. Imagined she felt a burning sensation each time someone touched her. When she entered her suite, the silence—compared to the earlier commotion—was nearly unbearable. Only Ruth remained in the lounge, arms crossed before her, hunched over, staring at the floor. Hearing Michal, she muttered, "I just can't believe it. How could we not …?"

Michal didn't respond, closing and locking the door behind her. She nervously glanced around, wondering what she should do. She knew Beth's bed needed to be stripped. That the sheets and blanket and quilt all needed to be washed. Manual work, using her hands, keeping herself busy, doing something—anything so that she wouldn't need to think. Making the decision to skip chapel and classes for the entire day, Michal rolled up her sleeves and went to work.

After putting the first of several loads into a washer, she vigorously scrubbed the mattress. Then she tackled the chair in the lounge where Beth had bled, followed by the floor. It wasn't until Michal was folding Beth's quilt that she felt the first stab of hunger, heard her stomach grumble in protest. Glancing up at the clock, she was surprised to see it was past dinnertime.

Flopping down on her bed, feeling the effects of the physical work without any food, Michal realized anew how wretched she felt. And how incredibly alone.

A soft knock at her door caused her to jump. "Yes?"

"It's me. Sam. Jenny, too. Are you all right, Michal?"

Michal took a quick glance in her mirror, wasn't surprised to see how disheveled she appeared. She was running a hand through her hair when she opened the door.

"Hey."

"We thought we should give you some space today. Just let you be alone for a while. But then we got worried about you."

Michal smiled, halfheartedly. "I'm okay."

"You haven't eaten anything, have you?" from Ruth.

"No. I just—" And then the tears came again, unbidden. Samantha and Jenny immediately put their arms around her. Ruth and Jessica joined in, and they all clung to each other, weeping, finding consolation in simply being together. They had just settled into comfortable positions in the lounge when the call came for Michal. "You have a visitor in the lounge."

For a moment, she considered not going. Her guilt was nearly choking her, and she knew instinctively Stephen wouldn't help. That he could potentially make it even worse. But she stood, resolutely telling herself, *I'm submitting to God's will. Isn't it about time I really listen?*

Ruth grabbed Michal's arm, forcefully warning, "I don't think you should … Michal, don't go to him just now. He's not … he's not good for you, can't you see that?"

Michal laughed the laugh that wasn't one again. Ruth winced in response. "My Aunt Sarah told me a story about running from life. And you know what? That's what I've been doing—avoiding life. I'm merely a bystander. A cowardly observer. I think it's about time that I jump in and … begin acknowledging the realities around me. And embrace them."

"So literally?" Sam muttered under her breath. After a piercing glance from Michal, the room went totally silent.

"I'll be back soon." And then Michal stiffened, held up her chin as she walked out.

Stephen was standing by the door, and instead of his customary removal of his hat and smile, he gave her a reproachful look. "I heard about Beth. Is it really true?"

Michal put her hands in her pockets, stared down at the floor like a guilty child.

"I can't believe it. How could you not know she was nine months pregnant? That she was having a baby in your room?"

She shrugged. Stammered, "I … I don't know. I just—"

Stephen took her arm and directed her to the outside door. Pulled Michal out onto a small patio bordered by thick bushes and a strand of trees that provided nearly complete privacy. He walked away from her and paced back, shaking his head the entire time. "This is simply unbelievable, Michal. You need to learn from this. We need to figure out what God's trying to teach you." He stopped within inches of her, close enough for Michal to feel his breath on her face. "What do you think that is?"

Michal was instantly intimidated, caught off guard by Stephen's question. More so, his proximity. "I don't know. I've been trying to figure that out all day."

He put his arms tightly around her waist, and she could feel her heart begin to pound. She struggled to breathe, feeling like she couldn't take in enough air.

"Figure out what?"

"My aunt said finding God's will isn't like this little point— something so small that's hard to find. And if we don't find that tiny little thing, then we're out of God's will and—"

"I don't think your aunt reads the Bible very much. That's not what I've been taught by lots of preachers." He tightened his hold on her waist, pulling her even closer. She could smell his scent. Feel the heat of his body pressed against hers and the need to breathe in tandem with him, they were so tightly wedged together.

The combination of not eating, working all day, and her sudden anxiety all combined to make Michal feel nauseous. She attempted to push away from Stephen, pleading, "I don't think we should be here, Stephen. I don't want to … please, let's go back inside, okay?"

She attempted to keep her voice lighthearted. Casual. But she was beginning to feel frightened. Of Stephen. And what he intended to do.

"I know this is God's will for you and me, Michal." As purpose-fully laidback as she had attempted to be, Stephen was the exact opposite. His intensity was an autonomous, demanding force. "I've been praying about it. You need to trust me more." He moved one hand up her back, worked it beneath her blouse. The other inched its way up the front.

"Stop it," she cried, tears stinging her eyes for the second time that day. But as Michal attempted to push him away, she discovered just how strong Stephen actually was.

"Don't tell me you haven't wanted this. And God wants—"

Out of nowhere, it seemed, powerful arms reached out to grab Stephen by the shoulders, lifting him up and throwing him out and away from her. Where he tumbled into the bushes at their feet.

Out of breath from the push of adrenaline, exertion, and fury, Allistair spat at Stephen through clenched jaws, "Now get out of here." Seething with rage, he added, "And if I ever catch you touch-ing her again ... if I ever see you near Michal again ... I promise you you'll regret it forever." His voice was thick with the threat. "Have I made myself perfectly clear?"

Stephen nodded, meekly. Scrambled to his feet and ran off, never looking back at either of them.

Michal, crying still, her legs suddenly weak, nearly crumpled to the ground when Allistair reached out to catch her. He held her around the waist, supporting her, but before he could open the door to the lounge, she stopped. Shook her head vehemently. "Don't. I can't go back in there yet. I'm just so ashamed."

"Michal, I never trusted that guy. I've been—truthfully, I've been keeping an eye on you because I was afraid he'd pull something like this." He retrieved a rumpled tissue from his back pocket, handed it to her. "Didn't your father warn you about creeps like him?"

She blew her nose. Shook her head no.

Allistair looked uncomfortable, glancing away from her wounded look. "When I first got the word that you two were … involved … well, I backed off. The first night back after spring break? I was planning to come see you when I heard about … his kissing you." He shrugged his shoulders. "I figured you'd made your decision. But I still felt like I needed to watch out for you. To keep an eye on him. Boy, am I ever glad I did."

Suddenly aware of his arm around her still, Michal backed away from his touch. "I know now I've been wrong about everything, Allistair. I failed my roommate. I thought Stephen was a godly person, the man I was supposed to have in my life." Her voice broke, and she cleared her throat, continuing, "And I thought I was this godly woman … a woman who … who was following the Lord's call back to Africa. What a joke." Her voice rose hysterically as she backed farther away from Allistair. As though she had an infectious disease, was intent upon preventing his catching it. "I'm the joke here."

"Michal, you can't—"

"I know now I'm not fit for the mission field."

"Please don't do this, Michal. Don't make a decision when you've just been through two horrible situations. It's been an unreal day.

Promise me you'll wait and talk with me about all this tomorrow, okay?"

She wavered. Stared into his eyes and wanted. So much. And then, determining to lie—to get away from him before she weakened—she nodded.

Allistair cradled her arm in his hand, gently and patiently guided her in. "Come on. You need to get a good night's sleep. I'll meet you tomorrow? Before chapel?"

"Sure." *It gets easier to lie once you start,* she thought.

His eyes were so deep, full of concern for her. Once again, she almost gave in. Knew she had to go right away, before she lost the courage to do what she had to.

"Well, good night then, Michal."

Taking him in, memorizing the wave of his hair, the crystalline blue of his eyes, the strength of the line of his jaw. The question struck her, *What would it feel like if Allistair kissed me?* She dismissed the wistful musing, but tucked every miniscule and cherished impression into her heart, knowing she would never forget how he looked at her that moment.

"Good night, Allistair." She started to weep again. And so she turned and fled. Not daring to look back, knowing that if she did, she would fly back into his arms.

The next morning, Ruth rapped on Michal's door. She'd heard no stirrings from the room and, becoming concerned, tried the knob. Discovered it was unlocked, and opened the door a crack to peek in.

Michal's bed was bare, the mattress particularly ugly now that it was stripped of the lovely star quilt. Panicking, Ruth checked the desks. Beth's still had textbooks and various items scattered across it. But Michal's was completely cleaned off, not even a pencil left behind. Jerking open the closet, Ruth noted Michal's meager assortment of clothes had vanished—and a drawer yanked open proved her dresser was empty also.

"Sam. Jenny, Jess—come here, quick."

"What?"

"What's wrong?"

When they entered the doorway, Ruth merely pointed to Michal's star quilt. It had been folded neatly and placed on Beth's bed, along with her other washed sheets, blanket, and the raggedy quilt. Attached to it was a note.

> I hope you can find it in your heart to forgive me, Beth. I wasn't the friend you deserved. Remember me when you wrap yourself in Aunt Sarah's quilt. I know she would've wanted you and your baby to have it. Love from Michal.

They looked mournfully at each other, sharing the ache of yet another loss.

Michal sat on the same bus she'd taken to Fort Myers before, though when she boarded this time, the driver noted Michal not for her joyous buoyancy and gregarious nature. Instead, he took in the red-rimmed eyes, her agitation, and how she ducked her head to avoid his eyes as she handed him her already damp, rumpled ticket. And then, pointedly ignoring anyone already seated, Michal hurriedly made her way to the very back seat. Where she slumped down and sat with her forehead resting against the windowpane, staring out with unfocused gaze.

As the driver watched Michal in the rearview mirror, he thought to himself, *Another down-'n'-outer, for sure, lookin' pretty desperate. Wonder what she's running away from? Or if she's in trouble?* He shook his head and sighed audibly. *And it's such a nasty morning, too. Bad weather … homeless—or worse passengers. I'm not thinkin' this day is gonna go well.* But he turned the key in the ignition, bringing the old bus to sputtering life, intent upon driving his daily route.

Michal sniffed loudly and wiped at her nose with the frayed cuff of a worn sweatshirt. At this point, she was numb, her feelings and thoughts so blurred that she hoped—assumed—sleep would rescue her from any blips of coherency. But then the sharp memory of the pungent smell of Beth's pooled blood came to mind … the feeling of Stephen's hands crawling all over her … the look of deep compassion on Allistair's face … and she nearly cried out loud. Instead, she leaned over, jamming the palms of her hands into her eyes hard enough to create vivid splashes of color against her eyelids. Until the pressure and pain made her stop.

She leaned back against the seat again, willing, insisting that sleep come to her. But as the bus rumbled through the city and ever closer to the bridge, the storm's increasing intensity would not let her body relax. Instead, the thunder and lightning constantly jostled

Michal, causing her to jump every time a particularly close strike highlighted the inside of the bus—acting like a spotlight on her and her alone, it seemed.

When a rumble of thunder and simultaneous flash of lightning felt like they actually pushed the lumbering bus sideways, Michal peered out the window, attempting to see ... anything. And then her heart leapt into her throat, for she realized they were beginning to fall—*Into the bay?* her mind screamed. Or did she cry it out loud? Suddenly, the entire bus erupted with screams of sheer terror. They were falling ... people were falling ... men, women, children. All tumbling about the bus as it fell headlong into the black depths below.

Only Michal was not floundering about, for she desperately clutched the back emergency exit handle, fiercely determined to not let go. Once again she was highlighted—by the bright beams of a Mercedes falling right behind the bus. But this time, she didn't cower from the light; instead, she sought out its glow as if it were a lighthouse. And she were the lost one following the luminous flare to safety.

ENDINGS

A Friday morning in May 2009

Captain Luis and his men stood like dumb statues, their limbs rigid with shock. Their minds refused to believe what was before their eyes, so they merely stared—mouths gaping at the sight of the broken roadway perched precariously above and the spot where the car, van, and bus had simply disappeared into the gulping, angry gulf below. Pleading with God that no others would dive from the precipice.

Another crash of thunder resounded. A flash of light followed, highlighting the surreal terror before them. It was enough to startle the captain into action—paralysis followed by a sudden burst of energy. "I'm going to send out the Mayday," Luis called out to his men. As he turned to run back to the pilothouse, he frantically shouted the command, "Jaurez! Everyone! I want every light we have pointed in the same direction. Where the vehicles went in—flood the entire area with light."

Jaurez needed to yell back as the pouring rain was still pounding out a loud, steady drumbeat. "But Cap'n—there's no way any of them—"

"Just do it, Jaurez. Now. I want the area thoroughly searched."

Jaurez shook his head at the senseless exercise, but who was he to argue with the captain? If Captain Luis was assuaging his conscience, then so be it. He set to work, directing his men to fetch stowed search lights and lanterns, flashlights. Anything they could think of to light the area where the doomed had plunged off the bridge to their certain deaths in the water below.

Meanwhile, Captain Luis ran into the pilothouse and grabbed his radio. In a voice filled with stark terror, he shouted into the mike, "Mayday. Mayday. Coast Guard, we have a Mayday. Coast Guard, we have a Mayday."

"Vessel calling Mayday. This is the United States Coast Guard, St. Petersburg, Florida." The operator's calm, measured answer was in juxtaposition to the captain's utter panic. "What is your position and the nature of your distress?"

"This is a Mayday. The Skyway Bridge is down. Get emergency vessels out to the bridge. This is an emergency. Stop the traffic on the Skyway Bridge. The bridge is down. I repeat, the bridge is down!" As Luis spoke the horrendous truth of the accident, his voice broke. "We've got vehicles in the water. We'll have more if the bridge traffic isn't stopped immediately. We're searching the water for survivors, but we're disabled. Send vessels to assist."

Overhead, miraculously, traffic had stopped. An alert driver noticed something was wrong, that the traffic ahead of him seemed to disappear. So he'd skidded to a stop on the slick pavement, accidentally—but fortunately—straddling and blocking both lanes of traffic. Managing to bring his large truck to a complete halt just a few feet before the pavement simply ended.

Those directly behind the truck braked quickly enough to keep from crashing into him, but several other vehicles behind them were unable to do so, causing a chain reaction. Though the drivers were angry about the damage to their vehicles and the delay, they had no idea of the tragedy they'd been spared.

Ignorant of this miracle above, Jaurez and his men repeatedly glanced up at the gaping hole. Solemnly crossing themselves, they prayed no more vehicles would plunge into the depths and turned their full attention toward those already in the water. Obediently following Captain Luis's command, despite their conviction of its futility.

Finally, the weather began to calm, nature's tantrum abating. The rain slowed to a drizzle, more annoying than dangerous. Despite the continued heavy cloud cover, the crew was encouraged to see more light in the east. The coming of dawn. Darkness had brought them destruction and death; they breathed a sigh of relief to see it diminish.

Morales, a seasoned member of the crew, leaned forward, straining to see into the water. He gave Jaurez a puzzled look, shaking his head in wonder. "It's not possible …" he mumbled.

"What? What's that?" Jaurez threw back at him, irritated.

"Did you hear—?"

A faint cry, carried on the sea breeze. Heartrending and plaintive.

"Mommy!"

Jaurez jerked forward, extending his body toward the source of the sound. Called out over his shoulder, "Morales, did you hear that?"

A look of amazement moved over Morales's features. His mouth dropped open. "I heard it. It can't be—but it sounds like a child."

"Stay right where you are, Morales," Jaurez instructed. He was pumping adrenaline now, every fiber in his being intent on finding survivors. Clicking into emergency drill procedure, he barked out, "Don't move your eyes from that spot—not even for a moment. Everyone—direct all the lights where the cry seems to be coming from. Where Morales is pointing. Anyone—John. Grab the life ring."

Morales kept his eyes peeled, while John hurriedly brought the ring to Jaurez. The two of them checked the strength of the rope's knot on the ring, tying the other end to a secure post on the *Wilder Wanderer*. "Is there anything—can you actually see anyone out there, Morales?"

"Mommy!" The mournful sound floated to them again, like a ghost gliding across the waves.

"Good Lord above," Morales whispered, his voice choking with awe. "There. Over there." Pointing, shouting, and nearly losing his balance in his excitement. "I see two—there's two—no, I'm countin' three heads bobbin' in the water. Gimme the life ring. Gimme the ring!"

Jaurez mechanically handed the ring to him, his gaze focused on the jutting waves. Squinting, he asked, "Where? I can't see a blamed thing out there but water. Morales, there's no way that … God in heaven," he suddenly muttered, crossing himself again. "If they're not ghosts, then they're angels sent by God. Get that life ring to 'em, Morales. Them poor souls. We gotta get 'em outta there, now."

Regretfully, he tore his eyes away from the bobbing heads, barking out, "Whatever you do, don't let them outta your sight. I'll be right back—going to tell the captain. Tell him to alert the

Coast Guard—we've got survivors." Before hurrying off, he grabbed Morales's arm, stared intently into his eyes. "God be with your throw, man."

All the crewmen stood with Morales along the bow, their eyes going back and forth from Morales to the survivors who appeared so small and fragile in the vast waters. Pointing, shouting advice and directives to the man entrusted with the all-important throw. Morales took a deep breath, then tossed the ring. Only to watch the wind catch it, pulling it far right.

"Get it upwind of them, Morales," a crewman offered, his tone like a reverent prayer. "If they's to have a chance, you've gotta get it just so."

Hand over hand on the rope, Morales frantically pulled the ring back to him. For a moment, he clutched it in his hands, lifted his eyes to heaven—offering a prayer. He drew back muscled arms and heaved it out over the waves. Only this time, he'd turned the direction of his body, pivoting left. The ring appeared to be in slow motion as they all watched it sail out and away from them. Miraculously, it landed a couple of feet upwind of the three. And they all watched breathlessly as a small hand reached out to grasp the ring, pulling it toward them.

They had it.

On deck, a raucous cheer went up. Jaurez and Captain Luis joined the jubilant crew, Luis shaking his head at the apparent miracle. "The Coast Guard's on her way," he said.

"Shouldn't we launch the *Wilder*'s dinghy? Try to get to them?" Morales asked. "We can't lose 'em now." He didn't take his eyes off the survivors, not even to acknowledge his captain's presence.

"There," Captain Luis shouted, his extended arm pointing through the haze hovering over the water. A reverberating blast of a horn announced the arrival of the Coast Guard vessel, its bow coming into view from the opposite side of the bridge.

"This is the captain of the Coast Guard," a voice called out through a loudspeaker. "We're coming to get you. A crew is on its way now. Hold on."

The crew quickly lowered the ship's rescue boat and made their way toward the survivors. As they grew closer, they could hear a child's voice, sobbing, nearly hysterical.

Finally pulling up next to them, they looked down to find two women and the child: a girl, her arms in a stranglehold around the neck of a woman with blood streaming from a gash on her forehead, and next to them, a younger woman. All three locked eyes onto the faces of their rescuers, blinking in shock, skin deathly white.

"Are you real?" the young woman asked.

"Ma'am, we're from the Coast Guard. And I can assure you we're quite real."

The crew reached to pluck the child first, the woman she was clinging to eager to hand the little one up to the rescuers. Then they pulled the two women into the boat, giving special care to the one with the wound, and wrapped them all in heavy blankets.

The child scrambled away from her rescuer, flinging herself back onto the woman's lap, desperate not to be separated from her. A kindly crew member wrapped a third blanket around them both, binding them together.

"What's your name, little one?" he gently probed. "Can you tell us your name?"

Wet hair plastered to her small skull, lips blue and teeth chattering, she whispered, "Aubrey."

He turned to the woman holding her with the same questioning look. One of the crew had already staunched the flow of blood; a bandage covered her wound. "And you are?"

"I'm Fran. Fran Thomason. My son. My husband. They're still out there somewhere. You've got to—you are looking, aren't you? Because they're still out there, in that awful water. Please, you've got to find them." She began sobbing, all the while hugging Aubrey to her. Needing to fill her empty arms. *Charlie* ...

"Ma'am, I promise you. We will continue to search. And we will find any survivors. But just now we need to take care of you. Are you hurt anywhere else?" To Fran's no he continued, "Are you sure there's nothing else we need to attend to? On you or the child?" She shook her head again and closed her eyes. Grasping the little girl as tightly as the child grabbed onto her. He turned his attention to the other woman. "And you are?"

"Michal. Michal McHenry."

The crew exchanged looks, a tacit agreement passing among them to wait, allow others to ask more questions later. When the survivors were carried and handed carefully up to others on the deck of the ship—the rescue crewmen shared the little they'd learned—the captain was eager to glean more information. News of the accident was now public, and he knew family and friends would be anxiously awaiting word of any survivors.

But first they needed emergency care, so Fran, Aubrey, and Michal were placed on stretchers—Fran and Aubrey sharing one, since no one cared to attempt separating the two—and carried to the ship's medical quarters. Once they'd been thoroughly examined, the doctor rebandaged Fran's head, the only wound of any significance in comparison to other minor scrapes and bruises. To the doctor's complete astonishment, he found nothing of consequence on Aubrey and only deep bruises on Michal's hands—nothing evidencing the disaster they'd just survived. Lastly, he started intravenous fluids for all three, though not without a pitiful cry from Aubrey at the prick of the needle. The doctor's heart wrenched at the sound.

The ship's personnel had already contended with Aubrey's hysterical demands to not be separated from Fran during the time it took to get them into dry clothes, to complete their examinations, to begin their IVs. Not until she was allowed back on Fran's lap did Aubrey begin to calm down, clutching Fran every bit as frantically as before. Finally, his ministrations to the two women complete and Aubrey's cries reduced to an occasional hiccup, the doctor nodded toward his captain.

Kneeling down on one knee before them, Captain Howard removed his cap, revealing a downy ring of white hair. He had kindly light blue eyes and a friendly smile, both of which he used to great effect when needed. He asked Fran, "Mrs. Thomason, is it? And this is your daughter, Aubrey?"

"No. Actually, she's—" Fran shook her head, and immediately winced at the sudden sharp pain from the gash on her forehead. One pain reminded her of the other, for Fran's eyes filled with tears and she sobbed out, "She's not my daughter. I honestly don't know who she is … and I lost … have you found my husband? My son?" She looked from the captain to the doctor to the others in the room, eyes searching, questioning. "Please? You'll keep looking?"

Softly, the captain answered, "Ma'am, we do have our crew continually on the watch for any other survivors. But we … we were amazed, really, to find you three. For the magnitude of the disaster …" He hung his head.

"So we're the only survivors you've found?" Michal asked, incredulous.

"Yes," Captain Howard said. "And quite honestly, your survival is nothing less than a miracle."

Fran continued to weep, and the captain reached out to put a comforting hand on her shoulder.

Concerned about Fran's reaction, the doctor intervened, cautioning, "Only a couple more questions at most, sir. I'm concerned she might have a concussion. And rather than do X-rays here, I think it best to wait and have them done ashore. At the hospital."

The captain nodded in agreement. "Just one more thing." Smiling, he peered into Aubrey's face and reached out to run a hand gently down her head, over the tangled mass of curls. "You're Aubrey, right?"

"Uh-huh." Never taking wary eyes off him. Nor relaxing her hold on Fran in the slightest.

"What's your last name, sweetheart? Do you know that?"

Insulted, she curtly replied, "'Course I do. It's Roberts."

Captain Howard replied in an "A-ha" tone. "So you're Aubrey Roberts. Am I right?"

Aubrey nodded her head yes. After acknowledging her response with a complimentary "Good," the captain glanced back over at the doctor, his mouth set in a grim line and a crease between his brows. "Hmm. The crew from the freighter indicated she was crying out, 'Mommy.'" He scratched his head, fluffing the ring of white. "None of this adds up."

"The angel tooked my mommy. And Rabbit," Aubrey interjected, exasperated. "I cried—" Aubrey paused a moment, shaking the curls, "—the angel said it was okay to cry. But then he tooked me to her," pointing a finger toward Fran's chest. "'Cause she has Mommy's eyes." Aubrey snuggled against Fran, a look of self-satisfaction blanketing her features.

"Oh. Well, then." Baffled, eyebrows raised and eyes wide, Captain Howard looked to Fran and then Michal for a plausible translation of Aubrey's story. But the expressions on both their faces showed they were equally nonplussed. Fran, wiping at her nose with a tissue, shook her head again—recalling too late the consequence would be pain. "Ouch. I'm sorry, I don't …" She put a hand to her head, gingerly feeling the bandage there. "I'm sorry, but I don't know what she's talking about because frankly, I can't remember anything."

"Not unexpected with a concussion," the doctor interjected.

And then nearly in complete unison, they all turned to Michal.

But Michal shook her head too, shrugging. "I remember hanging onto the latch of the escape door at the back of the bus."

"That explains the bruises on your hands."

"You were on that bus?" the captain asked, incredulously.

"Yes, in the very back. And I must've … must've gotten the door open, I guess? Honestly, like Fran, I also don't remember anything after clutching onto that handle. It's a total blank."

The doctor signaled for the captain to wrap up the questioning, but before he could stand, Michal grabbed his arm. "My aunt. Would you please call my aunt? Sarah McHenry. She lives in Fort Myers, but I don't know her phone number."

"Don't worry about a thing, miss. We'll find out and contact her straight away. For all three of you, we'll locate family and make those calls as soon as possible."

Glancing toward Aubrey, he noted her eyes fluttering closed. Michal was also fighting sleep, and Fran looked as though she could drop off at any moment. Captain Howard knelt there, spellbound, simply watching them. Thinking to himself, *These are miracles indeed. Two women and a small child. How on earth did they ... how could they possibly ...?*

He waited to make sure his charges were resting comfortably. Listened for the soft sounds of sleep, and left them to the doctor's care.

Several hours later, Fran woke. Allowing her gaze to wander, she realized she was in a hospital room. After taking in the metal cart at the foot of her bed and the IV still embedded in her arm, she turned to her left. A man and a teenage girl sat in chairs by the window.

The man glanced up, noted Fran had awakened, and instantly stood. "Colleen, go get the nurse, will you?" Fran watched her leave the room and then shifted her gaze back to the man—now standing next to her. "I'm Bill. And you're Fran? You're certainly due an explanation why I'm here in your room, first of all." He gestured toward Aubrey, who was still sound asleep and cuddled next to Fran, her fists tightly clutching Fran's gown. "Aubrey's my daughter. And at this point, she clearly doesn't intend to let go of you." He smiled, revealing a devotion to the little girl and a boyish charm in his grin.

Just then, the sun broke through a bank of clouds, pouring a ray of bright light through the window which highlighted Fran's face. She winced at the glare, immediately shielding her eyes. But she heard Bill's intake of breath, and before he turned to pull down the blinds, she caught the look of astonishment mixed with deep pain etched on his face.

"Is something wrong?" Fran asked.

He put his hands in his pockets and stared down at the floor. "I'm sorry. It's just that … you have the same unusual eyes as my wife does … did. Same color. And those dark flecks, like glistening gold, I used to tell her. It was like she …" Fran watched him swipe at the wetness on his cheek. "I'm not usually so emo—" He turned away, embarrassed by his weeping.

While sleep had been a temporary escape, Fran felt again the full impact of the knifelike ache for her family. Subconsciously, she tightened her hold on Aubrey. "Neither am I. But we don't usually have to deal with this type of loss, do we?" she said softly.

Bill shook his head. When he turned to her, his eyes were still glistening, his cheeks coated with tears. "Your husband—?"

"Yes. And my—son." Her voice broke, saying it out loud, making the truth too real. She closed her eyes and held her breath a moment, an attempt to stem the uncontrollable sobs for her precious son.

Fran's eyes still closed, Bill began to speak again. "My wife Maureen and I had this uncanny discussion just before she ... just before she left for Sanibel." He shook his head, a look of wide-eyed disbelief on his face. Wiping at more escaping tears, he choked out, "We were talking about being alone. That being alone is different from being lonely. And that being left isn't as frightening in the bridge of—"

"—*God's love*," they both finished in unison.

Their expressions exactly mirrored each other's: mouths open in shock, eyes still glistening with tears. An aura of complete awe.

The nurse nearly flew into the room, an anxious Colleen following at her heels.

"How are you feeling, Mrs. Thomason? Head hurt still?"

Fran shook her head—partly in answer to the nurse's question, but mostly to shake herself as if waking from a dream.

The nurse took Fran's blood pressure and pulse, busying herself with the IV and monitors. "Little one still sleeping? Best to let her wake up on her own, I'm thinking." She made a point of making eye contact with Bill. "The doctor will be in soon. He gave strict orders you weren't to face the crowd outside until he'd seen you first." She stood momentarily with hands on her hips, the only time she wasn't a mass of frenetic energy. "Sit tight. He'll be here in a jiffy." And with that, she was gone, racing out as fast as she'd flown in.

"Crowd? What's—?"

Bill coughed and then cleared his throat. "Reporters. Must be dozens." The sudden switch back to reality felt jarring. He handed a tissue to Fran and then used one to wipe his own face. "They've been anxiously waiting to interview you and Miss McHenry for some time. Tried to bully their way in at one point, but the Coast Guard posted some men outside the wing. No one's getting past those burly guys, that's for sure."

"Your eyes are just like my mom's," Colleen whispered.

Bill put his arm protectively around her. "This is Colleen, my older daughter."

"I'm so sorry about your mom," Fran said.

"I don't know how we'll ever thank you for taking such good care of Aubrey." Bill reached out to lightly put his other hand on Aubrey's back. He could feel her breathing slightly against his hand, the proof he needed that she was alive.

Fran shook her head. "Besides holding her head above water—the waves were frighteningly high—well, I don't recall doing anything. Michal—I think that's her name, but maybe I got it wrong—she was a big help too. She's a strong swimmer."

Colleen continued to stare at Fran as though mesmerized by her. "Michal is her name. I met her aunt outside," Colleen said. "Did you, um ... did you see my mom?"

"I'm so sorry, Colleen. No, I didn't."

Aubrey stirred. When her eyes fully opened and focused on Bill, she smiled. Let go of Fran. And stretched out her arms longingly to him.

Bill gathered her into his arms, where he rocked her back and forth, more silent tears falling down his cheeks. When Colleen put her arms around Bill's waist, he leaned down so he could hug both girls tightly to his chest.

"Daddy ... Daddy." Aubrey put a hand on Bill's cheek, demanding his attention.

"Yes, Lolly Pops?"

"The angel told me she would love me." She pointed to Fran. "And she'd love you and Collie, too."

Bill stared at her, momentarily speechless. "Aubrey, you shouldn't—"

Someone rapped on the door and then a woman peered in. "I'm so sorry to interrupt. But could my niece and I please come in for a few moments? We need to face these reporters soon, and Michal's just ... well, she tells me she needs to speak with you all. Is that all right?"

Bill looked to Fran, who nodded. "Please. Come in and join us."

After introductions, Bill motioned to chairs for Sarah and Michal. Sarah insisted she'd stand, so only Michal sat down, IV pole in tow. Michal turned to Fran, biting her lip. "I barely remember our rescue. The Coast Guard ship. The captain asking questions. Honestly, it's all kind of fuzzy. But I have this vague recollection of Aubrey saying ... well, something kind of ... strange? About angels?"

"Just one." Aubrey corrected her. "He tooked my mommy. And Rabbit, too—to keep Mommy comp'ny," she said as an aside to Bill. "And then he tooked me to her," pointing yet again at Fran, who couldn't help grinning back. "See, she has Mommy's eyes," Aubrey stated to Sarah and Michal, dramatically.

"Well, then. That explains it." Michal said smugly, leaning back and crossing arms over her chest. When she started to giggle, everyone in the room joined in to laugh with her.

Except Aubrey, who turned back to Bill with a pronounced pout. "Don't they believe me, Daddy?"

"Sweetheart, Mrs. Thomason, Michal, and you—the fact that you're here, with us—that's a miracle. No one is going to disagree with that."

Apparently satisfied, Aubrey hugged him again.

Suddenly fidgeting, smoothing her blouse and picking at a nonexistent piece of lint, Sarah asked Fran, "Did I hear correctly? Thomason is your last name?"

"Yes, my husband ... I'm sorry, this is difficult ... my husband was Charles Thomason Junior. Obviously his dad was a Charles, too. And we passed the name onto our son, Charlie."

Sarah just stared at Fran for an awkward moment. Then she calmly said, "Bill, I think I'll take the offer for a chair now and sit down. If that's okay."

Michal watched the freckles on Sarah's face begin to stand out, growing darker and more pronounced. *That's odd,* she thought. *Or is it that the skin behind them is turning lighter?* Alarmed, she asked, "Aunt Sarah, are you okay?"

But Sarah was solely focused on Fran. "I don't mean to pry, and this might seem random, but could you tell me please, did your father-in-law die of cancer when his son was eleven years old?"

Fran gasped. "Oh my. You're *that* Sarah?" she whispered.

Michal looked from Fran to Sarah, understanding dawning. "Charles Thomason. He's CK?" she asked. But Sarah had slumped over, putting her head in her hands.

"Sarah," Fran said, but Sarah didn't move, her face still resting in the palms of her shaking hands. "Sarah, please. Take my hand. It's okay—Charles and I talked about you, and he understood. You must've been hurting deeply too." Sarah looked up then, and her eyes were red-rimmed, wet. She reached out and took the offered hand between hers. "Sarah, this is … yet another miraculous gift." Fran's voice grew husky. "I can't tell you what this … you're a godsend to me right now! Can't you see you're a connection to Charles? Later, when we have time, I want you to tell me all you can remember about him. Everything—every detail. And Charles's dad—CK I think you called him? I want to hear—"

There was a tap from outside, followed by the doctor's abrupt entrance. "I see our patients are awake now." If he noticed the emotional weight hanging in the room, he didn't show it, for he immediately proceeded to examine Fran, introducing himself as Dr. Holms. "How you feeling? You do have a slight concussion, by the way."

Bill placed Aubrey on the bed so she could be quickly checked over also. The doctor tilted the little girl's chin up. Smiled as he peered into the bright eyes. "Hardly a scratch on you anywhere, little one. How did you manage that?" Then he gave Michal a quick perusal, pronouncing her nearly perfect too, except for the deep bruising on her hands. "You know, I can't say that I'm a religious person. But something or someone protected you three. Something bigger than any of us, that's for sure." He stood still for a moment, eyebrows raised. "Okay. Ready for the onslaught? They've been pacing the hallways like vultures."

He'd just reached for the door when Sarah blurted out, "Doctor, wait. Would it be possible for Michal and me to have just a few more minutes alone?"

"Absolutely. Take as much time as you need; they can wait. I'll beat them off with my stethoscope if I have to."

"Twenty minutes?"

"You've got thirty. Going back to Michal's room, are you? Then I'll meet you all in the lounge in a half hour."

Bill looked around the room at the small group gathered there. They were strangers—and yet, no longer. Intimates, in a way, but not that either. All touched by tragedy, now forming fledgling relationships for an unknown future—but one they would face with newly discovered hope. "I, um …" he stammered. Finding himself uncharacteristically without a sense of clear direction. Except for one thing. "Before you leave us, Sarah and Michal, is anyone else feeling this … sense of urgency like I am? That we six need to … to be together? To stay together, somehow?"

Vigorous nods and affirmations of "Oh, yes," from everyone followed. His gaze traveled from one to another, but he allowed it to rest longer on Fran and Aubrey. Aubrey had latched onto Fran's gown again, and Bill looked lovingly from his daughter's hand to the woman Aubrey had miraculously claimed as someone she would determinedly love. And who would in turn love her, Colleen … and *me?* Bill pondered.

Minutes later, Sarah helped Michal with the ungainly IV, tucking her back into bed, even though it would be a brief respite. Sarah took Michal's hands between her own, holding them tightly.

"Aunt Sarah, I … I need to talk to you about something."

Sarah smiled at her, reassuringly. "About why you were on the bus."

What she'd left behind came rushing back, and Michal nodded her head, her eyes flooding with tears. "Beth—" Michal could get no further, and abruptly stopped.

"I heard. Amongst the crowd waiting out there is a Miss Hamilton, your RA, I understand?" Michal nodded. "So Beth had a baby in the dorm. And no one knew she was pregnant. I take it … you didn't know either?"

Michal shook her head. "I had no idea, Aunt Sarah. And the night before I left, she had the baby right there in our room." It was a relief to finally tell it all, to let the truth come tumbling out. "She went through all that without telling me—being pregnant. Labor. Not confiding in me because I wasn't worthy of her trust."

"You shouldn't blame yourself, Michal. Beth made her own decisions."

"But that's not all. Something else happened too." She turned away, felt her face flush crimson.

"You know I'm just going to keep on loving you, no matter what you tell me."

Michal took a deep breath, still avoiding her aunt's steady gaze. "Stephen tried to … touch me." Her voice caught, and between sobs she choked out, "He said it was God's will. That I wanted it—that I'd led him on. I tried to push him away. But he was so strong.

"And then suddenly Allistair was there. Pulling Stephen off me. I hate to think what would've happened if he hadn't. But I was so ashamed that Allistair … what he saw. I don't think I can ever face him again." She turned, her eyes boring into Sarah's now. "So you see why I just had to get away from there. I don't want to ever go back. And please don't send me to Ethiopia either. Could I … could I come live with you? Please, Aunt Sarah?"

Sarah's eyes were soft, but her answer was firm. "No, Michal, you can't."

The unexpected rejection hit like a punch to Michal's stomach. But before she could utter a word, Sarah reached up to cradle Michal's face in her hands. "The feelings and memories will forever be with you. But hear me, Michal. Hear my heart. Following God means you may have to go where it hurts. Don't waste the pain, Michal. Follow it all the way to the cross with Christ."

Her voice flat, Michal stated, "You think I have to go back. To face Stephen. And Allistair." Michal squeezed her eyes shut, attempting to erase the images from her mind. The way Allistair had looked at her. The sympathy in his eyes. "I don't think I'm brave enough to do that."

"Yes, you are. You've survived boarding school, adapted to a culture on the other side of the earth, and then returned to a foreign home. And now you've survived a collapsed bridge. That's the brave young woman I know—and that's the same one who can face all her fears."

There was a knock at the door again. The doctor poked his head in, apologizing profusely. "I am so sorry to bother you yet again. But there's someone out here, Miss McHenry, who's insistent on seeing you before the others."

Sarah raised an eyebrow, and Michal, hastily wiping away tears, reasoned, "I don't know who it could be. I'm just not quite ready to—"

"Well, he's gotten … obnoxious, quite frankly. And that's saying a lot considering he's competing with reporters. Says he's from your school and his name's—" The doctor was abruptly pushed to one side of the doorway, and irritably snapped, "Hey. You can't just—"

Hair uncombed, clothes a rumpled mess, one hand clutching a large chocolate candy bar—he'd pretty much shoved the doctor aside in his impatience—he finally settled eyes overflowing with love on the one woman he'd been seeking.

"Michal? Oh God, I was so afraid I'd lost you."

She smiled through her tears. "Aunt Sarah. I'd like you to meet Allistair Fuller."

The six walked into the lounge together to raucous cheers, applause, and the flashes of dozens of cameras—three survivors and three family members, though each of the six would have firmly stated they were all present due to miraculous events.

Michal and Fran were in wheelchairs, Michal to the spectators' left. As soon as she entered the lounge area her eyes darted about the room, searching the faces. And when she found that one, her eyes lit up and a hint of a smile appeared as she relaxed back into her chair. Reddening, suddenly embarrassed, she studied the tightly clenched hands in her lap.

Sarah stood between Michal and Fran. She had one hand on each of the women's shoulders, lightly touching one of them. The other shoulder, the slimmer of the two, Sarah held so tightly that the tips of her fingers were white. A fan pushed Sarah's ever-escaping wispy curls across her nose, tickling her. But stubbornly, rather than remove a hand from either of the two women beside her, Sarah merely twitched her nose. She swallowed to keep herself from laughing out loud—appreciating the humor of how it must've looked—all the while keeping her chin high, her jaw firm, and one foot slightly in front of the other.

Fran cuddled Aubrey on her lap so tightly that it was nearly impossible to tell where one body stopped and the other began. Her cheek resting on top of Aubrey's head, those soft curls, she glanced now and then toward Sarah. And then Bill—though he appeared not to notice.

Aubrey still clung to the collar of Fran's robe, and she squeezed her eyes shut at the assault of glaring flashes. But when she peeked up at Fran, she was filled with wonder at the sparkle in Fran's eyes—partly due to the gold flecks, but mostly from the glistening tears.

Colleen had insisted on wheeling Fran's chair herself, and she gripped the handles as though she wouldn't be able to stand without their aid. Cowed by the intensity of the crowd, Colleen glanced up only now and then, keeping her gaze on the top of Fran's and her sister's heads. When Bill reached over to playfully pinch Colleen's side, she pushed his hand away—but smiled and giggled nervously as she did so.

The last in the tableau, Bill had come as the spokesperson for the group. He held a sheaf of papers in his left hand, some notes he'd jotted down concerning Aubrey's interpretation of the miraculous survival and a short testimony to the God of miracles. He cleared his throat as he began introducing himself and the others. And as he did so, he reached back toward Colleen. He touched her lightly and then—was he even aware of the movement?—his hand strayed toward the cold metal of the wheelchair and finally, the warmth of Fran's other shoulder. Where it rested, comfortably.

... a little more ...

When a delightful concert comes to an end,

the orchestra might offer an encore.

When a fine meal comes to an end,

it's always nice to savor a bit of dessert.

When a great story comes to an end,

we think you may want to linger.

And so, we offer ...

AfterWords—just a little something more after you

have finished a David C Cook novel.

We invite you to stay awhile in the story.

Thanks for reading!

Turn the page for ...

- **A Conversation with Carolyn Williford**

A CONVERSATION WITH
CAROLYN WILLIFORD

On inspiration

I'm often asked, "Where does your inspiration for a story come from?" and the answer is never a simple one. I can somewhat understand why the Greeks imagined a muse who delivered inspiration, for the creative elements of a story are always a bit indescribable—where core ideas and tangents and characters originate. We can't attribute that to the Holy Spirit, so does it come from one's subconscious? Submerged memories? The creative centers of the brain? I honestly have no idea, but I do know this from experience: It feels a tad mystical and wondrous. And it's tremendously fun and exciting when a muse "visits" me.

For example, when I first finished writing the prologue I had no idea who would survive the tragedy—and who would not. I felt a sense of intense anticipation, actually, as I watched the story take on a life of its own, eventually informing me who the survivors were.

Later my wonderful editor would have a say in that too. Ah, the jolt back to real life!

Source for themes

My themes for writing fiction and nonfiction generally come from my personal devotions. When I was studying the verse in Matthew 16:24—"Then Jesus said to his disciples, 'If anyone would come after me, he must deny himself and take up his cross and follow me,'"—I recall thinking that there were those with such poor self-esteem that they hadn't ever had a real "self" to deny and offer sacrificially to God. And then I thought of my own struggles—the times I've been so ill that I literally couldn't do *anything* to serve him, and how unworthy I felt as a result. Could I view myself as acceptable when all I could offer my God was a weak woman, in pain, lying on the couch? Clearly my own issues of *being* versus *doing* fueled my desire to explore those themes more in depth through the power of story. The parallel structure of the verse itself led me to think about a novel with three distinct yet intertwining stories.

The classic novel *The Bridge of San Luis Rey* by Thornton Wilder provided the pattern for a plot line, a guide for a modern-day tragedy. Though not often read in classrooms today (Wilder's better known for the inspiring *Our Town*), this engaging story of a bridge's collapse in Peru, the people who perished there, and the parallels in their pasts made a strong impact on me as a teen. If you haven't read it, you may want to do so to make your own comparisons with *Bridge to a Distant Star*.

The true story behind *Bridge to a Distant Star*

The last piece of the puzzle—*what modern-day tragedy to use?*—was quickly put into place with my fairly vivid memories of the Sunshine Skyway Bridge and the disaster of 1980. My parents lived in St. Petersburg for a number of years, and before they moved from Ohio, we vacationed on Treasure Island, which is just across the bay from St. Pete. So I had visited the area and traveled across the beautiful Skyway on numerous occasions, and when you've actually been to a place that later witnesses some sort of horrific tragedy, it's suddenly more personal, isn't it? Add to that the artistic shape of the Skyway itself; its inherent personality and style make it the perfect setting for a dramatic story.

If you Google Tampa Bay Skyway Bridge, you'll find articles on the day the bridge fell, including fascinating personal eyewitness accounts and pictures. In the real life disaster, sadly, there was only one survivor, and that was because his vehicle fell onto the freighter's bow before rolling into the water. (In *The Bridge of San Luis Rey*, no one survives the bridge's collapse. So though you may judge me harshly for having so many characters die, my story does allow for the greatest number of survivors!) Since my characters' vehicles fall directly into the water below, clearly no natural means would explain how Fran, Michal, and Aubrey survived. Thus my miraculous explanation: Aubrey's insistence on an angel. Literary license is a wonderful invention!

I also Googled, researched, and studied the physical form of the bridge itself (as a memory refresher, I located pictures of a drive onto and across the bridge), freighters and shipmates' vocabularies, and the transcript of the actual Mayday conversation between Captain Lerro (the freighter's pilot) and the Coast Guard. The more I read and viewed online, the more the event vividly replayed in my mind's eye. And the more I could picture this disaster happening to my cast of characters: Captain Luis; Maureen and Aubrey; Fran, Charles, and Charlie; and Michal.

One last comment on the tragedy and its consequences: I can't speak for all authors of fiction, but I would think it to be true of most storytellers that our characters become real people to us. After spending so much time with them, getting to know them intimately—what's in character for them to do and what's not—thinking as they do, putting myself in their shoes, so to speak, they become living, breathing individuals. To then have a character die is … nearly like losing a friend. I do hope my muse will allow all my beloved characters to live in my next novel.

He can take the villains as he pleases.

More Googling …

I also did extensive research on Ethiopian history, topography, and culture; metastasized osteosarcoma and its diagnosis and treatment; limb salvage surgery versus amputation with prosthetic devices; and soccer rules for youth leagues. For my first historical novel *Jordan's Bend,* I spent untold hours at several libraries, even traveling from Ohio to North Carolina to visit a library that had specific books I needed. For this novel I merely remained at my desk, continually going online to enter the endless resources on the Internet. Today's technology—what a wonderful gift in relation to the difference in time, energy, and available materials!

The idea for using averted vision must've come from my reading (I am *always* reading a book, and generally it's a novel; I can get almost panicky if I'm about to finish a book and don't have another waiting to begin immediately), but since I read so many books, I can't recall where I came across that fascinating anomaly. However, I remember feeling exactly that: fascination, and then a determination to weave the scientific phenomenon into all three story lines with a slightly different twist in perspective for each one. Adding the averted vision symbolism was like sprinkling fresh basil into my homemade pasta sauce: It's not absolutely necessary, but it would be bland without it. And that indefinable "something" would be missing.

Pulling from memories

I am a lifelong lover of beaches, particularly those on the Gulf Coast of Florida. Some of my earliest memories are of family vacations spent on the beautiful white sand beaches of Treasure Island where we collected shells (I still have jars full), body surfed the waves (with the scars to prove it), walked the boardwalk of St. John's Pass to view the catches of the day (unforgettable pictures of an impressive hammer head shark), and the feel and smell of caressing, salty breezes—which I can conjure up just about anywhere by simply closing my eyes and concentrating. As rich as the Internet is, it hasn't yet allowed my senses to feel the sun on my face … or taste the saltiness of the Gulf. Those I must pull from my memories—or experience once again.

My next novel, like *Jordan's Bend,* takes place mostly in the hills of Tennessee. I think I can already smell the honeysuckle … I can feel the just-picked, juicy blackberries I cradle in my hands … I can almost taste the skillet-fried cornbread, fresh from the oven. But I believe I need to experience it all firsthand again, don't you?

After all, your vicarious experience through my story is at stake.

A Final Note from Carolyn

On December 23, 2010, one of the brightest lights in my life went out.

I've often spoken about my fierce love for my three guys: my husband, Craig, and our wonderful sons, Robb and Jay. For a woman who expected to be the mom of girls, with their frills and dolls, I was surprised when God blessed us with boys—and the accompanying bats and balls, cars and trucks and trains, and military paraphernalia everywhere. But what joy I discovered in that all-male atmosphere, for I was treated like a queen. And oh, how I adored my guys, through every season of life, through every stage of life. And now … now I must learn how to live without knowing Robb's tender care (Need something? Need anything fixed? Robb would be there in a heartbeat), without hearing his laughter (I can still hear it in my head, but how I wish I could hear it for real), without watching him love his wife and play with his sons (Tricia, Tucker, and Tyler, he loved you dearly, and I loved watching him love you), without listening to him share his heart with Craig and me—his compassion compelling him to serve his Lord and Savior.

Robb needed emergency surgery to remove a ruptured spleen when he was a teenager. During his recovery, the nurses told us the first thing he uttered when regaining consciousness was *"Where am I, God?"* I believe that was a picture of Robb's faith: He trusted God, and trusted *in* God, knowing he was ever in God's care.

I have complete assurance that Robb is resting in God's care right now, and yes, that is so very comforting to me. But there is now a painful hole in my heart, and I will miss my sweet son until the day I draw my last breath.

I miss you, Sweetie.

TNT: How you were pushing Dad to get me a new high-tech cell phone ...

Love from Mom, forever